The Witches Damned

By

Sophie Tanen

ZMOK

The Witches Damned by Sophie Tanen
Cover art by Michael Nigro
This edition published in 2025

Published by Winged Hussar Publishing
Zmok Books
1525 Hulse Road, Unit 1
Point Pleasant, NJ 08742

ISBN PB 978-1-958872-70-3
ISBN EB 978-1-958872-71-0

Bibliographical References and Index
1. Fiction. 2. Fantasy. 3. Action & Adventure

For more information on Winged Hussar Publishing, LLC, visit us at:
https://www.WHPSupplyroom.com
Instagram: WingedHussarPublishing
Facebook: Winged Hussar Publishing LLC

Moments in Between

When a mortal endured the touch of a god, they would become something entirely new. Their old self burns away, replaced with the lingering presence of a divine being. The creation of a Hallowed is rare, and such an intervention on the part of a god leaves deep scars on the earth. The deepest scar created from such contact burrowed down into the sea, splitting the world into two realms.

The tale goes like this.

When the island was young, a single kingdom ruled over the lands, and the gods were content to watch the humans play with each other as they tended the land and helped it grow. The land thrived under the human's love and care, trees towering above to hold the gods up, the grasses green and the earth fertile. The gods had blessed every inch.

But the sea, filled with dark creatures that rarely broke the surface, moaning in their quiet loneliness, languished from the gods' neglect. Unloved and forgotten, the wretched sea creatures retreated into the depths, wasting away.

The god of the sea tamped his anger down for generations, but his resolve grew weaker as his territory and the lives within it began to fade. Balance had been thrown off between the land and the sea, a rope wrested taut between the Lord of the Sea and the Lady of the Land. The sea god sank into the darkness with the rest of his creatures, watching while his queen thrived. Eventually, he couldn't abide it any longer. He unleashed his power, refusing to rest until he saw the balance restored.

The storms hit as he bellowed. Churning hurricanes and towering tidal waves ate away at the blessed land, seeking to reclaim the power the land had taken for itself. For a long while, the mortals remained loyal to the Lady of the Land, praying only to her to save them from the violent tempests. Only when entire villages had been swept away did the people of the land fall to their knees, begging the sea for mercy. Only when the Lady of the Land's own people began to lose faith in her did she finally relent.

She gave a portion of her people over to the sea god's control. Half of all humans were transformed for the ocean floor, shifted to a new kingdom where they would live on to worship another god. Nysus, this newly-formed kingdom at the bottom of the ocean, grew from the seabed, grains of sand solidifying into sparkling glass walls and shimmering roofs. The island of Calypdon floated overhead, and Nysus spread out directly beneath in vibrant fields of coral and swaying forests of seaweed, spreading even past the boundaries of the island above, reaching out from beneath the perpetual shadow of the kingdom above, where the light could touch.

After the tumultuous ordeal, the sea god reached out and touched a man whose faith in the sea and its god had never wavered. He'd lived on the coast, in a cramped lighthouse cabin, and spent his days staring out at the waves and wishing for something better. With the god's touch, the lighthouse keeper was transformed, and the newly created Hallowed assumed the throne of the newly born kingdom.

Much later, in another place, and another time, a new Hallowed would at last be created. And the sea woman could attest; absorbing life back into her destroyed body was far more painful than dying could ever be.

Her body burned from the inside out, starting at the fatal wound deep in her stomach, incinerating flesh and sinew and bone. She was sure that when the pain at last faded away and she looked down at herself, there would be nothing left. Shadows crept into the edges of her vision. She prayed for unconsciousness to take her away and spare her.

No such relief came. She endured it all, until all she could feel was the touch of a goddess, reshaping a body that was only meant to contain a human soul.

She didn't know how much time had passed when she finally uncurled from the floor, slick with her own blood. The red dripped from her fingertips, smeared along the floorboards beneath her feet, and an onlooker might think *her* the monster of this story.

Coming to a mirror that somehow still hung untouched on the wall, she braced herself for what she would see and found an unrecognizable sight. What the woman saw in the mirror - it wasn't *her*. She should have foreseen such a repercussion of the agreement she'd made. When the goddess had reached down to even the score, to give her life back, the sea woman's original body had been ruined, dead on the floor where the Serpent Witch had left her when she ran. That burning had been true; her old body was gone, no corpse left to bury, replaced with … this.

Her eyes were farther apart, her nose had grown longer, and her brown hair was cut level with her chin. The goddess had gifted her an entirely new body to wreak havoc with. Still, familiarity lingered through pain as she beheld the scars that matched her remembered wounds but transferred onto her new body. The tears in her skin had healed, helped along by the magic of the goddess. But perhaps those final wounds couldn't go away completely. She remembered her old self as she beheld them, peering at a scar on her cheek, remnant of the witch's first strike. She remembered the moment it happened. The moment it became clear that the Serpent Witch had turned against her.

Lifting her shirt, she saw a similar mark just above her navel, where the Serpent Witch's sword had run her through, striking the killing blow.

Or so the witch had thought.

The woman took in the rest of the room, finding it surprisingly tidy. It looked mostly as it had the night before; when she'd shown up at the witch's door, when they'd -

She cut off the thought, choking it in her mind until it evaporated into mist. She returned to her assessment. An upturned chair here, a gash in the wallpaper there. It hadn't been a violent battle. In fact, it hadn't been a battle at all, not in the end. Once the Serpent Witch had chosen a side, once she had agreed to do what was asked of her, the war would always be over. She would always win.

And she had.

But something else was wrong. It had been dawn when the Serpent Witch attacked, golden light filtering through the lace curtains. The first thing the woman had noticed when she awoke hadn't been the sword pointed at her throat; it had been how beautiful the witch had looked in the early morning light. But an indeterminate amount of time had passed since everything fell apart. Night had surely come and gone and perhaps come again. The light in the room was strange, shimmering. There was a color to it, silver or blue or green, and glowing slivers spattered across her skin. Small fractures of light danced through the air, dotting her fingers for only a moment before darting away to target something else. But each ray of sun was interrupted, as if something was trying to block it out entirely. So unfamiliar in this room, and yet, the unusual qualities of light reminded her of something…

Those shadows that had crept into her vision during her transformation; they hadn't been unconsciously threatening to drag her down. No, they lingered even now, and the way they fell across the walls was familiar, somehow. It tickled a place at the back of her skull, a place in her mind that remained untouched by all that had transpired.

The Hallowed, newly formed and taking the first steps of her new life, turned slowly toward the window. The sight waiting for her was even more baffling than what she had seen in the mirror.

Over the past few months, she'd become accustomed to the view provided by the palace of Briarwood. Grasses and trees stretched out as far as the eye could see, the ocean too far away to make out. She'd even grown to appreciate the beauty of the vibrant greens and rich browns, the dryness of the cobblestones with weeds sprouting between the rocks.

But her heart skipped a beat, because now she could see the sea. It was as if the horizon had moved, shifting up above the land until it was visible over the trees. Sea foam frothed at the top, and she realized it wasn't the horizon; a giant tidal wave was hanging over the kingdom. It took up the entire window, and it reminded her of the years she'd lived on the ocean floor. Water extended up, almost as far as the depth of the ocean, blotting out the sun. A few rays snuck through as the waves rippled, and the familiarity almost kept the panic at bay.

Almost.

She tripped her way toward the window, legs longer and feet slimmer than she was used to, catching herself against the sill and nearly tearing the curtains down in the process. She threw open the window, leaning out and craning her head up, letting out a sigh when she found the end of the water, the sky visible once more directly overhead.

Blinking several times, she kept thinking the water would evaporate if she just concentrated hard enough. That this must be some sort of mirage, a trick of her new mind. Perhaps this was her way of mourning her old body, the one born of the sea. But that wall seemed to grow bigger with every blink, eating away at the sky.

Tilting her head, she leaned further out the window, nearly tumbling to yet another untimely death.

No, not bigger. Closer.

The water was moving. Like a wave lapping at the shore, it ate away at the land, swallowing houses and trees and any people in its path, no matter how fast they ran.

She had enough mind left to pull on a robe, her clothes having been incinerated along with her body, but she needn't have bothered. The halls were deserted as she sprinted barefoot through the corridors, finding her way easily around the palace that had become her home. She skidded around corners, only faltering when she encountered the first body slumped in the hallway.

More came after that. A lot more.

She let her vision blur until she burst through the large, main gates of the palace. There was blood on the handles, smeared across the wood, and she didn't let herself consider that for too long, either.

The smell of salt hung in the air, and being outside, surrounded by water but not *in* the water, was so much more horrifying. She had to crane her neck all the way back to find the top of the wall again, taller than any building she'd ever encountered. It was dizzying, and all encompassing, and the woman couldn't wrap her mind around it.

Well, not a woman. Not anymore.

A Hallowed.

Her breath picked up. Few of the Hallowed remained. Since the Ancient Rift, the gods had agreed to stop their meddling; that it had been their presence that had triggered the war in the first place. That perhaps, if they let the humans be, the sea god would remain satisfied with all they'd given him.

Apparently, the sea wasn't satisfied. It could never be satisfied, and with the help of its king, it had reared up, deciding to take everything that was left.

The woman ran down the hill, crashing into branches, thorns tearing into her skin, until she eventually found a clearing. And then she just watched, alone, because what could she do? She was no longer a woman of the sea, and even before, she had possessed no magic.

Torrents of saltwater ate away at the earth. It plowed across the lands, drowning all in its path–

Until suddenly, it stopped.

The ground shook when the water slowed to a halt, and the woman fell to her knees until stillness came once more and she found the courage to look up. As if the sea was held up by a towering sheet of glass, it sparkled in the sunlight, the murky blue cascading upward hundreds of feet. From some angles it looked as if it had solidified into ice, but there was too much movement, as if it was still trying to break free. It curved in at the top, bowing toward the capital, as if it could reach out and crush the rest of its victims into the earth.

All at once, the king's plan became crystal clear.

Calypdon had always been an island; large, surrounded on all sides by never-ending ocean, but now the water had become a cage. And she realized the goddess hadn't touched her with divine power out of the goodness of her heart, so she could complete her own personal retribution. She'd brought her back for this. After all, the goddess of battle could only truly be interested in war, and this would be the first in hundreds of years.

She could hardly complain. After all, she'd asked for this. With her dying breath, she'd sent up one last prayer. *Let this not be the end*, she'd begged. *The witch can't win like this*.

Apparently, the goddess agreed. She knew that, in the end, she would find her vengeance, too.

Two Hundred Years Later

The souls of the kingdoms sang to her, echoed in her veins, but the Serpent Witch had ceased responding decades ago.

The push and pull tugged against her blood, running through every bone and fiber. She would close her eyes as she stood at her open window, pale fingers braced beside the box of wilting flowers, face tipped toward the sky as though she could see past the shimmering, imposing barrier of water surrounding the kingdom; as if she could imagine a way through the walls that she herself had created.

Even with the stillness of the wind, the air cool and quiet, movement whipped around her. Souls of the living encircled her, locking her in a cage she would never escape. They floated through the boughs above and seeped through the wooden floorboards, into the soles of her feet. Each mortal life clung to her wrists and ankles like shackles. They spoke to her in quiet whispers. Begging. Pleading.

Praying.

Those murmurs had faded with the passage of years. Or perhaps she had just gotten better at ignoring them.

That phantom touch, though, always lingered. She could never quite escape it, the thrum of energy she felt with every passing contact, every interaction she had with the few people left in her village. Their blood reached for her, and when she felt their essence at the tips of her fingers, she recoiled. Many souls were loud and filled with sorrow. They felt happiness, too, but the people around her didn't share that. They kept joy to themselves.

Souls were far more fragile than most humans realized. Bodies were ephemeral, only a vessel to hold the powerful energy that made up a living creature. It wasn't only the destruction of flesh and bone that resulted in death. Sometimes, it started at the core.

The wooden steps creaked beneath Morgana as she descended from the tiny apartment she'd acquired decades ago, down into her reptile shop on the bottom floor. The air around her swam with the smell of decay, damp and muggy, an unflagging mist clinging to every surface. Taking over this place had been the last time she used her magic without restraint. She had erased the memories of the previous owners and inserted herself into the memory of every person in the town. It was a vague impression, of a quiet woman who kept to herself and sold pets to the village children. As if she had been there for as long as anyone could remember, as if she hadn't arrived out of nowhere.

She lowered her hood but left her dark cloak settled against her shoulders. Colder weather had begun to creep in, inching through the wooden walls and into her poorly heated home. Still, she smiled as she dropped down the last step.

"Good morning," she said to the shop at large, though she was the only human in the place. If one could even call her that.

Most wouldn't. *Witch*, they used to whisper in the streets, during the years when she had been in hiding, when they still knew her face. *Foul, vile, corrupt*. They shared stories of the woman who had cursed the lands, who had called the sea down upon them and drowned the earth. She had felt every ounce of their hatred in her soul. They'd infected her with hatred and fear and fury.

It didn't matter to her. Her reptiles felt the same beneath her skin, in that place she stored her power. She had a connection with the souls of every living creature, animals and humans alike.

Truth be told, she hated the rare day that one of her companions was sold, because once they left her shop, she could no longer lengthen their lives. She couldn't keep their steady hearts beating, pushing away the threat of age. She refused to extend her magic beyond the walls of this shop, not again. They became as mortal as any other beast when they left her, and she would lose them.

She would lose them all, one by one. Just as she had lost every other soul she had ever loved.

The Hallowed could not just ignore their powers. This magic was given for a reason, whether that immortal be blessed or damned. They'd be driven mad as that gifted power built up, desperate for control, for release. She'd felt the beginning effects of it once, had made rash decisions to avoid crawling out of her skin. She'd seen the destruction holding herself back could bring, and Hallowed could not afford to make the same mistake twice. She let out her power little by little, keeping her reptiles alive and the occasional visitor to her shop ignorant of her identity. She might obliterate the entire kingdom otherwise, with no means to stop herself.

So, she focused on her shop, making it into some semblance of a home. She cobbled everything she knew about humanity. She took what she'd learned about the lives of the people she controlled and made an invisible life for herself.

She swept through the store, flipping the chipped sign in her frosted window to indicate she was open. Even in the early hours of the morning, with the sun barely peeking over the rundown huts and onto the grass, people began to mill about through the cobblestone streets. Venders rolled out and set up for the day, gathering into markets for food, wine, wooden crafts. Children ran away from their parents with laughter. Children were few and far between, even now, but at least the people had begun to come outside again. It had taken decades, but within the rippling walls fracturing the rays of light, the Kingdom of Calypdon was slowly knitting itself back together.

The first eighty years of hiding had been horrid, because everyone had known her face. In the beginning, they'd hunted her ceaselessly. It was a miracle, on that first, shattered day, that she had managed to escape Briarwood, sneaking through the broken gates of a near-dead kingdom. After the war, after she'd done what she'd done, there had been an opportunity, an opening, and she had run. She had run and had not stopped; had not revealed her face until she'd crossed what remained of the island. There hadn't been much, a handful of leagues left untouched by the invading sea. She fled north for the cover of the dark, foreboding forest.

But slowly, the survivors of the cataclysm grew old and passed on, leaving fewer and fewer people who might recognize her. She remembered when the last survivor passed. She'd been passing through this very town when there was an uproar, and she felt his life force fade away. In the center of the street, as the townsfolk around her wept and the world stood still, she stopped and for the first time in years, she smiled.

One by one, everyone she had known from her first life had faded away, and she herself had lingered, emerging as a new woman who looked the same but who no one would recognize anymore.

She perched on a stool after going through and tending to the various snakes she had collected over the years. Most of them still slumbered, content in the enormous tank that spanned the far side of the wall, and she slumped behind her desk. Even in a cloak and simple dress, she felt the phantom weight at her hip, of something missing. Of a sword that she hadn't seen in two hundred years.

A sword she'd plunged into the only woman she'd ever loved.

Her thoughts were interrupted by the small, makeshift bell she'd fashioned by her door, and she looked up to see Cadence springing into the shop, her skirts sweeping behind her and her curtain of black, coiled hair bouncing over her shoulders.

Morgana sighed as the woman came in. Cadence lived in an overcrowded lodging down the street but survived alone in every other way. She remained the only person in nearly two centuries that Morgana had allowed into her solitary life. She had come one day about five years ago, when rain had been pouring down in thick sheets. Cadence had been soaked, shaking head to foot, but not from the cold. No, water had a much different impact on the land people since the rising of the ocean, and the near constant fear of drowning hung over their heads. With the torrential rains, it was easy to think those walls might come down after all.

Against every instinct, Morgana had offered her shelter for the night. It was the longest time she'd spent with another being in decades, and they'd spent much of the evening in companionable silence, listening to the rain. When morning came, light filtering onto Morgana's bed, she hadn't had the heart to touch Cadence's mind, to mold her memories to wedge that familiar distance between them, the careful boundary she maintained with everyone in town. Loneliness was a plague, and she'd been cured for but a moment. She hadn't been ready to give it up yet.

And so she had decided that she wouldn't lay a finger of magic upon Cadence, not until signs of aging began to grey one of their skin but not the other. After that, Morgana would have no choice.

Cadence threw her cloak off now, rubbing her hands together and pressing them to her rosy cheeks. "It's bitter out there. You're so lucky you don't even need to leave your house to go to work."

Morgana rounded her desk, lifting herself onto the wooden table and letting her legs swing beneath her. The threadbare fabric of her skirt ran over her skin, catching on her boots. "I'm sure you survived the two blocks separating us." Little more than two blocks separated anything in this village: in any village. They'd shrunk, after it happened, as people fled to the center of the kingdom, away from the ever approaching sea that ate away at Calypdon and any land-folk who stood in its way. Few villages lingered, and the ones that did consisted of perhaps fifty people, often less. "The first snow hasn't even fallen yet."

Cadence squinted out the window as she came further in. "Might come today."

Morgana hated talking about the weather. Still, she said, "Not cold enough. Rain, more likely."

Cadence grimaced, fingers raised to her hair, as if she, too, remembered that first day she'd come in. Drenched, wringing out her braid, sending droplets over the worn wooden floor. "Water's scary, isn't it?" She swallowed. "Given the whole…"

She trailed off, motioning vaguely in the direction of the looming wall relentlessly hanging over them. Morgana didn't need clarification as she gazed out the window. She almost couldn't see the monstrous wall of water through the mist.

"It is," Morgana agreed halfheartedly.

"I think it could be pretty," Cadence said wistfully. "Water and rain, the sea. In a world where the kingdoms were still split, and it didn't feel like we could drown at any moment."

Sometimes, Morgana would watch as rain flowed down the streets, over the grass and through the trees. She would try to track each drop as it spilled toward the sea, only a few miles away, but she could never follow it all the way. Morgana wondered what happened to water like that. If the rivulets would smash into that wall of water like glass, or if the sea would swallow that piece of their world, too. "Somehow it's the most beautiful and ugliest thing in the world at the same time."

"Do you think it will?" Cadence asked, gazing at Morgana as if she knew everything there was to know. Perhaps she could feel the differences that separated them in the air. Perhaps she somehow sensed the years that only a Hallowed could count. "Fall, I mean."

Morgana had gazed at her and decided to give a half truth. "Not in our lifetimes."

"I'll never have children," Cadence said after a moment. "Not when that wall could fall upon them. I'll live alone for the rest of my life so they don't have to spend every day fearing they will drown."

Morgana's eyes fluttered closed, regret echoing in the space between them. The pain of two women: one who would never see her future, and the other who could never escape her past.

Shaking off the melancholy, Cadence snapped at Morgana with slim fingers, a grin spreading across her face. "Enough of that. Where's my favorite snake?"

Morgana raised her hand, feeling the rattlesnake moving in the corner of the room, and Cadence hurried toward the small creature, scooping it up into her arms.

"Are you sure you don't want to take him home?" Morgana asked.

Cadence shook her head with a sigh, but her eye twinkled as she gazed over at Morgana. "If I took him home, what excuse would I have to come see you?"

Heat rose up the back of Morgana's neck, and she ducked her head. *A few more years*, she reminded herself. *That's all you get. This is what you'll give yourself until the water takes her, too.*

"Hey," Cadence said, leaning against the wall as the snake wove around her arms. She looked so comfortable with the creature, it tugged at Morgana's heartstrings. Not many people could hold reptiles easily, without fear. "I'm heading over to the tavern tonight for a drink. It's been a long couple of days with the cold. Care to join me?"

Morgana longed to say yes. Cadence stopped by at least once a week, needling her with questions, trying to find out more about her. Morgana humored her, laughing along with some of the jokes but never leaving the comfort of the shop, because the young girl was all she had. Morgana made up some stories about where she came from, claiming that she'd come from the overpopulated capital, deciding she preferred a quicker death by an impending tidal wave to starvation or disease. She gave only as much as Cadence demanded. Never too much. Never too detailed.

Never enough.

Cadence stood completely still, waiting for Morgana's answer to her invitation. She looked beautiful enough that Morgana began to open her mouth, to break the promise she'd made to herself in the beginning. But the memory of another woman echoed in the back of her mind, images of emotions that she had spent two hundred years of hiding trying to shove down. They always resurfaced.

The past had a tendency to do that.

Morgana turned away, hiding her face. "Perhaps another day."

Cadence would die soon, she reminded herself. She was tired of losing people to their miniscule lifespans.

Cadence tilted her head in concern, pursing her lips as she always did. But she didn't say anything more. She simply drew her fingers down the rattlesnake's back once more and disappeared back out into the cold.

Sometimes Morgana missed the excitement of her old life, the wars and the kings and the horrible things she had done. But then she remembered that peace was boring, and the ensuing violence wasn't worth her happiness. She spent the rest of the day alone, feeding the reptiles and keeping herself busy until the sun at last set. Until she could close the shop, go upstairs, and prepare to do the same thing the next day.

PART ONE
The Beginning
Morgana

Chapter One

Morgana once lived alone, deep in the woods on the outskirts of Calypdon, where she would be bothered by no one but the surrounding animals. They called it the Abandoned Forest, filled with rotting trees and wilted grasses, weeds and dead flowers since the Ancient War. The stories said that anyone who set foot on that land would be damned for all their lives, sinking deep into the earth they'd desecrated. This didn't bother Morgana. She had been cursed all her life.

Her mother had taken her there when they'd fled from those wishing to exploit her magic, finding comfort in the land that had housed the bones of their ancestors for generations. They made a home in a small, stone cottage nestled beside a winding stream. They were unbothered by the people who feared the woods. Her mother had told Morgana on her deathbed that she would be safer where no one could find her, where no one suspected. It would be better if no one knew she existed.

"They'll always know we exist," Morgana had countered, crouching next to her mother's bed, sending up prayers she knew wouldn't be answered. "Because they know you exist."

Her mother had pursed her lips, but they broke apart again with a hacking cough, blood glistening on her chin. Morgana brought pale fingers to the bloody lips, gently wiping the crimson away. "I fought for a noble cause. People are alive now because I revealed who I was, what I could do, and I don't regret that. I know you would do the same. Perhaps you will one day make the same choice."

Morgana wiped away a tear. Her mother had never tolerated crying; she said she'd lived too long to waste time on tears, regardless of whether or not they were her own. "And when that time comes, how, exactly, will I know if it's a noble cause or not? People lie, you know."

Chuckling, her mother gripped Morgana's hand. "They do. They always will. But … your magic will allow you to feel intentions. You will feel life, and everything that comes along with a person's soul. You will know when someone is worth it."

The magic of the Hallowed came from the gods themselves. Periodically, in times of great turmoil, they'd choose a vessel, sending a shard of their power down to stand for them in such moments. According to Morgana's grandmother, magic had once been far more common, with dozens of the Hallowed, those touched by the gods, existing at a time, scattered across every corner of Calypdon.

"The gods sent the Hallowed to work their will upon the land; to fight their wars for them." Morgana's mother had brushed a strand of hair behind her ear. "Many say the god of death cursed our ancestors, and there are times when I can't disagree with them. I'm sorry it now falls on your shoulders."

Morgana had asked what would happen if the fighting stopped.

Her mother smiled in a way that indicated she never thought such a time would come. "In a world without war, we would one day see a world without magic."

Her mother had passed away in the night. Morgana found herself alone the next day, curled in the center of her home in torment as the power that her mother had passed down transferred to her. She didn't have even a moment to grieve, left to deal with the agony tearing through her veins, weaving around her tendons, carving an oath into her bones. The weight of tens of thousands of lives, near and far, young and old, human and animal alike, found a home around her heart. It burned her up from the inside, and ate her muscle, drank her blood, shackled her wrists. The souls burrowed into her, knitting through her own, forging a connection with a world she had long ago exiled herself from.

And then it had all stopped. The pain ebbed out of her, leaving her weak and gasping, sweat lining her brow like an unwanted crown. Her strength came back, but the pull of those countless souls continued to drag on her as if gravity had multiplied. The walls of the little cabin bowed in toward her, pressed in by that ethereal weight.

Not knowing how much time had passed, Morgana groaned as she straightened onto her back, arms splayed out over the rickety wooden floor. Her fingers brushed something cool, and she rolled her head to the side to find the blade of a sword inches from her eye.

Exhaling slowly, Morgana ran the pad of her finger along the flat of the blade, down its silvery length. The blade itself was simple, long and straight, feeding into an elaborate hilt. A gemstone the color of blood reflected the light of the setting sun, set deep into the etched gold plating of the cross guard. Below, twin serpents with glinting red eyes twined around the handle, tiny scales etched in ivory, the tails rising to allow the wielder's hand to slip through. They were beautiful creatures, these snakes, but Morgana would never be able to look at this sword and appreciate its craftsmanship. She could only see the horror of what it could do.

Her fingers closed around the Serpent Sword. The air around her sighed as the weapon surrendered to its new owner.

Only after sliding the sword safely into its sheath did Morgana stand on shaky legs and leave to organize a service in the woods that no one would attend but herself.

A funeral for a mother who had almost completely decomposed by the time Morgana had awakened from her long, agonizing transformation.

She wrapped her mother's bones in her favorite blanket and carried them through the forest, trudging along for miles, kneeling when she finally reached a large patch of dirt. The Abandoned Forest didn't contain many empty spaces. It had no room for humans, with roots surging underfoot, winding around the graves of all the other Serpent Witches who had died before.

She dug for hours, thinking of all the funerals held outside of this forest, in the villages and towns and cities. Normally, someone else would do this, and more people would attend, and there would be someone to comfort her. But Morgana dug the grave herself, inch by inch, with each scoop of dirt, and buried her mother. She was sunk into the cursed lands where her kind belonged.

Her mother would remain damned even in death.

As she covered the bones, deep in the ground so no animals would disturb them, she felt movement along her foot, a scaly texture pulling over her skin, and Morgana kicked out on instinct, sending the snake flying.

It hissed as it hit a tree across the clearing, dropping like a limp rope in the waiting grass.

Morgana's hands flew to her mouth when she realized what she'd done, unsure if she should rush to the snake or give it space. A cobra, she realized, as she felt it shake itself off through her newfound connection to the souls of the world. She realized she could feel it breathe.

The snake lifted its head.

Her mother had spent the better part of Morgana's childhood teaching her about all the creatures in the world. "If you're meant to have control over them," her mother warned on more than one occasion, "you must understand them. You must never think of these creatures as less than you. You must know them as you know yourself."

Guilt dripped down Morgana's spine, and she rose to her feet, holding her hand out as the cobra flicked its tongue, tilting its head at her. Perhaps it could feel the connection, the link Morgana now had with everything alive.

"Hello," Morgana whispered, taking a step forward, trying to soothe the creature with her new power. But she didn't know how it worked. It churned within her, running through her blood, but she knew nothing of how to transfer it beyond her own skin.

She was nothing but a bridge between the gods and every mortal soul. A conduit that brought power down from the heavens and passed it along to all the souls in the kingdoms. With the god of death's curse came the responsibility to watch over those alive for as long as possible, until they one day passed into his realm. It wasn't a magic intended to be used, but that didn't mean she couldn't wield it with a little effort.

Anything could be wielded, when in the right hands. The link between her and each soul was a real, tangible thing, and she reached for it.

The snake curled up on the ground at the base of the tree, not taking its eyes off her. "I'm sorry," Morgana murmured, moving further forward. "You scared me. I thought you were my mother rising from the dead."

The cobra hissed again, but it didn't sound angry this time. Somehow, it reminded her of laughter.

Morgana lowered herself to her knees in front of the snake, extending her hands. She knew cobras were venomous, and that it could leave an ordinary human dead in the middle of this empty forest with a single bite, but she knew it wouldn't hurt her. Not that it could harm her, even if it wanted to. Before her mother's death, if the snake had sunk its teeth into her flesh, she would have dropped dead as a rock. Today, she would wince at the pain and wait until the burn of the poison faded from her blood. It made her want to test the new power.

Hesitating at first, the cobra slithered around Morgana's wrist, as if shaking her hand in greeting. Morgana exhaled, sending a silent message that she meant no harm. That she kept the snake alive with her every breath. The cobra must have understood, because it moved up her arm, settling on her shoulder. For the first time since her mother died, Morgana smiled.

"Would you like to come home with me?" Morgana asked, dragging a finger over the snake's skin. It hissed once more, and Morgana knew in her bones it meant yes.

With one last look at the dirt mounded on her mother's grave, knowing it would never be touched by another human again, Morgana swallowed and murmured, "All right, then." Turning her back on the past, she retraced her path through the forest, back to the cabin to figure out how to live this new life alone.

***

Several years passed. She stayed in her hut, scavenging for greens to eat and drinking water from the stream that wound past her cabin. It didn't matter what she ate or drank. She just needed something to soothe her human stomach. The cursed and immortal part of her would rid her body of any toxins, allowing her to survive on a diet that would kill any mortal woman, even on the days she didn't want to.

It was a boring life, and a lonely one, but it was simple, and it was peaceful. She had stopped aging when she reached twenty, as her mother had, and stopped looking in the mirror soon after. Humans only had vanity in the hopes of change. Or perhaps the fear of it.

She wiled away the days with the sun peeking through the golden leaves, swimming in the stream and hiking through the forest. Any activity she could think of, she would try, filling the minutes and hours with only herself and animals for company. She would coax foxes out of their caves to share a meal, tend to bears in the winter when their fur would mat. She whittled little wooden creatures with a kitchen knife, carving away soft wood taken from dying trees.

Most of the time, Coby, the snake she had found at her mother's grave, stayed on her shoulder, making a home in the hollow of her neck. Every now and then he would go out and explore, slithering through the forest where he had once lived. Morgana would close her eyes when he was gone, sorting through the souls of all the creatures in the woods. She could see them in her mind, like glowing balls of light wandering through the forest she conjured up in her mind, and Coby seemed to shine the brightest. On the few occasions he got lost, she would follow the link between herself and her snake and bring him home.

Only after several years, worn down by solitude, did she pluck up the courage to creep to the edge of the forest, where the hard packed dirt gave way to thick grass. The unfiltered sunlight burned her eyes as she approached, squinting so much she could barely see as the sun beamed down, filling the path animals had forged into the forest.

She didn't let herself step out, wouldn't allow the light to fall on her skin, unfiltered by boughs and twining branches. She remained, cloaked in leaves and shadow, hood obscuring her features, crouched behind a rotting stump.

There was a small village not far from the edge of the wood, but close enough that Morgana could feel their joy trickling over her skin. Their souls were like a forest fire, setting her hair on end. She watched from a distance, but it was still closer than she ever thought she'd be again.

Sinking deeper into the ferns, she rested her chin on the stump, fingers digging into the bark. She sat for hours, watching the people set up a market, bargaining for handcrafted goods and exchanging drinks. Her fingers itched for the trinkets on the carts, wondering what it would be like to own something made by someone else. To link herself to the world in such a way.

But the people seemed happy, and she could live with that. Perhaps steal just a morsel of their happiness for herself.

Only when dusk began to fall did something in her gut twitch. An overwhelming sense of *wrongness* surged through her chest, and she was halfway over the stump when a flash of silver caught the lingering light of the sun, bathed in oranges and ultramarine.

Something behind Morgana's ribs cleaved open, and screams burst from the street as villagers ran back and forth, taking shelter in their homes and leaving a single fading soul, splayed across the cobblestones. She felt the link between them beginning to dim.

One other person remained, looming over the prone figure, dressed in strange, unfamiliar finery, sword still drawn. It dripped with crimson, near black in the falling darkness.

There was nothing she could do. The man was already dead.

It was the first time since inheriting her powers that she'd been so close to a death, and she felt his soul leave hers. It wasn't soft and peaceful; the link between them didn't simply fade away. It snapped like a cord pulled taut, like the god of death himself had taken his blade and wedged it between them.

Morgana felt nothing of him after that; if she closed her eyes and used only her internal map of souls to gauge her surroundings, she might have believed the soldier was alone in the street. But because she didn't want to say goodbye to the man just yet, she stared hard into the fading light and watched as the soldier dragged his victim away.

The village stayed silent well into the night, and Morgana never ventured to the edge of the forest alone again.

Two years of lonely isolation went by before a knock sounded on her door.

She jerked from where she'd been lying on her bed, playing with Coby on her stomach. Coby turned his head to the door, too, as startled as Morgana.

"It's okay," Morgana told her snake, ignoring the tremor in her voice. "It was probably the wind. Did it look like a storm was coming–?"

She cut herself off when the knock sounded again, this time more insistent. Her mother had been positive that no one would disturb them here, so much so that Morgana had truly believed the stories claiming this land to be cursed. But no animal could summon that harsh, loud rap of knuckles.

Only a human would wait outside.

Warily, Morgana stood, pulling on some of the cleaner clothes she'd washed in the stream the other day, reaching for the Serpent Sword; she still had a hard time thinking of it as hers rather than her mother's. She hadn't had cause to draw it since her mother's passing. She shoved it into her belt, letting Coby slither from her arm and onto the table.

There was no window in the door. Why would there be, when no one came here but her? Steeling herself, she called through, "Who is it?"

There was a clearing of a throat, tension clear in the sound. The voice that spoke then was that of a woman, strong and confident. "My name is Aveline Combs. I am an emissary from the sea."

Morgana wrinkled her brow and swung open the door to reveal a tall woman standing a few feet away with her hands clasped behind her back. She, too, had a sword strapped to her waist, her dark hair pulled back with a ribbon. Opening her mouth, Morgana found she couldn't summon any words, the shock of seeing another person for the first time in so long overtaking her completely. She was close enough to touch, and the proximity to another soul took Morgana's breath away.

The woman, Aveline, just continued to stare, back straight and lips pursed. A few moments of silence passed before Aveline's eyes darted around, brow furrowed at Morgana's stunned expression. "Did you hear me?"

Morgana snapped her mouth closed and exhaled, movement coming back to her as Aveline's words at last registered. The only thing she could think to say was, "You should be dead."

Aveline blinked, eyes a dark brown in the dim light of evening. "I'm sorry?"

Throat dry, Morgana motioned around her. "This land is cursed."

Looking over her shoulder, Aveline shifted, clearly unsure of what to do with her hands or body, trying to remain as formal as possible despite her confusion. She wore a uniform of some sort. A soldier or a guard, perhaps. "The curses of the lands have no effect on the people of the sea. It was one of the conditions of the Ancient Rift."

The Ancient Rift.

Neither Morgana nor her mother had been alive during the war, but her grandmother had lived through those terrible years, over a millennia ago. Morgana had heard the stories through her mother. The split was true and absolute. One people had been torn into two, and ever since, the two kingdoms remained separate, rarely associating at all unless necessary. Those in Nysus, the sea kingdom, had learned to adjust to their new lives, and those left on Calypdon carried on as they always had. For those remaining on the island, they couldn't imagine anything different.

Which made it all the more confusing that it wasn't only a human, but a sea woman, who stood at her doorstep.

Morgana kept one hand firmly on the doorknob, half her body hidden behind the slab of wood and ready to slam it shut if the need arose. She tried to regain control over her galloping heartbeat and respond in a way this woman might perceive as normal. An ordinary human wouldn't be so scared of a soldier, would she? "Yes, of course. What can I help you with?"

Aveline slipped something from her sleeve, and Morgana was momentarily alarmed at the flash of metal, thinking it might be a dagger. But Aveline simply removed a small scroll from a silver cuff and unfurled it, reaching out to pass it to Morgana. Morgana didn't take it; one hand was still on the door, and the other would remain firmly on her sword until this woman left.

After several moments, when it became clear Morgana wasn't going to take the scroll, Aveline cleared her throat and pulled it back. "It's a missive from King Daegil of Nysus."

Morgana wanted to accept the scroll even less now. "What could the sea king possibly want with me? I live alone here, on the land. I've done nothing to offend him."

"You're not charged with any sort of crime," Aveline assured her. "He wishes for your aid."

Though Morgana's pulse quickened, she kept her face clear in the way her mother had taught her, calming herself, trying to make herself appear as non-threatening as possible. "That's worse, since he clearly has the wrong woman. I can barely keep myself alive out here, let alone aid a king."

Aveline folded her arms, and Morgana focused on the woman's fingertips brushing against her sword. "Interesting. If it's so difficult living out here, why bother? There are many villages that would be happy to have you. You could go anywhere."

Morgana scrambled to explain herself. "I prefer solitude."

"Please," Aveline said. "No lies. I'd like this to go as smoothly as possible. Especially since you yourself just admitted that this land is fatal to humans. Which you aren't."

Morgana truly began to panic. How could this woman possibly know about her powers, who she was? Sure, her line had been the subject of tales and stories for thousands of years, but how did this woman know about *Morgana specifically?* Morgana hadn't shown her face since she was a child, had never used her powers in front of others. When her mother had escaped, they'd made themselves virtually undetectable, unless–

Unless those in Nysus knew where they were all along, Morgana realized with a deflating heart. Unless their scouts had been following Morgana and her mother ever since they fled civilization, escaping into the Abandoned Forest.

They'd never truly escaped. They had never been free.

They would always be hunted.

"How did you find me?" Morgana whispered. "And what do you want?"

Aveline looked relieved at the admission, despite the desperation in Morgana's voice. "King Daegil has his ways and has had people watching over Calypdon for years. He has accumulated a lot of information, including your whereabouts, and including information about your king that you might be interested in."

"I'm not interested in anything you have to say," Morgana said, setting her jaw, but Aveline's hand now completely gripped the hilt of her sword. Morgana knew she could take this woman's life with a mere thought, but … she didn't want to. Her mother had done her best to never take a life, had only used her powers to heal and strengthen lives, except for the one time she'd had absolutely no choice. Morgana had always promised herself she wouldn't either. She went on, "And I don't care about your king's information. I don't belong to the sea as you do."

"No," Aveline agreed. "But from what I hear, you've not sworn an oath to the land, either."

"That's correct," Morgana said, voice raspy from years of only having a snake to talk to. "Because I don't belong to the land as land dwellers do, either. Although I wasn't aware I had to swear an oath anywhere."

Aveline nodded, looking past Morgana at the cabin strewn with dishes and discarded clothes. "It's clear that you haven't been involved with civilization in quite some time, and you have more than a little to catch up on. May I come in?"

***

"That's absurd."

Aveline had just finished summarizing the missive from King Daegil, since Morgana was still refusing to take the scroll. The sea woman had spent most of the time eyeing Coby instead of actually speaking to Morgana, and Morgana didn't know whether to feel offended or entertained that Aveline seemed to fear an animal over her.

Morgana went on. "You're telling me that the sea king wants to take over the lands? That he wants to be the sole ruler?"

"Not at all," Aveline said, leaning back in her chair. "He has no desire to rule over Calypdon. He simply wants to see the current land king unseated."

"But why?" Morgana asked incredulously, moving over to the kitchen to empty the mugs she and Aveline had been drinking from. "There are miles of water separating Nysus from us. We've been apart for centuries, contact is limited. What's there to gain by manipulating the land?"

"Nothing," Aveline said emphatically. "King Daegil just wants peace for the people of both realms."

Morgana snorted. "And his idea of peace is to bring about another war? I'm afraid we might have different definitions of peace. Do you not remember what happened the last time the balance was disrupted?"

Aveline leaned forward again, bracing her elbows on her knees, and Morgana thought she looked awfully comfortable in the house of a woman who could wipe away her life and soul with a thought. "No, no, you're misunderstanding me. The sea doesn't want a war; we want to *stop* one."

"You're contradicting yourself," Morgana countered sternly. "We've been at peace for centuries; the Rift satisfied the god of the sea. The sea got half, that was the bargain. Your king cannot take our people without breaking the gods' word. A war would be inevitable."

"This is not an issue of the gods at all," Aveline said, holding her hands up. "It's not the god of the sea, or my king, who desires more power. He has no qualms with the people of the land, only their ruler. He doesn't even want to claim the Calypdon throne. Everything else will stay exactly the same. The gods will remain happy with both the land and sea strong. He only wishes to take away power from an unjust king."

This caught Morgana's attention. "Is he unjust?" she asked curiously, leaning back against her counter. "I don't remember him being so."

"You also remember a different king," Aveline said solemnly. "The one you knew passed about twelve years ago, replaced by his son; King Wendell. A cruel man, who desires only to expand his own power and cause the fall of the sea. He cares nothing for the wellbeing of his people."

Morgana's brows rose as a memory came crawling to the edge of her mind. Of a scream in a village, blood on cobblestones. "If Nysus falls, then the god of the sea carries out his plan to destroy the lands. The Ancient War decided that one would never exist without the other."

Aveline looked uncomfortable as she informed Morgana, "King Wendell has no belief in the gods."

Morgana stifled a snort, her magic rearing up as if in opposition to her guest's words. Morgana was living proof that the gods plagued their world.

"Your king is the one who desires war," Aveline said, swallowing hard as memories seemed to flash behind her eyes. The kingdoms had been at peace for centuries when Morgana and her mother had left them behind, but that had been long before the rise of this new king, Wendell, when Morgana was only a girl.

Morgana thought of her grandmother's stories, passed down through her mother, of the horror and devastation of the Ancient War. Her grandmother had felt every death, every injury, every soul that had drowned in the sea god's attacks. She had referred to them as the lost years, because there had been nothing but agony until the Rift sealed the fates of both kingdoms and all their inhabitants.

Morgana would not see that agreement fail.

"King Wendell wants to return all humans to Calypdon," Morgana guessed. "He wants to undo the Rift."

"He refuses to call it that, to call it anything but a story. He believes he has a right to rule over them all."

Ludicrous, of course. Gods wrote history however they wanted. "What's he doing, then?"

Aveline's gaze darkened. "He's forcing each land dweller to travel to Briarwood to swear fealty to the land. But it's more than that; he's trying to reverse sea people back into land dwellers."

Morgana's throat went dry. "I don't understand. Is he a Hallowed?"

"No," Aveline said sharply. "He's descended from one, I believe, as both royal lines are, but, no, a god has never directly touched him."

"Then how could he possibly hope to reverse the act of a god?"

"I don't know. We don't know exactly what he's doing to them. Just that he's experimenting on them, trying to transform them back into something belonging to the land." Aveline swallowed, and for the first time, her voice shook. Her hand fluttered up to her neck, grazing over what looked to be a seashell strung onto a deep blue cord tied tightly at the nape of her neck. "My people, my fellow guards, are disappearing, captured by Calypdon soldiers. And they don't come back."

Morgana blinked and tried to wrap her mind around the implications.

Aveline went on. "He's become a tyrant."

It's a man who sees himself as one of the Hallowed but has no such blessing behind him.

Morgana stalked back to the table, lowering herself into the seat opposite Aveline. The other woman sat with her legs crossed, her fingers twisting together on the table. Morgana stared at them, at the whites of her knuckles. "You're nervous."

Aveline swallowed, a lump bobbing in her throat. "Yes," she rasped. It was as if her anxiety, now acknowledged by Morgana, had sapped her of all confidence.

Morgana studied her eyes, dimples crinkling her dark brown skin as Aveline pursed her lips. "You think I might kill you."

"I think you could," Aveline said, raising her gaze to meet Morgana's. Flashes of the setting sun shot through the window, turning the brown of her eyes into molten honey. Morgana felt suddenly self-conscious of her green hair, her different colored eyes. The oddities she shared with her mother and had since forgotten weren't normal. "And that's a lot of power for one woman to possess."

Morgana sighed, resting her elbows on the table, rubbing those eyes as if to wipe the color away. She had once asked her mother what caused these deformities, but she had simply said that magic manifested in different ways, that it was always looking for a way out. "It is. You think I don't know that?"

"I think you're new," Aveline said. "To your powers, to this life you've been given. I know you are. I was expecting a much older woman."

Morgana closed her eyes. "My mother passed away a few years ago, and her magic passed on to me."

When she opened her eyes, Aveline's brow creased in the center as she shook her head. "I'm sorry." Whether she was apologizing for Morgana's loss of her mother or the gain of her powers, Morgana couldn't tell.

Morgana shifted, not wanting to speak more on the subject. "There's a reason I live here, alone; why I've kept to myself all these years. I have no desire to hurt anyone." She lifted her gaze. "Moreover, I have no desire to fight in a war."

"Then *help* us," Aveline pleaded. She leaned forward as if she might grip Morgana's hand, but stopped halfway across the table. "Help me save my people. Prove to me you're not what I fear you are."

Morgana winced. Aveline spoke so sincerely that Morgana could almost believe she was someone to be feared. "Your fears are not my burden. I've done nothing to you."

"Your ancestors have done enough," Aveline said. "I've heard stories of wars in the past, wars that were decided by your kind."

"I don't give a damn about my ancestors," Morgana said harshly. "The only family– my kind, as you say– that I ever knew was my mother, and she only used her powers to help people. She saved many lives."

"You could save lives, too," Aveline said sadly. "People will die if you stay here."

People will die if I go.

Morgana considered her next words, needing a distraction as she reached out and tugged on the energy radiating from Aveline's soul. "And you're a lady of the sea?" Morgana asked. "You were born there, raised there?"

Aveline bowed her head. "I was. I've visited Calypdon only a few times. I only recently gained access to the portals." Her fingertips flitted back to the seashell at her neck.

Though the two kingdoms remained separate, travel between the two *was* possible. Certain areas of the land had been imbued with a thin veil of magic that brought travelers between the two realms. Morgana didn't know precisely where in the vast ocean Nysus had been created, but a portal could transport a land dweller there. Of course, they would need a way to open the portal, and a way to breathe once they arrived. A trusted few in either kingdom were given such a gift.

"And how did you sneak through Calypdon without capture?"

Aveline's eyes flashed. "King Wendell has many soldiers patrolling the streets, but he doesn't have the power to know where every life is at any given moment." She jutted her chin toward Morgana. "He doesn't have you."

"And you want me," Morgana said flatly, still trying to grasp this woman's soul. She had only ever experimented with her powers on Coby, to track where he went and where to find him on the rare occasion he got lost. She'd never dared reach out to a human with her powers, and she was about to give up when she struck a chord, a surge of energy within the woman seated across from her. The sea woman's heartbeat, the rush of blood in her veins, and the wash of emotions that took over Morgana's every fiber drowned out anything Aveline might have been saying. Desperation, hope, pride. Morgana sorted through the chaos and found nothing hidden, no ill intentions. Just a woman who had risked her life to travel to a new kingdom in the attempt to find a solution to her own kingdom's troubles.

"Are you alright?"

Morgana pulled back quickly, and the emotions fell away into the space between them, back to Aveline where they belonged. Morgana didn't have the time to decide whether she should feel guilty, whether that was betrayal of newfound trust. She just tilted her head and looked at Aveline. The sea woman sat chewing on her lip.

Morgana sighed, remembering her mother's words. *You will be able to feel intentions. You will feel life and everything that lurks within a person's soul. You will know when a person is worth it.*

Now, Morgana looked at a woman who had nothing but love for her people, nothing but hope for her world. "My name is Morgana," she said, and held out her hand.

Chapter Two

The sun had set by the time Morgana agreed to go with Aveline, if just to hear this sea king, Daegil, out. She would ensure that the Ancient War, a cause of such pain for her grandmother, had not been for nothing.

"I'm making no promises," Morgana said for perhaps the fifth time as they stood from the table. She knew the power of words, the ties they had to the soul. "I will listen to what he asks, I will consider what he wants, but you will not hold me in Nysus if I wish to leave."

Aveline listened to Morgana's conditions patiently. "I can assure you, the last thing we want is to harm you in any way. To hurt you in the pursuit of peace would go against everything we stand for. You will always be free to go if you decide you need to. Once you cross the threshold of my kingdom, you will know exactly where the portal is. Besides, we couldn't hold you even if we tried." She spread her arms. "There are no secrets from us. I swear it."

The tension in Morgana's heart eased, though it didn't go away entirely. Nodding curtly, Morgana peered out the window toward the waiting darkness. "How far is the nearest portal?"

Aveline sighed, and Morgana stiffened as she took her sword from her belt, but she only tossed it on the table. It clattered against the wood and then fell still. "A while. A day on foot, at least."

Morgana had feared as much. "Well, you must have had a long day, hunting me and all that - "

"I was not *hunting* you -"

" - so you probably need to rest before we set out," Morgana finished, pointedly ignoring the interruption. "The nearest town is over twenty miles away, so it looks like you'll be staying here."

Aveline blanched. "Oh, I really don't - "

Morgana shot her a look. "Scared I'll kill you in your sleep?"

The lack of response immediately translated into, *Sort of, yes*.

Morgana rubbed her eyes, and any resentment she had about her mother keeping them hidden away dissipated. If this was how people treated witches, with fear and distrust, maybe Morgana wanted nothing to do with them. "If I wanted you dead, you'd be dead. Did you forget that I could put you to sleep right now, and then kill you? Moreover, I could just kill you right now, and it'd be over and done with. You wouldn't even know it was happening."

"Maybe you want to catch me off guard," Aveline blurted out.

Eyes widening with incredulity, Morgana said, "Are you implying I'm a sadist? If you think that of me, you're sure putting a lot of questionable ideas in my head."

"I don't think you're a sadist," Aveline said quickly, not at all convincingly. "It's just unnerving to have an opponent that I wouldn't even have a chance to defend myself against. I'd be dead before either of us could draw our swords."

Morgana tilted her head. "I guess it's good we're not opponents then. Look - " She paused, taking her intricate sword from her sheath and delicately setting it next to Aveline's on the table, so they didn't touch. "I'm unarmed. You're unarmed. Let's agree that no one here wants anyone to die."

Aveline pointed at her. "Do you see where that doesn't really count, though? You're not unarmed. Your entire *being* is a weapon."

Morgana flung her arms in the air, almost impressed when Aveline didn't flinch. "Well, I can't really do anything about that, can I? You came to me, and I agreed to go with you tomorrow. Now, you need to sleep."

Aveline's breathing steadied, and she squeezed her eyes shut, probably questioning her life choices. Morgana was surely questioning hers. When Aveline opened her eyes again, she nodded stiffly. "I apologize."

Morgana tipped her head back toward the ceiling. "Don't apologize for being afraid of a weapon."

"Do you think of yourself that way?" Aveline asked. "As a weapon?"

Morgana spread her fingers across her stomach, over the warmth of the power rooted there. "You *just* called me one."

"I didn't ask what *I* thought. I asked what *you* thought."

Morgana was amazed at how brazen Aveline was being, asking so many questions, even as nervous as she claimed to be. Perhaps she really had started to believe that Morgana meant no harm. Morgana brushed her green-tinged hair away from her shoulders, trying not to wonder what Aveline thought of it. "I think there are two sides to everything."

"Even weapons?"

"Especially weapons. Sure, the blade of a sword is deadly, but the hilt offers comfort to the sword bearer."

Aveline nodded slowly, and at last allowed her muscles to relax. Morgana felt it in the energy radiating from Aveline, and her own heart rate decreased as energy between the women settled. "Okay, then. Truce."

"I'm glad we covered that for the second time." Morgana stalked toward her tiny kitchen. "Get some sleep. I'd rather travel by daylight."

No movement sounded behind her for several long moments, and Morgana at last glanced behind her to find that Aveline hadn't moved. She was ready to throw it all to hell and tell her to leave, but it all made sense when she saw Aveline glance warily at the extra, made bed that used to belong to her mother, where Coby had curled up on the pillow.

Morgana laughed, gliding across the room to scoop up the cobra, hugging him to her chest. He rested his head on her shoulder, and she felt his soul sing. "Oh, Coby won't hurt you. He's harmless."

"Cobras are deadly," Aveline countered nervously, backing away. Did they have snakes in the sea, or had Aveline anxiously researched anything from the lands that could possibly hurt her before making this journey?

Morgana just smirked. "Then don't do anything to make him want to bite you." Aveline's eyes widened even more, and Morgana laughed. "Relax, he won't bite." She wiggled her fingers. "I'll make sure of it."

Aveline didn't look encouraged by this, and Morgana thought it didn't make much sense for Aveline to be scared of a simple animal. They had droves of horrible, ancient creatures in Nysus. Sirens and mermaids who haunted the depths and stalked their prey through the shadows.

Morgana supposed that facing something different could be more terrifying than facing a familiar danger.

"Why a snake?" Aveline asked, still not moving as Morgana brought Coby closer to the sea woman. "You could welcome in dozens of animals, there must be thousands in these woods, and yet you choose a *snake*."

Coby's tongue flicked out, and Morgana ran a soothing finger between his eyes. "My mother loved snakes. She said any animal that humans feared was a powerful one, and one to hold close."

"Was that an attempt at reassurance?" Aveline asked incredulously.

"My conversational skills need some work." Morgana stopped in front of Aveline, extending the reptile to the woman. "Take him."

Aveline's eyes practically bugged out of her head as she recoiled. "I am *not* holding the snake."

Morgana didn't back down. "Consider this me proving my power. You know I have control over living souls, over people and animals both if I wish, but that control also includes the ability to calm them down, to forge connections between creatures."

"Please don't forge a connection between me and that snake."

Morgana forced herself to keep a straight face. "Look, you're expecting me to trust you. You plan to take me from my home tomorrow and into a foreign kingdom. I am putting all the faith in humanity I have left into you."

Aveline lifted her gaze from Coby to Morgana, and her eyes flitted back and forth, as if she couldn't decide whether to focus on the green eye or the yellow one. Morgana felt no judgment in that gaze, though, only mild irritation at the distraction as Aveline finally settled on the yellow eye. Morgana didn't blame her; it was far more interesting. "Why?"

Morgana thought the truth would be best. "Because I am able to feel others' souls, and I felt yours. I felt goodness there, so you can see how I'm at a disadvantage when it comes to earning trust in this partnership. You can't feel my soul."

Aveline brought a hand to her throat, as if she might reach into her own soul and find the goodness Morgana claimed to be there. She shifted her gaze to the green eye, and Morgana knew why. It was the human eye, and Aveline was trying incredibly hard in that moment to see Morgana as human.

"That's … very kind of you to say."

"I don't say it out of kindness," Morgana said. "I say it because it is the truth, and you should know that I never lie. If I'm going to trust you, you're going to need to trust me, too. Otherwise, this is going to end badly for both of us." She thrust Coby once more toward Aveline's chest, and he hissed. "Hold the snake."

Not taking her gaze from Morgana's, Aveline extended shaking hands toward Coby, who obeyed Morgana and immediately nudged his head into the cupped palms. Aveline cringed and squeezed her eyes shut at the cool texture, at the swift movement of Coby's body, but she didn't move away. Morgana brushed Aveline's fingers with her own, a lifeline, and Aveline forced her eyes open again.

Morgana said in the softest voice she could muster, "He's not going to hurt you, and neither am I."

Aveline nodded, allowing Coby to slither up and around her arms, Morgana letting go of his tail once she knew he wouldn't fall. Aveline sucked in a harsh breath as the full weight of the cobra settled on her, but she just held her arm up as Coby's head snuggled into her shoulder, his body winding around her waist. Chest heaving, Aveline tore her gaze from Morgana to peer down at the snake, whose eyes had closed, finding comfort in Aveline's body heat. She opened her mouth to say something, but the words lodged in her throat, replaced by stuttering breaths.

"It's often the people who are made out to be villains who are the most harmless," Morgana said, gazing fondly at Coby, who was already asleep. "More often than not, we make our own enemies with our fears and assumptions. Snakes won't hurt you unless you leave them no choice."

"That sounds vaguely like a threat," Aveline said, but a smile began to spread across her lips. Whether she smiled for Morgana or Coby, Morgana didn't care. She just basked in the feeling of seeing another person smile for the first time in years.

"It's not a threat," Morgana said, giving a small smile of her own. "Because I know you won't hurt me."

She shouldn't have been able to be wrong. And yet she was.

***

Morgana spent the night packing, gathering food and water for the day's journey and finding her sturdiest clothes. She had never bought new clothes; all the fabrics she owned had once belonged to her mother, resewed and hemmed and restored again. Once her mother had died, Morgana hadn't dared to travel to a village. She had convinced herself the people would be able to smell the magic on her, sense her *otherness*.

She had been gathering her things for less than an hour, when she dropped a pot, bringing Aveline rising groggily from her sheets.

"Sorry," Morgana hissed, cringing at the loud clanging, scrambling to pick the pot up.

Aveline squinted into the dark. "Are you planning on sleeping at all tonight? You're going to have just as long a day tomorrow as me."

Morgana secretly suspected that Aveline found it unnerving to be asleep while Morgana stayed awake, and she grimaced, because she knew she was about to make things so much worse. She'd been hopeful Aveline would fall asleep and stay asleep and be none the wiser.

Morgana turned away, clenching her shaking fingers. "Actually, I don't sleep."

Aveline didn't fall back asleep for quite some time.

***

The journey did, indeed take a full day, and Morgana regretted her decision to be the nice kind of weapon by the second hour. She was no stranger to long walks through the woods. She foraged into the trees often, whether to hunt for food or water, or to visit her mother's grave. But usually she brought Coby with her, who proved to be a much more personable companion than this woman from the sea. Throughout the early hours of the morning, the two women hiked in silence, with Aveline leading the way several paces ahead.

As the sun crept up and shone through the canopy of leaves directly above, Aveline suddenly whipped her head toward Morgana and asked incredulously, "You seriously don't sleep?"

Morgana sighed, quickening her pace to walk side by side with Aveline. She was jealous of the soldier's sturdy boots as her feet ached in her ill-suited shoes. "We talked about this last night."

Aveline kept her gaze trained forward. "I don't think it really registered until just now. I thought it might have been a dream."

"No wonder you've been so silent. You think I'm a demon in a woman's body."

"*No,*" Aveline scoffed. "I have actually been thinking the *opposite*, that you're more normal than I expected. The sleep thing threw me off."

Morgana tried not to think about how flattered she was by the word 'normal'. And then she tried not to think about how odd it was that she was flattered. "Is this your first encounter with magic?"

Aveline chewed on her lip. "It is. I've only heard stories of people blessed by the gods in the past, but all of them died long before I was born." She paused. "But you're not blessed, are you?"

Morgana hesitated, considering Aveline's question. "I don't know what I am, not entirely. In the grand scheme of things, I'm considered one of the Hallowed. After all, I've been touched by the gods, but it doesn't quite fit, either, because I would never consider my magic a blessing. It's a theory that one of my ancestors was once blessed by the god of death, and did something to anger him. In return, my line's been given the burden of holding the threads of all living souls, so he could focus on those in the Underworld."

Aveline's lips parted. "So … you're cursed."

"I'm not cursed," Morgana grumbled, kicking a rock into the trees. "I'm just one of many unlucky daughters who endures the burden of her elders' punishment."

Aveline ignored this. "So, you can't sleep because you're cursed?"

"I can't sleep because I don't *need* to sleep. Besides, it might not be a curse. There's another theory that my magic wasn't *meant* to be so scary. That we were made to be a bridge between mortals and immortals. We serve as this … passive conduit, a pathway for the life energy of the world. That theory says we initially couldn't touch the magic that passed through us. But over time, as the magic embedded deeper into our line, we gained the ability to harness it, though we try not to since nothing good can come from manipulating another person."

"You're not supposed to use your magic?" Aveline asked.

"In a perfect world? No. I think it's why we eventually die, unlike a true Hallowed; this is not a power anyone is meant to have, let alone forever." Morgana shrugged. "I suppose it's not the gods' fault that humans are constantly trying to turn it into a weapon. Don't make me out to be some tortured soul."

Aveline's lips quirked up. "I mean, you are a little bit." A tiny laugh bubbled from Aveline's through, the sound startling Morgana so much she nearly tripped into the dirt. It was the first true laugh she'd heard in years.

"Maybe a little," Morgana conceded, face burning. "But in the same way I have access to everyone's souls, I … well, for lack of a better word, I feed off them. Not literally," Morgana added hastily at the look of horror on Aveline's face. "Just … I gain my life force from the people around me in the same way they get theirs from me. And not just humans, all other living creatures as well. As you've pointed out, that's a lot of power." Morgana shrugged. "It never goes away, never gets depleted, so I never need to recharge. Hence, no sleep."

Aveline at last slowed to a stop, sinking to her knees on a nearby bed of grass. Settling her pack before her, she sorted through it for her water, and after a moment, Morgana did the same. "Don't you ever get tired?"

Morgana wiped her mouth, tossing her water to Aveline since she hadn't yet found hers. "Sure, after a long day I might need physical rest. But I don't fall asleep. I just need to sit for a few minutes."

Aveline jerked her chin behind them, as if she could point to the cabin they'd long since left behind. "Then what's the point of having one bed, never mind two?"

Morgana lifted her shoulder again. "I like to lie down."

In truth, her mother needed a bed once she'd taken ill after hundreds of years of life. She had been unable to stand in her final months. Morgana had built not one bed, but two, so Morgana could lie down with her mother and pretend they were human; so that her mother might feel less weak, and less alone.

They ate their lunch in silence before continuing on, Morgana's shoulders barking in pain as she resettled her pack on her back. She didn't have many belongings to bring to Nysus, but the food and water were more than heavy enough.

"You've really never been to Nysus?" Aveline asked a while later.

Morgana glanced at her, and at the necklace resting in the hollow of Aveline's throat. "No. I've spent most of my life in hiding. I've never even been to Briarwood."

"But you're connected to the sea, too," Aveline pointed out. "Our souls pass through you as well. Why did you choose the land?"

"I didn't," Morgana sighed. "My line lived long before the Rift, before the sea people were created. We were in Calypdon before, and we just … stayed."

Aveline furrowed her brow. "How old *are* you?"

Morgana scoffed. "Don't you know better than to ask a lady her age?"

"I do. No one says anything about asking a witch, though."

To Morgana's own surprise, she wasn't offended but rather burst into laughter. Aveline watched her warily as Morgana wiped her eyes. "Is that what you people call me? What do you think I am? A *witch*?"

Aveline's shoulders relaxed. "I suppose. Some of the kinder villagers call you a sorcerer, since there are stories of your ancestors helping in times of need."

"And I'm a witch because I, personally, haven't done anything?"

"*No*," Aveline said. "You're a witch because you have unexplained magic. And people don't like unexplained magic."

"No, they don't," Morgana said pointedly. "Unless they desire the use of it."

More time passed in silence, and Morgana found herself peering closer at the necklace between Aveline's collarbones. She realized that it wasn't a necklace at all. It was strung on a cord to make it appear to be a necklace, but the shell was actually embedded deep into Aveline's skin. A soft scar bulged out around the edges of the shell, perhaps indicating it had been there for a while. Morgana had half a mind to keep her mouth shut, to keep her distance from this woman who thought to use her. Curiosity, though, eventually got the better of her. She nodded to Aveline's neck. "Does that help you breathe air? The seashell?"

Aveline pulled back in surprise, her hand drifting to her neck, fingering the cord holding the shell. "Yes. The key to breathing in a foreign kingdom is to take a blessed token of your own, making it a part of yourself, so this new place can't overwhelm you."

"What will I do?" Morgana asked. "To breathe in the sea?"

Aveline shrugged. "Nothing, I presume. You are linked to all lives, all souls, including the sea people. I assume that will give you protection in our kingdom. At least where your lungs are concerned."

"And if it doesn't?"

"Then we come back and stick something in your throat. Probably a piece of bark."

Morgana shivered. "Let's hope it works. Was it painful?"

Aveline pressed on the seashell, shuddering. "Very. It requires great sacrifice to become a woman of two worlds. Not many receive that honor."

"And your king? He has it as well?"

"I should think so, although he's never been to Calypdon. He sends soldiers and emissaries for him. His true allegiance is to the sea, of course. He just wants the land to have a ruler that doesn't torment our people for sport." Aveline nodded to herself and let her hand drop. "We all do."

"I do, too," Morgana whispered, so quietly Aveline didn't hear.

The sun had begun to set by the time Aveline slowed to a stop once more, standing with her hands on her hips between two towering oak trees. They looked to be hundreds of years old, sturdy with huge roots spreading out at their base, thicker than Morgana's waist.

"Is this it?" Morgana asked in surprise, squinting into the space between the trees, trying to find some sign of water seeping through. "We're not even at the shore, how could this be a portal?"

"Most of Nysus exists under Calypdon," Aveline explained, situating herself so she stood dead center between the trees. "Calypdon is a floating island, with miles of sea beneath it. There are entrances at the shore as well, in rivers and streams, but Nysus is not in the middle of the ocean. It is beneath you."

Morgana had never thought about precisely where the sea kingdom was. She'd always assumed, with the sea god's hatred of the land, that he would have situated his kingdom as far from Calypdon as possible. "Okay, then. How do we get in? Does your shell do that, too?"

"It does," Aveline said, pressing her palm flat over the shell.

"Wow," Morgana said, approaching. "I think that seashell has more power than I do."

Aveline's lips twitched, but she didn't say anything; just let her eyes flutter closed.

Seconds passed, then minutes. The forest around them was completely still, the birds fell silent, the wind calmed. But nothing else happened.

"Maybe you have the wrong trees," Morgana suggested.

But it soon became clear that she didn't, because as soon as the words were out of her mouth, a watery blue-green light flashed at the base of each tree, sawing across the dirt, crashing together like flashes of lightning. Morgana watched in awe as she realized these lights weren't just lights, but cracks in the ground itself, giving them a glimpse of the world waiting beneath. The earth split apart, pebbles and blades of grass falling into the crevice as it widened, until the two cracks finally crashed together, creating one large fissure in the earth.

"Is that -"

Another light burst out, this time from Aveline herself. No, the light filtered out from between her fingers, from the seashell beneath her hand. The glow acted like water, dripping from her knuckles down her body, wrapping around Aveline, bathing her in an ocean breeze, in the ocean itself. And suddenly the light *was* water, water from the deepest parts of Nysus. Aveline lifted her torso upward, letting her head tilt back, looking entirely at home.

A woman of the sea.

Aveline glanced over her shoulder to where Morgana remained frozen, and Aveline extended her hand. Her entire arm was bathed in ocean water, but Morgana could make out the skin rippling beneath. "You'd better come now, or you'll be left behind."

Morgana stared with wide eyes, the ground rumbling as the fissure widened, inch by inch, until it was wide enough for two people to fit through. Or rather, jump through. "Maybe being left behind wouldn't be so terrible."

Aveline's eyes pierced Morgana's, looking so startlingly green that Morgana stuttered a step forward. "Do you trust me?"

Morgana glanced again at the glowing fissure, the pool of water that continued to gather. It bathed the whole forest with a blue light, shimmering in the darkening night. She managed a shaky smile "Is this your version of me asking you to hold the snake?"

"Maybe," Aveline laughed, the sound echoing through the water. It covered her nose and mouth now, but she remained perfectly at ease. Bubbles swirled around her lips, the last of the air escaping as she returned to her own realm. It was jarring to see Aveline breathe in water the way Morgana breathed in air.

When Morgana didn't move, Aveline's face grew serious once more, reciting the words Morgana had spoken to her only the night before. "I won't hurt you, and neither will this."

Morgana's heart pounded, but the words were enough, and her legs moved without permission. Reaching out, her fingers penetrated the icy cold water surrounding Aveline. She cringed at the cool liquid, but kept going until she found Aveline's fingers, gripping them with her own.

"To another world," Morgana said, still staring at those sea green eyes. She wondered if her own green eye looked different, if the part of her that took from the lives of the sea shone through, too.

"To my world," Aveline agreed, tugging on Morgana's wrist.

They jumped.

Chapter Three

They weren't falling at all. Time slowed around them as they drifted through the bright light, and the sensation of water was left behind. Instead, Morgana felt a cool breeze tickling her skin. Still, she refused to open her eyes, keeping them shut tight against the cool glow, too afraid that she'd look down to see a black hole of nothing beneath her.

A hand squeezed hers. She hadn't even realized she still held Aveline's. "Open your eyes. We're almost there."

"I'll open them when we're there."

Aveline's laugh sounded bubbly, livelier under the water as they continued their descent, Morgana seeing nothing but vague flashes through her eyelids. When her feet finally brushed something, she stifled a scream, only to realize they'd reached the ground.

Morgana's eyes flew open once her feet were secure on the ocean floor, boots sinking deep into the sand, and immediately sucked in a breath. It *was* dark. Craning her head up, she was reminded of a cloudy night sky, not a star in sight. But here, instead of clouds blotting out the sun, it was Calypdon floating above, casting all of Nysus into shadow.

But the dark wasn't absolute. Glowing rocks lit up a pathway leading down a hill, and little specks of light dotted the water around her like strange replacements for the missing stars. Morgana squinted closer, trying to make out more details, and gasped in delight. "They're fish!"

Tiny fish that seemed to flow with their own ethereal light swam above her head, diving down and weaving around her torso and between billowing strands of hair. They reminded Morgana of the lightning bugs she used to chase through the forest, and she felt a little less out of place.

Aveline, who had sat down and dug her fingers deep into the sand, smiled contentedly. "I thought you might like those." She pointed behind Morgana. "But the real view's the other way."

Morgana turned around, seeing they'd landed on a craggy cliff, tall and bathed in deep blue light, seaweed sprouting and tumbling over the edge. But Aveline wasn't referring to the cliff. Lifting her chin, Morgana gazed out at the city that lay below.

Seashell roads wound through the dunes, stamped flat from the passage of thousands of feet. Vibrant buildings of every color lined the pathways, as if the sea god had melted down a collection of seashells and poured out the material to form the structures below. Towers reached up toward the rocky underbelly of Calypdon, arched windows studding the walls. Everything around them had a soft glow to it, as if the materials were embedded with starlight, shimmering in the currents of the water.

"It's breathtaking," Morgana muttered, taking it all in. She was too distracted by the beauty to even notice the fact that she was breathing just fine, or to wonder whether she could even call it breathing. "It's…"

"Different?" Aveline asked, and Morgana looked at her to find the woman was breathtaking, too. Her hair floated around her ears, cloak fluttering like wings, her dark skin reflecting the deep blue glow of the city. She tilted her head back, brushing her fingers over one of two glowing boulders that Morgana hadn't noticed. The women had landed between the rocks, and the landmarks pointed up toward a swirling pit of water lingering over their heads. The dark mass nearly blended into the even darker mass of Calypdon far above. She touched her shell, and the portal closed in on itself, disappearing entirely.

Morgana just nodded, unable to speak. She'd never seen Briarwood, but now felt she would like to, if it was as beautiful as this.

Bubbles rose up between them, and Morgana jumped back with a startled laugh, her movement creating a sort of rippling wave. Her view of Aveline broke into fragments before coalescing, and Morgana's mind hurried to catch up. "I—"

"It's disorienting, isn't it?" Aveline asked, as if she knew exactly what had happened.

Morgana didn't move, not wanting to disrupt her surroundings again. The ceaseless motion was beginning to make her head pound. "Is that going to happen every time I move?"

"You'll get used to it," Aveline said, letting her hand slip away from Morgana's limp one. Her voice sounded different down here. It had an echoey, warbling quality, and there was a delay between the movement of her lips and the sound actually reaching Morgana's ears. "The currents, I mean. You'll adjust to them, and they'll start weaving around you once your movements become smoother. You'll be seeing clearly soon enough."

Morgana chanced a step, careful to be deliberate with her movements. She felt the water part for her, and although her vision wavered slightly, it didn't break up as it had before. She breathed a sigh of relief. "Let's move slowly, then. Where are we going?"

Aveline nodded to the largest building, built of elegant silver and shimmering gemstones. The palace was surrounded by walls crawling with glowing algae, but it rose higher than any other building, nestled on a large dune in the center of the city. "The palace of the sea."

Morgana swallowed roughly.

Aveline grinned, as if Morgana's nerves were a relief. "Welcome to Thalassa."

The rest of Thalassa spiraled out from the palace, curving roads branching out like veins from a heart. Aveline led Morgana down a path that avoided the craggy cliffside, and they walked through dark fields of seaweed.

Houses began to pop up as they approached the city, and clouds of shimmering algae floated through the water.

Morgana did her best to blend in as they walked, but the earth tones of her green hair gave her away. Observing her fingers, turning her wrist this way and that, she found that the verdant tint of her skin was more noticeable here, too. She tried to calm herself down. She didn't think it was possible to feel like more of an outcast than she did on land, but here she was.

She encountered more people walking down a single block of Thalassa than she had her entire life. She drank in the details, memorizing everything she could in preparation for the day when she was alone once more. She had had little exposure to those on Calypdon, but the sea people appeared to be remarkably similar. Simply … human. Humans who had to make a few concessions to account for living in water instead of air. Most wore their hair tied back, like Morgana would on a windy day, to keep the currents from blowing the strands into their face. Their clothes were heavy to counter the buoyancy that would cause lighter fabrics to float upward.

But there were other things, behaviors that Morgana could never witness on land because they weren't possible. When children played in the street, they could jump ten feet high, kicking their legs and swimming up to catch a ball. A woman didn't have to set her bag down to fix her hair, but rather let it float beside her. It had only sunk a few inches by the time she grabbed it again and resumed her walk.

Morgana kept close to Aveline, trying to ignore the curious looks people gave her even as she herself looked curiously all about her. But after the third person gave her a tentative smile in greeting, she realized that was all they were: curious. She found no hatred on their faces, no suspicion. She remembered that they didn't know who she was here. None of her kind had ever visited Nysus.

"Is it nice?" Aveline asked as Morgana grew more relaxed. "To feel like you don't have to hide?"

"I'll always have to hide, at least a part of myself," Morgana said, nodding to a young man as he passed. To her surprise, he nodded back with a smile. "I will always keep secrets, but … it is nice. To at least be able to show my face."

"You don't have to hide at all," Aveline murmured. "Not from me, at least, and not from King Daegil."

The feeling of freedom was intoxicating. Morgana smiled throughout the rest of the walk to the palace, and she didn't care who looked at her.

Getting past the wall surrounding the palace was surprisingly easy. All it took was one look at Aveline, and the line of guards, dressed in dark navy stitched with green, hurried to welcome her home. Morgana shrunk away from them, from their swords, even though she knew logically that those weapons couldn't kill her. Only one weapon could take her life, and she held it at her hip. Still … any other could cause a great deal of pain. In the right hands.

Shimmering green gemstones lined the pathway, lighting the way like fire. Morgana reached out a hand, letting the light glisten over her skin, absorbing the energy. She pointedly didn't look at Aveline, who appeared to be glowing all on her own.

Two more guards stood at the towering set of doors at the front of the palace, and one of them surged forward once they were close enough to make out.

"*Aveline*!" The young woman completely abandoned her post and flung herself into Aveline's arms. She moved in slow motion through the water, and Aveline jumped forward to bridge the gap. Morgana jerked back in surprise, giving the two women space and glancing awkwardly at the other guard.

The man merely grinned, and Morgana's nerves eased. "That's Helah. Her sister."

The young guard pulled away, holding Aveline's face in her hands. "You're okay? Oceans, you've been gone for *ages*."

Aveline pulled back a little, but kept their hands clasped together. "It was barely more than a fortnight. I'm fine."

Surprised, Morgana asked before she could stop herself, "It took you so long to find me? I thought you knew where I was."

Aveline turned back, spreading her arms lightly. "You've probably noticed, but gravity doesn't work the same here. I would have found you much earlier if I hadn't spent the first several days relearning how to stand."

Morgana laughed, but Helah didn't join in, staring at Morgana with wide eyes. "This is her?"

Before Aveline could answer, Morgana stuck out her hand with a smile, one she knew was sharp as a knife. "Yes, I'm the witch. No, I'm not going to hurt you or anyone else. We're not doing this again."

Unlike her sister, Helah didn't hesitate to grasp Morgana's hand. Her shake was firm, a warrior's grip. "I've never met a witch before. You must be charming, to have won over Aveline so easily."

Aveline snorted.

Helah glanced over her shoulder. "Reko, can you handle the post for the rest of the shift?"

"I think I can manage," Reko responded blandly, nodding to the considerably denser line of guards at the gate.

Looping her arm through Aveline's, Helah led them through the tall, wooden double doors. Morgana wondered vaguely how the wood didn't rot away, but quickly forgot as she stepped into the wide entrance hall. It spread out before her, at least ten times the size of her little cabin, with at least a dozen doors circling the room. Pillars flanked each doorway, disappearing into the gloom of a high ceiling.

The floor was a chessboard of pale white and emerald green, algae rooted in the molding between the squares. The trim of the walls was embedded with an array of glowing blue stones and seashells that spilled light onto the gleaming floors. The walls themselves were made of sturdy, deep black marble. The stone was shot through with streaks of white, weaving delicately around framed portraits and hanging sconces holding candles.

Morgana's mind stuttered at the sight, baffled at what seemed to be fire, but couldn't possibly be. How could the flames survive in the sea? Just looking at it made her more aware of the water surrounding her, the lack of air, and for the first time Morgana thought she might suffocate under the sheer newness of it.

But then a current rippled through the hall, making the flame waver as a breeze might, and Morgana saw a shield around it. Something about the area around the candle was lighter, less murky, and it shifted with the flickering flame. A bubble of air, shielding each small fire.

Morgana wanted to surge forward, to study this strange new magic, but several doors opened off to the left. Chattering voices echoed off the stone walls.

"The second shift guards are at dinner," Helah said in reference to the noise, tugging them along toward the staircase. "If we go in there, they'll never let you out." Morgana looked alarmed, but Helah added, "They'll talk your ear off with questions. Guards are a curious bunch because we're never told anything."

"The architecture is incredible," Morgana muttered, pausing for a moment to admire a winding, spiral staircase that led up the side of one wall. It was made of black steel, elaborate vines curling around the railing. "This is more stone and gems than I've seen in my entire life."

She didn't add that she hadn't seen much.

"Well, we make do with what we have down here," Helah laughed. "Limited options, I guess."

"I suppose."

"Is there someone you need to report to?" Helah murmured to Aveline. "The king is away, but I could -"

"Aveline, is that you?"

Aveline stiffened at the voice. Morgana narrowed her eyes at the voice coming from the staircase. A man had paused halfway to the floor. He stood in the glow of one of the sconces. It was odd to see someone cast in orange light in this world of blues and greens. Another guard, if his sword and uniform were any indication.

Aveline plastered on a smile but stepped ever so slightly in front of Morgana. Helah did the same. "Joao. How are you?"

"Better now that I've seen you safely returned," he said with a smirk, hurrying down the rest of the stairs and clasping her forearm. His dark eyes flickered to Morgana, a searching gaze, and Morgana leaned away. "And you brought a new friend."

Aveline wrenched her arm back, probably more aggressive than necessary, but Joao didn't seem to notice. His eyes now crawled over Morgana like he'd found a new prize, assessing her hair and eyes, everything that made her different. He, too, must have known exactly who she was.

Morgana didn't notice at the time, but she pressed closer into Aveline's arm.

Helah cleared her throat through the silence. "Yes! This is -" She cut herself off, turning to Morgana. "Sorry, I never actually got your name."

"Her name's Morgana," Aveline answered for her when Morgana stayed silent, keeping her narrowed gaze on Joao.

"You can call me the witch," Morgana added to the man, smiling sweetly, and Aveline coughed to cover a snicker.

Unfazed, Joao extended his hand to Morgana. "You're rather lovely for a witch."

Morgana took his hand, squeezing when he moved to kiss her knuckles, insisting on a simple shake. "Most are. That's what makes us so dangerous."

Joao retracted his hand, and joy sparked behind Aveline's eyes when he discreetly shook it out. "Well, we'll be working together quite a bit, so we'll have time to build that trust. My name is Joao, captain of the king's guard."

Morgana grimaced and glanced at Aveline. "Perhaps we should have discussed in deeper detail how I would be spending my time here."

Aveline jabbed an elbow into Morgana's side. "Morgana has agreed to help the king."

Joao's smirk didn't fade. In fact, it grew, as if he was looking forward to a challenge. "Very good, then. We weren't sure exactly when you would return, but we've been prepared just in case. I will show you to your rooms and send word to the King."

Morgana wanted to say that they were perfectly capable of bringing the news themselves, but Aveline's jab had been surprisingly painful, and she didn't want to push her luck. So instead, she just sighed, bit her tongue, and followed the man up the stairs. Aveline and Helah trailed behind.

"Perhaps I could interest you in a tour," Joao said as they circled the spiral staircase. At the top, he finally started down a long hallway. "There is much to see here in Thalassa."

"I'm here on business," Morgana said stiffly.

"Oh, I know," Joao said with a grin. "But there will be plenty of time in the evenings when you can do whatever you wish."

Thankfully, they reached a door before Morgana could answer, and he revealed a key, handing it to Morgana. "This opens this door, and this door only." He winked. "Don't go getting any ideas."

"Wouldn't dream of it," Morgana said flatly, taking the key and shoving it into the lock. It opened easily, and she fled inside, the sisters following.

Joao backed away. "I have duties to attend to, but I reside three doors down. Just in case you were wondering."

Morgana shut the door before she made some very poor decisions regarding her powers. She exhaled and turned to lean her back against the door, taking in the room.

Like the rest of the palace, the floor and walls were made of a kaleidoscopic mixture of marble and various stones. A wardrobe of glittering onyx sat pressed against the wall in the corner, the only piece of furniture beside the large bed in the center of the room. Morgana tried not to think too hard about how blankets survived under water. It probably had something to do with how it didn't really feel like they were underwater at all. She supposed when you lived your life in the sea, and you'd never been dry, you wouldn't notice the difference.

Morgana raised her eyes to where Helah and Aveline stood on the other side of the room. "Well, he's … nice."

Helah sighed and turned to Aveline. "I hate him. He sets my teeth on edge."

Aveline pinched the bridge of her nose. "Don't act as if I don't hate him, too."

"You weren't saying that when you -"

Aveline held up a finger. "Do not bring up the mistakes I made as a teenager. He's my superior. I can hardly do anything about it now."

"He's my superior, too," Helah muttered with her hands raised. "That doesn't stop me from ignoring him every time he opens his idiotic mouth when I'm off-duty."

"He's a bit of a creep," Aveline conceded, "and too ambitious for his own good, but mostly harmless."

Morgana wasn't convinced, locking the door behind her and praying he didn't have an extra key to her rooms. Once she was certain the door was secure, she stalked further into the room. "Okay, so what now?"

Helah leaned against the back wall. "Joao will send a message to King Daegil, and I'm sure once he receives word, he'll come right back. It should only be a few days."

Exhaustion tugged at Morgana's limbs, and she stared longingly at the wash room, where a basin presumably waited. Though she didn't need sleep, her body could certainly be worn out like anyone else's. "And in the meantime?"

Aveline understood Morgana's unspoken thoughts well enough. "For now, you rest, and tomorrow we can give you the tour." At Morgana's alarm, Aveline laughed. "Don't worry. We'll sneak out while Joao is on duty."

"Won't *you* need to be on duty? An assignment?" Morgana asked nervously, not wanting to be left alone in this new place. It made her feel pathetic, grateful that no one could feel her own anxiety.

Aveline moved toward the door, motioning for her sister to follow. "Until you meet the king, you are my assignment."

Helah smiled and bowed her head, and Morgana relished how naturally Helah acted around her. The guard must trust her sister a great deal. She began to duck out of the room. "Sleep well, Morgana. And welcome."

Aveline's words echoed from the hall as the door closed. "Oh, she doesn't sleep."

"*What?*"

Even in this unfamiliar place, Morgana sat comfortably on the bed, thinking that perhaps, if she helped them, she could make a home here.

***

"The king will see you tomorrow."

Aveline swept past Morgana as soon as she opened the door, inviting herself in without a word of apology. Morgana's heart ached at how natural she'd become, how comfortable. As if Morgana wasn't a monster. Aveline set her sword aside, next to Morgana's against the wall, and Morgana threw herself back onto the most comfortable bed she'd ever encountered. Her buoyancy slowed her every move, and she fluttered down onto the sheets. "Why tomorrow? Doesn't he know witches don't like to wait?"

Aveline rolled her eyes while Morgana grinned. "He sent a note, but he has business to finish. He'll travel back tonight, and tomorrow he'll hold a celebratory ball to welcome you."

Morgana sat up, moving back to lean against the wall so Aveline could sit at the foot of the bed. "Oh, no, that's entirely unnecessary. Please, is there a way that can *not* happen?"

Aveline looked incredulous. "You want me to tell the king you don't want to attend his party? Do you also want me to lose my position while you're at it? Get me kicked out of the palace?"

Morgana sighed, dropping her face into her hands as dread settled in. "You do realize I've spent my entire life avoiding the attention of other people, right? That's genuinely all I've done."

Morgana expected Aveline to laugh, but she just looked sad. "Maybe it's time to stop. To let other people see you."

Rolling her shoulders back, Morgana frowned. "Maybe. Or maybe it will go horribly and result in my execution."

This time, Aveline did grin. "You'll never know if you don't try." Her eyes flitted down to Morgana's tattered dress, floating around her. "First things first, you need to change."

Aveline had brought Morgana some clothes that would be more suitable for the sea, heavier ones that would fit better and not float upward. Morgana had spent much of yesterday holding her shirt down to keep it from drifting up in an unseemly way. Disappearing into the washroom, Morgana changed quickly, taking time to drag the fine comb through her hair, and spent a long moment getting distracted by the way the strands floated around her ears, fanning throughout the water. She marveled at how much lighter the color looked in the blue water; flecks of gold shone in the curls, dotting the forest green. The light from the gemstones tinted her skin with that same green tone, darker than usual, like the skin of a serpent. The color made her think of Coby. Then it made her remember her sword, leaning against the wall.

Morgana went back to the main room as casually as possible, stalking past Aveline to her sword, glad when the belt and sheath clicked easily into place around her new dress. The sword was amazingly light here, and it slid easily into place.

"You can leave that here, if you like," Aveline offered as she stood. "We're just going into town."

Morgana thought about complying, about hiding it in the dresser and traveling light for once, but she shook her head. "If everyone else in this place has a weapon, I'm taking mine, too. It's only fair."

Aveline didn't argue further. "We'll brave the dining hall for breakfast, but I want to get out of here as soon as possible. No use torturing you with small talk."

A smile tugged at Morgana's lips. "All you've done for the past two days was torture me with small talk."

"I meant small talk from others," Aveline said unapologetically, swinging the door open. "You'll have to put up with me for a while longer."

The hall was surprisingly crowded, filled to bursting with a mixture of guards, ladies in dresses, and men in long, fine coats. They chatted together comfortably, scooping from platters set in the center of each table, with servants constantly replenishing them. Morgana marveled at the sight of so many people, a little dazed. She wished she was wearing a hat, or a hood she could pull down over her eyes.

"If you keep freezing like that," Aveline muttered in Morgana's ear, "you'll lose your horrifying reputation."

"Shouldn't all these guards be … guarding something?" Morgana asked as she resumed her stroll. She'd hoped she'd only have to deal with a few people, not an entire crowd.

"The staff in the palace is large," Aveline murmured, comfortably dropping into the nearest spot on the bench and motioning for Morgana to join her. Morgana sat carefully on the marble bench. "Many guards are off duty at any given time. Especially this time of day."

Morgana bit her lip, looking around before asking, "And the queen? I know you said the king was away, but perhaps I could meet with her."

Aveline grimaced, ducking her head. "She passed away several years ago. It was horrible, but it makes sense that you didn't hear."

Sorrowful, Morgana said, "I'm sorry for your kingdom's loss."

"I suspect it was her loss that inspired the king to free the lands," Aveline said, beginning to serve herself. "He'd wanted to for a while, but it was a commendable task to attempt, to feel like he could still do something worthy without her."

Morgana nodded and decided once more she would do everything she could to help him.

"Good morning, ladies."

Aveline let out an almost imperceptible groan as Joao appeared, standing across the table from them, speaking far louder than necessary. Heads turned his way, noticing Morgana for the first time, and she did everything she could not to shrink in her seat, keeping her back straight. Just for something to do, she served herself some vegetables.

"Good morning," Aveline said for Morgana.

Joao ignored her, keeping his eyes trained on Morgana, who took a slow bite of her food. She kept expecting it to float off her fork, but thankfully the food was fixed firmly onto the tines. It was delicious, if a bit salty. She wondered what kind of magic was used to keep the food from getting soggy in the sea. "I hope your first night here was pleasurable, and that you had a rejuvenating night's sleep."

Morgana gleefully opened her mouth, but Aveline squeezed her thigh under the table, a silent message to *shut up*. Aveline was right, of course. Announcing to the kingdom at large that she didn't sleep would do more harm than good. No need to remind these people of such a stark difference between them. Swallowing the words, Morgana said, "The room was lovely, thank you."

He went straight to the point, hands clasped behind him. "I assume you've heard the news of the ball tomorrow."

A sour taste blossoming over her tongue that had nothing to do with the food, Morgana said, "I did. It sounds very exciting."

"Indeed. It's been quite some time since we've had such a celebration, and I've come to ask if I may accompany you to the event," he said. A slow smile spread over his face that made Morgana cringe. As if he knew she'd say yes, because she somehow owed him for what he deemed a kindness. Or perhaps because he'd asked her in such a public forum. "As the captain of the king's guard, it would be an honor to symbolize this new alliance."

Aveline sat straight as an arrow to Morgana's left, glancing between her and the man. Morgana remembered what Aveline had said last night. *The mistakes I made as a teenager*. Was he her former partner? Former lover? Aveline was clearly uncomfortable, that was for certain. The hall had fallen silent, too many people watching now, anxiously awaiting her response. She couldn't simply say no, could she? Was she allowed to decline someone of his status?

You have the power here, she reminded herself. *They need you. Do not forget who you are*.

Morgana smiled blandly, shoving her food around her plate. "My apologies. But unfortunately, I already told Aveline I would accompany *her*. After all, she spent so long trying to find me."

Aveline choked on her salad, frantically covering her mouth so she wouldn't cough it up all over the table.

Fire flashed in Joao's eyes as they flickered over to Aveline, reading the surprise written plainly on her face, but the rest of his face remained perfectly smooth. He straightened. "Of course. Do try to save me a dance."

And then he was gone, melting back into the crowd. Chatter resumed, but no one approached Morgana as she feared they might have. She supposed she could thank Joao for one thing.

"Funny," Aveline breathed out once the hall's volume returned to normal, and she thought they wouldn't be overheard. "I don't recall asking you to be my date."

Their elbows brushed, and Morgana winked. "If I'm stuck with you, you're stuck with me. You dragged me all the way here, the ball is your fault in the first place."

"*Actually—*"

Morgana grinned freely. "The least you can do is treat me to a party yourself."

Chapter Four

They passed Helah on their way out of the palace. She stood grumpily where they had found her the day before, this time with a different partner.

"Still here?" Aveline asked, pausing in the doorway.

Helah sighed. "I requested to be stationed here while you were gone, so I'd be the first to know of your return. But now I'm stuck here for at least another few days before they rotate assignments."

"Well, I'm sorry to have troubled you," Aveline laughed. "We were just on our way into town, do you need anything?"

The words only made her sister groan, flinging her head back. "You're rubbing it in. I haven't left the palace grounds in *weeks*. You get to have all the fun."

Aveline quirked a brow. "And whose fault is that? You let yourself get overworked. It's not my fault all you want to do when you get off duty is sleep."

"Just stay awake all the time," Morgana advised. "That's what I do."

Helah looked at her. "You and I need to have an actual conversation. I'm incredibly intrigued."

Morgana thought of Joao. "Everyone is."

The palace sat on a hill at the center of the city overlooking the rest of Thalassa, and Morgana followed Aveline down a winding path that cut through a field of seaweed and coral. Morgana extended her hand, letting her fingers brush along the soft plants as the women crossed from the palace gates into the bright streets of Thalassa.

Morgana looked around, up at the towering buildings and toward the bustling people. She could appreciate it all more this time, now that she had grown accustomed to moving without disturbing the water around her. A city of green, blue, and white, it extended out before her with shops and taverns at every turn. The crushed sea shells beneath her feet were well worn, faded colors of pale pink and purples washed out under years of treading feet.

"This is where you grew up?" Morgana asked in awe, turning in a circle, gazing up at the underside of Calypdon above, at the world she had left behind.

Aveline smiled fondly. "Yeah, I lived on a little side street on the outskirts of the city, just that way." She raised her arm, pointing south.

Morgana followed the line, squinting into the distance, trying to imagine the home in which Aveline and Helah had grown up, where their lives must have been so different from her own. Had they had friends? Did they go to school? Morgana's mother had done her best to teach her everything she needed to know, both history and sword work, but it had been lonely.

Morgana hesitated, trying to phrase her next question. She knew better than to assume anyone's parents were alive. "And … is it just the two of you?"

Glancing down at Morgana, Aveline grimaces. "It is, now. Our parents passed when we were children. I was ten, Helah eight."

Morgana closed her eyes. "I'm sorry."

Aveline pressed her lips together. "The palace sometimes takes in orphans, and we were especially lucky to be kept together. We were trained as guards so that we'd have a life off the streets." She looked back at the palace, her eyes shining. "I'm very grateful to the royal family."

"And do you enjoy your position? As a guard?"

"I do," Aveline said, but through the hesitancy in her tone, Morgana could tell there was little truth to it. "It can grow boring sometimes, like anything else." She smiled to herself. "I've enjoyed these past few days, though."

"Because I'm so entertaining?"

"Because you're good company. Many of the men I get stationed with have no desire to talk to a female guard unless they think I'll go to bed with them." Aveline rounded a corner and paused in front of the first shop. Beneath a yellow canopy, Morgana peered through the window at racks of dresses and coats of every color in shimmering folds of cloth, with dozens of people spilling in and out. "It's more crowded than I'd hoped, but it makes sense. No one wants to wear an old dress to the first celebration in years."

Morgana glanced at her. "And you require a new gown, too?"

"I have a gown," Aveline waved her off. "Too many, actually. Before we came of age, before we became official guards, we were often invited to parties in the ballroom. I even went to one or two when I was off duty, before the queen died." She fell silent and cleared her throat. "It will be nice to attend another."

Morgana smiled. "Maybe for you. The prospect of a ball makes me want to go back into hiding."

"You're just nervous because you have nothing to wear. Here, you'll have many options."

Morgana opened her mouth, hesitating on her words, but she forced them out. "I … I've lived alone for many years, I have no profession, I take no payment, I live out in the woods. I … I don't have any money."

Aveline merely laughed. "Oceans, Morgana, I *know*. Did you think I expected a witch to be rich?"

"Rich in power," Morgana reminded her. "Watch yourself."

Aveline huffed. "You're not as intimidating as you were two days ago. Lucky for you, I received a sizable bonus for hunting you down, which I feel guilty about spending since you weren't very hard to convince at all."

Morgana gaped at her. "Aveline, I can't take your money—"

"You can, and you will. But later," Aveline added, backing away as a group of women rushed past them and into the shop. "When it dies down. For now, let me show you the best part of the city. No one will be there, not today."

Morgana dutifully followed Aveline through street after street, her awe at the sheer magnitude of Thalassa only growing. She'd spent her life in a forest, contained on all sides, unable to see past the thickets of crooked, interwoven branches in every direction. Here, everything felt so … open, despite the tall buildings. The windows were open, and the streets were wide, and Morgana could see far into the distance. Cool water rippled around her, and it felt almost like wind.

The buildings got smaller and smaller as they approached the edge of the city, spreading further apart. Soon, her surroundings reminded her more of the village Morgana had been born in before they had gone into hiding. The coral and marble gave way to pebbles and seaweed as they rounded a hill, until -

The rocky terrain spread out in front of them, with plants poking out between gaps in the boulders and algae crawling up the side of the hill. The jagged gray stones rose up, and the women climbed up the cliff. What would have been a strenuous activity on land required almost no effort at all. Morgana hopped from rock to rock, letting the water lift her up until they finally reached the top of the plateau.

A bubbling pool of crystal blue was carved into the rocks. It was as if the center of the hill had been hollowed out. Bright blue gems studded the bottom of the pool, shining up with the same shimmering beams the portal had when it'd opened in Calypdon. The light reflected on pink seashells littering the surrounding rocks. Steam curled away from the surface of the pool, wafting over the rocks and around Morgana's ankles.

"Is this water … *in* water?" Morgana asked incredulously, crouching down to peer closer at the rumbling pit.

"No," Aveline said with a grin. "That would be a funny sight, though. This—" she hopped down onto a ledge that stuck out along the hole's side, like a bench, "—is one of the blessed air springs."

Morgana extended her hand toward the steam, through it, until she felt her fingers burst from water to air, heat drying her skin immediately. On the other side of the shimmering surface was a pocket of hot air. She sighed at the familiar, soothing sensation. Dumbfounded, she asked, "Is this like the hot springs we have in Calypdon?"

"Something like that. These are holy sites, sacred to your gods."

Morgana's brow furrowed. "My gods? We have the same gods."

Did they, though? Morgana had always considered the world to be one, even after it became two kingdoms. After the Rift, the god of the sea had abandoned the land, but Calypdon had never truly abandoned him, not wanting to risk his wrath again.

"We do," Aveline said. "The gods bless more than people, you know. Sometimes they bless places. Up on the land, every god is important, necessary. They get praised every day, for even mundane things. Even the god of the sea is praised above, when the people of Calypdon swim in his oceans, or pull fish from the sea to eat. Your people continued praying to him after the Rift, because his domain still pervaded your territory in the form of lakes, springs, and rivers.

"Once the humans were separated and the Ancient War over and done with, the gods believed in balance once more, in equality on all sides, but for a long time, the sea people only worshipped one god. This is the sea god's domain, after all. But the goddesses of the earth and sky thought that to own such a territory, to have it nearly all to himself, there needed to be some balance. In the same way that the land dwellers rely on water to some degree, the gods wanted to show the power of air, of earth." She jutted her chin to the bubbling, heated air. "If left alone for too long, these will bubble up and explode, crawling over the ocean floor and swallowing the villages and cities with air."

Morgana's mouth fell open in horror. "That can't be true."

Aveline shrugged. "It's what they say. Of course, no one's stayed away long enough to find out. People love to come here, to lounge in pockets of air for relaxation, to praise the rest of the gods. Just as the lakes litter the land; air found a home, here, too."

Morgana shook her head. "I swear, the gods are -"

Aveline shot her arm up, pressing her fingers to Morgana's lips, and she swallowed her words, suddenly too distracted by the calluses of Aveline's fingertips. "Careful of what you say here in this kingdom, at these sites." She looked up. "They listen."

Morgana took Aveline's hand from her lips, lowering it between them. "No, they don't. Do you know how often I pray to them, begging them to take away these powers, this life that I never even wanted? The gods don't listen, Aveline. They make their choices all on their own."

In the days following her mother's death, Morgana had cursed at the sky, screaming at the gods to set her free, or to at least let her know there was a reason for it all, beyond simple cruelty. She'd never received a response, other than the pulsating magic in her veins, threatening to tear her in two.

Aveline looked at Morgana sadly, their hands joined. The steam rose up between them, twirling around their fingertips, binding them together. "You don't want your life?"

Morgana looked up in the direction of the sky, trying to find it through the layers separating her from her home, but she could only see the underside of Calypdon. "Not always. Not this one."

"What if you could have another one?" Aveline asked urgently, taking a step closer. "A new one, here, where you didn't have to hide? Where you could live as all others do, as a sea dweller?"

The thought had indeed crossed Morgana's mind during the long hours of the previous night while she sat alone in her quiet room, gazing out the window at the silent city below. The glowing algae seemed to dim, as if even the magic knew the sea people slept. She imagined a new home, with friends, with people who knew who she was and didn't care.

But then, as it always did, reality came tumbling back, and she remembered the way Joao had looked at her on the stairwell. The greed, the desire for everything Morgana possessed.

"I admire the faith that you have in your people," Morgana said softly, delicately taking her hand away. "But people don't know the cost of power, and that makes them hungry for it." She chewed on the inside of her cheek. "Do you know why we went into hiding in the first place?"

"Your mother wanted to keep you safe," Aveline guessed. "She … thought people would try to use her powers."

"She didn't just think," Morgana said, looking down and taking a step away to settle on a curved rock. "She knew. She'd lived it." Squeezing her fingers together, not wanting to look at Aveline as she spoke, she drew a harsh breath and continued. "There was an attack on a village close to ours. To this day, we don't know who it was, or even what happened. The villagers managed to fend off the raiders, but the village went up in flames all the same." Morgana paused. "I didn't realize it at the time, but that was always happening in Calypdon, probably because the king was growing old and losing control even then, manipulated by his son."

Morgana shook her head, wishing she could shake away the memories, but they would never go. Everything within her would always haunt her. "Many of the survivors were gravely wounded. They wouldn't survive the night without a miracle." Morgana took a shaky breath. "I don't know how someone from that village knew about my mother, she always refused to tell me how they knew her true identity. But a rider came in the middle of the night to plead for her aid. She was the only one with the power to help them."

Closing her eyes, Morgana remembered her mother that night, flying from her bed and whispering with the messenger, casting a worried glance over her shoulder at Morgana. The commotion had awakened her and she stood in the doorway of the den. Her mother stayed there for several long moments, staring at her daughter before coming to a decision.

"I asked her not to go," Morgana said, raw. "I was young, but I remembered her warnings; revealing our magic would put us in danger. But she couldn't be convinced. I remember what she said as she knelt to hug me, 'This is not how any of those people were supposed to die. I feel that in my bones. I am not meant to lose them yet.' And so she went in the middle of the night, leaving me to wait at home. She tended to over a dozen wounded, all of whom would have died without her."

Silver tears lined Aveline's eyes when Morgana looked up, the other woman hugging herself as she listened. "Your mother sounds like she was a marvelously brave woman."

"She was marvelously brave on her best day," Morgana agreed, "and yet marvelously foolish on her worst. She went to that village, and she healed every single one of them, but they turned on her. They wouldn't let her leave. And before you ask," she said when Aveline opened her mouth, "she didn't want to hurt them. She could have put everyone in the village to sleep from the start, but that's not as simple as it sounds. With a wide array of ages and health conditions, the impact of her magic on such a large scale was impossible to predict. She spent days trying to think of a means of escape that didn't involve using her power as a weapon. She'd lived hundreds of years without doing so, after hearing her own mother's stories of war. She refused to give in so easily.

"Those men wanted to find out what she was. And she told them, told them of her powers, but using them through her wasn't enough. I guess they thought their best chance of claiming even a scrap of magic was through her own blood. Creating an heir. And you can just imagine, once they put that together, they tried to—" Morgana cut herself off, blinking rapidly. "She escaped that night. She knocked everyone unconscious, despite the risks. But she didn't have a choice. She had to get out before they had a chance to … force themselves on her."

Aveline stared at her with eyes full of sorrow and anguish. Her fingers shook where she held them in front of her mouth, reaching toward Morgana with her free hand like she might embrace her, but she held herself still. "Morgana…"

"One person, an elderly man who had brought her meals, didn't wake up. She felt him die as she was escaping. That was the first and only time she had used her powers to hurt people, to withhold the life force rather than providing it. And … her soul never quite recovered after that." Morgana frantically wiped her cheek. She didn't even know how she could possibly be crying, surrounded by water as she was, but she could feel the tears as she swiped them away. "It's horrible, yes, that we are seen as witches, sentenced to live by our differences only and never by our similarities. But we are seen like this because it is true. We are meant to live apart, to oversee your souls so you can all live free lives, instead."

Aveline reached out a shaking hand, fingers catching the tears glistening on Morgana's cheek. Morgana shut her eyes at the gentle touch, imagining yet again a life where she could allow herself this.

Aveline said, "This is not the life you deserve."

"It is the life I have," Morgana whispered, her voice cracking. "And it will be the life I have for many years after you are a mere memory. I will not let myself be put into a situation where I have no choice but to hurt people."

Aveline let her hand drop, water flowing between them. "You are stronger than me."

Morgana smiled sadly. "It's the curse of power."

Aveline opened her mouth, as if trying to find something to say, but in the end only exhaled softly. Leaning down, she unbuttoned her overshirt and kicked off her boots. She shed the button down, revealing smooth brown shoulders. Feet bare, she stepped smoothly into the pool of air, onto the bench lining the side, and sighed at the sensation. She sat down on the bench, so she was submerged in air up to her chin. Steam curled the ends of her hair, and she gazed at Morgana. "Give yourself an inkling of a blessing, then. Just a moment; a day, a week, maybe."

Morgana followed Aveline's example, climbing down beside her and sinking into the heat of the pool. Morgana held eye contact for a long moment before ducking her head under the surface, until her entire body was surrounded by air. She let out a sigh of relief, breathing in soothing gulps of air as the steam dried the lingering tears on her face. When she surfaced again, her heartbeat had steadied, and Aveline was smiling again.

Swallowing, Morgana admitted. "You've made existing easy enough. At least for now."

The steam formed tendrils around their hair and ears, rendering the whole world hazy. Warmth caressed Morgana's skin, dry dirt between her toes and a gentle breeze ruffling the ends of her hair that dipped beneath the surface. The familiarity of the land pierced her heart so deeply she almost started crying again. Aveline watched her closely, and Morgana managed a smile. It was as genuine as could be expected for such a moment.

"I will take you back to the dress shop later tonight," Aveline said, speaking with a newfound ferocity, "and you might discover something else within yourself."

Morgana snorted. "I'm no princess, Aveline. I don't even know if I'm one of the Hallowed, technically, as much as the people are convinced I am. No matter how much your king probably wants to portray me as one."

Aveline gazed at Morgana, and she didn't look away until Morgana allowed her own eyes to flutter shut, to give in to the steam of the air and the familiarity of the dry heat. "Witches and Hallowed are the same to me. They were just born into different lives, touched by different gods. Perhaps there's no difference between a blessing and a curse."

Chapter Five

Morgana and Aveline met Helah once her shift ended, at a tavern many of the palace guards frequented. Aveline led Morgana from the blessed air springs, declaring that they both deserved a nice meal. What appeared to be a run-down building nestled next to a sand dune on the outside contained a glowing, underwater cave when they walked in. Stalactites hung from the ceiling, crystalized and catching the light of the gemstones framing the entryway. Sparkling tables of purple and black were situated around the room, carved from hunks of quartz, and Helah waved them over.

"Finally," Helah exclaimed, already having ordered for them; three plates of dark meat and cooked greens sat on the table. "Being stationed at the front gates is torture enough, but knowing the two of you were out exploring the city? It was an extra-painful shift."

Aveline slid into an open seat. "You've seen everything, anyway."

"Not everything." Helah turned her attention to Morgana. "How do you like Thalassa?"

"It's beautiful," Morgana said, folding her hands in front of her to keep from fidgeting. This was the most she'd spoken since her mother died. "Everything shines here. It's like you recreated the night sky." Morgana blinked. "But I suppose you've never seen the sky, have you?"

"No," Helah sighed. "But Aveline told me all about the stars. I can't wait until I can see them."

"They're incredible," Aveline said. "While my body was adjusting to gravity, I just laid on the ground for *hours*, staring up at the sky. I couldn't believe it when they moved."

"I miss them," Morgana admitted. "I never thought about all the little things that would be different between the kingdoms."

Helah sat forward. "How different is Thalassa from Briarwood?"

"Truthfully, I've never been to Briarwood," Morgana admitted. "I didn't exactly like to leave my little corner of the forest."

Or rather, I didn't feel like I could.

The way Helah was staring at Morgana made her pause, as if she was studying the witch's soul. Helah finally said, "That's quite a sad life."

Morgana was struck by Helah's honesty. "It's a quiet life." She tilted her head. "You don't seem nervous around me at all."

Helah cracked a smile. "Should I be?"

"No, no, that's not what I meant. I just -" Morgana glanced at Aveline.

Helah followed the gaze before bursting into laughter. "Oh, was *Aveline* nervous when she met you?"

Aveline sputtered. “I was *not* -”

“She was,” Morgana interrupted. “I suppose I expected everyone to be … equally wary.”

“Aveline was nervous because you could kill us just by thinking about it, right?”

Morgana opened and shut her mouth several times before responding. “Yeah, that about sums it up.”

Helah shrugged. “So I wouldn’t be able to stop it anyway. Besides, you hid yourself away in a cursed forest so no one could find you. Something tells me you’re not interested in hurting us mortals.”

Aveline splayed her hands across the table. “I would just like to reiterate that I was *not* nervous.”

The corners of Morgana’s lips lifted. “You absolutely were. You even admitted it.”

“But I did an *excellent* job of hiding it.”

“Am I embarrassing you in front of your sister?”

Aveline hid her face in her hands.

Helah threw an arm around her sister, but didn’t shift her focus from Morgana. “I’m fascinated, though. How does it work?”

Morgana, feeling much more comfortable, swallowed a bite of her food. “My magic?”

Helah nodded eagerly. “Aveline filled me in a little bit, but it’s still so mysterious. You’re connected to our souls, right? You’re like an energy source for mortals?”

“That’s a good way of looking at it. Think of it like a tether. You might not notice it, and there are times when I don’t notice it either, but it’s a constant humming connection.”

Helah pressed a hand to her sternum, as if she might find a rope stretching from her soul into Morgana’s. “But you can reach out to it, right? Find that tether and tug on it? That’s what makes your power so … intimidating.”

“Sure,” Morgana shrugged. “If I concentrate. But I don’t like to do it. It feels wrong, invading someone’s soul like that without permission.”

“What if you had permission?”

Morgana cracked a smile at the pure excitement on Helah’s face. “What?”

Helah’s eyes had lit up, reflecting the glowing fish swimming around them. “What if I gave you permission to pull on the tether between you and me?”

Baffled, Morgana asked, “*Why*?”

“I want to know what it feels like.”

Morgana glanced at Aveline. “I don’t really -”

“Come on,” Helah said. “Don’t *you* want to know how your powers affect other people, too?”

Morgana's lips parted, because she'd honestly never thought about it. Her goal had always been to never use her powers on a human at all. It didn't occur to her that someone might give her permission.

"Are you sure?" Morgana asked, still looking at Aveline. As if Morgana needed permission from her, too.

Aveline was resting her chin in the palm of her hand. "You already reached out to my soul. For the record, I didn't feel anything. If you hadn't told me, I wouldn't have known."

Helah shoved her sister away. "Well, I want to try anyway. I can't imagine it's just … nothing."

"It probably is," Morgana laughed. "The connection is always there, so you shouldn't notice when I simply access it."

"So don't just access it. I want you to *tug* on this tether, Morgana. Make me stand up and do a little jig."

"Oh, if soul manipulation is on the table, I have suggestions," Aveline said.

"I'm not going to manipulate your soul," Morgana said. "Even with permission, it still feels wrong. But … I'll reach out. See if I can get you to feel something."

Helah sat back in her chair, bracing her palms against the table. She closed her eyes. "Okay. I'm ready."

Shaking her head with a grin, Morgana opened up her power. It was always there, ebbing and flowing, but she kept it tucked away so she didn't have to think about it. She brought it forward, homing in on the souls around her. Morgana brushed past Aveline's soul, her own soul sighing at the contact, before finding Helah's.

Helah's soul was similar to Aveline's; vibrant and pure.

"Feel anything?" Morgana asked.

Helah frowned, disappointed. "No."

Morgana reached further out, poking and prodding and pulling, until Helah jerked forward and gasped, "Oh!"

Morgana immediately let go. "I'm sorry. Did I hurt you?"

Helah was grinning ear to ear, rubbing her fingers over her sternum. "No, it didn't hurt. It was like there was something inside me, and the force pulled me forward. The force was hesitant, but it was there."

Aveline pouted. "I was really hoping you'd make her get up and dance."

Helah pointed a finger in Aveline's face as the two bickered back and forth. Morgana sat back, allowing herself a brief moment to bask in the souls around her. It was nice, not suppressing the magic as she was so used to. She felt a couple sitting a few tables away, their souls intertwining as they held hands. Her power shifted to a woman leaning against the wall, chatting to a friend. A man entered the tavern, and as his soul grew closer to hers, it seemed to shine brighter.

She paid a visit to each soul in the tavern, touching them lightly before moving on. None of them seemed to notice, and Morgana steadily eased into her magic -

Something shifted, and Morgana straightened. Behind her, the atmosphere soured. The soft, airy feeling of happy souls floated away, replaced by energy fueled with darkness. This new soul seemed to crawl up her spine, inching over her neck, as if it wanted to wrap its fingers around her throat.

Morgana whirled around, searching frantically behind her -

Only to find no one there.

Closing her eyes, Morgana maneuvered through the souls crowding her, finding that bitter soul that was reaching out to her. It was still in the same spot she thought it was, nestled against the wall in the corner of the room. But again, when Morgana opened her eyes, she found only empty space.

"Are you okay?"

Morgana jumped as Aveline's words jerked her from her thoughts. She blinked, glancing over her shoulder. Still, there was no one there. But Morgana could still feel them. Feel *something*.

"Yes," Morgana finally said breathlessly. "Yes, I'm fine. I'm still not used to tapping into my powers like that. It can get overwhelming. There are so many souls here."

Concerned, Aveline threw a smattering of coins on the table and stood. "Let's get out of here, then. That shop should have calmed down by now, and I owe you a dress."

But leaving the tavern didn't help. That sour, unsettling soul followed the women through the streets and into the dress shop, hiding away in the racks of gowns. But every time Morgana looked over her shoulder, peering through the fabric, no one would be there.

By the time they began to make their way back to the palace, Morgana was a tightly wound bundle of energy. Aveline kept sending worried glances her way, picking up on the sharp change in mood.

"Helah," Aveline said softly. "Could you take Morgana's dress back to the palace? There's one more place I want to show her."

Helah opened her mouth to protest, but at a sharp look from her sister, simply took the dress.

Morgana searched their surroundings as Helah walked away. "We should really go back to the palace. It's late, and I—"

Aveline grabbed Morgana by the elbow, pulling her into the space between two shops. Morgana's heart leapt into her throat.

"Okay," Aveline said. "Out with it."

Morgana tried to calm her pulse, trying to joke, "The place you wanted to show me was a dark alley?"

Aveline didn't laugh, searching Morgana's eyes. "You've been acting strange since you reached out to Helah's soul. Did we make you uncomfortable?"

"No! No, of course not."

"Then what's wrong?" Aveline asked tentatively.

Morgana bit her lip, checking one more time to see if a person had miraculously appeared in the place where that soul still hovered. When she found nothing, she leaned closer to Aveline and whispered, "There's someone following us."

Aveline stiffened, but otherwise didn't react. "Where?"

"That's the thing," Morgana said, near hysterical. "I can't *see* them."

"But you can feel them."

Morgana nodded. "I don't know what it is, but something's … off."

Aveline's eyes narrowed, thinking. "Show me where you think this person is standing. Be discreet."

Morgana nodded to her left, toward the opposite wall of the alley.

"I have a theory," Aveline said, loosening her hold on Morgana's arm. "And I'm about to test that theory. But if there's nothing there, it's going to look like I've lost my mind."

"If there's nothing there, then I *have* lost my mind."

Aveline nodded. "I'm glad I chose a dark alley for this."

In one swift movement, Aveline pulled a knife that had been strapped to the inside of her boot. She spun around, kicking off the wall beside Morgana to propel herself to the other side of the alley. Her free hand fumbled around in the space in front of her, until it seemed to catch hold of something. Aveline twisted her fingers around in the water, like she was clutching something in her fist, and raised her knife.

"Show yourself," Aveline hissed.

Perhaps they *had* both lost their minds.

But then the water rippled, and Morgana blinked in surprise. She hadn't moved, but the currents were fragmenting in the way they did when she moved too fast. But it was only the marble in front of Aveline that moved. The water shifted more, currents weaving over each other, until the view finally cleared.

Morgana reeled back at what she saw. Aveline was pressing a woman against the wall, her knife wedged in the hollow of her throat. The woman bared her teeth at Aveline, hands balled into fists at her side.

"I knew there was someone there," Morgana breathed, surging forward. She stepped up next to Aveline, gasping at the monstrous yellow eyes that came into focus. They were darker than Morgana's yellow eye and seemed to glow from within. "Who are you?"

"She's a siren," Aveline spat, tightening her hold on the woman's - no, *siren*'s - neck. "Only a siren would be able to mask themselves in the water like that. Why have you been following us?"

A smile spread across the siren's face. "Not you." Her eyes found Morgana over Aveline's shoulder. "Her."

"My question stands."

"King Wendell was curious," the siren drawled. "About your powers. When you would use them. *How* you would use them. I must admit I'm disappointed. I was hoping you'd wait until your guard dog here -" she glared at Aveline " - left you alone. I was so interested in what something like *you* could do to something like *me*."

"A siren is still a living being," Morgana said slowly. "So, I'd imagine the possibilities are endless."

"The King of Calypdon sent you?" Aveline asked. "Is this how King Wendell is killing so many people from Nysus? He has a siren on his side?"

"Oh, I wouldn't say I've picked a side," the siren drawled. "But the king of the lands does tend to give me some interesting missions. It seems I've failed in this one. I didn't even get to see the witch use her power."

"And you're not going to," Aveline growled, wrenching the siren around. Her eyes locked meaningfully with Morgana. "There's a reason she doesn't use her magic."

Morgana smiled sadly, reeling her power back into her chest, where she would let it rest once more. "Yes, there is."

***

Morgana discovered about three quarters through the next day that guards were posted outside her door. There hadn't been any guards the day before, or this morning when she went to the main hall for breakfast. But when Morgana had heard voices outside her door, she had peeked her head out and found two men there, standing guard.

"Oh!" she exclaimed. The men turned in surprise. "I'm sorry, I thought…"

"Apologies if we woke you," one of the guards said sheepishly.

"No, you -" She cut herself off as Aveline appeared at the end of the hall, dressed in her guard's uniform. "It's fine, it's fine." She walked back into her room, leaving the door ajar for Aveline.

"Hey, sorry I'm late, Helah convinced me to cover her post for a few hours -"

"Why are there guards outside my room?" Morgana demanded, whirling back toward Aveline with her hands on her hips.

Aveline's mouth snapped shut. "I … thought you knew they were there?"

"Am I a prisoner?" Morgana asked, stomach in her throat. "Because you said yourself that this would only work with trust, and I -"

"Whoa," Aveline laughed, holding her hands up and coming closer. "Okay, first of all, *no*. You're a guest. And a valuable one at that. The guards are not there to keep you in, they're to keep people like Joao, and the *siren that tried to attack you last night*, out."

Heat rose in Morgana's face. "Oh."

"Yeah, *oh*," Aveline teased, dropping down onto Morgana's bed. "She's in the dungeons, by the way. Joao is questioning her."

Morgana wrinkled her nose.

"I know, but I was told I'm *'too close to the situation.'* Anyway, I suppose I should have told you the guards would be there, but you said it yourself. There are a lot of people whose intentions are not as pure as mine."

"The jury's still out on your intentions," Morgana grumbled, rubbing her eyes, the anger and adrenaline sapping out of her as she fell on her back next to Aveline.

"Are you really dreading this ball that much?" Aveline asked with a grin, leaning toward Morgana. "Did you - for lack of a better phrase - wake up on the wrong side of the bed?"

"Ha-ha. I was born on the wrong side of the bed."

"Well, get reborn or something," Aveline said, extending her hand. "You have a ball to prepare for. I believe the king is sending people over to assist you."

"Because the witch who spent her whole life living in the woods doesn't know how to dress herself?"

Aveline looked apologetic. "Yeah, that's exactly why."

When the maids arrived, they sent Aveline on her way. She left with a smile, heading back to her room to get ready.

"I'll return in an hour to escort you to the ball," Aveline said with a slow smile as she left. "Since I'm your *date*."

"Oh, don't look so smug about it. You're my only friend; it's not like you had any competition."

With Aveline gone, Morgana turned back to the three maids and their supplies.

"So…" she said, rocking back on her feet. "Where do we start?"

With a bath, apparently. Once they'd thoroughly washed her hair and scrubbed her skin raw, they sat her at the end of her bed, complaining at the lack of a vanity desk.

"Maybe they gave me one of the smaller rooms?" Morgana tried to explain, although she had no idea what a bigger one could possibly look like. "This being a temporary stay, and all."

The maids chatted together as they bustled around her, leaving Morgana to sit awkwardly in silence. How could she start a conversation with three people who were clearly friends, who she would probably never see again? She decided not to bother. And with the frenetic way the women bustled about the room, Morgana doubted she'd get a word in if she tried.

Instead, she settled on watching herself slowly decorated through a mirror hanging on the wall. They spread glittering green powder over her eyelids, lining the lashes with a pure black and painting her lips a dark green. She wondered whether they were going overboard with that particular color, but she caught on before she could ask. They were trying to make the hair stand out less, to blend in with her skin. To make it look normal on her.

Two maids left to press and fan out the dress, and the other climbed onto the bed with an array of hair products that Morgana would never be able to tell apart. The maid knelt behind her, sorting through the strands, separating the hair into locks.

"Your hair is beautiful," the maid said as she brushed through the wet curls. Morgana had overheard one of the other maids call her Joasia. "A very unique color."

Yeah. Unique.

Morgana cleared her throat. "Thank you. Not everyone thinks so."

"Your thoughts are the only ones that matter. No one can change you. No one can order you around." She tilted her head. "Not even a king."

"No," Morgana said softly, narrowing her eyes. "I should hope not."

"You will be the gem of the night," Joasia said with a soft smile. "There's no doubt about that. You'll draw every eye, and it will have nothing to do with the color of your hair."

Heat rose on Morgana's neck, and she stammered out her gratitude as the door opened again, the other maids coming in with wide grins. They held the dress Aveline had helped Morgana pick out the day before, and it still shocked her whenever she saw it.

"Enough staring," the maid holding the dress said. "You can stare when it's on."

The soft fabric slipped easily over her skin, the material settling against her shoulder as she turned to the mirror and opened her green painted lips.

The dress fell over her in shimmering silver, made of layers of floral lace, stitched with glowing embroidery. The flowers fanned over her breasts on a sheer neckline, cinching at her waist before fanning out in sweeping skirts that tickled her toes. Stars dotted the material, glowing as everything did in Thalassa.

"Do you know how to walk in heels?" one of the maids asked, wrenching Morgana's attention to several pairs of shoes. The look on Morgana's face at the three-inch heels must have been answer enough, because the maid gave an amused nod. "Flats, it is."

Morgana ticked the seconds away as the ever-dark Thalassa darkened even more. Though no sun ever touched the city, the lanterns knew when night fell, and dimmed to a slighter, atmospheric glow. The lights of bright blues and greens faded to ultramarine and deep purples filtering through the sea water. Her maids fussed around her, perfecting her rouge and smoothing down any stray hairs. She wondered how they managed to apply blush on the cheeks and charcoal around the eyes in the water without them smudging. There must have been a hundred pins in her hair, keeping it still despite the waves' determination to drag the strands along with the currents. Morgana sat quietly through it all, because if there was one thing her life had taught her, it was patience.

The maids backed away when a bell tolled outside. It echoed for far longer than any beel would on land.

"That's the signal that the ball is about to start," Joasia said, hurrying to the window and squinting down at the crowded streets below. "People are making their way towards the palace; the king will want you in the ballroom soon."

Morgana had asked earlier if she should meet him in private before the ball, but apparently, he would be arriving after the party began. Besides, royalty loved a spectacle.

Slipping her shoes on, Morgana tried not to pick apart her appearance in the mirror, admiring the silver clips Joasia had used to sweep up the upper half of her hair. Shouts and laughter drifted from the entrance, but Morgana kept her focus trained on her door, even after the maids left.

Several more minutes passed by the time footsteps sounded outside, and Morgana swung the door open before Aveline could even knock.

"I know I'm late, I -"

Aveline's words died in her throat as she stared at Morgana, standing still in her finery, leaning against the doorframe. Morgana found herself similarly stunned, taking in the first bit of vibrant color she'd seen Aveline wear. Dressed in skirts of pale blue, they layered in different shades so when the hem brushed her toes, it looked like an ocean shore. Silk and lace intertwined up her arms, draping from her shoulders and down to her wrists, and a bodice of blue and white gems hugged her torso. It was almost as distracting as Aveline's eyes, which traveled from Morgana's face, down to the dress, all the way down her feet, and heat spread over Morgana's neck.

"You are late," Morgana agreed at last to break the silence, voice hoarse. "But you look beautiful enough to make up for it."

Aveline brushed a strand of hair away from her face, breathing, "Your beauty has nothing to make up for. It just is."

Needing a distraction, Morgana smoothed down her skirt. A dress that would normally be incredibly heavy on land was as light as a feather in the sea, and Morgana glided forward, extending her hand. "Forget beauty. I was promised a party."

Aveline smiled, her eyes still roaming in admiration over Morgana, but then they caught something else. Aveline cleared her throat, gesturing to the sword hanging at Morgana's side. She'd insisted her maids stitch a few loops into the skirts, to hold her sword belt steady. "It's not customary for guests to attend celebrations at the palace armed."

"It's not customary for guards to accompany witches to a palace ball, and yet here we are. Besides -" Morgana spread her arms, twirling in the doorway so her dress brushed against Aveline's legs. "I think it completes the ensemble."

Smiling too widely to argue, Aveline snatched up Morgana's hand. "I won't bother disagreeing with that." She led Morgana down the hallway. "I'm off duty tonight."

The ballroom seemed to hold half the kingdom by the time they arrived, a string quartet playing soft music from the corner. The music took its time reaching her ears, as if the sound trapped itself in bubbles and had to maneuver through the water in order to burst next to her ears. The strings sounded quieter than such instruments did on land, but at the same time far crisper. She was so distracted that she almost didn't notice that the surrounding conversation fell silent when she appeared, heads swiveling her way as the guest of honor arrived.

"This was what I was afraid of," Morgana sighed.

Aveline tapped her chin. "Put your witch mask on. If they're afraid of you, they won't approach you."

"I don't *want* them to be afraid of me."

Aveline pressed her lips together, looking amused. "You do tonight."

Delicately lifting her skirts up, Morgana made her way into the ballroom, down the three steps that led into the hall. The music continued, whispers picked up, and Morgana didn't spare a single person a glance, weaving a path step by step until they had crossed to the center of the hall.

The ballroom was similar to the entrance hall, decorated with gems and marble, but here, a dais sat at the back, a single throne on top. Morgana wondered what had happened to the queen's throne. When had they finally decided to remove it? But she was more focused on the fact that the sole seat remained empty.

"I was told he would be arriving late," Aveline murmured in her ear, lips warm against her hairline. "He had a long day of travel today."

Morgana nodded absentmindedly, wondering what they could possibly do while they waited for him, and where he could have gone.

She must have said her concerns aloud, because Aveline swung toward her, dress sweeping around like a hurricane of silk. "I have an idea. And it's a really crazy one, so you have to bear with me. *How about* ... you *enjoy* the party? No one will try to talk to you if you're dancing."

"Valid suggestion," Morgana tried to say flatly, but a laugh bubbled out anyway. People drifted past, twirling each other toward the dance floor. A few people moved as though to approach her, but Morgana turned her back on each of them, moving Aveline around with her as she did so. "Unfortunately, I've never been to a party."

Aveline didn't let go of Morgana's hand, and Morgana obeyed the tug as the guard moved them toward the growing group of dancers. "Lucky for you, I've been to a few. I can keep you distracted for at least a few hours." Morgana's eyebrows crept toward her hairline, and Aveline blushed deeply. "I didn't -"

"Oh, I'm sure you did," Morgana said, and though she didn't know what she was doing, excitement took over as she plunged them into the throng.

Aveline trailed after her, pulling Morgana toward her once they were fully lost in the crowd, where no one looked twice at Morgana. The people around them were engrossed in their partners. The music had grown louder, swelling after Morgana's arrival.

"I've never danced before," Morgana admitted in Aveline's ear, trying to pitch her voice loud enough to be heard over the music, but soft enough that only the other woman could hear. "Not really. My mother used to twirl me around the living room, but we never had any music."

Bodies pressed in around them, forcing them together, and Aveline giggled as she stumbled, catching Morgana's waist. Morgana glanced down at the hem of the other woman's dress. "It's because you're wearing heels."

"It's because I've already had a drink or two," she said, hand secured around Morgana's waist. "And for the record, it's not the music that matters. It's the partner."

Taking her cue, Morgana looped her arms around Aveline's neck. She found it was easy to enjoy the party after that, to get lost in the music and the dancing and Aveline's smile. It occurred to her more than once that everything moved too fast, that she needed to keep her wits about her for the king's arrival, but then she remembered how her mother had never let her go to a ball, how she'd never had reason to attend one. Maybe Aveline had a point, and she should enjoy the bits of life she could. No matter how small or how brief.

Morgana caught sight of Helah over Morgana's shoulder, stationed at the edge of the room, and Aveline's sister gave her a wink.

The music swelled, and bubbles rose up around them, weaving between bodies to the rhythm of the strings, forming stars above their heads. Morgana accidentally brushed her fingers along the nape of Aveline's neck, over the sensitive skin beneath her hair line, and Aveline's breath hitched in her chest. She tightened her hold on Morgana. Her hands spread across Morgana's back, over the skin exposed by the dress, drawing circles across the spine with her rough calluses. Morgana shivered.

"You have the hands of a soldier," Morgana whispered in Aveline's ear, resting her chin on the woman's shoulder.

Aveline's shoulder shook with a small laugh. "That's because I am one."

"No, you're not. You're a guard."

"The king trains his guards like soldiers."

Morgana pulled back just enough to squint at Aveline's face. She hadn't even realized the lighting had changed, the hall growing dimmer and the gemstones glowing brighter. "Have you ever had to fight in a battle?"

Aveline tilted her head. "No, actually. No one's ever been foolish enough to attack the palace, and there hasn't been a war in my lifetime. But with the way things have been going, with King Wendell's aggression towards our emissaries, I'm afraid it won't stay that way for long. There's been whispers of conflict for years."

Morgana's brows furrowed. "But isn't that why I'm here? To make sure you *don't* have to fight?" Because Morgana was as good as a volcano ready to erupt, worth an entire regiment of soldiers on her own. Enough to secure success for whatever side she chose.

It was why she decided she would always refuse to choose a side.

"That is, indeed, our goal," a deep voice rumbled behind her. "But my kingdom prefers to take precautions."

Aveline and Morgana sprang apart, Aveline's eyes wide, staring at someone over Morgana's shoulder. Morgana had been so caught up in Aveline that she hadn't noticed the hush fall over the crowd, the music stuttering to a halt, the dancers stilling around them. With hundreds of eyes on her, she spun around to face the king of the sea.

"Your Majesty," she forced out as she took in the tall man before her. He did not look much older than her, but his sea green eyes held the wisdom of a ruler. His dark green finery was trimmed precisely around muscled arms. In his hand was a curved staff of driftwood, embedded from top to bottom with tiny, shimmering seashells.

With tanned skin and dark hair, he smiled a royal smile and bowed his head. "I am King Daegil. Forgive me for not welcoming you to my home upon your arrival."

That's when Morgana realized that the rest of the room had bent at the waist, bowing to their king. But this was not her king, so she stayed upright. She simply lowered her head in return, taking in again the king's outfit. It stuck out amid the crowd of lighter colors. His finery was the same shade as Morgana's hair.

King Daegil smiled, noting her gaze. He spread his arms. "I was told this was the color to wear tonight."

Morgana kept her arms at her side, resisting the urge to run her fingers through her hair, to cover her green eye. She chewed on her lip, unsure of what to say.

King Daegil didn't seem fussed as he lifted his head, pounding his staff against the marble floor, which his people seemed to take as a cue to stand. Aveline rose gracefully but remained behind Morgana, letting her fingers brush against Morgana's arm.

The king's voice echoed around the room. "You must be the Serpent Witch."

Chapter Six

Morgana tried not to stiffen at the name, but it was impossible. She'd heard it before as a child, when they still lived among people. There had been whispers in the village, talk of a witch older than time who carried the Serpent Sword, but they hadn't known it had been her mother. They hadn't known that the Serpent Witch was actually a line of witches, that the power and the name were passed down through blood and bad luck.

Keeping her features smooth, Morgana lifted her chin. "Is that who I am?"

Daegil's dark eyes flashed, and Morgana found a strange echo of familiarity there. "It's who your mother was, and your mother's mother, and so on. I suppose you yourself have done nothing to earn the title yet."

"Are titles earned?" Morgana asked, looking him up and down, at the silver crown on his head. "Or are they given and inherited?"

The king's smile spread, but it was slow and calculated, with nothing natural about it. "Right you are." He tilted his head, assessing Morgana, and suddenly he didn't look nearly as young as he had. "Well, whoever you might be, whatever you prefer to be called, I'm charmed to at last make your acquaintance, to welcome you from your previous life of solitude."

Morgana had trouble finding words, and she didn't know why. "Your kingdom is lovely, your majesty." She glanced at Aveline. "And the people I've met, even more so."

"They are. I'm honored to rule over them." Daegil lifted his gaze, looking out over the crowd in the ballroom. "Return to your festivities, please. This is a party to celebrate an end to years of unease between Nysus and Calypdon. Soon, the Serpent Witch will ensure freedom for all, and to thank her—" He stepped forward, extending his hand. "I hate to steal you away, but I must insist we share a dance." He winked, and Morgana was suddenly reminded of Joao. "To signify your union with our people. Welcome to my kingdom. May you find a home here."

The crowd cheered, and after a moment, Morgana stepped forward, taking Daegil's arm. His large hand engulfed hers, and he guided her to the center of the dance floor. The crowd dispersed around them, taking their partners, and Morgana watched over King Daegil's shoulder as Aveline disappeared into the throng of people, hands wringing at her chest. Wrenching her gaze away, Morgana allowed the king to place one hand at her waist, holding her fingers securely with the other. Couples resumed their dance around them but gave them a wide berth. The king leaned in to speak.

"How are you enjoying your stay?" Daegil asked. He was eerily beautiful, not a flaw on his young face. The sight struck her again when she forced herself to look up.

"It's been marvelous," she said, honestly. "Absolutely beautiful."

"It must be rather different," he said, sweeping her around, his steps easy and graceful. "Jarring, after spending a lifetime on land."

Morgana relaxed a little, because this was a conversation she could keep pace with. "I can hardly describe it, feeling so light, although I suppose my magic helped me adjust faster than others might."

Daegil chuckled. "Yes, I can attest to the strangeness of such a transition. I might be biased, but I think the transition from land to sea is far easier than the opposite. Although perhaps that's only because I am so used to the sea. You'll have to tell me your thoughts once you go back to Calypdon."

Morgana couldn't help but laugh at the thought, remembering how Aveline had had to relearn how to stand. "To be honest, I'm not looking forward to the return of gravity. Does that mean you've been, then? To Calypdon?"

"Oh, yes," Daegil said, eyes sparkling. The verdant gemstones turned his green eyes even more vibrant, and for a moment, his eyes reminded her of a snake's. She thought of Coby, and her heart ached. "Also rather beautiful, I must admit."

"I think I've seen more of Nysus than I have of Calypdon, at this point," Morgana admitted softly.

Daegil squeezed her hand. "I'm glad you took some time to explore our city." He grimaced. "There won't be much of that in the coming days as we plan our foray to Briarwood."

Morgana's stomach soured as she remembered her true purpose here. Still, through the dread, she said as confidently as she could, "And what exactly is it you want to do in Briarwood? I'm assuming you'll want me to … immobilize the king. If it's nothing more than that, we'll be back in your wonderful kingdom soon enough."

He tilted his head. "Immobilize him?"

Not risking looking over her shoulder, even as she wanted to find Aveline for reassurance, she lifted her chin. "Yes. Not only is taking him as a prisoner more humane than murdering him, if he is alive, he can give you information. Although," Morgana said, looking around with an expression she hoped looked sheepish, "this probably isn't the setting to have such a discussion."

"No," Daegil agreed. "But you can give me your oath to assist in my cause, yes?"

Something slithered down Morgana's spine, but she kept swaying to the melody. "An oath wouldn't mean much, I don't think. Would you really trust a witch's word?"

He chuckled, and it made the hairs at the nape of Morgana's neck stand on end. "I suppose a good ruler doesn't trust anyone's word. We must trust our instincts. You, too, are in a position of great power. I'm sure you must understand."

She did, but somehow, she thought that their instincts were miles apart. "And what are your instincts telling you?"

He looked up and around the ballroom, at his smiling people. "It's telling me that the Rift was a temporary solution. That the Ancient War never truly ended."

Morgana blinked. "Of course it did. With the creation of your kingdom, the gods found peace with each other. The violence stopped, the drowning stopped, and the world healed. There has never been another war of that magnitude."

"Perhaps for the gods it is over," King Daegil said, his eyes drifting somewhere far away. Somewhere darker, a place even Morgana, with all her darkness, couldn't follow. "But in the sea, we've never truly recovered."

"Recovered from what?" Morgana asked, curiosity getting the better of her. "Your kingdom is incredible."

"It is sealed away from the outside world," Daegil said, and for the first time, bitterness entered his voice. "There are more gods than just the Lady of the Land and Lord of the Sea. There are dozens more, and their blessings upon the land far outweigh what has been given to us down below."

Incredulous, Morgana looked around. "He gave you everything. He forces the Lady of the Land to give you humans."

His mouth twisted. "Humans are not everything."

Morgana's heartbeat echoed in her ears, the ground tilting beneath her as she processed those words, unsure at first why they threatened to send her into a panic. It didn't take her long to realize it was because humans *were* everything. At least to her. All she'd ever done in her sad and lonely life had been for them.

Daegil went on when Morgana didn't, taking her silence as curiosity. "The Rift was about equalizing the territories, giving the sea what it lacked. But, when the sea is ignored by all gods but two? Well. That's not a very balanced kingdom, is it?"

"No," Morgana said faintly. "I suppose not."

He nodded, as if she'd said what he expected. "The lands have been corrupted by those blessings, by the greed that comes with them. Only when the sea gains everything they're owed will the Ancient War truly come to an end. I know you want that," he added, inclining his head, "considering all the war did to your ancestors."

The music faded away. "What could you know of my ancestors?"

"Stories," he shrugged, but any nonchalance that had been there before disappeared, and he stared at her with the weight of a thousand years. "I can't imagine the pain when all those souls shifted and came to the sea. We will do all we can to eliminate that pain for you."

"Pain?" Morgana asked.

"To restore balance," Daegil elaborated, "we will take a sliver of their land. A larger chunk of the population. Perhaps if you are inside the sea when those people are remade for the sea, there will be less discomfort."

"I will not harm them," Morgana burst out, heart hammering against her ribs as she tried to wrap her head around everything the king had said. But she had to wonder … did the Ancient War truly continue? Would there soon be consequences even worse than before, if they did nothing to balance the kingdoms? "I will find the king, I will speak with him and put him to sleep if I must to keep him from tormenting your people further, but I won't touch the innocent, or those who have simply done what they must to survive under a tyrannical ruler."

The king momentarily lifted his hand from her waist, using it to wave at the room. "Look around you. Does living here seem like such a horrible fate for those trapped on the land?"

"If it is against their wishes, then yes."

He shook his head. "The lands are a threat to us, more than you know. The king has tainted them with lies of the sea and has made us his enemy. His people don't know what they want. We all deserve a clean slate, don't you agree?"

His words reverberated in her mind.

A clean slate.

Morgana nodded dumbly, murmuring, "Yes, we do," but her magic curled around her. She reached out, in the same way she'd done to Aveline, searching for truth in the king's life and heart. He didn't seem to notice, and Morgana's mystical touch reached his skin, inching into his blood -

Her magic recoiled from what it found there, shrieking with agony.

Morgana's eyes widened, but she didn't let her body flinch away, just carried on dancing in Daegil's arms. Flickers of information flashed behind her mind, imprints from what she'd gathered from the king's soul, and only one thing stuck out.

Death, death, death. Morgana could see intentions, could feel them in her bones, and when she sorted through his, that simple word was all she saw.

He had no intention of taking only some of the land. He desired all of it.

His eyes flitted down her body, and Morgana wanted to cave in on herself, to hide every exposed bit of skin, but his gaze only fell on the sword at her hip. "It's a beautiful weapon."

Morgana froze. "It is. It's very dear to me."

"So I've heard." His lip curled. "I've heard many things about that sword, actually. I've thought about it extensively, the things I might do with it if the opportunity arose. If that blade were taken from your beautiful hands."

Morgana's blood ran cold, and she resisted the urge to run, to take that sword in her hands and hug it close to her chest. Even as fear crawled up her throat, she managed, "It is only a sword, Your Majesty. A gift from my mother, so I find it to be a particularly important sword to me. But to anyone else, it is nothing but a decent sword."

"You are not the only one to deem that sword of high value. And it is here, within reach. Perhaps you should keep that in mind, if you are called upon to make any decisions tonight."

Any decisions. He could feel it, then, Morgana's disgust at what he planned. He didn't want refuge for the land dwellers, Morgana realized, regardless of whether they cooperated or not. He didn't want them if they didn't bow to him.

He wanted to wipe out Calypdon entirely. Become a part of the sea or face death. And he meant to use her to do it.

Daegil stared at her, that bland smile still on his face, but something had shifted. "Is there a problem? Witch?" He said the name like an insult, not with the curiosity Aveline had. "Cooperation is key in this plan. From everyone. Do you understand that?"

Morgana felt a fire rise up within her, and she pressed her lips together. "Perfectly, Your Majesty."

When a new song started, Morgana made her escape as the tempo picked up, the violinist sawing on her instrument. She stepped out of his embrace but had to yank her arm away to free her hand. He let go unwillingly, tilting his head.

"I think I'll step outside for a moment," Morgana said numbly, unable to look away from what she had found behind his eyes. Her magic couldn't feel it anymore, but she could see it well enough as King Daegil's mouth set into a thin line.

"Should I accompany you?"

"No," Morgana said calmly, and then let out a fake, hopefully charming laugh. "I've been surrounded by people for days now, Your Majesty, and I'm just feeling a tad overwhelmed."

He bowed his head. "I imagine it's difficult to shift away from a long life of solitude."

Indeed. A life of solitude that she should never have left.

He took her hand in his once more, lifting her knuckles to his lips. They were icy cold against her skin. "Take all the time you require on this night." He squeezed her hand so hard she had to bite her lip to keep from crying out. "War begins tomorrow."

It's not a war if the other side stands no chance. And they won't stand a chance against me.

Morgana backed away from the king, heart pounding in her throat, staring at him until he was at last swallowed by the crowd. As soon as she felt those eyes leave her, she spun on her heel, pushing through what seemed to be an ever-growing mass of people, confining her on every side as she tried to fight against the dancing guests around her.

Whipping her head from side to side, she searched for Aveline but couldn't see above the crowd. She did a double take at every blue dress, every head of dark hair, but each new face was unfamiliar.

"Are you okay?" a man asked her as she stumbled over his foot, but she ignored him, hiking up her skirts and carrying on. His voice echoed after her, his concern seeping into her bones as she battled inside herself, reconciling with how this place could seem so beautiful and *good*, but hold such darkness at the core.

What if King Daegil wasn't entirely wrong? What if the gods had a fate even worse than this in store for the kingdoms?

She escaped the crowd at the foot of the stairs, and she sighed in relief at the sight of a way out. Had Aveline left? Was she still in the crowd? Had she gone somewhere else to wait for her? Morgana didn't have time to think too hard about it, couldn't hear her thoughts above the rapid pounding of her heart, the roaring in her ears.

The king must have lied to Aveline, because Morgana would not do this for them, and Aveline had to know that, especially after yesterday. She wouldn't, and she would go now, before she found herself any deeper in the king's bloody plans.

Holding herself upright, Morgana kept her gaze trained forward as she climbed the stairs, moving away from the music and nodding pleasantly to the guards manning the towering entrance. Only when she'd passed the threshold, turning the corner out of sight, did she break into a run.

She supposed it was good she'd said no to the heels.

Morgana had become passingly familiar with the castle over the past days, but she'd moved too quickly, and her vision broke out into shattered fragments as it had when she first arrived in Nysus. She slowed as much as she dared, squinting as her view of the hallway reformed. She skidded to a halt at the sound of voices, catching herself against the wall just before she came to a corner. She had no desire to explain herself to anyone at the moment.

"A new order from the king."

The voice echoed through the otherwise empty hallway, familiar and unwelcome at the same time. Joao. Morgana stayed frozen, pressing her body into the icy wall. The marble brushed against the bare skin of her back, so starkly different from Aveline's warm hands.

"Now?" another voice asked incredulously. "Why? Everyone's in one room."

"He lost sight of the witch," Joao growled, venom lacing his words. Morgana didn't chance taking a step back as she wrapped her fingers around the hilt of her sword. "He said to find her at all costs, and under no circumstances allow her to leave the palace."

Morgana's eyes widened, thinking of the guards posted at her door, of Aveline almost constantly at her side. She thought of King Daegil's promise of council, of planning, of ending the Ancient War once and for all.

She was not a guest at all. She was always a prisoner. A weapon not to save Calypdon, but to destroy it.

And they didn't plan on giving her a choice.

Her mother had been so sure Morgana would know when the right person came to her door. And yet, she'd been wrong.

A hand gripped her by the shoulder, and Morgana swung around, freeing her sword in one quick motion and holding it to the throat of her attacker. At first, she couldn't see who it was because the image before her fractured again, but her hands shook even more when she could at last make out Aveline's frightened face. The sea woman lifted her hands by instinct, eyes wide as she stared down at the point of the sword a breath from her neck.

"Morgana?" she gasped out, chest heaving. "What -"

"Did you know?" Morgana cut her off, pushing her against the wall. She listened for the other guards, but they must have moved on. Swallowing, Morgana blinked away tears, Aveline blurring before her. "You must have. Did you know?"

Aveline's eyes darted around her, forehead creasing, her mouth gaping like a fish. "Know *what*?" Her voice came out strangled, probably from trying to move her throat as little as possible in the presence of the sword.

Morgana let out a hysterical laugh, wanting nothing more than to be back in her home with Coby, where she was safe and everyone else was safe from her. "That King Daegil means to eliminate not just the land king, but all of the lands? That he wants to expand his kingdom, until there is no air left? To make the land dwellers either join the sea or drown? Was that your plan all along, to trick me into making some sort of deal, to *force me* into killing thousands?"

Aveline tried to take a step back, but she was trapped between the wall and the blade. Morgana pulled the sword back so she could speak. "What are you talking about? That is *not* the plan, he wants to *help* -"

"He wants to *kill*," Morgana shouted, shaking the sword in a full frenzy now.

Oh, gods. What if the king somehow got his hands on her sword? There's no way he could know that secret, too, could he?

"And he wants to use me to do it."

"That's absurd. He wants the kingdoms to come together as one -"

"No," Morgana said with a humorless laugh. "He wants *one kingdom*, a kingdom where the entire known world is of the sea. He thinks it will end the Ancient War, that true balance was never reached. And he has no desire for the lands to take any part of it."

Aveline looked around crazily, as if she expected someone to melt out of the walls and explain this all to her. "I don't know what you've heard -"

"What I've *heard*," Morgana stressed, jabbing the sword forward, "is that your king issued an order to capture me. To keep me here, by any means necessary. Although I'm sure you knew that, given your position."

"I haven't heard *anything* from the king," Aveline said frantically.

"*You* brought me here," Morgana cried. Her entire body trembled, and she knew she should probably lower her sword. She might make a terrible mistake in her state, but she had no idea who to trust. No idea who cared for her safety and who didn't. If anyone did at all. "You brought me here under the guise of freedom, of a *life*. It would have been one thing if you'd kidnapped me, but this? This was *cruel*."

Morgana's heart wrenched. She hadn't realized how lonely she'd been, how much she had wanted something new, something better, until the brief glimpse of it had been snatched away. It was that promise of freedom that had made her lower her defenses so easily. "Were your orders to keep me distracted? To - to make me think I could have a life you never actually planned to give me?"

"I had nothing to do with this!" Aveline shrieked, her hands still held high, eyes pleading with Morgana. "The sea means you no harm, I *know* it -"

"It's true. We don't."

Morgana finally took the sword away from Aveline, only to turn it on Joao, who leaned casually against the wall a few feet away, his sword held loosely in his fingers. He stood comfortably, as if Morgana weren't a threat at all.

"And we won't hurt you," Joao said, taking a step forward. "Not if you cooperate."

Aveline sucked her breath in, because she'd heard it. The clear, shameless threat. "You won't hurt her *regardless* of her choices," Aveline snapped brazenly, and guilt dripped down Morgana's spine for holding the sword to her throat for so long. "Let us pass."

Joao pushed off the wall, securing his fingers tighter around his sword. Morgana watched it carefully, keeping hers poised ahead. "You know I can't do that. Orders are orders."

"Don't do this," Morgana said, stepping in front of Aveline, who was unarmed. Unarmed and off duty, Morgana remembered. She wouldn't have heard any orders from the king on this night. "Let me go, and no one will get hurt."

"No one will get hurt either way," Joao said, so cocky that she wanted to punch his teeth out.

"Does she need to remind you who she is?" Aveline asked, stepping up beside Morgana. "You could be dead with half a thought. This whole palace could be."

"But she wouldn't," he said with a wicked smile, moving further forward, dragging the tip of his sword along Morgana's own blade. "I truly believe you don't want to hurt anyone with your powers. It's what makes you such a terrible witch."

Morgana swallowed. Would she have the will to kill him? Or anyone, if it came to that? She gripped her sword tighter, knocking his away. "I am leaving and never coming back. I will go somewhere you will never find me, and you will forget I ever existed."

"The king will never stop hunting you."

"I'm used to being hunted."

Joao bared his teeth, the amusement sapping away as his expression hardened. "Enough of this."

He lunged.

Morgana ducked, slashing her sword up and across his torso, then kicking him back toward the wall. Shoving Aveline further down the hall, Morgana rushed forward to distance her friend from the fight as much as possible. She vaguely heard Aveline screaming at her, but couldn't make out the words, too focused on deflecting Joao's jab, the sound of steel-on-steel ringing through the hall. Joao fought with a cold precision that Morgana had never learned, sword moving nearly faster than Morgana could track. She stayed on the defensive, slashing his sword away with every attack, searching for an opening.

She desperately tried to call her magic, to stifle his life force, to weaken it, but she couldn't focus long enough to reach him. She couldn't locate the thread that linked her to Joao, couldn't sort between him and the other guards and everyone else in the ballroom. Every time she tried to take a moment and find it, she nearly got her head slashed off. Her parries were clumsy and untrained, and his sword at last drew blood from her arm.

Morgana jumped away, warning, "Careful. You can't kill me anymore than I want to kill you. The king would have your head."

"Maybe I'll take your head for myself," he snarled. "Because I can't kill you at all, right? No one can. I think you'd just stitch back together. It would be a fun experiment."

Morgana had always wondered what would happen if someone ever managed to behead her, if she would just live the rest of her days in two parts, or if her magic wouldn't allow her body to be separated. She didn't particularly feel like finding out.

"You'll be left to deal with King Daegil," Morgana hissed. With Joao distracted by her words, Morgana jabbed forward, the tip of her blade catching Joao's sword arm. He cried out in pain, clutching the wound as blood seeped into his fine white dress shirt.

"Morgana, we have to go *now*—"

Morgana turned to find Aveline running toward her. She had just enough time to see Aveline's eyes widen, a shout on her lips, when pain exploded in her side.

A scream wrenched from Morgana's throat. Her knees buckled, the Serpent Sword tumbling from her hand and skittering across the floor. She felt around her waist for a different sword; the one now lodged in her body. Black tinged her vision, and her numb fingers found the cool metal lodged just above her hip. She looked down as red blossomed over her once beautiful dress.

The blood spread over the silver, rising up in tendrils that weaved through the water. Wispy clouds of crimson shrouded the area around her torso, and it became more disorienting the more it spread, as if the sea itself was leaching the blood from her body.

Hands reached for her, grabbing her shoulders, trying to haul her up. Joao still knelt over her, grabbing his sword and wrenching it roughly from Morgana's flesh.

"That is a taste," he hissed. "Don't make me do it again."

He glared at Aveline, who stared on in horror as she struggled to get Morgana to her feet,

But Morgana couldn't focus on either of them as panic wrapped a tight fist around her chest, her empty fingers and weightless belt crying out to her. *My sword.* Morgana scrambled about weakly, blindly, searching for the cool, familiar feel of the snake inscription. *I need my sword.*

Joao inched closer, shoving his face into hers, his hot breath spreading over her clammy skin. "You're ours now, witch."

I will be, truly, if I don't find my sword.

Where is my sword?

Steeling herself, Morgana gathered everything she had and swung her legs out, catching him in the gut with her heel and sending him toppling over. Her vision swam, and it had nothing to do with the water around her, but she stumbled to her feet, leaning on Aveline.

"Morgana," Aveline said desperately, hands roving over her face. "We need to go." Morgana coughed, sending a small billow of blood flowing through the water by her lips. Aveline steeled herself, supporting almost all of Morgana's weight. "We need to -"

"*Stop them,*" Joao bellowed, and Morgana sluggishly looked up to find two more guards sprinting down the hall, weapons poised, ready to box them in.

The cloud of Morgana's blood staining the water was all that separated them. It looked like so much more blood, spread out like this, than she imagined a pool of blood on dry land might. Through the crimson, Morgana's eye caught something glinting on the ground. She felt a distant twinge of relief and one last burst of energy surged through her limbs.

"My sword!" she screamed, lunging away from Aveline and scooping up the weapon, nearly losing consciousness in the process. Aveline didn't loosen her grip on Morgana's arm, being pulled after her. Morgana fell to her knees, her strength giving out, stars dotting her vision, barely managing to maintain her grip on the weapon.

The guards scuttled closer as Joao stood, fury contorting his face. Morgana shrunk into herself, because he stood between the women and the exit.

They wouldn't escape this place.

As if on cue, her hand burned where she held the sword, and Morgana watched with her limited vision as the metal began to glow, heating with magic, strands of light wrapping around her hand, securing the sword to her skin.

Power thrummed through her, vibrating through her veins, and Morgana looked up slowly to see Joao gaping at her, taking a step back. But Aveline was there, shoving him away as she watched in awe.

Morgana's arms shook, and she didn't bother lifting her sword. "This magic is not something you want anywhere near you," she snarled.

Embracing the pressure building in her chest, she lashed out blindly with her power. Joao collapsed to the ground, her grasp on his life force just enough to send his body kicking and thrashing to the ground. Her magic spread over him, and she just had enough mind to veer it around Aveline. He screamed into the silence that fell in the hall. The other guards watched in shock, unsure what to do with their commander writhing on the floor.

Joao managed to glare at her, mumbling, "Witch," but she squeezed her magical fist around his heart, shoving him further against the ground. Only then did another guard rush forward to help, but he barely made it a step before Morgana latched onto his soul, sending him slumping against the wall.

Her magic, even after years of being ignored and stifled, obeyed her every command, now easily flowing from her as it was meant to, and she felt somehow lighter and heavier than she ever had at the same time. It had a mind of its own, as if it knew Morgana wouldn't have reached for its help unless she was in desperate need. It scared her and invigorated her at the same time as she lurched around the hall, addressing each member of her audience.

"You will let us pass," Morgana said in the most forbidding voice she could muster, finding that the anger made it come easily despite the pain still thrumming in her side. "You will let us go, or meet the same fate as your friends."

Each guard carefully stepped away, so she didn't bother wondering what she might have done if they hadn't.

She stumbled a step back, swaying, searching for Aveline. Perhaps she'd scared her off. Morgana had scared herself, too.

But Aveline wasted no time as she came up behind her, grabbed her hand, and they took off running. Morgana screamed as they went at the magic tearing through her and leaving a trail of sparks behind them. But as they moved, Aveline didn't let go of her once, leading her through a string of unfamiliar corridors that had none of the grandeur of the rest of the palace. Passages for the staff, probably. They burst out of the palace through a side door hidden in stone, and the magic leached out of Morgana.

The light of her magic vanished along with any strength she had left, and she collapsed, barely avoiding skewering herself on her own blade.

Everything was so much darker now, and Morgana couldn't move, her cheek pressed against a piece of coral. Hands pressed against her shoulder blades, and panic seized her, but the fingers were calloused and familiar, soft and kind as they scooped Morgana up into surprisingly strong arms.

"Aveline," Morgana whispered, the name a prayer on her tongue. She couldn't see her, but she could feel her. She didn't know what she held tighter, her sword or Aveline's shirt.

"It's okay." Morgana's head lolled against Aveline's chest as she hurried away, jostling Morgana with every stumble and trip. "It's okay, you're going to be okay."

She thought of Joao's pain, how she could feel it, how it had only made her squeeze him harder. She thought of the fear in the soldier's eyes. "I'm sorry," she moaned.

"No," Aveline shushed her, panting. "Don't. Don't speak, save your energy."

Morgana managed to look up, to make out Aveline's wretched expression, the anguish written on her face. She opened her mouth, but it took so much effort to move. Black clouded the edges of her vision, and she tried to blink it away.

Darkness pulled her under.

Chapter Seven

Voices mingled around her, filtering through the fog filling her mind. They blended together, the words slurring as she tried to make them out over the ringing in her ears. Her eyes wouldn't open, too heavy, and her limbs refused to move. She felt as though she'd been turned to stone.

Fingers dug into her arm, sharp enough to startle some clarity into her, and slivers of light filtered through her eyelids. It was brighter, clearer, and more yellow than she remembered, and the realization that they'd somehow made it back to Calypdon jerked her out of her stupor.

Her eyes flew open. She didn't have the strength to sit up, or even move very much. She forced her neck to turn, struggling to take in her surroundings. The room was small, with a glass dome set into the ceiling, the blue-sky visible overhead. Streams of light pierced through the room, warming her skin. She'd think it was a dream if it weren't for the pain in her side, roaring for attention.

The fingers squeezed her forearm, moving to her hand, but their touch wasn't enough to distract her from the growing agony of her wound.

"Aveline," she rasped out, but when she rolled her head to the side, it wasn't Aveline who sat there.

It was a man she could barely make out, merely a silhouette with the sun from the window beaming behind him. For a moment she was afraid that they'd failed to escape from the sea after all, that King Daegil somehow sat before her, wearing a slightly different crown. But then he leaned forward, the rays shifting so they slanted across his soft features. He smiled, and it was a true smile, lighting up sparkling green eyes.

Morgana glanced further down at his throat and found a jagged piece of bark embedded, in the same spot Aveline's seashell sat.

"You're awake," he sighed, his unfamiliar voice lilting through the room, calming Morgana's pounding heart. "I knew you would get there eventually, you being who you are. But after so long, I was starting to get concerned."

Morgana opened her mouth to speak, but was immediately overtaken by a coughing fit, the wound in her side pulling painfully. The man rubbed her shoulder, brow furrowed as Morgana regained control over herself. "Who are you?"

"Who am I?" the man laughed, lifting his hand to poke at his crown. "Well, I don't wear this thing for fun, do I? It's actually rather uncomfortable, if I'm being honest."

Morgana gaped at him, wide-eyed as she tried to scramble away. Her arms and legs ignored her. The king of Calypdon freely let go of her arms as she struggled to sit up, braced on her elbows. She broke into a sweat. "You're… you're -"

"You're awake!"

Aveline rushed into the room, dropping the blanket she had been carrying and kneeling at Morgana's bedside. Aveline leaned over the bed to frame Morgana's face in her hands, tentatively laying a palm on her forehead as confusion filtered through the woman in the bed, unable to decide whether to look at Aveline or the man. Aveline didn't seem bothered at all by the presence of the king, examining Morgana's sweaty face, hand pressed to Morgana's forehead as if to check for a fever.

Morgana batted her off. "Stop that. I can't get sick."

"Maybe not, but clearly you can get stabbed," Aveline said, lowering her hands to Morgana's shirt and lifting the hem to reveal a mess of bandages wrapped around her torso. "Badly."

"My body is still a human body," Morgana groaned, trying to sit up wholly but failing, falling back into the pillows. The overwhelming relief of seeing Aveline alive and well threatened to overwhelm her senses. "What happened? How did we—"

"I told you she'd panic," the king said, stunning Morgana speechless at how casually he spoke to Aveline.

"No, I'm pretty sure *I* told *you* she'd panic," Aveline said pointedly.

"That was when *you* were panicking," the king waved her off. "That doesn't count."

"What is going on here?" Morgana croaked, put off by the humor in the king's voice. He looked to be a few years older than Morgana, perhaps nearing his thirties, but he somehow looked ages younger than King Daegil.

"The first thing you need to know is that you're safe," Aveline said, squeezing Morgana's hand. "We both are. Thanks to him."

Memories came back in fragments. Blood shrouding her vision as it billowed through the surrounding water. Aveline holding her up because Morgana was too weak to stand. Joao's sneering face, his sword stained with Morgana's blood.

The vile taint of King Daegil's soul, as if it was a tangible shadow.

Morgana's voice cracked. "What happened?"

Aveline motioned to the king of Calypdon. This didn't make Morgana feel any better. But something nagged at her mind, telling her to listen.

"We have contacts in Thalassa," the king said, sitting back and smoothing down his shirt. He wore casual clothes, similar to the clothes Aveline was wearing. "We have ever since -" he cut himself off as a strange expression flickered across his face. He covered it quickly, clearing his throat. "Anyway, when we received word of King Daegil's intentions -"

"How could your contacts possibly know the king's intentions? Because even Aveline, one of Daegil's trusted guards, didn't know." Her eyes flick to Aveline, her doubts resurfacing. "Right?"

Aveline squeezed her hands in answer. "No. *No*, I didn't know, I swear. I -" The words caught in her throat, eyes glistening. "I still don't understand why he…" She trailed off, ducking her head as she collected herself. When she looked up again, anger had replaced the sorrow. "I didn't know that he intended to keep you against your will, or his true intentions for your power."

The land king - Wendell, Morgana remembered - leaned forward, inserting himself between them. "If you don't mind, I'd like to hear exactly what King Daegil's intentions were. Aveline told me all the details she could, everything you relayed to her, but I don't think you had a chance to tell her the full story before you lost consciousness."

Morgana's eyes flew to this new king, another man she knew nothing about. "Why should I tell you anything? What do *you* want with me?"

The king sighed. "You're right to be wary after everything you've gone through. Let me be honest with you; I *do* want something from you."

Morgana simply stared at him. "I already knew that. I asked *what* you wanted with me."

A shadow passed over the land king's face. "Your sea king -"

"He's not my king," Aveline and Morgana said at the same time, the witch more aggressively than the sea woman. Aveline just sounded resigned, and Morgana's stomach flipped.

"*King Daegil*," Wendell corrected, bowing his head and lacing his fingers together, "has been instigating violence all over Calypdon and casting the blame on me. It took me too long to see what he was doing. Believe me, I feel as foolish as you surely do." He dropped his hands to his knees and clenched them into fists. "This is what we get, I suppose, for wishing to see the best in people."

Morgana flinched, but didn't look away from the land king. "I think you'll find that I've learned my lesson."

King Wendell's gaze hardened. "So have I. And yet here you are, protected in my palace. If I wished you harm, I could have simply turned Aveline away; or have you murdered while you were still helpless."

"I was in Nysus for several days," Morgana shot back. "But Daegil bided his time because he needed, and still needs, my cooperation. Perhaps you have similar intentions?"

"I didn't even know your existence was more than a myth until my contacts informed me of your arrival in Nysus." He huffed, shaking his head. "I'd heard rumors, when I was a child, of a Hallowed that holds our souls in her hands." His eyes softened. "Never did I imagine such power would lie in the hands of a young woman."

Morgana was struck by the pity in his voice. "I'm a bit like you, I suppose. You, too, inherited an … unfortunate situation."

The king barked a bitter laugh, removing his crown and running a hand through his tousled hair. "That's putting it mildly. Morgana - may I call you Morgana?"

The question caught her off guard. “I, um, yes.”

“Morgana,” he continued, his tone soft. “King Daegil must have been planning this for well over a decade. He must have known you were in hiding, that you would know little of Calypdon’s situation, and he knew to use your ignorance to his advantage. He could be as vile and twisted as he liked in the light of day without you knowing, because you were tucked in the shadows of the woods.”

“And what of your actions? I saw a man executed in the street. We know people from Nysus have been killed by your people. Are you claiming innocence?”

“Yes,” the king said, and for the first time, fury raced across his face. “None of that was my doing, nor the actions of anyone loyal to Calypdon.” His throat bobbed. “I don’t know who you saw executed, but I can assure you, it did not happen at the hands of one of my soldiers.”

Morgana’s head throbbed, too much floating around in her still exhausted head. “Why in *either of the kingdoms* should I believe you? I’ve already been fooled by one king. I won’t allow it to happen again.”

Aveline made a noise, a squeak that broke into a sob. “Because it was Daegil.”

Alarmed, Morgana looked at Aveline with concern. “What?”

Aveline took a deep breath. “King Daegil’s agents have been killing his own emissaries, casting the blame upon Calypdon and King Wendell. He sacrificed his own people to fabricate an excuse strong enough to convince you to come.”

Wendell placed a hand on Aveline’s shoulder. “He only needed to appear better than me.”

“And is he?” Morgana snapped back. “You make your own people fall to their knees at your feet and swear a vow. What kind of king does that make you?”

For the first time, King Wendell’s face cracked wide open with real sorrow. He no longer looked like a king, but rather a young, lost man. “A desperate one.”

The grief on the king’s face stunned Morgana into silence.

Wendell ducked his head, raising his hand to his throat. He laid his palm over the bark there, as if he wanted to yank it out or push it further into his flesh. “King Daegil has someone … very important to me, trapped in Nysus.”

Though Morgana’s heart panged with sympathy, she didn’t back down. “That’s not a claim of innocence.”

Aveline’s eyes softened. “No. But I think you and I can both understand doing things we don’t want to do for … people we care about.”

Morgana stared at Aveline for several seconds, finding sincerity there and realizing that the sea woman must have already heard this story. She turned back to Wendell. “Who does he have?”

"She's my..." Wendell trailed off, clearing his throat. "She's a very dear friend of mine. We grew up in the palace together, we were inseparable. Her father was the captain of *my* father's guard, and she knows more about running this kingdom than I do." He cast his gaze skyward, full of regret. "That's why I brought her with me to Nysus."

Morgana remembered what Wendell said, about the consequences of seeing the best in people, and she sighed. "What happened?"

"We travelled to Nysus nearly a year ago to meet with King Daegil. He invited us saying he wanted to strengthen relations between our two kingdoms." He tapped the bark in the hollow of his throat. "He was actually the one who told me where to find this. He sent us to a waterfall just south of Briarwood, with a great weeping willow growing from the riverbed. A piece of bark from that tree is Calypdon's version of Aveline's seashell." He shook his head, brow furrowed. "I still don't fully understand why he granted us access to Nysus in the first place; we weren't able to open the portal, of course, he had to let us in."

Morgana pressed her lips together. "King Daegil will go to great lengths to gain a person's trust. It sounds like it worked."

"We went to Nysus and brought several trusted guards. Not enough, of course. Not nearly enough. It all stayed quite normal for the first evening, but Thyra never came to breakfast the next morning. I found only King Daegil, and let's just say he had ... conditions."

Morgana put the pieces together. "One of which was making your people swear oaths of loyalty, in exchange for her life."

Wendell was doing a decent job of keeping his composure, but his fists clenched at his sides. "I didn't really know why at the time, of course. I couldn't know it was part of his plan to trick you, so I did what he asked. It wasn't directly hurting anyone, and if people didn't come to Briarwood, they would face no repercussions."

No one said anything for several moments. No one wanted to say that King Daegil was likely punishing them in Wendell's stead.

That was likely the case for the man Morgana saw executed.

"But yes," Wendell said, lifting his head once more and looking Morgana in the eye. "For that, I am guilty, but I never thought it would harm anyone. I only wanted to save her."

Morgana studied his eyes, his body language. "I understand," she finally said quietly. "I've discovered that we all have our breaking point. But this is all still..." She trailed off, shaking her head and letting it fall back onto her pillows. "I don't know who to trust."

Aveline reached out and gripped Morgana's hand. "You should believe him because he saved both of our lives two weeks ago."

"I -" The words died in Morgana's throat. "Two weeks ago?"

To her surprise, Aveline's eyes welled up. "That's how long you've been unconscious," she said, voice cracking. Morgana noted the bags under her eyes and wondered how much sleep she'd gotten during those two weeks. "I think it had more to do with the magic you used than your wound, but I … we couldn't do anything to wake you up."

Morgana's throat tightened, thinking of the power that had charred her insides. Aveline ducked her head as she looked away.

King Wendell spoke up, his composure once again locked down tight. "My contacts in Nysus wanted to get you out that very first night, but we knew you'd never come willingly, not until you found out the truth about King Daegil. The last thing we wanted was to try to bring you here against your will. We didn't realize quite how badly you would react to being lied to." He actually smiled at that. "An admirable trait, I assure you, even if it did annihilate our plans."

"And what exactly were they?" Morgana asked. "Your plans. They must have involved this other woman, rescuing her?"

"Thyra," Wendell said softly. "That's her name. And truthfully, we thought you might be our best chance of getting her back."

Morgana couldn't even hold that against him. He was probably right.

"One of your maids was going to linger in your room after helping you get undressed. You were placed in a room with a secret passage behind the wardrobe, and she would have led you out of the palace."

"My maids -" Morgana faltered, and a memory flitted back. "Wait … Joasia?"

The king nodded. "It was her that found you and helped Aveline carry you out through the servant's passages"

Morgana craned her neck, trying to look through the door. "Is she here, is she safe?"

Aveline's face fell and tapped the hollow of her throat. "She couldn't come through without a shell. And to be honest, I didn't trust her enough at the time to take her with us anyway."

"I'd been waiting by the portal when Aveline came through," Wendell said. "Hoping to discuss going back for Thyra. But you were unconscious, and Aveline promptly tried to kill me."

"You understand," Aveline said apologetically. "I tried to kill a lot of people that day."

Morgana wanted to go home. She wanted to go and scoop Coby up, to bring him with her as far away from kingdoms and kings as they could get. Morgana's voice was embarrassingly small as she shook her head, and asked again, "What do you want from me?" Because everyone wanted something. And she had a lot to give, a lot to be taken. "You want me to get Thyra for you?"

"Yes. But more than that, I want what King Daegil told you he wanted," he said simply, leaning forward. Morgana scrutinized his eyes and found nothing but honesty there. "I want peace, and he needs to be dethroned in order to do it."

"That's the same exact story the other one told me. This feels a little too convenient."

King Wendell held up his hands. "Test me."

Morgana stared. "You *want* me to use my powers on you?"

"Well, you can leave my soul in one piece," the king laughed, and she was shocked to find not a hint of discomfort there. "But yes. Aveline told me what you can do, how you could read both King Daegil and her. I'm assuming it all went sideways when you actually met him?"

Morgana nodded, and realized King Daegil's late arrival had surely been by design, to give her a false sense of comfort and security within Nysus.

King Wendell spread his hands. "Excellent. Then read me."

Morgana glanced at Aveline, who nodded in encouragement.

"Do you think it'll knock me unconscious again?" Morgana asked, nausea rising in her throat as she remembered what had happened in Thalassa, at the debilitating weakness that had locked her in sleep for two whole weeks.

"I don't know," Aveline said in wonder. "You were hurt, and overwhelmed, and it all sort of … rushed out. Maybe you used too much, too fast, and you didn't have full control."

"And you're healing," the king said. "Your side, I mean. We should be able to take the stitches out any day now."

Swallowing, Morgana leaned forward, pushing away the agony in her ribs, extending a shaking hand. She didn't need to, she knew that, but it made her feel better in the moment, helped her focus her power on the king. Tendrils of magic that only Morgana could see reached out, entwined around the king's neck and sank into his blood as she braced herself, ready for the shock she'd felt in the ballroom, for her magic to draw back in fear.

But nothing happened. Her magic sank into his soul, sighing contentedly at his spirit. It felt exactly as Aveline's had, if a little more authoritative, a little less whimsical.

Morgana drew back, let her body drop back against the pillows. "Thank you."

King Wendell seemed surprised. "For rescuing you?"

"For being a decent man," Morgana corrected him tiredly. "The first one I've met, actually. The world is clearly lacking in them."

The king chuckled, and he clapped his hands together. "If only you'd been awake when I first met Aveline. That conversation would have gone a lot faster."

"Kings have to be eloquent," Aveline said dryly, crossing her arms. "Consider it a test."

The king smiled wider and extended his hand to Morgana, who didn't hesitate to take it. "My name is Wendell. Welcome back to Calypdon." He glanced at Aveline, who still sat curled into her chair. "I'll leave you two alone. Aveline, I trust you'll fill her in?"

Aveline nodded at the same time Morgana exclaimed, "There's *more*?"

Aveline's jaw set as the king swept from the room, shutting the door behind him. Morgana made a mental note to check for guards later.

She closed her eyes at the silence that surrounded them, and decided she needed to say this now or she'd never say it. "I need to go."

Aveline's mouth snapped shut, cutting off whatever she'd been about to say. "Go?"

"Go home, go back into hiding..." Morgana buried her face into her hands. "That skirmish back in the sea could have ended ... far worse than you realize."

The intoxicating song of her magic had come back to her in her dreams, the way her own soul had swelled as she'd crushed Joao's, absorbing bits of him as she had almost bled him dry. She hadn't been able to see through the light, the fractured elements of her mind and soul, blinded by her magic, and she knew in that moment, with the lines of souls getting jumbled in her mind, that she could have killed every one of them.

Aveline leaned forward. "But it didn't. Everyone's okay, you're okay. *I'm* okay."

"It will happen again," Morgana said gravely, shaking her head. "When I used my magic like that, it was this ... tug inside me, impossible to ignore." She raised her gaze. "I stopped myself that time. I cut it off, but even though I can't die, it felt like it would kill me. My magic isn't supposed to be used like that, but it was as if when I gave it the option, it became its own beast."

"But you're stronger," Aveline whispered, and Morgana wished she shared her friend's confidence. "There were half a dozen men that night trying to take you, and you wounded *two*. You could have done far worse."

It still made her sick, how she'd nearly destroyed everyone in that hall, that palace, that kingdom, how she could have lost control so easily. Worse, she could have just *done it*, and her magic-addled brain wouldn't have had the presence of mind to remember that she didn't want to.

Shaking her head, weary and filled with sorrow, Morgana repeated, "This will happen again. And again, and again, until someone succeeds."

"How would they -"

Morgana cut her off. "I need to go home."

Aveline wasn't having it. "You can't. King Daegil knows where you live."

"Then I'll go somewhere else—"

"He'll find you," Aveline said harshly. "You said it yourself, it will happen again and again, and I promise you that he has his ways. We need to do *something*."

Morgana lifted her head, squeezing her eyes shut, battling within herself, even as she realized Aveline was right. If Morgana ever wanted to see the day where she could live out the rest of her life only using her powers to calm down an animal or two, to help instead of hurt, she had to stay.

Aveline drew herself up, sitting straighter in her chair. "I did invite you on a mission to unseat a corrupt king. I'm still game if you are."

Morgana exhaled, gazing up at the dome in the ceiling, as if the sun itself might rescue her. When no help came, she looked back at Aveline. "No surprises this time."

"If it helps, I was as surprised as you were."

"And," Morgana said loudly, "if it ever happens, and I lose control in any way like I almost did last time -"

"You didn't."

"You said it yourself, it all just came out of me. Maybe it was the physical injury, maybe it was just me, but we can't be sure. I had *no* control."

"You had enough," Aveline said, a little desperately.

"And if I don't next time," Morgana said, voice thick and determined, "I need you to stop me."

Aveline didn't hesitate. "No."

"Fine," Morgana said. "Not you, then. King Wendell, *someone*. Just don't let me hurt someone who doesn't deserve it."

Because that second man, who'd only moved to help a fallen comrade, certainly didn't deserve what Morgana had done to him.

Aveline swallowed, eyes glazed over. "I'll think of something, but I won't hurt you."

Satisfied, Morgana scooted toward Aveline, wanting to reach for her hand as she had at the dance, but not knowing whether that was appropriate now that they were back in ordinary clothes, in an ordinary room. She returned the conversation to what King Wendell had mentioned. "Okay, then what? What is it?"

"We have to act quickly," Aveline said, back to business, throat bobbing. "We had to leave rather abruptly, but we left a lot behind. I'm going to get them out."

Morgana shot up. "Good. For Thyra and Joasia?"

"Yes. The other agents Wendell's developed since Thyra's capture, as well." Aveline swallowed, and when she spoke again, it was at a near whisper. "And my sister."

Guilt dripped down Morgana's spine at Aveline's anguished features. She gazed at the shell nestled at Aveline's throat, a symbol of her home that would never truly leave. Would Aveline have made the decision to escape if Morgana hadn't been so gravely injured? She didn't think she wanted to know the answer, but the facts still echoed around in her skull. Aveline had left her home, everyone she knew and loved, to save *her*.

Morgana had taken Aveline away from Helah, her sister, her only *family*. Morgana hadn't had a family in many years, but she still knew what that meant.

"I will do whatever I can to help you get her back," Morgana promised, voice thick. "I won't sacrifice others for myself."

Aveline's eyes hardened. "*You* won't be doing anything for several more weeks. You're lucky Joao missed anything important."

"It wouldn't have mattered," Morgana said flatly. He had come at her with the wrong weapon.

Wait.

Her sword.

Morgana jerked up, scrambling beneath her covers despite the pain flaring in her side, but there were too many layers weighing her down. She couldn't tumble from the bed no matter how much she flailed.

"What?" Aveline asked, alarmed, reaching out. "What?"

"My sword," Morgana said, breath coming quicker now, her throat closing up. How could she have forgotten? "I need my -"

"It's here," Aveline said cautiously, lifting the Serpent Sword from where it had been placed on a nearby side table. She held it out to Morgana. "Although you did a stupid thing, diving after it like that. No relic is worth your life."

Morgana couldn't take her eyes off the sword as she relaxed into her pillows. The serpent on the hilt stared right back. "You have no idea."

Chapter Eight

It turned out Morgana's wounds healed much like those of an ordinary human. Just as painfully, and just as slowly.

Aveline came to see her every day, insisting on bringing her food and fussing over Morgana's skin temperature, giving her updates on the councils she couldn't yet attend due to her injuries.

The king stopped by, too, every now and then, but he was a busy man. He mostly came to check on her progress and to pester her for more details about her time with King Daegil at the ball. Morgana told him everything she could remember, and he caught her up on the recent history of Calypdon.

"I was crowned several years ago," he informed her, "and inherited a mess. It's why King Daegil set his plans into motion when he did. We've been vulnerable since my father died. Ties between Calypdon and Nysus have always been shaky, considering how Nysus was first created. But when I came to power, King Daegil clearly saw an opening."

"It came as a total shock to me, when Aveline said war was brewing," Morgana said. "Things were stable before my mother took us into hiding. Of course, I was young, so maybe I just didn't know better…"

"They were," Wendell said, running his hands through his sandy hair. "King Daegil is … an incredibly patient man. He knows when to bide his time, and when to strike."

"I hope the same can be said about you."

He grinned. "I'm fully trained in battle strategy, if that's what you're asking. Although my patience could use some strengthening."

"You and me both."

He was easy to talk to, probably because he always said whatever was on his mind.

"I started to believe you were a myth," he said with an airy laugh. "My mother told me stories when I was a child, but it had been so long since anyone had seen or heard anything of you. The last people to see your mother's powers were the inhabitants of one small, isolated village. We thought perhaps they had fabricated it, to … I don't know, perhaps to get in my father's good graces."

"What an honor," Morgana replied with a smile and a roll of her eyes. "To be so legendary that people doubt my existence."

"I think you just hid yourself well." He furrowed his brow. "I wish you hadn't had to do that, that you'd been able to be a part of our kingdom."

Morgana pressed her lips together. "If these past weeks have taught me anything, it's that I made the right choice. I will stay here to remedy the mess I made by leaving my cottage in the first place, but after, I must go again. I won't be responsible for another war."

He leaned forward in his chair. "What if there was a way to hide you in plain sight? To, I don't know, pass you off as someone else, someone ordinary?"

"Maybe," Morgana said softly. "But what would I do when you all aged around me, and I remained the same?"

He didn't have an answer for that.

***

Morgana couldn't escape the guilt she felt every time Aveline walked into the room. She was the reason the sea woman had left behind everything she thought was good. While the council planned for Aveline's return to Nysus, Morgana wished to go in her place. She wanted to keep Aveline here, where they at least thought it was safe. But Morgana wanted Aveline to have her sister back more.

Aveline came into Morgana's room dressed in full gear, borrowed from the Calypdon armory, early in the morning. Morgana was instantly filled with a convoluted mixture of relief and dread.

She sat up, taking in the vision of the powerful sea soldier Aveline had once been. Her appearance made Morgana's heart hammer. "Today's the day?"

"You know it is," Aveline murmured, leaning against the bedpost.

Morgana had known. She'd asked relentless questions about the plan, needing to know every detail so she could play it out in her head. She wanted to know the timing of every aspect of the plan, to know how long each element should take. If they didn't come back when they were supposed to, she'd know things went wrong.

"It won't go wrong," Aveline said, for what must have been the dozenth time. Her hand drifted up to her neck, to the rosy seashell embedded there. She did that a lot. "Helah received my message. They know where Thyra is kept. She'll be waiting for us at the portal with Joasia and the others."

Helah needed help because her shell had not yet been fully activated. To gain the power to open passages, the bearer of a shell had to become a soul of both kingdoms. They needed to breathe both air and water before an artifact could reach full power.

"How did you open the portal the first time?" Morgana asked curiously.

"The king himself," Aveline said bitterly. "The ritual is meant to be an exercise in trust; you cannot gain access to a kingdom that doesn't belong to you without someone first letting you in.

"It won't even be a fight," Aveline went on, reading the worry on Morgana's face. "We'll be in and out. I promise."

Morgana shook her head, her throat surprisingly tight. "Stop making me promises you don't know you can keep."

Aveline sank into the chair she'd been using for weeks. Though Morgana could move a bit on her own now, Aveline still insisted on coming to her, to give Morgana as much rest as possible. "I'll keep on making promises and do my best to keep them. That's all I can do."

Aveline's hands rested on the edge of her bed, inches away from Morgana's. It would be so simple, for Morgana to reach out and brush their knuckles together, to intertwine their fingers. But Aveline had to leave, and Morgana thought if she took hold now, she wouldn't have the strength to let go.

So Morgana settled for a tearful smile and a nod. "Then I'll promise to be there for the next fight."

Footsteps sounded in the hallway, and Wendell poked his head in. For a king, he was awfully casual. "We're leaving, Aveline. Now or never." He shot Morgana a meaningful glance before ducking out again.

"Now, then," Aveline breathed, standing. She gazed down at Morgana, opened her mouth as if she might say something more, then nodded. "One hour. We'll be back in one hour. You'd better be here waiting."

Morgana swallowed. "One hour."

And then Aveline was gone.

Morgana stared at the grandfather clock towering in the far corner, slicing away each second. Accounting for traveling to the portal, and getting each of Wendell's people up through the gate, they had decided that the rescue couldn't possibly take more than an hour if all went smoothly. Most of the work - freeing Thyra, getting out of the palace unnoticed, sneaking through the gates, finding the portal - would fall on Helah, Joasia, and the others.

Morgana sat up as soon as a full hour had passed. She'd spent the time fiddling in her bed, constantly glancing at the door, waiting for the sound of footsteps in the hall, longing for the door to open. The clock had ticked the seconds away, and it had taken every bit of self-control not to spend the hour staring at it.

She rubbed gingerly at her side. The wound had healed nicely, the skin stitching together over the last few weeks. A thick scab still remained, a bloody mass that would soon form into a jagged scar, but she could move around now with only a slight twinge of pain.

Another minute passed. Then two. When five more minutes had gone, she hopped out of bed, already dressed. She strapped her sword to her side and laced her boots up her calves. She took a ribbon from the desk, one that Aveline had left behind after a day of training and tied up her hair at the nape of her neck. Morgana had promised King Wendell she wouldn't follow until she was certain they were overdue. But she hadn't told the king she couldn't say much for her patience.

Morgana followed the thread of Aveline's soul through the halls and out to the palace gate.

Morgana would find her.

***

Portals into Nysus were scattered across Calypdon, and Aveline had clearly led her party to the nearest one. Morgana paused to breathe just outside the palace gates, at the edge of a winding path, marveling at her surroundings.

She had known, on some level, that she was in Briarwood. But that realization hadn't quite hit her, confined to her room as she was. Not until she stepped byong the palace walls and into the city streets. She stared at the wooden buildings from her position at the top of the hill, and the city layout was very similar to Thalassa. It was constructed with different materials, of course, and hundred-year-old trees sprouting up in every spare nook and cranny, but otherwise, the similarity was uncanny. She recognized twists and turns in the streets, the path leading down the hill from the palace. It was almost an exact replica to Nysus's capital city. Morgana wondered if this had been intentional during Nysus's creation; when the gods divided the kingdom, did Thalassa rise from the ocean flood, a mirror image of the city above? She took the time to pause at the end of the path, gazing even further out at the people below. They were so small from here, so far, but they seemed happy.

Although, the sea people seemed happy, too.

She melted into the forest, weaving through the trees as she followed the trail of her magic. She conjured up the tether between her and Aveline, made of it a tangible thing, and followed it. Sun pierced the canopy of leaves, but the cover above loomed thick. Morgana pushed into the deepening shadows of the forest, the tug in her gut leading the way.

Morgana stopped at a winding river; a shifting, blue-tinged light shone through the trees. The glow of the still-open passage illuminated the greenery, and the portal carved through a riverbed. It drank down the water, the flow of the river pouring through the rift. It roared like a waterfall, as if the fresh water was protesting its collision with the sea. Morgana wished she had time to create a dam; to reroute the water around the crevice so it could continue on its journey.

Morgana looked around at the deserted landscape. Why hadn't they left anyone to guard this side of the portal? Someone to call for help if they didn't come back? Morgana knew why, of course. Only the king, Aveline, and two guards had gone. They wanted to keep their numbers as small as possible, to keep the circle of knowledge to only those necessary. Daegil had spies everywhere.

Nerves seized her as she stared at the flashing portal, river water still roaring through the rift as if it couldn't get enough. The idea of returning to the kingdom that had caused her so much pain nearly paralyzed her with fear, but she gripped her sword tighter and took a steadying breath. She remembered what she had said to Aveline, weeks ago when she first woke up.

I won't sacrifice the lives of others for my own.

Taking a deep breath, she stepped through. She slid gracefully into the sea, this time keeping her eyes open as she drifted down to the ocean floor. Nausea roiled in her stomach as shades of blues and green and purples swirled around her, growing darker the deeper she fell, fragmenting with the speed of her movement. The water burned her eyes in this in-between place, and as she tried to blink away the blur, she struck the sand and collapsed in a bed of seaweed.

Aveline, Wendell, and Helah were nowhere to be found.

Adjusting her movements to the ocean currents around her was just as troubling as it had been the first time, and she strained to keep her body grounded despite her buoyancy. Her head pivoted furiously, searching for a hint that Aveline had been here, but only succeeded in fracturing her vision further.

"Your friends were foolish to come to Nysus."

She whirled, homing in on that familiar soul and squeezed it tight. Joao snapped into an eerily still stance, with only the ocean's currents providing any movement to his hair and uniform. He snarled from where she'd caged him a few feet away, although a hint of fear flickered in his eyes.

"Where are they?" Morgana growled, drawing her sword.

"Not here," he said, that superiority coming back. "We have spies, too."

Ice trickled down Morgana's spine, and she stalked toward him, though her movements were hesitant as she struggled to accustom herself to the depths again. She watched his fragmented image as he struggled against her invisible bindings; to find the movement she'd taken from him. Morgana reveled in the sight and wondered what else she could do with her powers, how she might play with her enemies.

Shocked, she reared back, drawing in her power to only that necessary to hold Joao in place. *You won't do anything to them*, she said to herself. She repeated it in her mind like a mantra, even as she threatened aloud, "Tell me where they are, right now, or I swear I'll kill you. And you have no idea what a witch can do. I will tear your soul into tattered shreds. I will leave you nothing but a howling echo, fading into the darkness. I'll make sure you feel every bit of your soul being torn away, until there is nothing left but the fading memory of anguish. Our last encounter will be *nothing* compared to what I will do to you today."

"You don't have it in you," he spat.

"Careful," Morgana drawled, trying to maintain her calm as she twirled her sword, even as dread pooled in her stomach. "We wouldn't want a repeat of last time, would we? I'm sure neither of us want to find out what I can do to you without a stab wound hindering my powers." She kept her voice steady, masking just how much she didn't want to make good on the threat.

"What's so important about that sword, hmm?" Joao asked, staring at it, and the question surprised Morgana enough that she almost released her hold on him. She resecured the bindings. Joao went on, "You nearly got yourself killed going after it last time. You wouldn't do that for any old weapon."

Heart pounding, Morgana said as casually as possible, "It was my mother's. What can I say? I'm sentimental."

His eyes flashed. "I don't think so. The king has mentioned it, too. I think he might want it at least as much as he wants you."

Morgana's heart stuttered, because now there could be no doubt. Daegil knew the secrets of the sword. But *how*? It had always been the most closely guarded secret of the Serpent Witch line, knowledge for only the witches who possessed the sword. She cleared her throat. "If I needed any more indication that Daegil is insane, you've just given it to me."

Somehow, he smiled, despite her hold on him. "I'll figure out what it is. "

"You're acting mighty confident for a man who can't move," Morgana hissed, raising her blade.

He smiled wider. "I can move my mouth." And then he whistled.

The water rippled behind him, currents flowing over each other and bubbles lifting toward Calypdon, lost in the darkness overhead. The mirage was swept away. Aveline, Wendell, and their two guards were revealed, held by two soldiers of Nysus, each at knifepoint. Aveline was staring at Morgana in horror, mouth slack as she stood completely still, her chin tilted back with a blade pressed into the skin above her shell. Helah, Joasia, and three others were there, too, held a few feet away by half a dozen guards. An unconscious woman lay on the ground, her blonde hair fanned over the sand, her wrists bound by rope.

Wendell smiled tightly, his gaze flickering frantically between Morgana and the woman on the ground. "Quite an effort, Morgana. You couldn't have known we were here. I won't hold it against you."

His two guards stared at her warily, and Morgana thought about the things she'd said, the threats she'd made, but she was too afraid to feel any shame. "How…"

Morgana's eyes fell on a woman behind Aveline, who raised her hand in a wave, sneering.

The siren.

Aveline squeezed her eyes closed. The knife dug further in at the movement, and her eyes flew open again.

"They intercepted your message, they were watching me, I'm sorry," Helah burst out, all in one breath, before one of the guards behind her twisted her arm until she cried out in pain.

"I will consider this an official act of war," Wendell was saying, eyes dark. "I will not hold back any longer."

Joao scoffed. "King Daegil isn't afraid of you."

Wendell snarled. "Take Morgana, and he will be."

Joao's smile widened, walking over to kneel next to the unconscious woman. "Maybe I'll just take Thyra back. I've *so* been enjoying the pleasure of her company."

Wendell lashed out, tearing desperately at the guards holding him.

"Let them go," Morgana croaked out, lifting her hands toward the guard holding Aveline, and Wendell fell still.

"You try to control him, that knife will go right into your lover's neck," Joao snarled.

Morgana didn't have the presence of mind to correct him, but she dropped her hands. Her panic lasted only a moment before an idea sparked. "Let them go and take me instead."

Wendell's eyes flew open at the same time Aveline shouted, "*NO!*" The guard holding her pressed his knife hard enough to shed blood.

Morgana didn't look away from Joao. "That's what you want, isn't it? Why you kept them here instead of bringing them to the palace? You were waiting for me, and you knew I'd demand to see them alive or I wouldn't agree to go with you. Well, it worked. Set them free. Let me watch them pass safely back to Calypdon with those they came to retrieve, and I'll go with you freely. Close the portal behind them, and I won't have a way out."

Something flickered in King Wendell's eyes, and his mouth opened slightly. Morgana silenced him with a glare.

Joao's eyes glinted gleefully, and Morgana could tell she had calculated correctly. They'd fallen perfectly into his trap. "Oh, I don't know. To give up the king of Calypdon? The soldier who betrayed her own kingdom?" He gave Aveline a dirty look. "Are you really worth that?"

"Spare me," Morgana snapped, clenching her fists. Seeing Aveline so close to death was enough for Morgana to give up everything without a second thought. "I know my value, and so do you. That is my offer. Take it or leave it."

Tears streamed from Aveline's eyes, pooling in glowing silver. And though she couldn't move under the guard's hold, Morgana could have sworn she was shaking her head. Morgana averted her gaze, unable to stomach watching any longer, and when she saw the triumphant look in Joao's eyes, she knew she'd won.

Joao lifted his chin. "Take her."

Two of the guards by Helah rushed forward, snatching up Morgana's arms and pinning them behind her. They wrenched her shoulders back, and she gritted her teeth as their swords poked at her, ready to run her through if she gave them an excuse. Someone clasped iron chains around her wrists, and she almost laughed. She remembered stories she heard as a child, something about iron having a dampening effect on magic.

Not just stories, actually. Not entirely.

"Don't do this," Aveline whispered as Wendell looked up at Calypdon, as if he was praying. "Please, don't do this."

Morgana refused to look at her, wishing she'd taken her hand that morning. Maybe if she had, she wouldn't have let her go on this insane mission.

"Now let them go," Morgana said stiffly. "Open the passage, allow me to watch them go through, and then I'm all yours."

"And if I don't?" Joao grinned.

"Then you'll never be able to use my power," Morgana said. "You need me to cooperate; you need me to be compliant. Let them go and I'll do what you ask."

Wendell looked sick, and Aveline was angry enough to burst. "No. Morgana, *no*, you *can't*."

Morgana's lip wobbled, but she swallowed hard. "Let them go."

Satisfied, Joao jutted his chin out toward one of the sea guards. "Take them through the portal, but don't remove their chains until you're on the other side. I don't want any surprises."

"*Morgana*," Aveline shrieked as the guard shoved her toward the portal, fighting against her bonds now that there wasn't a knife pressed to her throat. "*Morgana, please don't, please—*"

Morgana forced herself to look at her. "It's okay."

Because it would be.

The sea guards swam up toward the portal above, pulling Aveline with them before pushing her through. Helah followed, with a nod to Morgana that she knew meant *thank you*, and slowly, they each disappeared through the portal.

The tension in Wendell's shoulders released as soon as Thyra passed out of sight, and he turned to face Joao, treading water before the passage. "We will return." The light of the portal illuminated his hair, and Morgana understood why he hadn't bothered to fight for her. One life was nothing compared to the ten lives he would save by agreeing. And when she met his eyes, he nodded gravely. "For her, and for you."

And then he, too, disappeared, leaving Morgana alone with her enemies.

Perfect.

Joao returned his gaze to her as the portal closed with one last flash of brilliant blue. He stalked toward her, reaching out and drawing a finger up Morgana's sword. "Your humanity will be the death of you," he murmured.

"It might be," Morgana agreed. "It's a good thing there is so little of it inside me. Less than you know."

Joao rolled his eyes, stroking the hilt now, swiping the pad of his thumb over one of the snake's ruby eyes. "I have a feeling I just won myself two prizes."

Morgana tilted her head. "No."

Joao scoffed. "Enough of the act. I know this sword has some sort of power. Perhaps it was made by the same god who made *you*."

"I'm not denying that," Morgana said sweetly, eyes darting toward where the portal had been. "I'm denying that you won any prizes at all."

One of the guards squeezed her arm, so tight she began to lose feeling in her hand as Joao straightened. "You're stuck here. You either help us or live your days out here as a tortured woman, and I promise, we have methods that would make you cave eventually. You don't believe you're the biggest prize all over the two kingdoms?"

"No, I am." Morgana narrowed her eyes at Joao, and smiled. "You just didn't win me."

"You - "

Morgana clenched her fists, gathering her magic, pushing away any hesitation. "Contrary to how other magic works, how iron might smother the power of an ordinary Hallowed, I don't need my arms to be more powerful than you. I don't need a body at all. And I certainly don't need anyone else to open that passage for me. I'm a woman of all worlds, including yours."

A guess. A guess that she was not entirely certain would work.

She lashed out and took hold of the threads binding her to all those around her, striking first at the guards behind her, squeezing her magic around their lives until they gasped and sputtered, drifting down to the ocean floor. She froze their souls, sinking them into the sand, but made sure they stayed breathing. Her mind clouded as it had last time, as the haze of magic rose up between her and the surrounding world, but she kept herself grounded in the moment by focusing on each of the heartbeats around her. She counted them one by one as she floated off the ocean floor, staring down at Joao, who stood dumbly in front of her.

"The … the iron," he sputtered, stumbling back and falling into the seaweed. "It should cut off your powers, it's the weakness of witches…"

Morgana smiled wickedly, even as her hands remained chained behind her. "I have no weaknesses."

She slashed him down, sending him tumbling into the pile of soldiers. They would wake up, eventually. They would be found. But they would remember what she could do. Joao cried out, and she relished it, too angry to think about how hurting him should disgust her, too overwhelmed by the magic.

She kicked him away from her, sending him sprawling down the hill, and she looked after him, furious. "I'm tired of being hunted," she murmured to herself, and turned toward her new life. Toward the place where the portal had disappeared.

She'd been able to breathe just fine in the sea, drawing from all the souls of the sea people that were contained within her, Aveline included. She drew from them now, and they sank deeper into her bones. Her body vibrated with the power of them, and she tried to imitate what she had once seen Aveline do, drawing herself up and closing her eyes.

The ground shook, and when she opened her eyes again, the lightning-wreathed whirlpool had reappeared, the glowing hint of what waited above.

She stumbled out of the passage several moments later, splashing into the freezing river. Her arms were still chained behind her back, so she couldn't catch herself when she stumbled to her knees. Aveline looked up from where she'd been sobbing on the ground in a puddle of water, Helah trying desperately to get her to stand. Wendell, Thyra, and one of the guards were gone, probably already returned to the palace. Those remaining jumped at the sudden noise, the guards drawing their swords, but Morgana didn't have the energy to raise her defenses.

"Hey," she said instead, brushing herself off, shaking her hair out. "What did I miss?"

Aveline stood in wonder, shaking off her sister's grip.

Helah's face split into a wide grin, slapping Morgana on the back. "I should have known. You gave in way too easily."

Morgana met Aveline's eyes, and the message was clear enough. Morgana would have given up that easily, even if she hadn't had a plan, if it meant their safety. Her safety.

Aveline didn't say a word for several long moments. "You … you got away?"

Morgana shrugged sheepishly, but her shoulders felt heavy now, still weighed down by the chains. "Witches always have a trick up their sleeve."

Aveline staggered. a few steps forward, one at a time, and then launched herself into Morgana's chest. Aveline clung to Morgana like a lifeline, and since she couldn't hug Aveline back, she settled for burying her face in the crook of Aveline's neck.

"That was stupid," Aveline croaked out, her fingers digging into Morgana's shoulder blades, and Morgana relaxed into the pressure. Her magic still thrummed inside her, but at Aveline's touch, it faded away. "Really, really stupid."

"It's not stupid if it works," Morgana said, unable to hide the quaver in her voice.

Because she really could have gotten stuck there. And she would have, willingly, as long as Aveline got out.

"Are they dead?" Aveline murmured against her shoulder, in a way that suggested she didn't much care what the answer was.

But Morgana could tell the truth, and breathed back, "No."

Aveline didn't let go for several long minutes.

Chapter Nine

Aveline was the only one Morgana trusted enough to smash the iron manacles, taking a large rock from the river. It took several swings, the iron rattling against her bones with each impact, but on the last attempt the cuffs burst into fragments.

To Morgana's surprise, Helah launched herself into Morgana's arms the moment she was freed.

"Thank you," Helah whispered into her neck. "For keeping my sister safe when I was a kingdom away, and for bringing us back together."

Morgana pulled away, hands on Helah's shoulders. "Don't thank me. I'm the one who put her in danger in the first place."

Aveline slid her sword back into its sheath, throwing an arm around her sister. "I take full responsibility for all the danger I've been in, thank you very much. And I'd say it was worth it."

Helah picked up a piece of the chain from where it had fallen at the base of the tree. She rolled it between her thumb and forefinger. "I have just one question, though. Why doesn't iron impact you like it does the rest of the Hallowed? *Are* you one of the Hallowed?"

Morgana sighed, rubbing her wrists. Blood had started to ooze from where the cuffs had rubbed her flesh raw. "That's a point of contention, and I'd say it depends on your definition of the Hallowed."

Aveline stilled Morgana's hands, wrapping the wounds with a piece of cloth torn from her own jacket. "I'd define the Hallowed as anyone touched by a god or goddess. You certainly qualify."

"True, but no other Hallowed passes their magic down through blood. They are fully immortal, and if they are eventually killed, the magic becomes diluted. The blessing lingers, but any heir they bear is mortal."

"But you inherited every bit of your mother's magic," Helah said. "You're different."

Morgana nodded. "In more ways than one."

Every immortal being other than the gods had to have some sort of weakness, the gods would have it no other way. For most of the Hallowed, it was iron. The Serpent Witches, of course, had an entirely different weakness.

She didn't say any of that out loud, though.

Aveline just shook her head. "I don't think I'll ever fully understand how your power works."

"If it helps," Morgana said as they began the trek back to the palace, "I don't think I will, either."

Hours later, Morgana lay on her bed, thinking of all the ways everything could have gone wrong. What if Joao had just decided to stab Wendell, or Aveline, or Helah? What if iron actually *could* hurt her, as it could the other Hallowed? Her mother had always said it didn't, since there was only one thing that could hurt them, but she hadn't known for certain.

She wanted to see Aveline again; sitting alone in her room was becoming unbearable, but the two sisters were huddled in Aveline's room, crying tears of relief, and Morgana figured they could use the space.

A knock sounded at the door. She sat up, her lead filled feet dragging over the wooden floorboards until she wrenched open the door, revealing Wendell leaning against the frame. He wore a loose white shirt and slacks, his crown slightly crooked on his head.

"I knew it," he said by way of greeting. "As soon as you said you didn't have the power to open portals, I knew what you planned. I kept trying to tell Aveline, but she wouldn't listen." He took in Morgana's plain clothes with a frown. "Shouldn't you be celebrating?"

She stepped back, and Wendell swept in, lowering himself into Aveline's usual chair at her bedside. Morgana shook her head as she closed the door. "It's hard to celebrate when it could have ended so horribly."

"But it didn't," Wendell said, and his face lit up with a triumphant grin. "Today was a resounding success, as far as I'm concerned."

Morgana managed a tired smile. "How is Thyra, then? Shouldn't you be with her?"

"She's resting," Wendell said. "They were keeping her unconscious, and it will take some time for the potion to wear off. The physician sent me away. 'King's aren't supposed to hover,' were his exact words."

"You're not great at taking instructions."

"No," Wendell agreed. "But I also know that today would have ended *far* differently if not for you. Thank you."

Morgana didn't deserve his thanks. "You're lucky you're even alive."

He tilted his head. "I'd say the same for you, but you don't need luck to stay alive."

Morgana huffed. "I'd need luck to die, I think. If it ever happens."

Wendell sat back in the chair, considering her. "The more I speak to you, the more I realize that you don't seem to give a damn about your own life at all."

Morgana collapsed on the foot of her bed, tucking her feet beneath her. She wished she could fall asleep, if just to get a damn break. "Of course, I do. I have to. My life is everyone else's life."

It was true. In the same way she received her power from other's life forces, the world sustained their life from her magic. Wendell seemed to put this together and furrowed his brow. "And is that the only reason?" he asked.

"Beyond that, there's never been a life to value," Morgana said honestly, surprising even herself with her honesty. She'd normally never say it out loud, but Wendell was so painfully genuine that he wrenched the words from her. "That's the bargain, right? The curse? I sacrifice my life so everyone else can have one."

Wendell shook his head, looking down. "No. No, you're worth more than the life you give to others."

"I don't *give* life to others," she said flatly. "They take it from me. You're doing it right now, whether you want to acknowledge it or not."

The king stared at her, solemn, and he flexed his fingers as if he could somehow feel it, that piece of her.

Morgana shook her head, looking down. "I'm used to it now, but there's this … relentless pull on my chest. A weight, the weight of tens of thousands of souls, the weight of all this ... *control*, that I never wanted. Do you know what that feels like, Your Majesty? To have the lives of everyone alive at your fingertips, every life but your own?"

"A bit," he said softly. "It sounds kind of like being a king, but with none of the rewards."

Morgana cracked her knuckles, adjusted her weight. Her body had always felt wrong, too confined for what she was. "I suppose you never signed up for what you are, either. But at least people admire you for it. They praise you, instead of fearing you."

"For what it's worth," the king said, leaning forward, resting his elbows on his knees. "I admire you a great deal. Both for your power, and for your willingness to give up endless pieces of yourself so we can have a sliver of life."

Morgana leaned back against the bedpost, and it dug into her spine. There would always be reminders of her human body, an ill-fit for her immortal soul. Immortal, until she had an heir.

"I'm not celebrating," Morgana said after a few moments of silence, going back to his initial question, "because we may have won, but I think we lost a great deal."

"How?" Wendell asked curiously. "No lives lost, not even the lives of our enemies. How is that not a win?"

"They didn't know that iron doesn't hurt me," Morgana mourned, rubbing at the marks left by the manacles, red and raw. "That advantage is gone. They learn more about me every time I have to use my powers in front of them, and that's not safe for anyone."

And Morgana feared herself more every time, too, and that wasn't safe for *her*.

"I don't suppose it really matters," Wendell said, rubbing his jaw. Stubble had spread over his skin, grown darker than usual. "Because there's nothing that can take your powers, anyway. That's the whole point."

Morgana swallowed down her retort, pushed down the truth. As much as she'd come to trust him, as much as she liked him, that was a secret she would never divulge. She'd carry it to her death bed.

If things went poorly, that end might come sooner than anticipated.

"Even if that is true, we've lost the leverage," Morgana said seriously. "If Ave— if any of you are captured, there won't be anything I can do. They might resort to less humane methods to get me to cooperate."

"And would they work?" Wendell asked, face blank.

Morgana refused to look him in the eye, instead casting her gaze skyward, to the lingering rays piercing the dome above as dusk approached. "Let's hope it doesn't come to that."

They both knew that was answer enough.

***

When Morgana attended her first war council a few days later, it became apparent that Wendell's assembly of trusted advisors was painfully small. It consisted of Aveline, a man named Kadri, a woman named Ida, and Thyra.

"It used to be bigger," Wendell informed her, having met her at her room to show the way, "but given how things went the other day, we decided to keep any plans locked down tight. I know it couldn't be helped, the message was intercepted in Nysus, but I'd rather play it safe. Any soldiers we need will be informed on the day of the mission. You and Aveline need to be here for obvious reasons."

They weaved through the halls of the palace. It all felt strangely familiar, and she soon realized that the layout of the palace in Briarwood was eerily similar to the palace of Thalassa. The great hall, entrance, the ballroom, the guest chambers; their locations mirrored each other. But the design couldn't have been more different. Where Thalassa had been all blues and purples and bright greens, gemstones and marble, Briarwood's palace appeared as if it had been molded directly from the earth. Brown, earthen walls rose up on either side as they walked, roots weaving in and out to hold the sconces lining the corridors. The ceilings were high and arched, with delicate engravings of gold foiled leaves. Footsteps echoed hollowly on the wooden floorboards, cut from polished oak.

"It's comforting," Morgana noted to Wendell. "If I blur my vision, it's almost like I'm back in the forest."

"Do you wish you were?" he asked.

"Sometimes," Morgana admitted. "We'd all probably be better off if I was."

Wendell snorted and opened the door to the council chamber. He nodded, not at all subtle, to Aveline. "Not everyone."

The room fell silent as Morgana crossed the threshold. The four people in the room were crowded around a rectangular table with a map unrolled across the surface. The woman with short cropped brown hair, who must have been Ida, had paused with her finger jabbed at the map, now wholly focused on the entrance of the witch.

Aveline broke the silence, pushing away from the table to pull Morgana further into the room. "Come in. We were just going over all the known portals between the kingdoms."

Thyra fell into her seat, her long blond hair braided down her back. "The answer is too many."

Wendell sat down next to her, and the woman's eyes softened when he rubbed a hand over her shoulder. "Before we get to that, how about some introductions? I don't think you ever had the chance to properly meet."

She barked out an unfriendly laugh, turning to Morgana. "I'm pretty sure we all know who she is."

Morgana reeled at the open hostility, but recovered quickly, addressing the whole room. "But I've only heard some names, and I don't know who's who."

Aveline jumped in, pointing to the woman with the short, cropped hair. "This is Ida, captain of the guard. That's Kadri, he's a cartographer charting the kingdom, finding all possible entry points between Calypdon and Nysus." Aveline nodded to the blonde woman next to Wendell. "And you know Thyra, of course." Aveline didn't specify why Thyra was here, but given how close she was sitting to Wendell, Morgana could hazard a guess.

Morgana sat down gingerly. "Thyra, I'm glad to see you up and moving. Are you feeling better?"

Thyra rolled her shoulders back. "At least I'm conscious. Although with how things are going here, I might have been better off in the dungeons."

"I get it," Morgana said, addressing the rest of the room. "I wish we were meeting under different circumstances."

"We all do," Kadri said softly. "But I think I speak for all of us when I say that we're glad you're here now. And not there."

"And while you're here," Ida said, leaning forward and locking eyes with Morgana. "I don't plan to waste time. Do you actually have the strength to kill King Daegil?"

Morgana blinked. "I - yes, my magic -"

"I'm not asking about your magic," Ida cut in. "I'm asking about your *will*. From what I've gathered, you're surprisingly tender-hearted for a witch, and a number of people have almost been killed because of your unwillingness to use your magic."

Gritting her teeth, Morgana said, "But no one did. I exhaust every other option before resorting to using my magic that way. My power is meant to give life, not take it."

"But you could, in theory, end King Daegil's life without putting a single other life, even yours, at risk, correct?"

Morgana raised her eyebrows. "No. What makes you think that?"

Kadri cleared his throat. "From what I understand about your magic, you have a deep connection with every living being in both kingdoms. And if you focus on their souls, you can affect their lives."

Warily, Morgana said, "Yes, I suppose that's a good way to sum it up."

"In that case, and forgive my candor," Thyra said, assessing Morgana from head to toe, "but can't you just … kill him from here? Right now?"

Morgana braced her palms against the round table, shaking her head. "It doesn't work like that."

"But you could kill me right now with a mere thought. If you wanted."

Morgana sighed, and decided she didn't like this woman. She respected her courage, though. "The ordinary Hallowed only use their magic by calling it into action. It is a tool, a tool that fuels their life force every time they use it. Mine is in constant use. There are no breaks; no pauses. It fires off in thousands of directions at once, all the time. It infused our kingdoms with its touch. Every corner."

Wendell leaned forward. "But you *can* feel King Daegil right now."

The magic nestled in her ribs slumbered, rolling over. "Yes. I have everyone, during every second of every day. But there is an inherent balance to my everyday life. I don't have to work to keep each of you breathing." She looked each of them in the eye, except for Aveline. She couldn't bear it. "There's a bridge between me and every living being that connection is there, whether they like it or not, and whether I think about it or not. And that's exactly the problem; there's too much to sort through. Too many barriers in the way. Like, for example, two entire kingdoms."

"But you know what his soul feels like," Aveline put in. "I saw it, that night -" She stumbled over her words, choking on them. "That night at the ball."

Solemn, Morgana said, "There are many wicked people in this world. They get muddled together."

A light went off behind Wendell's eyes. "You're saying you could accidentally kill the wrong person?"

"I'm saying I could accidentally kill *everyone*."

Everyone in the room flinched. Even Aveline.

Morgana didn't let the reaction faze her. "And that's not what we want. We want a single casualty; specific. For that, our connection has to be stronger." She swallowed roughly. "I have to be close."

The meeting disbanded quickly after that. Nobody wanted to be in the same room as Morgana after an implication like that.

A plan formed over the following weeks. They would not be invading Nysus again. If King Daegil had plans to attack, they would wait, and make the sea come to them. This battle would happen on their land, on their terms.

And for the first time, she would use her powers to kill.

Morgana spent her nights thinking about it, wrapped up in the thought of what collateral damage might occur on that day if she couldn't keep herself on a leash. If the king wounded her, and the magic rushed out of her as it had before... During the days, she did her best not to think about it at all.

She spent her time training; with Wendell, with various guards, and Aveline. Days turned to weeks as Aveline trained Morgana in everything she knew. Thalassa guards fought differently from those on land. Sea guards had to factor in the drag of the water on their sword, leading them to train in stabbing maneuvers rather than slashing. They had to prepare for how blood could cloud up and obscure the vision. The two women spent their days in the courtyard surrounded by guards, never sure if the soldiers were training as well or simply stationed to watch them.

Because there were *always* guards watching them. Well, Morgana. Morgana's words, the threats she'd made during the confrontation in Nysus, had spread through the ranks, and no one would quite look at her. Though they didn't have guards stationed outside her door, they did periodically check on her throughout the day, offering to accompany her to various points around the palace. Though it pained her to accept, she didn't particularly want to increase their suspicion, and she already feared she'd get lost in the halls on her own, even after all this time.

After a few weeks, when meetings grew sparse and all they could do was wait, Wendell accompanied her to the main courtyard. "No meeting today," he said, looping his arm through hers. He'd taken to doing that, and Morgana wasn't sure if he did it to have more control over her, or to clarify once more that he trusted her. "We've planned all we can, down to every detail. All there is to do now is wait."

Morgana sighed, following him down the now familiar halls to the training courtyard. Aveline was already there, breaking a sweat with Ida. It was too early in the morning for many people to be there, so Aveline noticed when they arrived, catching Morgana's gaze. The slight distraction was enough to cost her, and Ida knocked her flat on her back.

"That is why we'll keep you two separated on the day of the battle," Wendell called. "Too risky."

Aveline's gaze turned murderous at the reminder, fighting against Ida with a new vigor. One of the main points of contention when developing their plan was Aveline's insistence on being Morgana's second, to accompany her on her hunt for the king. Wendell denied her every time, explaining that they couldn't take the chance that Morgana might be distracted if Aveline was in danger. As he said more than once, she had already proven herself prone to 'stupid, self-sacrificing gambles.' He had a point.

"Careful," Morgana said now, drawing her sword. "She might forget you're the king and do something she regrets if you don't stop talking to her like a friend."

"She *is* my friend," King Wendell said. "And somehow, so are you."

Morgana scoffed. "You have to say that, because everyone's worried I'll switch sides and murder everyone."

"No one thinks that," he said, and when Morgana lifted her brows, he sighed. "Okay, perhaps some people, but they don't think you're a bad person."

"They don't think I'm a person at all."

"They're wary," he said, stalking over to a rack of weapons, pulling two fighting knives as he rolled his sleeves up. "You're … new."

"You can call me a witch," Morgana said, tired. "I won't be offended."

"I don't believe you." But he said it with a fond smile, and it loosened the anxiety knotting in Morgana's stomach.

Morgana held her sword up, waving it in front of his face. "Enough chatter. I came to beat you into the dust."

"I'd say that's insubordination," he sighed, "but you'd just make me fall over."

Morgana snorted. She'd taken to doing that, sapping him of the energy to stand whenever he upset her. It was exceedingly entertaining, especially when his crown fell off.

It calmed her down to use her magic in ways that caused no harm, that instead made the people around her laugh. She missed the days when all she needed her power for was to find Coby when he had slithered too far into the woods.

Morgana lifted her hands. "I won't use my powers. I promise."

She'd been training like a regular soldier, learning how to defend herself with only her sword. She knew the odds of getting through a battle without magic were slim, but she'd told Joao that she didn't have any weaknesses. She wanted to ensure that was true.

Not only that, but she'd started to prefer fighting with her body over her magic. At least she'd never lose control of her sword.

Wendell flipped his knife in his hand, catching it easily. He'd been holding weapons since he was a toddler, and Morgana had not yet defeated him without her powers. "Then let's spar."

They danced across the courtyard, running through exercises that made Morgana's thighs and biceps scream. Though she'd tried to train in her little cabin in the woods, she'd never been able to push herself nearly as hard practicing by herself. Now, with someone to push her and push back against, muscles filling out her arms and legs as she improved by the day. Slowly, she'd become better at fighting than talking, and she didn't know what that said about her.

She kept her back firmly facing Aveline, not needing the distraction. She'd been doing that a lot lately, because every time she looked at Aveline she thought of Joao's words, about how Morgana had made her a traitor.

Sensing her thoughts, Wendell puffed out, "I'm having trouble following the relationship between you two." He said it absentmindedly, but Morgana wasn't fooled. Every king she had ever met had been a calculating bastard. Both of them.

Morgana swung the sword, slashing it against the king's blade, and a loud clanging sound filled the air. "We're kidnapper and kidnappee."

"She didn't kidnap you."

"I never said she was the one who did the kidnapping."

Because that was how Morgana thought about it. She'd as good as stolen Aveline away from her life. It seemed a good life. She shook her head, hissing when Wendell's knife tapped her forearm.

Wendell's brow furrowed. "She went willingly. You were passed out when it happened, but I can attest to that. She was beside herself, thinking you wouldn't make it."

This didn't make Morgana feel any better. That sounded more like obligation than willingness, to her.

Gritting her teeth, Morgana lunged, effectively ending the discussion.

When they finally stopped, Morgana felt as if they had been sparring for hours. Morgana looked over her shoulder to where Aveline was sparring with Helah, laughing as they fought with wooden swords. Helah appeared to be winning. "I need a bath," Morgana said to no one in particular, and left before anyone could offer to escort her. She felt their eyes on her, though. Every guard stationed throughout the palace, watching her with bated breath as she went by.

Chapter Ten

With each passing day, Morgana realized it would never get better. They would never fully accept her. She wondered whether it was real or just the product of her paranoid imagination. Even so, she felt every odd glance or shift away from her as a pang in the chest. She kept to herself, locked in her rooms as often as possible. She rushed to her room now, taking a long bath before flinging herself onto the sheets, thinking that if the loneliness didn't kill her, boredom might.

She didn't know how to fit in here. She'd felt it, briefly, in Thalassa, but she couldn't find a way to feel it again. The happiness, the *life,* was out of reach, when all she could focus on was it all being taken away.

A knock sounded on the door, and Morgana didn't like the way her heart hammered in her chest. She hated how she never felt relaxed anymore, never felt safe. With a resigned sigh, she opened the door.

Aveline paused where she'd been pacing in front of the doorway, her eyes falling on Morgana's rumpled appearance, the bags under her eyes.

"Hey," she said after several long moments.

Morgana shifted. "Hi. Does the king need -"

"The king doesn't need anything," Aveline said, her voice sounding raw and wobbly. "This isn't about the king."

"Okay…" Morgana trailed off.

"I haven't seen you in a while," Aveline said, fiddling with the hem of her shirt. "Every time I try to talk to you, you run off."

Guilt pierced Morgana's muddled state, and she ducked her head, stepping back to let Aveline in. "I've been … adjusting."

Aveline brushed past her, walking toward the bed, leaning against the bedpost at its foot. "Adjusting?"

"I … yeah," Morgana said slowly. "I feel like just yesterday I was in hiding, and then suddenly these months go by, and -"

"Do you blame me for what happened?" Aveline blurted out.

This surprised Morgana enough that her melancholy cleared, and she stared. "What?"

Aveline gestured helplessly. "The fact that you're here, that you're stuck in a war that you want no part in. Do you blame me for that?"

Morgana gaped incredulously. "*No*. You … you got me *out* of there! I know you had no part in their plan to hurt me." She hoped her surprise conveyed her sincerity.

Aveline swallowed, lowering herself to the bed. "Then why haven't you been able to look me in the eye?"

The words stuttered through Morgana's chest as she realized they were true. Morgana hadn't just turned away from the people in the palace: she'd turned away from everyone. She had turned away from Aveline.

Morgana walked to the wall, leaning back so she could gaze at Aveline, so she could look her in the eye and ask, "Do *you* blame *me* for what happened?"

Aveline pulled up short. "How could I -"

"I took you away from your home," Morgana rasped out, letting the worries of the past weeks pour out. "You'll never be welcomed back in Thalassa; you turned your back on them because of *me* -"

"And I'd do it again," Aveline said fiercely, standing again. "A million times over, I'd do it again. Anything to get you out. Morgana, we didn't take each other away from our homes. We rescued each other from situations we didn't even realize were bad. Things that would have destroyed us in the end."

Morgana scoffed, looking down. "Maybe we wound up in something worse."

"How could this be worse than a king trying to use you to exterminate an entire kingdom?"

Morgana let her head rock back against the wall, gazing up at the wooden ceiling and smoothing her shirt down. "I hate it here."

Confused, Aveline asked, "Why?"

Morgana pressed her lips together, a lump forming in her throat. "Do you see how people look at me here?"

"No," Aveline said simply. "I've been too focused trying to get *you* to look at *me*."

Morgana's breath hitched, and she made a mental note to circle back to that later. "They treat me like a monster, like a volcano that might erupt at any moment." She chuckled dryly. "I suppose I am, but it's like they think I'd *choose* to hurt them, even though I came here to *avoid* doing that."

"I think they just need to get used to being around your … power," Aveline tried. "Remember, it took me some time."

"It took you less than a day," Morgana said flatly.

"Not everyone is as extraordinary as I."

The corners of Morgana's lips twitched up, but they fell back down just as fast. "I'll never be more than a witch to them. You trust me because you grew close to me, but I can't do the same with everyone in this kingdom, there's not enough hours in the day or patience in my bones. At least in Thalassa, they didn't look at me like that, because they didn't *know*. Not really. My ancestors never went there, Nysus had never experienced the bitter parts of my magic. But here…" Morgana trailed off helplessly, her hands falling to her sides. "They're afraid of me."

"I'm not afraid of you."

Morgana looked back down to see that Aveline had hesitantly taken a step forward, her fingers slipping off of the bedpost. "I'm not afraid of you,"

Aveline said again, and Morgana let the words sink into her skin, her bones, as Aveline trailed across the room.

Morgana watched as she approached, the seashell still in her throat flashing in the lamplight, and she thought she heard Aveline mumbling something under her breath. Morgana inched forward as if to meet her, but Aveline just shook her head and shoved Morgana up against the wall, fingers curling into the shirt hugging her shoulders. Morgana only had time to think, *oh*, before Aveline tipped Morgana's chin up with a gentle finger and brought their mouths together.

Morgana kissed back without hesitation, finding it as natural as breathing. She wrapped her arms tight around Aveline's back, registering the softness of her lips, the fullness of them. Aveline drew Morgana's breaths from her chest, and Morgana pulled her closer, obliterating any lingering space between them, until Morgana's entire torso heated with the feel of Aveline's skin, the pressure of her body. After weeks of letting walls fill the space between them, she wanted to tear it all down.

There was too much going on at once, too many points of contact, and Morgana's head rolled back as she was fixated on Aveline's fingers trailing up her side.

They melted as one, two candles braving the flames together, and Morgana gasped when Aveline grabbed her waist like their lives depended on it.

Aveline trailed kisses along Morgana's jaw, lower and lower until she reached the hollow of her throat. Her lips moved over Morgana's skin, each kiss a gentle caress, a whisper of a message. Morgana heard them echoing with every touch, in each silent moment until Aveline finally voiced them aloud.

"You're not a volcano," Aveline murmured against her collarbone, scraping her teeth over bone, and Morgana let out a strangled moan. "You are not destructive. You're no more a monster than I am."

Morgana wrestled the words out of her throat. "I might start thinking you're a monster if you don't stop messing about and kiss me again." Morgana couldn't think of anything else. In that moment, Morgana cared nothing for her magic or otherworldliness. She just wanted to kiss Aveline.

Aveline smiled into the crook of Morgana's neck, but she still didn't move, letting her lips brush over skin with every word. "You are not a monster."

Morgana couldn't take it anymore. Reaching out blindly, Morgana grabbed a rough hold of Aveline's chin, wrenching her back up for a searing kiss. It was rougher this time, more intense, and Morgana tangled her fingers into Aveline's hair, tugging softly, trying to find any way to ground herself. Aveline's hands roamed over her body, under the hem of the shirt, skimming over her stomach and the waistband of her pants.

Deciding she might not be able to stay upright for much longer if she went any lower, she pushed against Aveline's hold on her, propelling them forward, and Aveline stumbled back readily. Maybe it was that Aveline didn't flinch away, didn't shy from anything Morgana did, but Morgana's fuzzy mind gathered into a distinct clarity. She thought that perhaps nothing else would matter if she could just keep this. If they could just have this.

The back of Aveline's knees hit the bed, and she fell onto the sheets, laughing as Morgana barely managed to keep from falling on top of her. But she stood frozen above her, Aveline gazing up with wide, shining eyes. Her pounding heart stuttered to a stop as her mind caught up with her body, wondering what the hell she was doing, how she could possibly -

"This isn't what the universe wanted for me," Morgana couldn't help but say, mesmerized by the woman before her, the humanity of her. "Cursed witches aren't supposed to be happy."

Aveline sat up on her elbows. "Then it's a good thing you're not a witch. Or cursed. You're a woman, and you're worthy of everything I am. We're worthy of each other."

"I'll end up hurting you," Morgana whispered.

"Don't start doubting yourself again now that I'm not touching you. I had you nice and distracted for a moment there," Aveline breathed, a hint of cockiness edging her voice, and Morgana couldn't blame her. Morgana would probably be mighty proud of herself, too, if she had seduced a reclusive witch.

"Your hands and lips are pretty distracting," Morgana said, unsure of where exactly to look before finally settling on Aveline's kiss-swollen lips.

"Well, if that's what it takes." Aveline surged up, but she didn't even have a chance to grab at her before Morgana let her belt and weapon slip down, tossing them aside, settling over Aveline with her hands on either side of her head. Green curls fell over Morgana's shoulder, brushing against the exposed skin above Aveline's neckline, and Aveline ran her fingers absentmindedly through the strands.

It was true. That might be what it took, because Morgana's mouth fell lazily onto Aveline's, and they laid there for what could have been hours, twirling within the bedsheets and within each other.

Morgana thought that she might never find a home in a place, but perhaps she could find one in Aveline.

***

"We should organize another ball."

Morgana jerked away, but Aveline didn't let her go far, her arms wrapped tightly around her shoulders. "I nearly bled out at the last one, and you think we should *repeat* that?"

"First off, you can't bleed out, so that's not even a good argument. Secondly, I think we should do the opposite of repeating it." Aveline shifted so she leaned slightly over Morgana, who sank back into the pillows. "I think we should have a total do over. Balls are really lovely under the right circumstances…" She trailed off, face contorting.

Clambering for her hand, Morgana let her fingers slip into Aveline's, squeezing tightly. She kissed her hairline. "One day, this will be over. And once it is, you can throw all the parties you want. I'll only complain a little bit."

Neither of them mentioned what Morgana might have to do once the conflict was over. Neither wanted to think of the life of solitude Morgana would likely have to return to.

"If you could have a life," Aveline said into the silence. "If you could have a life unhindered by your powers, what would it be?"

Morgana scoffed. "That's a bit of a cruel question, isn't it?"

"I don't think so. I think it's a hopeful one."

"Witches don't hope. They live immortal lives with nothing to show for them."

Aveline sat up, gazing down at Morgana, who refused to look at her, casting her eyes downward. "Tell me anyway."

Morgana pressed her lips together, stretching her arms over her head. "I'd own a reptile shop, a place filled with all kinds of beautiful snakes. That's how I lived many years of my life, alone in my hut, with Coby as my only companion. I'd enjoy making a life out of that. A better one, where other people are welcome, too."

Aveline smiled sadly at the thought. "And me? Would I be welcome?"

"Ideally, you'd run it with me. If just so I could torture you with Coby's presence a little more."

Aveline laughed. "Our House of Reptiles. But mostly yours."

"Mostly mine," Morgana smiled, voice soft and longing. She gazed up at Aveline, lifting her hand to stroke slowly down the soft skin of her cheek. Aveline's eyes fluttered closed at the touch with a small sigh. "Will you hate me for it?"

Aveline's eyes opened again, brow furrowed, and she settled back down into the pillow. Morgana shifted too, turning on her side. "For what?" Aveline asked softly.

"When I kill him." Not if. When. The words still felt uncomfortable on Morgana's tongue, sour and unnatural. She'd always sworn she'd never harm anyone, and yet here she was, planning a murder.

Aveline didn't flinch away from the sentence, just kept her eyes trained on Morgana's "No. I'd kill him myself, if I could."

The words settled over Morgana's chest, and she could read the sincerity on Aveline's face. She didn't regret a thing.

As Morgana watched Aveline fall asleep, she decided that maybe she didn't, either. Not yet. But monsters can't escape their fate, even for the briefest of moments. Morgana had always felt in her bones she'd live long enough to see the world burn.

She would watch it drown, instead.

PART TWO
Two Hundred Years Later
Aveline

Chapter Eleven

Warriors were seldom content being patient. They certainly weren't meant to chase the same weapon for over two hundred years.

Although Aveline discovered she could be *quite* patient, when the weapon she was chasing had once been used to kill her.

Aveline crested the hill leading to Goran, her horse rearing up as the village came into view, cast in rippling shadows from the wavering wall of water towering above. It was even smaller than most, and nearly as far as one could get from the capital of Briarwood after the war with the sea. From her vantage point she could see exactly where the border ended on the other side of the valley, where the land was swallowed by the dark, piled up ocean. It rose from the shore, stretching high into the sky and past the trees, churning against the invisible barrier holding it back. Tiny wooden shacks littered the landscape, nestled in the valley, and snow-covered cobblestone streets wove between them. Dots of townsfolk went about their day, unaware of the fugitive they harbored.

And yet even from here, she watched as those people raised their heads up to the great, looming wall that had been encroaching on their village over the past two hundred years. It inched over the ice even now, eating up the hard packed snow and melting it back into the waves. They were running out of time.

Would the villagers move? Would they try to flee to the center of the kingdom, to the already overflowing capital? Many didn't bother, deciding to die in the only home they had ever known, and Aveline bristled at the reminder that no matter the amount of magic in her veins, she might never bring the kingdom back from this.

Even then, she would live to be one of only three souls to see the end. Someday, whether years or centuries away, that blood magic protecting the last broken shards of the kingdom would fade, and the rest of Calypdon would go with it, sinking beneath the waves.

"You're sure she's here?" her lieutenant asked, gazing down in doubt at the innocent looking village. He'd never visited this place before, rarely leaving Briarwood once she had convinced him to join her forces. Aveline always insisted on going alone on her scouting missions.

"Positive."

Aveline's blood thrummed within her, and she barely noticed the bitter wind through the anticipation. She couldn't feel the lives of others as the Serpent Witch did, but her sharp eyes didn't lie. She saw the name of the shop, a shop that sold reptiles, of all things, in the center of the town square.

So few shops remain in the kingdom these days, with even fewer people to buy *anything*, let alone reptiles.

Micah sighed, sensing the fury radiating from Aveline's skin. He smoothed down the mane of his horse - whether to soothe himself or the horse, Aveline didn't know - and they rode onward. The hills of Calypdon were endless, wilting under the thick cover of snow, and they stretched between the two riders and their goal. Wet flakes pelted their faces, turning to streaks of water against the snapping gusts, and Aveline gritted her teeth against it.

She wondered how her horse felt, if he ached from the hard day of riding, his hooves grinding into the ice. If he missed the stables back in Briarwood. If he was glad that Aveline claimed him as her own. She constantly found herself marveling at the thoughts of animals, trying to get into the mind of every one she saw. She couldn't help trying to think like the witch. She was the only other Hallowed that Aveline knew.

They only stopped on the outskirts of the village, under a ring of evergreen pines at the edge of the forest, when the sounds of life began to filter toward their ears.

"Do you really plan to go in unarmed?" Micah asked at her side, dropping down from his horse and moving to offer her a hand.

Aveline scoffed, shoving his fingers roughly aside and landing gracefully in the slush without so much as a sound. Even the crunch of snow yielded to her magic. "I've fought in more battles than you have years, Micah. I can get off my damn horse."

Micah simply brushed his hand off on his thigh, as if her touch were poison, but he grinned. "You've fought in *one* war, and I seem to remember being told you were unconscious for most of it. And then you *died*."

Aveline glared.

Lifting his hands with a laugh, he added, "I'm nothing if not a gentleman, even to someone as old as you."

Aveline ignored the jab at her age. She would never get used to looking in the mirror and seeing the same face she'd seen just after the war, after the transformation. She longed to see lines creasing her skin, to know what she would have looked like with the chance to grow old. "To answer your question, yes. No weapons. We leave them here, at least until I get her out."

"Are you sure that's wise -"

Aveline held up her hand, and Micah fell silent. He had distinguished himself only a few years ago, as the lands slowly gathered themselves and regained some of their power. After all, without the Serpent Witch, Nysus would have a difficult time claiming the rest of the land. Aveline had waited, watched some of the lingering fear bleed away as generations died, hope born into the new generations, until she felt like the lands might be able to make something of themselves again.

Micah had been one of the first to join her. She'd found him on one of her scouting missions, after she watched him spear a squirrel through the eye.

He was a tall, sturdy man who joined her in the palace to train. A palace that hadn't housed a king or queen in two hundred years. Heavy white flakes dotted his dark eyelashes, and he straightened under Aveline's sharp gaze.

"Bringing a sword would be useless," Aveline said after a moment. "If she decides to kill me, no weapon would save me, anyway."

Micah swallowed hard. People who had only heard stories about the Serpent Witch forgot exactly what she was capable of. She'd faded once more into myth; only Aveline knew for certain that the tale came from something real.

What she'd done. To the people, to the entire kingdom, to Aveline herself. The Serpent Witch had rained such devastation down upon the land, leaving only a small, shattered territory free from the waves. The survivors huddled in the nooks and crannies of the city ruins, hiding under the cover of trees as if leaves could protect them from millions of gallons of water.

Drawn to the sea, Aveline looked back over the village. There was nowhere she could look that didn't feature the tall wall of water towering above, as it had for over two hundred years now. Aveline could only see one side from her vantage point, but she knew that it extended all around. It made a ring around the ruins of Calypdon, fighting against the magic granted to the royal bloodline.

To the first of the Hallowed.

The blessing given by the old god of the earth lingered in the royal bloodline. Someone in Wendell's lineage was still living and breathing. Hiding, perhaps, or unaware of who they were. But somewhere. Even after the witch's massacre.

That bloodline grew weaker with every passing day, evidenced by the tightening of that cage boxing them in. It crawled slowly, almost imperceptibly, but Aveline had taken note over the past two hundred years. In that time, the wall had swallowed miles of land, absorbing fields and roads into the rot of the sea. It had decimated almost as much of the kingdom as Morgana had decades before. This village, and dozens of others around the perimeter, would soon follow.

Aveline rolled her shoulders back, unsheathing the sword at her waist and handing the hilt to Micah. Her eyes caught on the ivory for a moment longer, the weapon she'd carried for two hundred years now, swearing she would use it to cut down its previous owner.

She would make it hurt.

The serpent winding around the hilt glinted in the sun, winking.

Micah took the sword warily. He didn't know the history of the sword, just that Aveline never let the hilt stray far from her hand. "I still think this is a bad idea."

Aveline ignored him. She did that a lot. "Keep that sword out of sight, at least for now. Don't let her see it."

Because if the Serpent Witch saw her old sword, none of them would make it out of here alive.

Micah swung the sword around his hand before shoving it into his own belt, fastening his olive green coat around it. If Aveline squinted her eyes, he almost blended into the pine needles around him. "And I still think it's irritating that you won't tell me more about all of this."

Aveline exhaled, turning away. "Live another hundred years. Then we'll talk."

Micah had the nerve to roll his eyes. "And what, exactly, makes you believe that she *won't* suck your life away as soon as you step foot on her property? She doesn't know you, you're not from her village. This is a woman who's been in hiding for two hundred years. You're wearing armor, Aveline, she's going to feel cornered."

Aveline simply began her trek forward, dragging a deep path through the snow as she left Micah behind with the horses. "Good."

***

She made her way through the streets, the echoing of her boots against stone getting lost in the surrounding chatter. Someone had swept away the fresh fallen snow, tents set up to protect trinkets sold from various carts. Children bumped into her as she tried to keep her head down to avoid suspicion, but Micah was, regrettably, right. People shot her odd looks, assessing her leathers and unfamiliar face.

The people of Calypdon didn't have much reason to travel. Everyone remained as isolated as possible, as if creating an imaginary barrier around their village could protect them from the invading sea. What remained of the land-folk split further, between those who hid from the wall and those who lived as though there was a chance it wouldn't one day overtake everything.

Back when the rise of the water was still new, and people remembered the original shape of the land, there had been outcries in the villages, calls to action against the sea. But the numbers hadn't been strong enough to do anything at the time. Aveline herself had spent years locked in an abandoned palace, watching it crumble around her, with the remnants of Wendell's soldiers standing guard as she had tried to adjust to her new body.

Besides, they'd tried once to fight the sea king, and failed.

How could they wage war against the sea itself?

An icy chill ran down Aveline's spine that had nothing to do with the snow covered ground. Aveline wrapped her cloak tighter around her torso.

Making her way into a quieter part of town, Aveline drew closer to where the witch had created her sanctuary. Subconsciously, Aveline dragged her fingers along one of her scars, tracing where it still bulged slightly above the surface of her skin. Beginning on the left side of her forehead, the sword wound sliced through her eyebrow, mercifully missed her eye, and resumed down her cheek, ending just at her jaw. A cruel joke, Aveline thought, to carry this and many other scars onto her new body for the rest of her immortal days. Or maybe the goddess of battle left them as reminders of what this new life had cost her, an imprint of what would soon enough fade into just another ancient war.

Drawn from her thoughts, the air blew out of her lungs as something struck her in the torso, and her hand flew to her side before she could stop herself, reaching for the ghost of the sword she had left behind. She hadn't even realized how attached she'd grown to it until she was separated from it.

She looked down to see a child. A young girl, no more than ten, staring up at her with wide eyes. She was bundled in a tattered pink coat, the color so faded it was more like a blush-beige, a woven headband secured around her ears.

"Sorry, ma'am," the girl squeaked, assessing Aveline.

Aveline actually laughed at the shock on her face, feeling somehow lighter at seeing a small child playing in the streets. "No harm done."

But the girl didn't move, shuffling her boots. Aveline narrowed her eyes and noted the wide hole at the toes. "Are you a soldier?"

Aveline clasped her hands in front of her. "I am."

"But we don't have an army."

Aveline knelt down, her knees popping from spending days on horseback. Most would think that being blessed by a goddess would make her body immune to little twinges, but no one could be so lucky. "What made you think that? Is that what people say?"

The girl nodded. "We lost the war a long time ago."

"And where did you hear *that*?"

"School," the girl said, a little bit of pride edging onto her face. "I'm a good student."

"I'll bet," Aveline said, though her heart ached. By school, she knew the girl must refer to a class of perhaps five children, taught by one of the older women in the village. "But I'll tell you a secret."

The girl came closer, eager.

Aveline let the words drift along the cool wind. "There's always something to fight for."

The girl jerked back, and Aveline didn't think it was possible, but the whites of her eyes grew, completely surrounding the irises. She looked over her shoulder, up at the sea visible even from here, an ominous wave above them that never went away. "Is there a war, ma'am?"

Aveline stood, brushing her knees off. "I hope not."

There wouldn't be, no. Not if this next conversation went her way. With the Serpent Witch, there was no fighting. There would be no true battle. The world would be split into two halves: the one who lost, and the one the witch fought for.

Without another word, she brushed past the girl and prayed the child stayed in this village forever, away from Briarwood and, once Aveline took the witch to the capital, away from the Serpent Witch. Aveline gnawed on her lip, imagining what would happen if the witch struck this whole town down in order to protect herself.

She needed to get that woman out of this village. She prayed the rest of her way through the town, casting her gaze to the cloudy sky, if only so she wouldn't have to look at any of the others on the streets. She prayed, but in vain, because the only goddess that had ever heard her would never listen to those pleas. Her goddess would never say no to more soldiers, to more wars.

That's why she had chosen Aveline. Because Aveline couldn't really say no, either.

She lowered her eyes when they at last fell on the wooden sign swinging above the door. The corners were worn from years of wind and snow, rain and sleet, rotting at the edges. Aveline wondered how often the Serpent Witch had manipulated the souls of these people, to adjust their memories, so she could stay here. Disgust bled through her on behalf of the people, whose lives became only a half-life as soon as they had let this woman into their midst.

Still, she couldn't take her eyes from the sign, painted roughly with chipped block letters. She imagined the Serpent Witch standing on a stool, a brush in hand, painting that name at some point in the past decades. The thought was enough to make Aveline's heart ache. A reminder of the witch who had once been a person.

Our House of Reptiles.

Aveline stiffened, averted her gaze, and moved toward the door.

"I wouldn't go in there, if I were you."

Aveline glanced over her shoulder to see a nervous looking man paused in the street. Aveline didn't wait for an explanation. She simply responded, "I don't want to," and pushed through the door.

What waited inside was the most well-tended part of any village she'd seen in a very long time. All of Calypdon was worn down; it had never recovered from what the witch had done. With so many dead, there had been no one to love the buildings or the streets or the abandoned shops.

But the tiny reptile shop had been tended to with all the love and attention the rest of the kingdom lacked. The small den expanded on the inside, extending back with a large tank glowing along the side of the wall, rounding the corner and continuing along the back. The glass took up nearly half the store, snakes and lizards lounging about together, small candles lit in the corners to keep them warm. They wouldn't go near the flames. They wouldn't attack each other, even the predators. The Serpent Witch could ensure that.

The Serpent Witch.

Aveline finished her examination of the room, eyes landing on what appeared to be a young woman seated on her desk, gripping the wood beneath her with narrowed eyes. Her dark green curls tumbled over her neck, down her back, the color of wet moss. The witch tilted her head, sending shadows over her pale skin, and if Aveline didn't know better, she'd think the two different colors of Morgana's eyes were a trick of the light.

But Aveline had seen them up close, studied the dark green eye and the bright yellow one as if they each held the secrets of the universe. The green one had flecks of molten gold, flashed through with deep forests, and the yellow one held the sun itself. Perhaps if she'd looked a little deeper, beyond their startling beauty, she would have found something real. A lump lodged in Aveline's throat at the familiar sight, at the pure indifference in those eyes.

The Serpent Witch swung down from the desk, her cloak sweeping behind her, revealing the bark brown peasant dress she wore beneath. Cloth woven into a layered long skirt approached the floor, brushing the toes of her boots, a vest tucked into a thick belt of dark leather. Aveline had to shake herself at how purely human the witch looked. How mundane.

"Good afternoon," the Serpent Witch spoke, and her words sparked something buried in Aveline's chest. That deep voice rasped out of her throat, as if she rarely used it anymore. "I don't think I've seen you here before."

Aveline lifted her chin. "Or felt me, either."

The witch froze, her fingers clutching the clasp of her cloak as she studied Aveline. With pursed lips, her fingers fiddled with the strings by her neck, and all at once she shed the cloak, tossing it on her desk before twirling to face the soldier. In the watery light of the sun filtering through the window, the sage undertone of her skin shone. "I take it you're not here to look at the snakes."

Aveline removed her own coat, allowing the witch to take in her fighting leathers and her empty weapons belt. She tucked the coat under her arm, standing straighter, trying to keep her face blank, to keep the rage simmering just beneath the surface from showing. "No. I come from Briarwood."

The witch sucked on a tooth, once again leaning back against the desk and folding her arms. "I haven't heard word of a battle."

Aveline stalked further into the room, past the snakes, but keeping a wide berth of the tank. With a flick of her wrist, the Serpent Witch could send twenty serpents flying at Aveline, each ready to sink their fangs into her neck. "Not yet, no. The land has spent these years rebuilding, preparing to take back what was taken from it during the last battle."

The Serpent Witch tilted her head. "What do you know about that battle?"

Aveline stared at her. "Enough."

The Serpent Witch exhaled, running long fingers through her hair. "Then you know that the sea won, and devastated more than enough of the land to secure hundreds of years of control."

"I believe that was you," Aveline said flatly, and Morgana showed no sign that the words affected her at all. "Regardless, it *has* been two hundred years. Your time is up."

The witch shook her head. "I will not go with you."

Aveline flicked her brow up. "Won't you? I hear you enjoy a fight, that you reveled in the fall of the land. And yet you didn't join King Daegil under the sea."

Morgana stilled, but didn't let anything else show on her face.

"I believe you made a deal," Aveline said carefully, "and the king abandoned you. As he discards all who have outlived their purpose."

The witch squinted, fists clenching. "Who are you, exactly?"

The lie came easily. She'd rehearsed it a thousand times in the past two hundred years, and she bowed her head. "My name is Ailani, commander of Calypdon's armies."

"Calypdon's armies were destroyed," the witch snapped, harsh, if just to cover her surprise. "There were no survivors within the palace walls."

There was one survivor.

"There were many survivors," Aveline fought back. "The king didn't order his entire army to the palace during those last days, that would have been foolish. Despite the blind faith he put in you, he took your power's limitations to heart. He sent enough into hiding that they were able to regroup, rebuild over the years. My father passed his title to me."

Technically true, her father had been the first to put a sword in her hand. But her parents were long dead, even before the war, even before she actually became a soldier.

"I won't hold it against you that you couldn't tell, couldn't feel them," Aveline went on. "It must get disorienting, feeling so many lives at once. They hid far enough away that you couldn't locate them. And you were busy utterly destroying an entire army, weren't you? An entire city?"

The witch's nostrils flared. "I will not go with you."

"Right," Aveline drawled, thinking of that day, of all the bodies. "Because your allegiance is with King Daegil?" She shrugged. "Where are your allies now, abandoning you to dry out on the devastated lands all these years?"

The witch turned away, gliding past Aveline to the tank. For someone so deadly, her grace always shocked Aveline. "My allegiance is to no one." Her hands remained still for a moment over the tank before she opened it, giving something to the snake inside. Food, probably. The snake flicked its tongue out, a loving caress. "My powers shouldn't be used for war."

Aveline barked a humorless laugh but swallowed it quickly. She placed a hand to her hip, the one not holding her cloak. "It was your powers that lost us the war in the first place. You *were* the war."

"Exactly," the witch snapped, turning back to Aveline. Her hair framed her face in wild curls, the green glowing from the candle behind her like a dark halo. "I won't participate in human charades again."

"You made your choices," Aveline growled. "You do not get to hide from them now."

Morgana moved to Aveline, so fast the witch was there before she could take a step back. "You know nothing about my choices, *commander*."

Aveline swallowed, heart hammering at the mere inches of air separating them. "Thousands of people died on that day. Stories didn't."

The Serpent Witch didn't move. "I will not go with you." Her eyes remained trained on Aveline's face, but Aveline didn't miss them flickering to her cheek, scrutinizing the mark there.

Aveline cleared her throat, stepping back as heat rose in her cheeks. It took all her power not to raise her hand to her face, to try to cover the scar. "It's rude to stare."

"I don't bother with manners," the witch said flatly. "You wouldn't, either, if you'd lived as long as me."

I have, Aveline thought bitterly. Because of the witch, but she could never know that. Could never know who Aveline actually was.

"Where'd you get such a scar?" the witch asked. "There's been no fights, no battles. No reason to draw a weapon."

Aveline was prepared for this question, too. "Training gone wrong."

"Training," the witch snorted. "Training for what? Do you really plan to fight the sea king? He'll never come to land, you know, and you can't get to Nysus. You'd drown before you got the chance."

"*You* wouldn't," Aveline said. "Morgana."

The name stung her tongue; the first time she'd said it in decades. She'd taken to calling this villain of the war, the villain of her life, the Serpent Witch. It was the name people called her in the tales, remembering her distinct, ivory sword. Aveline lumped herself in with the public as they swore Morgana off in fear, as if she could distance herself from the witch, as if the betrayal might hurt less if that's all she had ever been.

Morgana at last stepped back, running her fingers along her skirts. "I haven't been called that name in many years. I didn't think anyone remembered it."

Aveline spoke through the memories. "Like I said. Stories have a longer lifespan than people." She paused at Morgana's murderous stare. "Most people."

"Some stories get twisted."

Morgana's look, a mixture of anger and sadness, struck Aveline. Maybe she'd been hoping that Morgana would recognize her, that the bond they had once supposedly shared would linger. But Morgana had no idea who she was, hidden behind the transformed face of her Hallowed body.

Some relationships were only skin deep, and Aveline's old flesh had burned generations ago.

"You own this store by yourself?" Aveline asked, shifting topics abruptly.

It had the desired effect. The Serpent Witch furrowed her brow and looked over her shoulder. "Yes. I've been on my own for a very long time."

Aveline walked to the window and looked up toward where the sign for the store hung. She couldn't see it anymore, but she knew the name well. She'd been there when Morgana first came up with it. "'*Our* House of Reptiles'. Not '*My*.'" The word *our* caught in Aveline's throat.

In another life.

Morgana snarled, resolve breaking as she stalked toward Aveline and shoved her into the window, so hard Aveline thought she might fly through the glass. But the window caught her, ice cold, her head bouncing off the panes as Morgana held her by the throat. "What do you know?"

Aveline did her best to keep calm, but she remembered all too well the last time she was on the receiving end of Morgana's fury. Needless to say, it hadn't ended well. "I know that there were more survivors than you know on that day. I know that a certain soldier lived to tell the tale. I believe her name was Aveline?"

Morgana stood like a statue, and as hard as Aveline tried to decipher the look on her face, she couldn't. It was too complex, riddled with remnants of two hundred years of separation.

Two hundred years since she had murdered Aveline in cold blood.

"No," Morgana whispered, grip slackening. "That's not possible."

Aveline resisted the urge to shove Morgana off. "Morgana, you've been in hiding for two hundred years. You have no idea what's possible anymore."

Morgana pushed away, turning to hide her face, but her shoulders rose and fell rapidly with her harsh breathing, the gasps loud in Aveline's ears. "I could kill you with a thought," the Serpent Witch said, her hand reaching to her side, but she found nothing there. Aveline knew the sword that haunted her. It haunted Aveline, too.

"Kill me, and my people slaughter this town."

"You'll be dead before you get the chance to finish the job." That empty look in Morgana's eyes was so different from the wary curiosity of their first meeting. The last time Aveline had journeyed out and pulled the witch from her home. It was as if she could see the souls of countless ghosts locked behind those eyes, rather than the living souls she tended.

"I know," Aveline said calmly. "But your home will still be destroyed. Besides, kill me, and you'll never know what Aveline said about that last battle."

You'll never know what you really started. Neither of us will ever know if that day could have ended differently.

A goddess's blessing would only protect her from Morgana once.

Morgana took a few more moments, gathering her breath, gathering her thoughts. Gathering her options. Then she stalked over to her desk, took her cloak up in her arms, and took something else from a drawer. Metal flashed, but Aveline only had time to confirm that it wasn't a knife.

Morgana straightened, mouth set into a straight line. "I will go with you."

Aveline didn't smile. She had always known the witch would.

Chapter Twelve

Micah waited for them exactly where Aveline had left him, dozing beneath a nearby tree. The walk through the village had been silent, and no one had stopped to talk to Morgana. When was the last time she had so much as left her shop, let alone spoken to the people whose lives she must have disrupted?

"So, where's this army you were telling me about?" Morgana had asked blandly once they left the main street. She must have been reaching around for any souls hidden in the surrounding forest and only found one waiting for them.

Aveline shook her head, staring ahead. Morgana's presence was painful beside her. It was different, somehow, now that Aveline had magic of her own. It was as if their magics recognized each other. She forced herself to focus on the weeds bursting up between the cobblestones of the walkway. The first attempt of spring breaching the layer of snow. "I knew I wouldn't need them. Revenge is a powerful motivator."

Morgana's gaze was bleak and cold. "Indeed."

Micah hopped to his feet as soon as they came into view, his hand flying to his waist to make sure his cloak still covered the sword. Aveline winced at the suspicious movement. Morgana didn't seem to notice as she took in his wary look.

"Calm," Morgana ordered with a roll of her eyes, her voice strong and steady, colder than Aveline had ever heard. Was that a suggestion or a magic-induced order? Micah's face didn't change, so she relaxed and assumed the first. Morgana continued, "If I wanted you dead, you'd be dead."

Aveline groaned inwardly, remembering how Morgana had always been so straightforward, so deadpan. But then she reminded herself that she had never really known Morgana at all.

Micah chuckled uncomfortably, straightening. "But you could do it before I even knew what was happening, yes?"

"Yes," Morgana confirmed, folding her arms loosely over her chest. "But I won't."

Micah pressed his lips together, breathing out as he turned away, "Sure. Let's trust the witch. That's smart."

Something ugly shifted in Morgana's face, and Aveline knew she was probably remembering the first time Aveline had called her a witch. She'd taken it much better, then.

Aveline strode past Morgana, pushing away her own memories, and jerked her head to Micah. "You ride with him." They hadn't brought an extra horse. They barely had enough room for all the people hiding in Briarwood from the constant threat of the towering waves. Only so much space could be spared for animals. Not for the first time, she wondered what Morgana would think of that. The witch always, even during the days she'd pretended to have humanity, made it clear that she preferred the company of animals over humans.

Micah blanched at the thought of sharing his horse with the witch. He looked like he wanted to protest but quickly thought better of it. Whether it was fear of Morgana or fear of Aveline that he kept his mouth shut, she didn't care. As long as they got on these horses as quickly as possible, and everyone shut the hell up.

They did, and they rode in painful silence. She thought of her first journey with Morgana, how Aveline had spent most of the time trying to think of something to talk about, to pry words out of Morgana's mouth about anything and everything. It only worked about half the time, but she had still learned more about the witch than anyone else ever had.

Aveline snapped the box holding those memories closed, grimacing to herself, wondering how in either of the kingdoms she'd ever survive this.

She breathed easier the further from the wall of water they got, even though she knew logically that it didn't matter how far they travelled. If that magical barrier ever fell, if they couldn't stop its steady progression toward the center of the kingdom, there would be nothing stopping the sea from flooding every inch of free land left. Nothing would be safe.

Doing her best to keep her own eyes trained forward, she couldn't ignore Morgana's angry gaze on her the whole way. Even in the shadows of the tall trees, the piercing glow of it distracted her, somehow slowing time and speeding it up all at once, making a mess of the two hundred years that separated them. They weaved through the small paths between trees for hours, only making camp outside another village when the sun finally set. She didn't know which one.

The villages all looked the same, anyway. Small, run-down, and utterly devoid of hope.

Micah sat down next to Aveline, watching as Morgana dropped down from the horse and turned, staring back at the village she'd left behind. She'd been there a long time, as far as Aveline could tell. Longer than she'd ever been anywhere else.

"Watch your back," Micah murmured in her ear, watching Morgana like a hawk. "I don't trust her not to run off into the night but if we wait long enough, she might fall asleep."

"She doesn't sleep," Aveline said absentmindedly, and Micah whipped his head toward her.

"But *you* sleep?" he checked incredulously. He dropped his voice. "How did you get any rest when you knew her the last time?"

Aveline sighed, settling back for a long night of keeping watch. Now that she was Hallowed, she could do with less sleep than normal, but she wasn't like Morgana. Her magic didn't eat at her the same way Morgana's did. Aveline wasn't too far gone. "With too much trust. Add that to the never-ending list of mistakes that brought me here."

***

They rode into Briarwood barely halfway through the next day. Calypdon had been razed to almost nothing, and the entire kingdom took less than four days to traverse.

Aveline glanced at Morgana. She tried not to do it, but found it harder and harder not to, the more that Morgana's eyes glazed over her, as if she was nothing. As Morgana gazed at the palace, Aveline saw the first flicker of emotion since Morgana threw Aveline into the glass.

"You rebuilt," Morgana said in awe. "I didn't see much of the city in my time, but … it looks…"

It didn't look the same, Aveline knew. But it probably looked better than Morgana had expected. Better than what she had left behind, with bodies littering the streets, collapsed in homes and shops when the witch had decided their time had come to an end. At the time, Aveline thought it would have been better if there had been blood, if Morgana had torn them apart limb from limb. Somehow, she found chaos easier to deal with than silence.

Aveline couldn't help but glare. "A lot of people came together to repair the damage you did." When the land dwellers had dropped dead, any number of further disasters had resulted. Fires under stoves were left unattended, their flames escaping, spreading, and burning down entire streets. Animals from the surrounding forests stormed through, seeking refuge from the advancing sea.

Morgana's mouth snapped shut, jaw hardening, and she turned away.

Aveline wanted to rage at her for what the witch did. She wanted to fling her off the horse and grind her to dust, make her feel the pain she'd inflicted on Calypdon, on the people who had taken them both in when they'd needed it most. But more than that, she wanted to hurt her, she wanted to understand. To understand why Aveline had fallen asleep in Morgana's arms, in *love*, but had awakened to a genocide, with a sword pointed at her chest.

Morgana had killed everyone else with magic, reaping their souls instead of their bodies. But with Aveline, she'd used a blade. She'd used her hands.

Aveline and Micah flanked the witch as they escorted her into the palace. It was a bit haphazardly pieced together, the years taking their toll on the walls and old furniture, but it stood tall and huge. Aveline had found a way to call it home; to take in others from surrounding villages, and gift it as a home to them, too.

Calypdon had lost over three quarters of its land when King Daegil had raised the waters and flooded the earth. The people couldn't run from a tidal wave, though they had tried, and the sea had swept them away. They had been left with only a few hundred miles spanning a perfect circle, with the capital of Briarwood at its center.

But that wall of water loomed over the people, thousands of feet in the air, shimmering and rippling. It moved like the ocean, a reminder that there was nothing solid about this wall. Years passed, decades, and the generation that had feared Briarwood, where the horror had all begun, dwindled away. Instead, the new generations came to fear the outlying villages. Few wished to remain so close to the sea, and most eventually moved themselves and their families to the capital, as far away from the wall as possible.

Aveline had watched them come from the shelter of a small hut she'd built in the woods surrounding the capital. She hadn't wanted to stay in the palace, unable to bear living with the ghosts of all those who had died there. Once Helah had passed away, there had been truly nothing left. But the people from the villages filled the space left by the dead, searching for shelter throughout Briarwood and gazing over at the deserted palace. Only when the surrounding ruins had reached near bursting did Aveline enter the palace for the first time in over a hundred years, flinging the doors open for anyone who needed a place to sleep. She had unlocked the many abandoned rooms in the palace and the empty houses of the dead.

For a while, it had been enough, but years continued to pass, and more people crowded in. Some even had children, and suddenly they had to put two families to a house, and then three, and then four. People slept in the halls of the palace on makeshift mattresses, in ramshackle huts made of branches and leaves. Sickness ran rampant through the close quarters, food became scarce, and Aveline had feared they'd wipe themselves out before King Daegil had a chance to finish the job.

They had found a way, somehow, as the old and the weak passed away, and fewer and fewer children were born. It wasn't a good way, it wasn't a happy way. They simply found a way to survive.

Aveline began recruiting for an army once the chaos had begun to die down, when everyone had had a roof over their heads and she'd had time for more than scavenging for food. She had searched for a way to win a war that had loomed over them for two centuries. Perhaps victory wouldn't grant them happiness, but she had aimed to at least ensure their survival for as long as the gods blessed her with life.

Aveline led Morgana through the grand doors of the palace. Sound clattered in Aveline's ears with the chaos of the afternoon. She found Rike, Castor, and Verona waiting for them in the large main hall. Others milled around, coming from training or headed toward the dining hall, and they waved to her as she passed. Some she recognized, others she didn't, and she didn't have the energy to feel guilty. Instead, she ignored them, focusing on the remaining members of her crew.

She'd done a lot of recruiting in the past few years, but only four had achieved the status of her inner circle. They looked as uncertain as Micah had, glancing furtively between Aveline and the witch. They were young, about the age Aveline had been when this all started. Rike and Castor shuffled from side to side, not knowing how to proceed. Verona actually had the nerve to give a deep, exaggerated bow that made Aveline want to slap her.

"We don't bow to monsters," Aveline snarled.

Verona rose gracefully, crossing one ankle over the other as she leaned against the staircase. She looked bored, as she always did, but Aveline imagined that the past several days of waiting weren't helping much. She nodded to Morgana, tossing her long, dark braids over her shoulder. "Consider it a 'thank you' for not killing everyone."

When they had first met, Aveline had been drawn to Verona's sheer indifference to whatever might happen to her. She had been a scrappy little thing who grew into an even scrappier young woman. The way she laughed as she fought, taunting her opponents, spurring them on. She didn't care about her own wellbeing as long as life remained interesting.

"You're late," Castor said impatiently, jerking his head toward the waiting hallway. His blond curls bobbed with the movement, and he rolled the hilt of a knife between the palms of his hands. This one was new; he'd probably forged it while she was gone, desperate for a distraction. "We're already short on time." He had absolutely no patience for going off schedule.

"We can't be short on time when we have no idea when they're going to attack," Aveline said.

"I'm pretty sure that means we're always short on time."

She met Rike's gaze over the other's heads, and she found reflections of herself in those familiar, dark eyes, the same shade as the ones she used to have. Rike sent her a silent message with those eyes. *Are you okay?*

Rike was the only one who knew the exact nature of the relationship Aveline had with Morgana and was the only one she felt comfortable showing a hint of vulnerability to. *I'm just about ready to burn myself alive.*

Rike's lips curved up at the corner, and she looked so much like her ancestor that Aveline's heart ached, wanting to rush forward and hug the only piece of her sister she had left.

Aveline didn't know the events that had led to her sister's survival, just as she didn't know most of the events of that day. All she knew was that when she had awakened from being resurrected as a Hallowed, Helah had sat with her, bone tired, and knowing no more than Aveline had. Still, Aveline hadn't even asked any questions until much, much later, simply clinging to the only person she'd had left.

Verona jabbed Aveline in the ribs. "Again, you're late. Let's move."

Morgana's gaze turned to Aveline, asking coldly, "Late for what? Is this the part where you tell me why you dragged me back here?"

"No," Aveline snapped, pushing down her emotions as her eyes burned. "This is the part where we lock you upstairs and decide exactly how to deal with you."

With a long sigh, Morgana said, "Thinking ahead is an important attribute for a leader. What was your position here, again?"

Aveline's blood boiled. "A high enough rank to keep you in line."

She wanted Morgana to get angry. She wanted her to scream, so Aveline could scream back. But the witch just rolled her eyes in what appeared to be heavy exhaustion, and asked, "Where are you putting me, then?"

Verona swept in. "Follow me."

Aveline was fairly sure Verona had a death wish, looking no more bothered by Morgana's presence than she was by anything else. But perhaps she just wanted an excuse to be late for the meeting.

Morgana nodded curtly and followed Verona toward a side door without so much as a backward glance. Aveline was about to turn back to the rest of her circle when she heard Morgana mutter, "You shouldn't, you know."

"What?" Verona asked, fading down the hall.

"Bow to monsters. They'll get the wrong idea."

Their voices faded as the door swung shut behind them, and Aveline slumped against Micah.

He shoved her off. "Don't be so dramatic. You're acting like a jilted lover."

Rike clamped a hand over her mouth to stifle a laugh. She looked at her three remaining companions, and they suddenly seemed different. They'd become comrades, friends, in their time working to find Morgana and plan a war against the sea king, but they suddenly looked so … young. Untouched. As if seeing Morgana had plunged Aveline back into the past, to when she was as young and naive as these three were now.

Aveline took a deep breath. "If there's no news, then there's no point in meeting at all. I've had … an incredibly long day, and I'm running on the three hours of sleep I got four days ago and pure rage." She scanned them. "Is there news?"

Castor's lips pressed into a thin line. "Should we lie and say there's nothing so you can sleep?"

Immediately alert, Aveline clapped him on the shoulder, and said, "I knew it. Castor's been itching to get an eye on the witch for months now, I knew as soon as Verona beat him to the offer of escorting her alone that he must have something more important to say"

"It could be that," Micah said. "Or, we could consider that Castor is a coward."

Castor scoffed, unbothered, because it was true enough that he didn't like a fight. He preferred strategy. "As if you haven't been dying to know how she operates, too. How her magic works. I'd take her apart vein by vein if I could. Wouldn't you?"

That she would.

***

Aveline paced along the length of her bedroom, all fatigue gone after the meeting she had just endured. For once, she was grateful that no one had wanted to share a room with a Hallowed, too intimidated by her or annoyed with her shortened sleep schedule. To make up for it, she had moved herself into the smallest space she could find, more of a broom closet with a tiny bed and bathroom than anything. Consequently, her room to pace was limited.

Thoughts ricocheted around her skull as she tried to adjust to the new information.

She'd assumed wrong, mistook Castor's silence for excitement. It wasn't good news.

She pressed her face into her hands, kicking herself for waiting so long, for hesitating for the days as she had spent on the outskirts of the village, just … watching and wasting time.

Aveline had found Morgana nearly a year ago.

It had only taken her so long because for decades, she didn't even bothered looking. She'd assumed Morgana had found sanctuary with the sea king, beneath the water that had overtaken the lands. Only after decades had passed, and Morgana and King Daegil had still not attacked again, did Aveline consider that they might have separated. That Morgana had never returned with the king, that the king had abandoned her and left her for dead.

Well, not dead. But something as close as an immortal witch could get.

She hadn't told anyone at first, holding the information close to her chest and praying she was wrong. She hadn't wanted to be told that she had spent all that time being wrong, thinking Morgana was still held by King Daegil, still serving him. She didn't want to admit that she'd wasted so much of Calypdon's dwindling time.

Still, she had kept her mouth shut, scouring the countryside herself, claiming she was studying the encroaching wall of water and taking note of its movements. She'd known the witch was still in Calypdon the moment she'd seen the shop's worn sign. She'd missed it on her first two visits to the village, the sign so run down from years of exposure she could barely read the paint. But it was its age that gave it away, drawing Aveline's eye as even more worn than the rest of the village. And though she had to squint to find it, past the chipped paint and worn wood, she had known when she had read that title.

Everything reminded her of Morgana then, once she had found out that she still haunted the land.

Only when Aveline saw the painted letters on the reptile shop sign, when she had known for certain without even needing to see the witch, did she ride furiously back to the palace, bursting into a meeting she'd told her group to conduct without her. They had stood, seeing tears streaming down her face for the first time. They came around her, even Verona, brows furrowed with concern as they asked what in the world had happened, what could have possibly surprised a two-hundred-year-old warrior.

She'd told them almost everything that night, everything she knew about the Serpent Witch and the role Aveline had played in Calypdon's fall, withholding only the fact that Aveline herself had once loved her. Their relationship aside, Aveline had still been the one to bring Morgana into Nysus. Aveline had still trusted her.

Her bonds with these new comrades had been solidified that night, when they didn't hold the sins of her past against her. When they didn't blame her for trusting a witch no one had known well enough to doubt.

A pounding on her door interrupted her thoughts, and she wiped her eyes only to find nothing there. She hadn't cried since she had found Morgana living so close.

She gathered herself and smoothed her hair before pulling the door open, revealing Rike with mussed clothes and particularly impressive bedhead.

Though her face looked murderous, Rike's words were concerned. "Are you okay?"

"Fine," Aveline lied airily, lingering in her doorway.

"I live below you, remember?" Rike said grumpily, shoving past her relative into the tiny room. "Need I remind you that I can hear *every. Cursed. Step?*"

Aveline winced, rubbing her elbow. "Sorry. I need to move to think."

"That's your problem," Rike said, collapsing on Aveline's cot and pulling the blanket into her lap.

"Moving?" Aveline asked tiredly.

"Thinking. It's kept you up for the past two hundred years. Give it a rest for one night."

Rike was the only one who knew the full story, who knew exactly what Morgana had meant to her before … everything. Aveline was surprised Rike kept her features so pleasant upon meeting the witch, probably so as not to give Aveline's identity away. Rike had a knack for fooling those who shouldn't have been able to be fooled, making her tall frame look small, wiping her face to neutrality. Aveline would bet that Morgana hadn't even noticed her.

That's why she was Aveline's best spy.

Aveline buried her face in her hands. "That woman ran me through with a sword. I spent decades trying to get that image out of my head, but now it's *all* I can see."

"I can't say I blame you," Rike tried for humor. "Most people don't live long enough for their murderers to haunt them."

Aveline threw her hands in the air, barely hearing the other woman's words. She pointed at the scar on her face, then to the one on her stomach, hidden beneath her shirt. "She did it with this … completely emotionless expression on her face, as if she didn't care at all that she was going against everything she had claimed to stand for, like none of it had meant *anything*."

"You have to stop blaming yourself for the actions of a woman who lied to you," Rike said harshly, as Aveline sat next to her. "Your hands are clean. Hers are not."

Aveline shook her head, casting her gaze upward. She missed Morgana's old room, with the window in the ceiling. At the time, she'd convinced Wendell to give it to her instead of Aveline, insisting that the witch needed more sunlight to heal. She considered taking it when she'd moved back in, after all was said and done and the palace rebuilt, but she'd thrown up her dinner the single time she'd stepped foot over the threshold.

While she had built walls in all the other huge rooms, dividing them to provide groups as much privacy as possible, she'd kept that room untouched and empty. She wouldn't curse anyone with that space.

Except an already cursed witch. That room was where Verona had taken Morgana.

Aveline's throat bobbed. "I brought her out, I…"

Rike shook her head sadly. "King Daegil won. He won her over. Aveline, that might be all there was to it."

But Morgana was here anyway. She just had to find out who the witch hated more: Aveline or the king who had betrayed her. Aveline cut her gaze to the two swords leaned beside her bed; the Serpent Sword and the plain one she'd have to carry in the presence of the witch. The ruby eye of one of the snakes seemed to wink at her.

Rike leaned forward, jostling Aveline with her shoulder. "You hear me? Aveline, sometimes monsters are just monsters."

But it couldn't have been just that. The night before Morgana had murdered her, Aveline had been curled into the witch's side. She'd told her over and over that Morgana wasn't a monster, that Aveline wasn't afraid. There had to have been a reason for Morgana's act. For leading Aveline on. But no matter the excuse, it could be nothing but cruel.

Rike squeezed her hand, and her slim fingers felt so similar to Helah's that Aveline leaned into the touch, letting her head fall against Rike's shoulder. She tried her best to love Rike only for who she was, rather than her relationship with Helah, but sometimes Rike was Aveline's only reminder that despite it all, Helah had survived. And though she had passed eventually, fading as all humans do, Helah hadn't died by Aveline's hands. By her actions.

That, at least, she didn't have to atone for. But she would make amends for everything else when she pulled Calypdon from the water.

And killed the witch and the king who had taken it from her in the first place.

Chapter Thirteen

Aveline hadn't been awake for most of the attack, unconscious in Morgana's bed. But she'd witnessed the rushing tide of water surging toward Briarwood. It blotted out the sun, rising up from the shores and plowing inland. The water had drowned Calypdon, crashing through every crack and crevice of the earth, swallowing everything in its path. It had climbed higher and higher, and for the first time, she'd been afraid of the water.

Aveline lifted her hand to her throat and slipped it beneath the scarf she wore to cover the shell shaped scar on her neck. A flash of pain, a memory, haunted the space between her collarbones, of a sword slipping beneath the breathing relic and popping it free. The agony had been incomparable, not just because of the shell ripping from her skin, but from her body rejecting the air that the shell had been allowing her to breathe.

But Morgana hadn't given Aveline the chance to suffocate. The witch wanted to take her life herself. She hadn't wanted to leave it to nature.

Aveline stared out her bedroom window at that wall of water in the distance. From certain angles, it took up the entire view. There were moments where she could almost convince herself she was back in Nysus, so all-encompassing was the water. She'd watched as it slowed, then stopped, too. As she'd stared in horror at the great tidal wave cascading toward Briarwood, fast and unforgiving, magic at last sent it screeching to a halt. The water seemed to congeal into a perfect, wavering circle that rose thousands of feet into the air.

She couldn't see the wall moving anymore, not at its slow pace, but Aveline knew it tightened its hold every day. She hadn't realized at first, not until she started to receive word from the surrounding villages that their buildings were slowly being swallowed. Towns folded in on themselves, becoming as small as possible as they inched away from the water, but it kept coming. Soon, entire villages were lost to the sea. One of two things happened to the people within them. Either they fled to the city, or they stayed and went with their home into the ocean.

Every day the kingdom went on without an heir on the throne, the lungs of the land people burned, anticipating the moment they would no longer have air to breathe. Every day that the blessing protecting Briarwood grew weaker, the sea grew that much stronger.

One day, it would swallow the remnants of Calypdon whole. Maybe it wouldn't be soon, maybe it would take years. But Aveline, hallowed as she was, would be alive to see it, and so would Morgana.

Aveline turned on her heel, moving to grab her cloak and sword. By instinct, she nearly put the Serpent Sword into its usual sheath but corrected herself at the last second. She wrapped her fingers around the sword she'd picked out in the armory and grimaced. The simple golden hilt felt unfamiliar and too light in her hands. She'd carried Morgana's old sword for two hundred years now, and each time she left her room without it, it was as though she was leaving a limb behind.

Stalking from her bedroom, Aveline pushed the rest of her many questions away. It was agony, waiting for King Daegil to return. As far as she was concerned, there was nothing stopping him. The army she'd managed to scrape together would never be enough against him and his forces.

She nodded angrily to the guards posted at the witch's room and rapped on Morgana's wooden door so hard her knuckles barked in pain. The door was familiar; it was the one room she'd kept empty. She hadn't wanted to curse anyone with the desolation of the witch's room.

Aveline knocked again, harder. "Get up. Now. I know you're not sleeping in there."

Footsteps sounded, and the door swung open to reveal Morgana, dressed in clean trousers and a loose shirt, the top half of her hair tied in a knot at the back of her head. It'd grown longer, the green sweeping over her back in loose curls. The sight of Morgana's irritated face still managed to inspire a fire deep in Aveline's stomach, something that wasn't entirely made of hatred. "Good morning to you, too."

Aveline ignored the words. "We have a council meeting."

Morgana looked past Aveline's shoulders, her gaze darkening at the presence of the guards. Once more, her fingers fluttered to her side, searching for the sword she'd last seen in Aveline's chest. "And I'm invited to this one? Ailani?" She said the name like poison.

"You're being told to go," Aveline corrected. "I didn't bring you here for your protection, or to give you the answers you seek on a silver platter."

Morgana tilted her head. "Actually, I wasn't seeking anything until you showed up. I was living quite the quiet life."

"Witches aren't meant to live quiet lives," Aveline snapped. She thought of Morgana's wish for a simple snake shop, for a life without the weight of responsibility for thousands of souls and wondered why that hadn't been enough.

Morgana's voice was soft. "And what do you think I'm meant for?"

Aveline's heart pounded, because she honestly had no idea. She had once thought she'd known. She had believed Morgana could be meant for something better, for a life of blessings rather than curses. She had thought Morgana might be meant for her. "Death, it would seem. So you're going to kill someone for *me* this time."

Morgana snapped her gaze back to Aveline. "I won't kill innocents."

Aveline's blood turned to ice. "I'm *so* glad your philosophy has changed," she fired back. "That would have made things a lot easier about two hundred years ago."

Morgana reeled back as if she'd been hit, eyes widening with a flash of *something*, but she masked it so quickly Aveline didn't have time to decipher it. The reaction stunned Aveline into silence.

Morgana recovered quickly, though, plastering indifference over her face. "If you are planning some sort of retribution toward the people of the sea, some sort of *life for life* revenge scheme, then you can find someone else to help you."

So, her allegiance is still with the sea.

Aveline straightened. "I'm not. Just as you claim, I have no interest in killing innocent people, sea or land. Most of them had no part in this travesty. I only have my eyes set on their king."

Morgana's stoic expression didn't change. "You're out of luck. I can't kill Daegil."

Aveline's brow furrowed, unable to stop the confusion blossoming over her features, but she didn't bother asking why Morgana would lie about such a thing. Or perhaps she wasn't lying, and had just replaced *can't* for *won't*. Stepping back, she motioned for Morgana to come out into the hallway. "Then it seems we have a lot to discuss."

With a heavy sigh, Morgana followed Aveline down the long hallway, glancing back over her shoulder. "How did you know that was my room, anyway?"

"Verona told me," Aveline said impatiently, wishing more than anything that they weren't alone, and she picked up the pace. Morgana's proximity was steadily becoming torturous.

Morgana rolled her eyes. "No, I mean, how did you know that was my room when I was here … before." The words seemed to die in her throat, fingers clenching at her side.

Aveline cursed herself even as she wondered at the pain in Morgana's voice, the way she said *before.* "Don't ask how I know things," Aveline snapped, jerking her head down the hall. "In fact, don't ask anything at all. Just keep your mouth shut."

"You have a lot of nerve," Morgana said, but she didn't sound angry. She just sounded tired, as if she was making a vaguely annoyed observation.

Aveline lifted her chin and spoke with cold determination. "You don't scare me."

She'd said it once before, but for entirely different reasons. She'd once spoken out of love, but now it was nothing more than resignation. Because if Morgana killed her, then so be it. She'd already done it once before.

It was hard to be terrified of something that had already happened, of a fate she'd already faced.

Morgana didn't look at Aveline. "That's rare. Of the people in history who knew me, there haven't been many who didn't fear me. Even less who didn't hate me."

Aveline pursed her lips. “I can’t say the same about the second one.”

“You don’t know me, you know only what you’ve heard. How is it that you hate me already?”

“Sometimes, the stories are enough.”

Morgana stopped in the hallway, whirling around to halt Aveline’s long strides. She stumbled to a stop, reaching out to catch herself on Morgana’s shoulder, but switching to the wall at the last second. Aveline moved to push past, but Morgana stood firm, nostrils flaring. “Stories are nothing but words. I know nothing of why you need me, or how you know of Aveline’s fate. It is only because you knew her name that I agreed to hear you out. Take care how you treat me, or I will disappear again. And you won’t find me a second time.”

Aveline’s heart pounded, and she had to catch at the flood of sour words rising up through her throat and onto her tongue, the thousands of vile things she wished to scream at this woman. But she pushed them down, because Morgana was right. Though Aveline had reason after reason to hate Morgana, Ailani had nothing but stories passed down over two hundred years. Stories that, as far as Morgana was concerned, Ailani had no proof of.

Taking a deep breath, Aveline motioned to herself. “Then use your powers. Read me, or whatever it is you do.

Morgana sucked on her bottom lip, letting her eyes flutter closed. She spoke softly. “I won’t.”

Exasperated, Aveline flung her arms in the air. “*Why*?”

Morgana turned around, resuming her pace, and Aveline hurried forward to lead the way. “My magic has been wrong before. I don’t trust it anymore.”

Aveline narrowed her eyes. Who had it been wrong about? The sea king, perhaps? Morgana’s reaction that night in Thalassa, at the welcome ball, had told Aveline more than enough about what she found buried beneath his soul. The way she’d reared back, as if King Daegil’s touch had been poison.

Maybe she only feared him because her own evil had recognized itself in him. Evil for evil, monster for monster.

“You were not the first soldier to pull me out of hiding,” Morgana said, stiff and sour. “Remember this as we go forward: I haven’t agreed to anything yet. Don’t consider it too great of an accomplishment.”

Aveline didn’t. She wished Morgana had turned her away that first day two hundred years ago, but she knew it would have been useless. King Daegil would have just sent someone else, someone more ruthless and less gentle, to fetch the Serpent Witch. Aveline might have forfeited her life by failing in such an important mission, but she would have saved her heart.

But Morgana would never have turned Aveline away. She knew that now, because Morgana clearly had never actually had a problem with killing. She wondered if that horrible story Morgana had once told her about her mother was even true.

"You were hardly hiding this time," Aveline decided to say.

"I was. For many years, until everyone who had survived that horrible day had died. My previous attempt had failed so miserably, I thought it might be better to hide in plain sight."

"Or perhaps you wanted to be found," Aveline said. "To pay for your crimes."

Morgana's jaw twitched, and she paused, slowing again to look at Aveline. "Remember this as well, Ailani. If I were to find out that you were lying about Aveline's fate, the results would be very bad for you, indeed. I don't take kindly to being played with."

Aveline tried not to laugh hysterically at the irony of it all, and they walked the rest of the way in silence.

***

They'd set aside a tiny, cramped room in the east tower for their council meetings. It was a cozy space with an oversized fireplace and an assortment of worn-out chairs. Aveline sighed when she entered the familiar space. A fire flickering in the corner cast a warm orange glow over the hearth and the forest green walls. If Aveline could block out the witch walking in behind her, she could almost pretend everything was normal.

The rest of her council waited for her, clearly irritated at her tardiness. Aveline had spent much of the morning struggling with herself, trying to force herself to go and fetch the witch.

Castor grinned broadly, and Aveline didn't know if it was directed at her or Morgana. "Good morning, ladies. Shall we get started?"

"Please," Verona sighed. "I want to be done before lunchtime."

Aveline rolled her eyes and sat down in her usual chair. Morgana remained standing, leaning back against one of the walls. Aveline caught Rike's gaze, a twinge of sympathy there, and quickly looked away. Aveline cleared her throat. "Yes, yes, let's get started."

"Good," Morgana said, her voice hauntingly quiet in the echoing room. "Then you can start by telling me exactly who you people are, and what you want from me."

"We'll start," Aveline said through gritted teeth, "wherever I say we start."

"Are you a queen?" Morgana asked, annoyed. "Are you in charge here?"

"No, and yes," Aveline said. She would never name herself queen. Their mission would ensure she'd never have to. "I am in charge, temporarily."

"You're not," Morgana said, sweeping across the room and perching on the only remaining chair, folding her legs beneath her. "You're not in charge, because I am."

Aveline pressed her lips together, as Verona stifled a laugh.

But Morgana wasn't finished, leaning forward to look around at the small council, sitting before them like they were equals when they all knew they were insignificant compared to her. "This is how this is going to work. You will tell me what you want, I might decide to do it, and then you will give me what I'm owed."

"Straightforward," Micah nodded, trying for a joke even as his nerves shaded his tone. "Nice. Most witches aren't."

Morgana glared at him. "And have you met any other witches to test that theory?"

He didn't respond, shifting and sinking into the cushions.

"Right," Morgana hissed. "You haven't, because I'm the only one of my kind alive. I can control each and every one of you, whether you know it or not. Your blood, your souls, your lives … it all slides through my fingers."

Ice dripped down Aveline's spine, because she saw her, then. The immortal, all-powerful witch that Morgana had kept hidden for so long. Morgana seemed to tower over the room, despite being seated like the rest of them, her face twisted and beautiful and haunting all at once. This was what she was, Aveline reminded herself. This was what she always had been, and Aveline had just been too blind to see it.

Morgana sat back again, crossing her arms over her chest. "I may be immortal, but I'm no longer as patient as I once was, nor will I allow you all to think yourself more powerful than you are. I know the power I hold, and from your looks, so do you."

"And yet you haven't used it in two hundred years," Castor mused, more out of curiosity than anything, but Aveline still stiffened. Castor was an inherently curious soul, born to fiddle with broken things until he fixed them, but Aveline always worried that he'd eventually be shattered in the process.

With an exasperated puff of breath, Morgana considered him. "No," she conceded. "I have not. They are not abilities to be taken lightly. I have learned from my past mistakes."

"You call murdering thousands … a *mistake*?" Micah asked incredulously, cringing as soon as the words fell from his mouth.

Shockingly calm, Morgana bowed her head, but Aveline had a feeling it was more to hide her face. "That was not the mistake I meant," she said, almost to herself.

Aveline's fists clenched, wanting to punch her even more for being so cryptic. Did this always happen to people with age? Quiet superiority had nestled into the witch's bones, angles of her body sharp and harsh in the places she had seemed soft and kind before. Was it happening to Aveline, too?

Morgana lifted her gaze once more. Her mismatched eyes, one glowing yellow and the other a vibrant green, flashed in the firelight, burning deep in her skull. "I won't kill anymore, but I'm not above knocking you all out for several years. You will obey when I say: tell me what I want to know about

Aveline's last moments, or I will leave."

Rike's eyes widened, glancing at Aveline and mouthing, *Several years*?

Several years was nothing to an immortal. Aveline could feel it herself, how she might step away for a decade and come back unchanged.

Micah cleared his throat, shifting uncomfortably as he shot a furtive glance toward their leader. "You know what happened the day King Wendell fell."

Morgana's eyes turned into dark pits. "I do."

Aveline kept her composure, even under Morgana's molten gaze. Aveline barely recognized the Morgana she had known in the worn, angry woman sitting before her. No more than Morgana could recognize Aveline as Ailani. "When the sea came to conquer Calypdon, it couldn't take Briarwood, it couldn't take the core of our lands." She motioned toward the churning wall of water, beyond the remaining miles of fields and mountains waiting outside the window. "Briarwood remains protected from the waters."

Morgana barked out a laugh. "A cruel twist of fate, yes. I can't say I bothered to find out why that happened, why this sliver of land was saved."

"Was that why your king abandoned you?" Aveline couldn't help but ask, glaring at the witch. "Because you couldn't give him everything he wanted, couldn't give him the entire kingdom?"

Morgana stared at her, biting her lip so hard she might have drawn blood. A battle raged behind her eyes, until she finally stated, "I have no king."

Aveline supposed that was true.

The witch went on. "But I figured it must have been enough for Daegil, because I haven't felt him stir in Calypdon in all these years. He's stayed in Nysus."

Micah pursed his lips, scratching his jaw. He always had to be doing something with his hands, a man of action born out of the resignation of the villages, a fighter born from a generation spending their lives waiting to drown. He usually fiddled incessantly with his weapons, but Aveline had forbidden any of them from entering today's council armed. The last thing she needed was some sort of threat making Morgana explode like a volcano. Again. "Yes, well, he doesn't need to. After all this time, he might soon have the means to bring down the rest of the water."

Morgana didn't flinch. "If he couldn't do it then, how could he do it now? Nothing's changed. Briarwood seems to be protected."

"And you don't know why the center of the lands survived?"

"No," Morgana said flatly. "Some sort of magic, I assume. Maybe the gods decided that someone as horrible as the sea king shouldn't take everything."

"Did you know that Calypdon was once blessed by the goddess of the earth?" Aveline asked. "That the first king was one of the Hallowed?"

Morgana rolled her shoulders back. "I did. Thousands of years ago, though, so I'm not sure what that has to do with anything."

Castor scowled. "For an immortal being, you don't know much."

Glaring, Morgana looked murderous. She constantly looked murderous these days. "Just because I'm immortal doesn't mean I've been alive for thousands of years. Not yet, anyway."

Aveline reclined back in her plush chair, rubbing her eyes. "You should know more than anyone that magic, particularly magic sent by the gods, doesn't just disappear upon the death of the bearer. It is passed down through the blood."

Morgana's eyes narrowed.

Nodding, Aveline looked away, choosing to scrutinize the flames eating away at the logs instead of the witch. The bright lights burned her eyes, but she ignored them. "The blessing meant that the land would forever be protected by the goddess, that it would stay lush and green."

Morgana actually snorted, but there was no humor in the sound. Aveline didn't think she'd ever get used to the vacant, dead look behind the witch's eyes. The look that told her the soul Aveline had thought she'd loved had never been real. "Well, someone should go up there and tell the goddess the blessing was faulty."

Verona leaned forward, plucking a few grapes from a bowl on a side table and tossing them in her mouth. She was the only one eating. "The Hallowed are immortal, but they *can* be killed. We can assume he was eventually, but magic lingers in the bloodline. Each descendant of the Hallowed received a sliver of that blessing, but as more time separated the line from the source of the magic, the blessing became weaker. With every generation, it did less -"

"So when Daegil attacked, it didn't protect the entire land," Morgana finished for her, resting her chin against her fist. "Just Briarwood and the surrounding territory."

Aveline nodded. "It remained with the one true heir to Calypdon's throne, hidden somewhere in the surviving city or villages."

Morgana stared at her before shaking her head. "That doesn't make sense. Wendell died childless; he never had the chance to marry."

Aveline wanted to snarl at her, to scream that she didn't deserve to say his name, but she held her tongue at Morgana's curious gaze. "Well, that's reassuring. At least he didn't tell you everything."

Irritated now, Morgana asked, "And are *you* going to get to the point?"

Castor grinned mischievously. "King Wendell *did* have a child. A son. His lover was pregnant when he died. Before the battle, he hid her away in a distant village where she would be safe."

Morgana stared at them, dumbfounded, and Aveline wanted to laugh at the stricken look on her face. It almost made her look human again. "So, the royal bloodline lives on?" she whispered.

Aveline nodded. "Somewhere out there, an heir who evaded your slaughter lives on, whose line has survived long enough to protect us from you."

Morgana sat back in her chair, slowly, staring off at some vacant spot on the other side of the room. At last, she blinked and returned her gaze to Aveline, who saw something like grief there. "I'm surprised you didn't throw me in a jail cell, considering how you think of me."

Aveline reeled back at the raw emotion in Morgana's voice but nevertheless responded with the harsh truth. "You wouldn't have let me. You'd have stopped my movement before I had a chance to get you to the dungeons."

Morgana pressed her lips together, nodding. "I suppose that is what you'd think." She turned away, instead focusing on Verona, of all people. "Then what's the problem? You have a bloodline; your lands are safe."

"The *problem*," Verona spoke over Morgana, "is that the heir was kept a secret. The mother never came back to Briarwood. The current heir doesn't know who they are, and neither do we."

"And why do you need them?"

"Because our lands *aren't* safe," Castor said, jerking his chin meaningfully in Morgana's direction. "We need to ensure the safety of the heir in order to protect what we have left. Perhaps the goddess would strengthen her blessing if she saw them assume the throne."

"And," Micah added before Morgana could shoot that idea down, "Calypdon needs a ruler, beyond a general, if we ever hope to rebuild, to take back what we lost."

Aveline noticed that he was careful to say *what we lost*, instead of *what was taken*. "So, there it is. That's what you're here for, to act as the tracker of the last remnant of the king's bloodline."

"A tracker?" Morgana asked, shocked as she sat back. "Interesting."

Aveline nodded curtly. "You can do it; I know you can. You could find anyone in either kingdom."

"No, I can do it," Morgana waved her off. "It's simply that most people mean to use me as a weapon. It's a nice change of pace."

"Well," Micah said dryly. "We'll see how the search goes, and then we'll talk."

Chapter Fourteen

Aveline found Morgana's entire demeanor off putting.

It all seemed so … calm. So tired, so unattached. So unlike the Morgana that Aveline had once known. And it made sense, considering Morgana had clearly never been the person Aveline thought she was, but it still disoriented Aveline to see that body with a completely different soul inside. If Morgana even had a soul.

Aveline supposed she must. If she held a tiny morsel of every living soul, shouldn't some of that humanity have bled into her? Even a little bit? Aveline had contemplated more than once whether having a bit of everyone else's souls was enough to fuel one for herself.

"I think she does," Micah said. She'd brought up the subject as they trudged down the tower stairs, Verona having escorted Morgana back to her room. "Have a soul, I mean."

"What makes you say that?"

He gave her a half smile. "Because as much as you want to deny it, you seem to think she has a soul."

Aveline snorted, even as her heart twisted.

Not fooled, he exclaimed, "See? You don't have it in you to deny it."

Aveline sighed, murmuring, "She once said that the soul was the only part of a person that mattered, that our bodies' only purpose is to hold something more important."

"Probably true," Micah agreed. "You saw firsthand what happens to a person without a soul, when the witch took them. A soul makes a person. And she possesses bits of everyone's souls."

It made Aveline sick, to think that Morgana, to this day, had that same tight grip over her as she had on everyone else. That she would never truly be free of the witch. "Yes."

"Maybe she doesn't have her own soul," Micah decided. "Or maybe she does, but it's filled with our souls, and it gets … confused."

It was a sad thought, Aveline allowed herself to muse. That Morgana would only ever be made of others, and not of herself.

But Aveline supposed they all were made of the witch, too.

Knowing where Micha was heading, Aveline nodded. "If she has a bit of everything, I think that probably means she had the bad, too." She imagined a war waging in Morgana's chest, a battle that never quieted, of good and evil souls fighting for domination. Perhaps she truly had been good in the early days that Aveline knew her, before the bad in the world overtook everything.

"I think," Micah whispered, "with a war looming on the horizon, with people hating her and cursing her … It's a wonder the evil side of her didn't win sooner."

***

The council reconvened the next day. Morgana had demanded some time to think over what they were proposing, to decide how she felt about it, and she seemed to have landed on disbelief.

"Let me get this straight," Morgana said as she shook her head, waving her hands in front of her. "You want to find the heir, the one person holding your lands together, and you want to expose them … to me?" She stared at Micah like he must have been born yesterday. Compared to Morgana's lifespan, he might as well have been.

Micah sighed, dragging a hand down his face with a grimace. "I'll admit it's not an ideal plan."

Staring at them with incredulity, Morgana asked, almost accusatory, "How do you know I won't turn around and finish the job? That I won't bring the rest of the sea down on what little we have left?"

Aveline didn't miss the way she said *we*, but just looked at her, steady. "We don't. In the same way those people you betrayed two centuries ago didn't know then. But from what I've gathered, you went back into hiding as soon as you believed Aveline to be dead."

The witch's throat bobbed, fire guttering in her eyes. Flashing an odd look toward Aveline, Morgana turned her body away. Wary of the angry woman's depth of knowledge, she focused on Verona instead.

Aveline didn't back down. She hadn't backed down for two hundred years, intent on plunging forward until the deed was done. "You tried very hard to kill Aveline. It's clear you'll do … quite a bit to know what really happened to her. I'm sure you're quite curious what she had to say about *you*."

Though the rest of her crew ducked their heads, reminded that they were in the same room as their general's killer, Morgana kept her face impassive. It was infuriating.

Micah spoke instead, leaning forward onto his knees and weaving his fingers together in front of him. "We need to find the heir, and we have something you need, too. Something you've come out of hiding for."

Morgana didn't seem to care about Aveline at all, though. Not when she looked like Ailani. And why would she? As far as Morgana was concerned, she was a different woman with a different name, who hated her. At least Verona had offered to walk Morgana to her room the night before.

Aveline didn't have it in her to feel bad about any of it. Not when she knew what she knew, not when she had lived the life she had lived these past two centuries, before her current crew were even born.

Taking Verona's cue, Morgana leaned forward and plucked a single grape from the table, rolling it between her index finger and thumb. "That's smart, that you're considering how your actions might affect any decisions I might make. But let me ask you this." She pointed the grape at Verona. "What makes you think there's any logic to my decisions? You've all said it yourselves, I've killed thousands. There's no logic to that, is there?"

Silence filled the room.

"No," Verona said softly. "None that I can think of."

Morgana sat back. She moved so slowly and meticulously now, as if she had all the time in the world. She clearly didn't mind making mortals wait. "The question stands. Do monsters follow logic, or do they just do what they want? Because they can?"

Tossing the grape into her mouth, Morgana waited in the quiet as Aveline tried to figure out what game the witch was playing. What did she have to gain by convincing them all she was mad? Or maybe nothing stood to be gained at all, and the fact that she at some point lost her mind was all there was to it.

Verona wasn't having it. "Monster or not, you think about what you do. Whether that makes it all worse or better, it's the truth."

"Is it?" Morgana asked quietly. "There are many things your kind doesn't know about mine. That, at least, I know for certain." And Aveline might have imagined it, but she thought Morgana reached almost imperceptibly toward her phantom sword.

Verona shook her head. "It's not about your kind or mine, it's about *you*. I can see it in your eyes, the way you pause before responding, the way you're taking us all in, even now. I bet you've seen quite a bit in your years, done a lot of people-watching, and that you could tell me more about me from the hour we've spent together than I'd like."

"I can tell you a lot of things about a lot of people that you wouldn't like," Morgana said. Every word was a whisper, so everyone had to lean forward to hear.

Verona shrugged, lounging back into her chair. "I believe that all creatures have a bit of monster hiding inside them, in their own right. Humans are capable of doing horrible things just as much as witches. You just did it more efficiently."

Morgana rubbed her jaw, considered the girl across from her, before turning back to Aveline. "The blood will be thin."

Startled out of the back and forth between two of the most mysterious women Aveline had ever met, she jerked up. "What?"

"The blood of the heir," Morgana sighed. All at once, she became entirely focused. "It will have thinned out, just as the magic of their ancestors has. Much more diluted than the king I knew."

"But it's there," Micah said, squeezing his hands together. "It's the same blood."

"In theory," Castor added, poking his cheek with a pencil. Aveline had no idea what he could possibly have been taking notes about. Probably Morgana's every move. "But it will have been contaminated by the blood of each heir's spouse. The heir possesses less and less of the royal blood every time it is passed on."

Morgana nodded, sucking on a tooth. "Had you come to me a few generations earlier, I would have been able to make do, but it's been so long that my connection with him has long since faded." She waited a moment, and Aveline knew. She saw it in the way Morgana's face contorted that she was using her powers, trying to reach out in search of the lost heir. The atmosphere sizzled around them, crackling as the ancient power thrummed through Morgana's veins, branching out to everyone near her.

Castor realized, too, blurting out in awe, "Are you using magic?"

Verona chucked a grape at him, and Morgana collapsed back in her chair as she shook her head. "The blood won't work, at least not now."

"Why not?" Aveline snapped. "His blood is on your hands."

Rike shot Aveline a warning look, as if she could sense the words Aveline *really* wanted to say crawling up her throat. Seething, Aveline sat back and clamped her mouth shut.

Morgana didn't flinch at the outburst, paying her no mind as she chewed on her lip, considering. It made Aveline even more furious, the way Morgana looked right through Aveline in this new body. It shouldn't have, considering she had clearly been nothing to Morgana in her old body, either.

Morgana exhaled sharply through her nose and brushed her hair out of her face. The energy had sent some of the strands flying. "Because he has been dead for two hundred years. I am only linked to the living, if you'll recall. And it's true, I can access every soul, but the dead fade away more quickly than you might think. I lose contact the second they are gone from this world."

"You can't do it," Micah said, shoulders slumping. For years now, they'd each been held up by the hope of finding the heir. Aveline watched it slip away, piece by piece, from every single one of them. "You can't find the heir."

Morgana rolled her eyes. "I never said that." With a flourish that *really* made her look like a witch, she stood and walked around her chair, surveying the walls of the room and peering through the window. "Magic is impacted by distance and knowledge. I can feel every soul in the kingdoms but sorting them out becomes difficult when they are far from me. Echoes of energy and life linger all over, even long after a soul has passed on. Everyone and everything leaves an imprint on this world. Souls go to … wherever they go, but bodies and the things we've loved during our lives stay here, and echoes of a person's soul cling to whatever they can find."

Micah turned greener with every word. "Are you telling us that we need to find his body?"

"It would be the most helpful way of reconnecting with his soul," Morgana conceded, "but no. I will need something of his, something that has lasted all these years, something to bring me back to him. To … to bring him back to me." Her throat sounded suspiciously tight, but Morgana shook it off. "The clothes he was wearing that day would be covered in blood, or the weapon that killed him. But there's something else that's inherently linked to this kingdom, to the royal line that has been passed down for generations."

It didn't take long for them to realize what Morgana was implying.

"His crown," Rike breathed out.

Morgana snapped her fingers, turning away from the window and the fog waiting beyond it. "Yes. It has been in Wendell's family for generations. The day he was murdered, the crown was covered in King Wendell's blood. I saw it."

It took everything Aveline had to keep herself from flinging herself at the witch. She'd never known exactly how Wendell died. Had she killed him, too? Had she skewered him with that same sword, the one hidden under Aveline's bed, where it had remained for decades?

She must have. Because the thing was, most of her victims hadn't bled. She didn't inflict damage on their bodies. She took away their souls.

Castor leaned forward. "And what exactly did you see of King Wendell's death?"

Dangerous territory. Not just for Morgana, who clearly had no desire to speak of the events that had transpired two hundred years ago, but for Aveline. The facts of Wendell's murder threatened to break her. She didn't want to mourn him all over again.

Morgana's jaw twitched. "Enough to know that the sea king shattered Wendell's skull on the floor of his own throne room."

Rike sucked in a sharp breath, hands flying to her mouth.

Castor just looked intrigued. "Then you didn't kill him yourself."

Aveline found herself braced for the answer, even though it wouldn't actually make a difference. What was one life in the face of thousands?

"No," Morgana said steadily, a solid answer about that day when she'd been unwilling to give any others. "King Daegil kept that kill for himself, to secure his power over the kingdom. He thought, perhaps, the blessing would go to him, since there was no heir."

Castor huffed. "Or so he thought."

"Yes," Morgana agreed softly. "But I don't know what became of the crown. The last I saw it, it was beside Wendell in the throne room. I presume King Daegil took it as a prize."

Micah pressed his lips together. "That does seem the logical answer."

A logical answer that proved what Aveline had thought she'd seen in her drugged state. A picture of King Daegil wearing a crown that didn't belong to him, smiling as he watched Morgana kill her.

Rike sighed. "And an inconvenient one."

"Why?" Morgana asked tiredly. "Of course it would be in Nysus. That's where Daegil is."

Aveline steeled herself. "That brings me to the bad news." The bad news she'd received the day she returned from fetching Morgana.

A razor gaze ripped toward Aveline, and Morgana said, "This has all been bad news. It's been bad news for two hundred years."

"This is new bad news," Castor sighed. "Especially if we have to sneak into Thalassa."

Morgana stiffened at the first direct mention of returning to Nysus. Aveline could imagine the witch dreaded returning to the king who had abandoned her. Aveline wanted to laugh.

But she didn't, the solemn tug in her chest overwhelming everything else. "We have no way of getting into Nysus right now. No way to open a portal, and no way to survive underwater. But we could pass messages with those from Calypdon who now live in the sea. *They* could travel to Thalassa and bring back information."

Rike's eyes shut, and Aveline recognized the pain well. Other than Aveline, Rike was the only one whose lineage could trace, in a way, back to the sea. Helah had married Dorian, one of Wendell's surviving guards. Sharing blood from both people, their children, and their descendants, could breathe in either kingdom. But Rike still felt that tug, as Aveline did now, of a life that could have been. "They were discovered. A message we sent was intercepted, they…" She stopped, casting her gaze downward, throat bobbing.

Micah took over, voice quiet. "They were slaughtered. All of them. The most casualties we've had since -" They deliberately all looked away from Morgana.

It was easier for them, Aveline realized, to ignore it. To ignore Morgana's past. They hadn't seen it. This new world was all they'd ever known. But in that moment, she saw Micah's face as he remembered all that Morgana had done, all the destruction she had caused.

"A terrible tragedy," Morgana said.

"It was," Castor said harshly to Morgana, as if he didn't believe a word she said. "Before you turned up, before we knew for sure you weren't in Nysus, we thought you might have been responsible."

Unfaltering, Morgana said, "Good theory. You've thought I was with King Daegil all these years?"

"We only recently found out that he didn't grant you asylum. Otherwise, we'd have searched for you years ago. And bad news gets worse, because without a breathing artifact, we can't open a portal." Castor cleared his throat. "Which is another thing we need you for."

Morgana sighed. "I'm afraid you're out of luck. I can't open a portal to Nysus."

Aveline jabbed a finger toward Morgana's chest. "You've opened a portal before, so I *know* that's a lie."

Morgana held up a placating hand. "You're quick to make accusations, aren't you? What I *mean* is that I can't open a portal to Nysus *anymore*."

Aveline blinked. "What?"

"Several years into my exile, I tried to… Well, it's not important. I wanted to return to Nysus, but when I went to the portal in the Abandoned Forest, it didn't open. It was strange. It was as if the portal wanted to respond to me, but there was a barrier blocking me out. It felt like what I imagine iron would feel like to an ordinary Hallowed."

Gaping, Castor asked, "He blocked you out. How? Why?"

Morgana shrugged. "I don't know. As for why? Probably for his own safety."

Verona snorted. "Well, we all know your revenge isn't pretty."

Aveline leaned forward, rubbing her eyes. "So what I'm hearing is; we have no way in, and no way to survive if we *could* get it."

"Technically," Morgana said, holding up a finger, "even if he's created barriers against me, I'd be able to breathe fine once I'm in there. My connection to his people still stands."

Micah licked his lips with a sigh. "Yeah, well…"

Resigned, Morgana said dully, "But you won't let me go alone."

"We can't keep you from doing anything," Verona said with a shrug. "But, yeah, we'd prefer to keep you away from the king, should old alliances come up and cause any. … confusion."

Morgana stared down at the floor with something like dimly muted shame. "You don't have to worry about that."

Aveline would worry anyway.

Shaking away whatever feeling had come over her, Morgana straightened, patting down her cloak. They all watched her warily, searching for hidden weapons that they might have missed earlier, despite the fact that she wouldn't need anything but her mind to kill them. After a few moments, Morgana nodded and brought something out of her pocket, holding it delicately, like a valued treasure. She cupped it in her palm, pursing her lips and admiring it as she dragged her finger over the crevices. She hesitated for only a moment before holding it out. The pendant dangled on a thick string. "Will this help?"

Aveline stared. And stared and stared and stared as her heart jumped into her throat, as her mind sent her two hundred years into the past, to the moment she'd been awarded the artifact. From Morgana's slim fingers fell a seashell. *Her* seashell. The seashell that used to be a part of her, embedded into her skin, a symbol of the vow she had taken to a king when she was young and foolish.

"You still have it?" Aveline croaked before she could stop herself.

Rike shot Aveline a warning glance, but Morgana was too engrossed in the pendant to notice the outburst, watching it swing before her eyes. "It does look old, doesn't it? It belonged to a … to someone I once knew."

Aveline sat incredibly still. Each member of her council held their breath.

Morgana lifted her eyes. "I took it from her body after she died. After I pried it from her neck."

Wincing, Aveline resisted the urge to reach for the hidden scar.

"King Daegil didn't notice me take it." Morgana shook her head, letting her fingers envelope the shell once more before tossing it haphazardly toward Aveline. She caught it; the feeling of the shell's ridges hauntingly familiar. "If we can figure out how to get that on one of your necks..."

"Then we have our way in," Micah finished for her, staring at the shell. Aveline knew Micah was making the connection between the shape of the shell and the shape of the lingering scar on her neck. Aveline would have to find a way to hide the scar while Morgana put the necklace on her.

Verona smiled slowly. "How is it that you have everything?"

Morgana sighed, reaching toward her belt before forcing herself to stop. "Not everything. But you can gain as much as you lose when you live a long life." She stood, then. "Does this conclude our meeting?"

Castor flipped his journal closed. "For now. We'll have to reconvene, figure out how the hell to get that device on Ailani's body."

Morgana nodded curtly. "Good." She waited a moment, but no one moved, and eventually she sighed, tipping her head back toward the ceiling. "I'm assuming I'm not allowed to walk myself back?"

Verona moved to get up, but Aveline beat her to it, the words *someone I once knew* still echoing in the back of her mind. "You catch on quick. I'll bring you to your rooms, and someone will bring your midday meal to you."

Waving her off, Morgana headed to the door. "I figured." She glanced back at the rest of the council, who remained stiff in their seats. "It was nice to make your acquaintances. It's been a long time since I encountered people with hope."

She swept out of the room.

Aveline scrambled after her, but Morgana knew the way well, weaving through the hallways as if their stay here had been only yesterday. The council room wasn't far from Morgana's rooms, and they'd arrived before Aveline could even get a word out.

Morgana opened the door, brushing past the guards, and whirled around to face Aveline. "Am I dismissed?" she asked sarcastically.

"What did he promise you?" Aveline couldn't help but ask, leaning against the wall across from the doorway with her arms crossed. She kept thinking about her mannerisms, the parts of her that didn't die with her old body, worrying that Morgana might pick up on the similarities. Then she remembered that Morgana had never cared about her, and would never notice. "King Daegil. It must have been a pretty remarkable deal, even if he didn't follow through."

Morgana stood perfectly still in her doorway, but her fingers were clenched at her side. "The king had his ways. I could not stop him."

"Maybe you could have, if you'd tried," Aveline snapped. "You had a lot of nerve just then, speaking of hope."

"No," Morgana said, still not turning. "I couldn't have." Morgana straightened and glanced over her shoulder. "You will learn, with time, that there are so many things the people of the world don't know. So many twisted turns, and endless possibilities of betrayal and loss."

"That's a lot of talk for someone who murdered thousands."

Eyes flashing, her lids fluttered shut as she exhaled. "It is not an honorable past," Morgana said softly. "But then again, what past is?"

"Most aren't," Aveline agreed, thinking of the mistakes she'd made. "But most are not like yours. Most people do the best they can."

Morgana turned away again, disappearing into her room as the door swung shut behind her. "I did."

Chapter Fifteen

They had no idea how to attach the shell to Aveline.

"Tell us how they did it the first time," Rike said when Aveline sat down to eat with her crew in Verona's chambers, using an oversized chest as a makeshift table.

Gazing out the window to the forest beyond, boughs weighed down by fresh fallen snow, Aveline pushed her food around her plate, appetite disappearing. "There was a ceremony where they inducted some of the guards into higher positions, into the king's inner circle." The words tasted sour, knowing how much pain the sea king had caused later. "We were charged with finding a shell near the blessed land springs, following the pieces that … called to us."

Aveline had spent three days camping out by the blessed springs of air like the one she'd taken Morgana to. She searched in exhaustion for the perfect shell, for a piece of the sea that would never fail her once she braved the lands for the first time. Legends said that they needed to take a piece of the sea from the spot blessed by the goddess of the land, so the artifact would allow a sea person to reach both kingdoms. She had journeyed for miles, her legs weakening beneath her as she passed shell after shell, not feeling that tug anywhere. Other soldiers had described it to her, the pull that would come when the shell showed itself, but after two days, she had started to think it was just a myth.

But on the third day, it had hit her. She had awakened groggily to a violent wave of nausea. Squinting, she looked around, thinking she might be sick from the way her stomach was turning before she'd realized that it was not sickness at all, but rather the tug she'd been waiting for.

She had followed it, inching over the rocks, blearily searching for a piece of the sea to carry with her forever. The shell she had finally found was angular and ridged, sharp in the palm of her hand as she lifted it from its perch at the edge of a pool. She might have imagined it, but she had thought it glowed in response to her touch, rumbling its agreement that, yes, it would keep her safe.

Such artifacts were specific to one person. The artifacts didn't give them the ability to breathe air, they brought the protection of the sea onto the land. Her crew would never have been able to gain access to Nysus. Aveline knew of the weeping willow that provided artifacts for the land dwellers, but it had been swallowed by the sea.

Leaning her elbows against the table and rubbing her eyes, Aveline sighed, "I found it, after a ridiculously long time. I think it must have been just another test, to see who was willing to endure the search for days at a time."

Verona snorted into her drink. "I have a hard time picturing you devoted to his cause."

Sitting back, her hands gripping the bench, Aveline murmured. "You and me both." She shook her head. "Anyway, the shell was bonded to me from that moment, but it needed to be linked to my throat, so I could access its powers, both for opening the passages and for allowing me to breathe." She grimaced as the ghost of smooth fingers slipped over her collarbones. "The king did that."

"How?" Micah asked intently.

Aveline shrugged helplessly. "I always thought it was some sort of magic inherent to the blessed land springs, to the place I found the shell. That's where the ritual was performed after I found it. It could have been that, but it could have been *his own* blessing that gave him the ability. All I know is they strung the shell onto a necklace, tied it around my neck, and the sea king pressed it into my throat. There was a bright flash, a sort of golden light, and a whole lot of pain. When it went away the shell was … a part of me."

She would always curse herself for going along with everything so easily, for not questioning *anything*. Maybe if she had, she'd have more answers. Or maybe she'd have gotten herself kicked out, and she'd be mercifully dead by now.

"It's extraordinary how unhelpful that is," Verona pointed out. Also unhelpfully.

"I suppose it's too convenient to think you just need to hold it to open the passage?" Castor grumbled.

"Nothing is convenient," Micah said around a piece of chicken. "Except for the fact that our witch doesn't know about the link between the shell and Aveline here. Hopefully she'll just think we could attach it to any old land person."

"But what she *won't* know," Rike interrupted, "is how Aveline can breathe in the water. The shell grants sea folk access to the land, not the other way around, remember?"

Aveline stared at her last living relative. Damn. She felt an extreme headache coming on.

Micah braced his hands against the table. "Right, so this is what we know: we've spent the past several years operating under the assumption that Morgana was on the other side, and that we wouldn't have to hide Aveline's blessing."

"Maybe we don't?" Rike suggested. "Just because Aveline has been blessed doesn't mean she's … who she actually is. It probably wouldn't even occur to Morgana."

But Aveline was already shaking her head. "Blessings occur in crucial junctures of history, they don't just … happen. As soon as Morgana finds out I'm Hallowed, she'll put it together, especially considering how much we seem to know about 'Aveline.' At the very least, she'll know I'm from the time of King Daegil's attack. She's not a stupid person."

"She's not a person at all."

"My point still stands."

"Anyway," Micah continued, "we'd hoped that we'd be able to bring any sort of fight here. The last thing we wanted was to have to fight him in his territory, even if we *did* find ways to gain access. We still want that; she just needs to get into Nysus long enough to get the crown."

She. "I'm not risking sending Morgana into our enemy's hands on her own. Not because I'm concerned for her safety, but for everyone else's. For every living person in Calypdon who survived her first slaughter. I won't let it happen again. She *won't* go without me." She pushed away the panic growing in her throat, clenching her fists.

Castor jerked up from where he'd been fiddling with his fork. He was a small man, easily forgettable when he didn't make himself known. But when he did, he rose high enough that he could not be ignored, and they all turned to him. "Maybe she won't have to."

"Did you not hear me? It's not even an *option* -"

Flicking his fork to signal he had more to say, he waved his hand. "I was just being dramatic for effect. I know she won't have to."

Micah raised his brow.

Slowly, Castor turned to Rike with a feral grin. "Little Water Sprite, I have an idea."

Water Sprite. They'd taken to calling her that when she'd revealed herself to be a descendant of the sea. As far as they were concerned, Aveline didn't count. The body she was in had only ever lived in Calypdon.

Rike was so unsettled by Castor's smile that she didn't even have the mind to correct him on the nickname she hated.

***

"Is there anything else that you could possibly use to track the heir?"

Morgana was disheveled when she opened her door that night, hair mussed from her pillow. There wasn't much to do in her room besides lie on the bed.

They'd spent hours going over the logistics of Castor's plan, which involved a lot of yelling on Aveline's part and even more soothing on Rike's. Micah had grudgingly agreed to the plan, despite the fact that it hardly involved him and he liked to be in on the action. Verona had ended up stalking out halfway through the argument, telling them to come get her when they'd settled down and had a job for her.

Aveline had to admit that Castor's plan wasn't a *bad* plan. At least, not objectively. But Aveline had a hard time being objective when it came to Rike, just as she had with Rike's mother, and her mother's father, and so on. All the way back to Helah, who had died over a hundred and fifty years ago.

The witch blinked at her now, a blanket wrapped around her shoulders. "Do you even know how to say hello?"

Aveline paused, surprised enough by Morgana's question that she said, "Hello. Is there anything else you could use to track the heir?"

Morgana stepped back, allowing her in. "It's possible. If we were to find something else with a strong connection to the bloodline, or, like I said, his bones, then maybe. But I can't be sure when it comes to dead people. They're not my domain."

Aveline remembered the story Morgana had told her, of the theory of how the Serpent Witch's powers came to be: a curse from the god of the dead. When people lost their lives, they left Morgana's control and went to him.

"Can we at least try?" Aveline said, ashamed to be pleading with the witch; at the way that even after all this time, she still needed her.

Morgana stared at her, gnawing at her lip before dropping the blanket. She was wearing a thin tunic and tight pants, her hair braided down her back. Two hundred years later, and she looked the same as she had at twenty-two. "I will, if you tell me one thing."

Aveline knew better than to make any promises, than to make any more deals with witches than she had to. Then she already had. "That depends on what it is."

Morgana leaned against the wall next to a pile of discarded clothes Verona had provided her. Morgana had thrown them onto the floor where the dresser had once sat. It was a small pile since Morgana had brought nothing with her. Nothing, aside from Aveline's shell pendant. "Why aren't you afraid of me? Why are you so confident I won't hurt you? And most importantly, why are you putting any sort of trust in me after all you think I've done?"

Those were loaded questions, and all Aveline could think to say was, "That was three questions."

Morgana rolled her eyes. "Fine, then answer one of them. I'll even let you choose."

Aveline avoided looking at those mismatched green and yellow eyes and instead focused on a strand of hair that had slipped free from her braid and brushed over her cheek. "I'm not afraid of you because I've already lost everything," she said honestly, hating the raw tone of her voice. The pain of decades before somehow still lingered, still surprised her. "There's nothing left for you to take from me."

Pressing her lips together, Morgana nodded. She didn't look angry, or vengeful, but only resigned. She jerked her chin toward the door. "Lead the way, then. We'll see what we can find."

There was only one place a replacement for the crown might be found, and even then, it was unlikely.

Wendell's quarters were much the same as they'd been when the king was alive, and yet the room felt wrong. Darker, somehow, less loved, even with the people living in it. They had done what they could when they had restored the palace, using Aveline's memory to guide their way, but they could only do so much after decades of neglect. The carefully carved furniture had been ruined with age, replaced by whatever makeshift fixtures she could find. She had spent a lot of time in these chambers during her first few weeks in the palace. She stared at the room now, still struck by how empty it felt without Wendell.

"Do you often bring strangers to your room?" Aveline had asked when King Wendell welcomed her inside for the first time, gathering a pot of tea and cups from the table in the corner.

He'd poured her a steaming cup, and it had warmed her hands when he'd handed it to her. "Only when they refuse to go to their own room." He picked up his own mug, raising an eyebrow meaningfully.

Affronted, Aveline had said, "I'm just concerned for her. I won't have her dying on someone else's watch."

"And I'm concerned for you," Wendell had said. "Our dear Morgana will be of no help to me, or you, if she wakes to find you dead from sleep deprivation. I imagine that would indeed end horribly for everyone involved."

Aveline's eyes had drooped at the mention of sleep. "It's off putting, you know, for you to be so casual. So … welcoming."

Wendell had grinned. "It's also what makes it bearable to be around me. Tell me, would you ever have followed your king to his quarters? Willingly," he added after Aveline hesitatingly opened her mouth.

"Not a chance," she'd realized. But she always assumed kings were meant to be feared.

Aveline shook the memory away, feeling so small in the large suite, trying to imagine the new heir in these still familiar chambers.

Aveline turned to Morgana. "Walk around, there's a few rooms branching off of this one. Do you … I don't know, feel anything lingering?"

Morgana didn't answer for several long moments, so long that Aveline turned to make sure she hadn't simply walked away. But Morgana was there, staring around at the room as if she'd seen a ghost. Her different colored eyes were wide, her fingers lifting to brush against her lips, and all at once, she looked young again.

Aveline's gaze went cold. "You aren't allowed to mourn him."

Reeling her expression in, Morgana came further into the room. She moved around, brushing her fingers along each piece of furniture. "Most of these are replacements," she noticed immediately, sniffing around the room. Not for the first time, Aveline wondered exactly how Morgana's power worked, what it felt like. If it was overwhelming, if she drowned in it.

Folding her arms, Aveline nodded. "They are. But see if you find yourself drawn to *anything*. We've had to work to maintain the palace after so many years, but you and King Daegil didn't destroy it that day. You may have killed everyone in the city, but you left the palace intact."

Morgana hummed. "I find arson melodramatic."

"You didn't destroy the palace because you didn't need to," Aveline corrected bitterly. "We only replaced things because they'd been … worn, from years of abandonment."

Morgana poked her head into another room, one that Aveline knew to be a large sitting room that housed several families. The witch shook her head and shut the door. "Why did it take so long for Calypdon's people to rise up again?"

Aveline followed Morgana's movement closely, picking up on every reaction. "Morale was low, for … a very long time. For generations, the people remained scattered and unwilling to come out of the shadows. Only when those alive during the event had all died did we stand a chance to truly rebuild. That's when the people started moving to Briarwood in droves. From what I hear," Aveline added, hopefully not too quickly.

"I wouldn't know," Morgana said, low and under her breath. "I was hiding by the wall of water in those days. I didn't see another human for … at least ninety years."

Because they might have recognized her.

"Consider it a blessing," Aveline murmured. "That you didn't have to see the aftermath." Aveline had seen it all, had lived it. Had hid like the rest of them for far too long with only Helah at her side. She hadn't known how to step past the threshold in a world where water might come crashing down at any moment.

Morgana's back went rigid where she'd stood by the bed, smoothing down the rumpled sheets and blankets. "I didn't need to see it," Morgana whispered. "I felt it."

"You did?"

"Every second." Morgana's throat bobbed as she swallowed, licking her lips. "I feel it even now, the grief. I feel it in you."

I'm sure you do.

Morgana looked around, blinking. "Worse in here, I think."

"He was a good man," Aveline said with a trembling lip, gazing into the corner as if Wendell might appear, might take her hand and bring her back in time with him. "He was an even better king."

A muscle trembled in the witch's jaw, and she circled around to the door to look at the room again as a whole. "I agree."

Aveline felt Morgana's shoulder brush against hers as the witch walked past, and the contact sent every muscle and nerve on high alert. She wouldn't return to this room anytime soon. "I hope you suffer for the turmoil you caused. You did this to us."

Several long moments passed, and Aveline felt Morgana's presence like a second skin. As if their souls had knitted into one, two hundred years ago. Try as Aveline might, she hadn't quite shaken herself free. Hadn't successfully sliced through every stitch.

"I did," Morgana finally whispered, and before Aveline could grapple with what she'd seen, before she could even insist on accompanying her or sending guards, Morgana disappeared into the hallway.

Chapter Sixteen

"And what makes you think I can even do this?"

For the first time since arriving with Morgana, Aveline and her crew took the witch out into the forests that weaved through Briarwood, shielded by the tall trees towering over even the highest of buildings. Though it was technically a city, nature infiltrated every spare inch between the lingering signs of civilizations, remnants of the blessing bestowed upon Calypdon millennia ago. Flowers burst up between the cobblestones, vines wrapping around every surface they could reach. Trees grew out of the walls of every house, many acting as support beams, branches holding up the roof.

Winter had settled heavier over the kingdom in the past week, but even through the dusting of snow, hints of greenery awaited around every turn, branches and pine trees reminding her that life would come back with the warmth. Aveline leaned against a bare tree, in a clearing about a mile from the palace. The sun streamed through the roiling water above her, the golden yellow melting into the blue of the waves. They figured it would be better to get Morgana's magic away from the people settled there, in case of any … unforeseen reactions.

Morgana's magic was odd enough as it was, and they had no way to know what would happen if she attempted something beyond her usual abilities. Especially since, according to the witch, she had used her powers as little as possible in the past two hundred years.

Castor surveyed Morgana, then the pendant Aveline had just shoved into her fingers. "According to what we've heard about the ceremony where the sea soldiers were bonded with their shells, it's the sea king that melds them together."

Rike shivered. "You make it sound so creepy."

Unperturbed, Castor said, "That's because it is. Regardless, it's probably safe to assume he drew magic from the sea in order to do it."

Morgana folded her arms. Despite the cold, she wore a light, simple dress embroidered with dark green flowers. "Unfortunately for you, I haven't been blessed by anything."

Verona snorted. "No, you definitely haven't."

"Regardless," Castor spoke over her with a glare, "you have an intense connection with the people of the sea, including Daegil himself. If you can draw from his life, it can be assumed you can draw from his power."

"I don't know if you realize this," Morgana said, looking around at them all as if they were ants, "but I've done very little experimentation with my powers, beyond what I know I can do. They're strong, yes, but I don't know if I can hone them down to one specific thing like that."

"And I don't know if *you* realize *this*," Aveline said, "but yours is the only magic we've got."

Well. The only magic left to try. Aveline had already tried in vain to attach the shell to herself, to use whatever powers the goddess of war's blessing had granted her, but unsuccessfully. Probably because her magic had no link to the sea. Her power gave her long life, and an advantage in battle, but those gifts were nothing to what Morgana possessed. Morgana held all the souls of two kingdoms in her cold heart.

Morgana gripped the necklace tighter, so hard the shape would probably leave an imprint on her palm. "I will try, on one condition."

Aveline rolled her eyes. "What is it?"

Morgana's mouth set into a thin line. "You have to give it back to me. When you're done with it."

Anger flared in Aveline's chest. On *what grounds*? That shell was hers. It had always been hers, and Morgana had *stolen it* after Morgana had brutally taken it from her dead body. "That's not how this is going to work."

"It is not yours to keep."

Rike slapped a hand over her mouth, and Castor nudged her.

Every muscle in Aveline's body twitched, but how was she supposed to explain that it *was* hers? Through clenched teeth, she said, "I will do what I can, but I make no promises."

Morgana considered her for a few moments, eyes narrowed, before eventually nodding curtly and stalking forward. "Okay, then. Walk me through it."

Letting the necklace unfurl, Morgana secured the string around Aveline's neck, making sure to center it in the hollow of her throat, over the powder she'd applied to hide the scar. Aveline sighed at the familiar weight, at the pressure she'd grown used to missing. Her fingers drifted up to the shell, pressing it into her skin, but nothing happened.

Morgana glanced at Verona, who seemed to be the one she hated the least. She'd brought a thick blanket out on their excursion and laid out a few feet away, craning her neck to look up when Morgana addressed her. "What now?"

Verona shrugged as best she could lying on her back. "Push it in?"

Castor waited inches away, looking like he would press right up against Morgana to get a closer look if he could. His eyes narrowed in concentration, searching for any signs of magic.

Micah rolled his eyes, grabbing him by the collar of the shirt and tugging him back as he addressed the witch. "Draw whatever you can from the sea. You must still have quite the connection with the sea king."

Morgana's eyes darkened. "You have no idea."

"We have a little bit of an idea," Verona murmured.

Micah, ever the peacemaker, pinched the bridge of his nose and held out a silencing hand. "He's below us, probably closer than you think. Find that connection with him and drag it up here. Or … something like that." He looked questioningly at Rike, who let her head fall back in exasperation.

Morgana ignored them all, and Aveline felt her train her eyes on her chest. Aveline resisted the urge to recoil under the intensity of the gaze, trying not to think too hard about all the other times Morgana had stared at her. How many of Morgana's actions had been an act?

Or worse, if Aveline let herself consider that it hadn't been an act, then … what had happened?

"Stop moving," Morgana murmured, close enough that her breath caressed Aveline's neck.

Aveline clenched her teeth. "Your proximity is unsettling."

"If it makes you feel better," Micah offered, leaning against a tree and hooking one ankle over the other, "she could kill you just as easily from across the clearing as she could touching you."

Glaring, Aveline squeezed her hands into fists.

Morgana flicked her gaze up briefly before returning to her work. "He's right."

The clearing fell into silence. Aveline could do nothing but stare up at the trees above, squinting at the sun filtering through the branches. Blotches of gold scattered over her friends' faces and made the coat of snow on the ground glisten. Admittedly, she still felt a bit odd calling them her friends, considering she was two hundred years older than them, but they'd fallen into a comfortable enough rhythm. Even after she'd told them the truth of her past, they hadn't fled from her, hadn't started avoiding her gaze, hadn't trusted her any less.

"I knew you were too wise to be twenty-three," had been Verona's exact words after listening to Aveline's long winded story. "I need whatever you have. Your skin looks great."

"Don't feel bad," Micah had said at another point, when Aveline couldn't find the right thing to wear to a meeting. "You don't look a day over two hundred and seven."

Castor had just asked for a blood sample. She'd said no.

None of this was enough to distract Aveline from the green head bending over her, poking and prodding her neck, grunting with the effort of trying to use unfamiliar magic. Rike gave her a halfhearted thumbs up, but as more time passed, her shoulders steadily deflated.

Morgana snatched the pendant back, squeezing it so hard Aveline feared the shell would slice into the witch's skin. "It's not working. Nothing's happening."

"Well spotted," Castor said dryly, sitting back and tugging his cloak closer. His nose had turned a bright red from the cold.

Aveline sighed, rubbing at the raw spot where Morgana had pressed the shell. "What were you doing? Could you feel the king?"

"I can always feel the king," Morgana snapped. "It's constant in a way that no other connection is, like he's … here."

The hairs rose on the back of Aveline's neck. "But he's not … right?"

Morgana shook her head. "No, he's below. I can feel him there, but I feel him here, too. Like a part of him ingrained himself into Calypdon's dirt on that day."

"And which part are you drawing from," Castor asked suddenly..

Morgana shrugged. "Whatever's closest."

"Don't, then," Castor advised. "Go to where he really is, not to … whatever bond you made with him two hundred years ago." He shivered at the thought and looked away. Aveline didn't blame him, not liking to think too hard about that bond, either.

Gritting her teeth, Morgana placed the shell back against Aveline's neck. She gave one last push, digging the fingers of her free hand into Aveline's shoulder for leverage.

The effect was instantaneous.

Morgana's power had never come slow, at least not in the few times Aveline had seen it firsthand. It had burst out of her, as though the witch spent most of her time struggling to keep it contained and was finally allowed to set it free. The magic burst forth from Morgana's skin in a blinding blue light, illuminating the trees and bathing the forest with an icy blaze. Aveline flung her arms up, shielding her eyes, but the light only glowed brighter, distracting enough that she almost didn't feel the faint burning on her neck or the press of Morgana's fingers.

Head spinning, Aveline squeezed her eyes shut as the magic filled her veins. It inched beneath her skin, spreading from the shell and encompassing her entire body. She didn't remember it being this intense the first time, just painful. Aveline swayed on her feet, only remaining standing because of Morgana's iron grip.

Forcing her eyes open, Aveline looked down to see Morgana, breath catching in her throat. Green hair flew around her as she grimaced, chest rising and falling as she put everything she had into Aveline. The light grew brighter between them, almost masking Morgana's face, but her yellow eye glowed, mingling with the blue luminescence of the shell until the illumination on her cheek turned green. Aveline could still see the lines of concentration on her forehead, the dimple on the left side of her mouth as she frowned. The magic enveloped them in a ball, caging them in, and Aveline could see nothing else, could feel nothing but Morgana's soul and her own.

It stopped just as quickly, as Morgana closed her eyes and drew the magic she had unleashed back into herself. Aveline tried to catch her breath, but it was as if Morgana was taking the air as well as the magic. Worried that the shell had reacted poorly to being joined with the body of a land dweller,

Aveline lifted her hands to her throat in a panic, but then the air came rushing in, her Hallowed body not letting her down.

The light winked out, and Morgana swayed slightly. gripping Aveline even harder to remain upright. Aveline fought against the instinct to reach out, to steady her. Silence filled the clearing, and Aveline looked over Morgana's slumped shoulders to see four awed faces. Rike looked slightly terrified, and Castor appeared moments away from losing consciousness, leaning on Micah with his hand to his mouth.

"I wish I was a witch," Verona finally moaned.

Morgana cast a pained look up to the sky, as though whatever god had cursed her might finally grant her mercy. Nothing happened, and her mouth twisted as she turned away.

Aveline peered down at her neck in exhaustion. "I was almost hoping you wouldn't be able to do it."

Morgana gaped at her, her hand dropping to her side, the glowing fingertips slowly fading.

Sighing, Aveline motioned for the others to follow her. "Then, at least there would have been limitations to your powers. It would have been reassuring. A huge issue for us, given the circumstances, but reassuring."

A strange, convoluted look passed over Morgana's face before she shrugged, trudging back toward the palace. "If you ever find the limitations, let me know."

***

Later in the tower room, Morgana agreed to the plan with a drone in her voice. She listened to Aveline speak but didn't look at her, focused on a far-off point in the room. She would go with Rike into Nysus, and as far as the witch knew, no one else would be accompanying them. Morgana then stood abruptly from the table, shoving her chair back, and glided from the room. Micah sent a pair of guards after her.

Aveline stared as the witch left, fists clenched, because it was so hard to conceal this level of hatred. To hold back how much she had wanted to scream and shout and spill her guts like Morgana had spilled Aveline's. This hatred, this need for revenge, had become a part of her, embedded in her soul when she was reforged into a new body.

"You look angry."

Aveline glared at Micah, who immediately held his hands up in mock innocence. "I'm just saying," he went on. "Maybe you'd find this whole ordeal easier to survive if you told her."

Aveline didn't bother responding. The moment Morgana found out who Aveline really was, Aveline wouldn't survive to find the ordeal easier.

Pushing away from her chair, she stalked to the fireplace, leaning down to adjust the wood and sending sparks flying up the chimney. She waved them away and kept staring at the flames until her eyes watered with the burning, if just for something to do. If just for something else to hurt her, something new besides the dull pain she'd lived with for two centuries.

"You'll kill her as soon as we're done with her." Rike's voice drifted across the room, soft and understanding, and a little bit lethal, too. "Won't you?"

Aveline didn't turn around, just kept staring and staring, so hard her eyes began to burn and water. "Yes. And I'll do it slowly."

"I still don't understand why you have to go into Nysus in secret," Micah said, blessedly changing the subject. "Why can't you just go in with Morgana and Rike?" He motioned to her neck. "You have the shell."

Aveline tapped the artifact on her neck. "This shell is not meant to allow a land dweller to breathe in the sea. It is meant for those from Nysus, but it carries the blessing of the land. That's why we had to hunt for the relic at the blessing air springs; it is the god of the earth that permits us access to his domain."

"But it's a breathing relic," Micah argued.

"It only allows sea people to breathe on land. King Wendell had a piece of bark from a blessed willow tree embedded in *his* throat; that was how he breathed in Nysus. And that's what an ordinary land dweller would need in order to survive beneath the sea."

"And Morgana knows that," Castor added.

"Right. The shell, at this point, is only acting as a means to open the portal. I'll be able to breathe in Nysus not because of my relic, but because a part of me is from the sea; the same reason as Rike. But the witch can't know that."

A crash sounded from the hallway, and Aveline spun up, hand flying to the knife sheathed at her waist. Her crew jumped to attention, Castor moving behind Micah, Verona rolling off the couch and letting twin blades drop from her sleeves. Footsteps echoed, coming rapidly closer, and Aveline drew her blade too. Her heart pounded at the thought of an attack, the first attack on the palace in two hundred years -

Morgana burst through the door, more light spilling in from the hallway, framing her and setting her curls ablaze. The sight did nothing to calm Aveline down as the witch marched into the room, whipping her head wildly around, her fingers flexing at her side.

"Calm down," Verona said instinctively, now holding her knives together in one hand and holding her free hand out to Morgana. "Whatever you're thinking of doing, I promise you, you don't want to do it."

Morgana ignored her. "I knew I recognized you," she said breathlessly, chest heaving, voice rough around the edges.

Aveline went rigid, as did the rest of her crew, as her hand slackened around the hilt of her knife. How had Morgana recognized her? What had she done wrong? Could Morgana *feel* that Aveline wasn't who she said she was?

But Morgana's eyes were not on Aveline. She was looking at the opposite end of the room, to the only woman who didn't have a weapon on her, backed up against the wall.

Her eyes were on Rike.

They hadn't thought about this, hadn't even considered the possibility that Morgana would recognize the great, great, great granddaughter of a woman she'd only spent a handful of days with. Rike's eyes widened, hands lifting as if to profess her innocence.

Morgana didn't give her a chance to say anything, slamming the door shut behind her and approaching, head tilted as she took in every detail of Aveline's distant niece. Morgana probably hadn't given Rike much thought these last few days. She had stayed quiet most of the time, inclined to let Micah or Verona do most of the talking. It would have been easy for Morgana to overlook her.

Until Rike had become the center of their entire course of action.

Morgana stuttered. "I never … I thought you were born of the land -"

"I was," Rike said, voice wavering, still pressed into the shelf behind her. She glanced at Aveline, but she was at a loss for words, mouth gone completely dry. "My ancestor's connection to the sea was from long ago, I don't see how you -"

"Long ago," Morgana said faintly. "I think you mean two hundred years ago?"

Rike swallowed. It was answer enough, though she tried to play it off. "What are you talking about?"

Morgana lifted her hands to her hair, tugging at the roots in distress, chaos churning behind her eyes. "He let her live. I never knew for sure."

Aveline exploded, "*He*?"

Morgana kept looking around, like she might find the answers hidden in the crevices of the room. "You … you're descended from Helah -"

Fire exploded in Aveline's veins, making her vision go white, and before she could stop herself, she grabbed a handful of Morgana's shirt in one tight fist and shoved the witch roughly against the wall. Morgana was surprised enough that she didn't fight back, staring with an open mouth at Aveline's furious face.

"Don't say her name," Aveline spat, their faces close enough to brush noses, Morgana's ragged breathing hot against Aveline's neck.

Wendell, Helah, and everyone the witch had killed. She didn't deserve to even think about them, let alone say their names as delicately as she'd said Helah's.

Morgana craned her neck, still trying to look at Rike. "You are, though. I know I'm right; you have the same exact eyes."

Aveline's fury guttered. She used to have those eyes, and had to stop herself from blinking too fast, her new eyes suddenly uncomfortable in her skull.

Rike drew herself up, eyes squeezing closed. "Yes. Helah was my great-great-grandmother."

Looking back at Aveline, at the way her mouth contorted, Morgana's brows furrowed. "And what do you know of Hel—" Aveline's harsh glare was enough to cut Morgana's sentence off. "And what do you know of her? Why should you care?"

"I told you," Aveline explained with a shaking voice, her closing throat threatening to betray her. "I've heard many, many stories. That's all we've had for hundreds of years. Rike has told me enough of her great-great-great-grandmother that I know you're not worthy of even remembering her."

Morgana's nostrils flared as she exhaled sharply. "I remember enough."

Shoving Morgana away, Aveline turned to Rike, still frozen where she stood. Verona's knives had disappeared, but she eased herself in front of Rike, gaze icy and guarded as Morgana straightened.

"I never knew she'd survived," Morgana said, staring at Rike, and Aveline wondered if the witch saw her there, too. If, had Aveline's eyes not changed along with the rest of her body, Morgana would have made that connection as well.

"She did," Rike said, bowing her head. "Though of course, I never knew her."

Morgana dragged a hand down her face, and Aveline's breathing stilled as Morgana stalked toward Rike.

"Careful," Verona warned.

Morgana shoved past her, but didn't touch Rike. Stiffening, Rike looked around for some sort of escape but found none. Morgana did the last thing Aveline would have expected.

She bowed.

She didn't drop to the floor, didn't fall to her knees, but the dip of her waist was indication enough. Morgana bowed her head forward, hand pressed over her heart and stared at the floor.

"Your ancestor did more for me than you could ever know," Morgana said to Rike's feet. "More than even she knew. Since I could never thank her, I'll thank you in her stead."

Rike stared in awe, unsure of what to do as her eyes flickered from the witch before her to Aveline across the room. Verona gaped.

The sound wrenched Morgana out of her stupor, and she jerked up, gazing once more at Rike. She swallowed, nodded, and turned away.

Aveline wanted to tackle her again, wanted to demand an explanation, but there was no way to ask without appearing suspicious. No way to release the turmoil constantly growing in her gut without exposing herself.

In reality, she couldn't bring herself to ask the question for fear of getting an honest answer. She didn't want to think that it was possible that Helah had helped Morgana in any way. That her sister had betrayed her, too.

Morgana swiped a hand over her cheek. It almost looked like she was wiping away a tear. She looked at Aveline's neck, at the shell she'd stared at for the entirety of their meeting. It unnerved her, how this Morgana stared at her necklace instead of at her. Morgana motioned to Rike. "If she's descended from the sea, why didn't we put the pendant on her?"

A good question.

"I didn't want to risk it," Aveline said quickly. "In case it went wrong, I'd rather put myself in harm's way."

"Leaders are like that," Verona said dryly, but Aveline could tell this was the most worried she'd been since Morgana arrived. "The self-sacrificing types."

Morgana swallowed again, jaw setting. "This is how you know what happened to Aveline, then? Because you have her great, great niece, or whatever she is?"

Sure. Aveline could run with that.

Morgana's gaze flew around the room, narrowing in confusion. "Tell me what happened," Morgana growled, this time at Aveline. "Tell me *now*."

Aveline had always wondered what it meant that Morgana had spared Helah and not herself. Helah had tried her best to relay the story of that day, of seeing Morgana in the throne room with the sea king, but she had been as heavily influenced by the poison as Aveline at that point, and remembered almost nothing. Nothing but Morgana kneeling in front of her briefly, shoving her aside, and then walking away.

"No," Rike snapped back, her stare cold as ice. "We had a deal, and you've yet to fulfill your end."

Morgana huffed out a humorless laugh, looking away. "Your great aunt would know all about not fulfilling one's end of the deal. I learned from the best."

And then she left, slamming the door behind her. The rest of the council stared at each other, once again trying to figure out what in the world they had missed, and what was possibly going on in the witch's head.

Chapter Seventeen

Morgana didn't grace the council with her presence again, informing them that she would be ready when the time came, but to otherwise leave her alone.

"I agreed to find your heir," she'd said. "I never agreed to be your ally."

Aveline had responded, "I don't recall ever asking for an alliance."

Aveline hadn't seen her since, avoiding Morgana's wing of the palace. Aveline had left her a note the night before they were set to go to Nysus, telling her to come to the armory at midnight. Aveline didn't worry about Morgana running off, she'd had plenty of chances in the past week and hadn't taken them.

"Are you going to let me go in armed?" Morgana asked upon stalking into the armory, scanning over the racks and tables with a slight slump to her shoulder.

"Is that a real question?" Aveline asked. She motioned to the witch. "You don't even need to be here right now, your entire being is a weapon."

Running her fingers along the blade of a sword, Morgana's mouth twisted. She picked up the sword, testing the weight in her hand. "I'm aware of that, which is why I prefer to use weapons when I can. I feel better about fighting someone when we're both using the same tactics."

Aveline remembered Morgana's fight with Joao in the hall of the sea palace, fighting only with her sword and completely ignoring the powers that could have knocked him clean on his back until she had been given no choice. It was a moment that heightened her confusion over Morgana's betrayal even more.

She tugged her cloak tighter around herself, the better to hide her weapons. Though she'd left Morgana's Serpent Sword behind, not wanting to chance Morgana seeing it, Aveline thought it would be best to hide that she was armed. She wasn't supposed to be a part of any fight that might take place in Thalassa. She wasn't even supposed to be there; Morgana had no reason to think Aveline could survive in Nysus, so she would have to go in secretly. "I didn't think witches were concerned with whether a fight was fair."

Morgana tossed the heavy blade aside, choosing a lighter one. The silver blade glittered in the candlelight, the hilt carefully carved with swirls and shapes, but Aveline couldn't tell what they were from this distance. Aveline knew why Morgana drifted toward that one. It looked extraordinarily similar to the Serpent Sword.

She felt oddly powerful, now that she possessed both the sword and the shell. Before, even though Aveline hadn't realized it until recently, it was like they'd switched roles, switched prized possessions. Aveline relished having the two things Morgana seemed to want most.

"I'm not actually a witch, so that might explain it." She leveled the sword out, pointing to the wall, testing it with a sharp swing. Aveline wondered what Morgana had practiced with all these years, in the absence of her beloved sword. If she'd bothered practicing at all. "The Serpent Witch is merely a name people took to calling my family … to explain something different than them. They didn't want to call us monsters outright; in case the day came when they needed us. And they couldn't just call us some of the Hallowed, even though that's what we technically are, for nothing about our existence is a blessing."

She strapped a sheath to her side, shoving the sword in, and turned to Aveline. "It makes you feel better, doesn't it? To think that you're working with a witch instead of a monster."

It did, Aveline admitted inwardly. *The first time.*

Before Aveline could respond, Rike rushed into the weapons room, followed by Verona. Rike had dressed in one of Helah's old guard uniforms, refurbished by Castor who was surprisingly handy with a needle. A knife was strapped to her thigh; Rike preferred a bow and arrow, but those would be useless in the water.

"Sorry I'm late," Rike breathed, halfway through braiding her dark hair back. "I barely slept."

"Knowing you're walking into certain death will do that to you," Verona said, leaning against the doorframe. At the flippant comment, Aveline resisted the urge to throw multiple knives at her.

Tying her braid off and letting it flop over her shoulder, Rike rubbed her eyes. "Hilarious, Verona. Must be easy to joke when you're staying nice and safe here in Calypdon."

"I'm pretty sure we could all die at any time if that wall of water decides to fall, so there's no such thing as safe, is there?" Verona paused. "Ironically, you're the only one who *might* survive if that wall comes down."

Rike, Morgana, and Aveline. They would be the only land dwellers who could survive a kingdom made of only water.

Aveline took care of avoiding Morgana's gaze. The witch was wearing another of the old Nysus uniforms. The pieces didn't fit quite as nicely as they did Rike, but they did the job. Helah and two of the other guards they had rescued had been wearing their uniforms that day, and Aveline had preserved them, figuring they might prove useful someday. She had almost discarded them on several occasions over the past two centuries, convinced their presence was causing her more pain than they were worth.

Rike and Verona were still bickering, and they drew Aveline back into the conversation when Rike stuck her elbow into Aveline's ribs.

"Can you make her leave?" Rike asked, seriously.

"She's just doing her job," Micah said as he came in, wrapped in a large cloak big enough to serve as a blanket. Castor was nowhere to be found, off securing a hiding place for Aveline.

"Verona has a job?" Rike asked, deadpan.

"Sure," Micah said, hopping up to sit on one of the tables, somehow managing not to stab himself with the weapons littering the surface. "She considers the worst-case scenario, and then lets everyone else figure a way out of it."

Verona leaned against the back wall. "It's my great talent."

"It won't be a problem." Aveline said, deciding it would be best to just ignore them entirely, sweeping across the room to take Rike's hand. "First, it won't come to the worst-case scenario, so there's that. Second, even if it does, we'll yank you both back before you can drown."

"Totally reassuring," Rike said miserably, shoving her feet into the fighting boots that had been tucked under her arm when she came in.

Morgana rolled her eyes, folding her arms across her chest. "This whole ordeal could be avoided if you would just send me alone. I'd be far less likely to get caught that way."

"You wouldn't get caught because you'd run straight to the king," Rike snapped. She'd been far less patient with Morgana since the witch found out about Helah. Morgana didn't deserve the kindness of Rike's ancestor, and Aveline agreed.

Morgana didn't fight back against Rike's outburst. Tapping her fingers against her sword, she just shrugged. "It was worth a shot."

"I'm a little surprised you're not putting up more of a fight," Micah said, narrowing his eyes.

"Oh, don't start again," Morgana sighed. "It's suspicious if I fight, and now it's suspicious if I don't?"

"Witches are inherently suspicious," Verona pointed out helpfully.

Morgana huffed, marching toward the door. "I'd rather get this over with, wouldn't you?"

Morgana had no problem leading the way. She remembered where the portal was from when she had followed Aveline and Wendell all those years ago, suspicious - not concerned, Aveline carefully reminded herself - after they hadn't come back on time. She wove through the trees, path lit by a lantern she carried to guide the way. Aveline reviewed what they knew in her head as she walked, holding Rike's hand.

First? King Daegil had taken Wendell's crown two hundred years ago. It had taken a while to convince Morgana that they knew for certain it would be in Thalassa. It became easier once Morgana recognized who Rike really was, telling Morgana that Helah had seen the king wearing the crown to mock Wendell, wearing the crown so as to mock King Wendell.

Second, the sea king likely had the crown displayed as a prize. It was nothing but a piece of frivolous jewelry to him, and a reminder that after so long, he had finally won. Aveline figured it would be in the palace, perhaps in the throne room or in the ballroom. Regardless, it would be in a place people would be able to see it.

There wasn't a third point, because they didn't even need to *steal* it. They just needed to find it so Morgana could touch it long enough to pick up a trace of the heir.

"Do you think we're rushing into this?" Micah murmured in Aveline's ear, nerves grating on his vocal cords.

"Yes," Aveline breathed back. But they didn't have a choice. The more the water closed in around them, the more crowded the remaining villages and city became, every shelter overflowing. Aveline had done what she could, welcoming people into the palace and ordering more buildings to be built, but they would soon run out of space. There would be too many bodies and not enough space, not enough hope.

Micah exhaled. "Yeah, okay. As long as we're on the same page."

Castor waited by the passage to Nysus, leaning against a nearby tree and shivering in the cold. The river flowed at his feet, ready to be ripped open by magic. "Did we really need to do this in the middle of the night? It's always dark there, regardless of the hour."

"Be that as it may," Aveline sighed, "they still sleep when the sun goes down. Better to get in when people are drunk and stumbling home, and leave when the streets are busy at sunrise."

They'd argued over the timing, finally deciding that the sea king was most likely to be asleep in the hours just after midnight.

Castor shifted, revealing vines and shrubbery he'd planted at the edge of the portal, ivy climbing up the inside of the tree. Despite the obstruction, the portal would split the ground beneath it, stretching out and opening a tiny area past the tree. Anyone would be able to slip through it to the other side of the tree without knowledge. Aveline nodded, letting him know it would work.

Aveline made quick work of opening the portal, having done it many times, but it still felt somehow … foreign. As if her new body was trying to get used to the presence of the sea. Morgana watched with careful eyes as the passage opened at her feet, spilling blue light over her boots.

She shook her head. "This is all too familiar. I don't like it."

"If it makes you feel any better," Castor said, "*none* of us like this."

Sucking on a tooth, Morgana lifted her eyes to Rike. "I've been deceived by your line before, brought into this very kingdom under false pretenses. I know you claim to hold no allegiance to Nysus, and I believe you, but I plead with you just in case: do not turn me over to them."

Rike was so shocked that she stammered out an agreement before her mind could catch up, glancing at Aveline.

Seemingly satisfied, Morgana nodded. "In that case, into enemy territory we go."

Aveline didn't watch them prepare. She'd already slipped through.

***

As Aveline fell back into her old realm, she felt like her stomach was trying to escape up her throat. She understood, for the first time, how jarring this transition had been for Morgana. The lack of gravity tugged at her, the buoyancy battling against this new body.

She didn't have much time to dwell on it, though, scrambling to hide herself behind a clump of rocks before her companions passed through to join her. There had never been any chance that Aveline was going to allow Morgana to take Rike into Nysus alone, but Morgana was under the impression that Aveline, as Ailani, would not be able to survive underwater. She would just have to follow quietly.

Aveline watched as Morgana came through first, floating gracefully to the ocean floor. Her cloak fluttered around her, and she shed it almost immediately. Though winter still had its claws deep in the sea, a piece of fabric could hardly offer protection against the water. The cloak floated behind Morgana, weaving through the ends of Morgana's curls, before settling on the seabed. The bioluminescent light of Nysus was eerie on Morgana's face, when Aveline had once thought it to be beautiful.

Aveline could live to be a thousand and never finish reliving all the mistakes she had made when she was young.

Rike came next, and Aveline held her breath, anxiety traveling up her spine as Rike seemed to refuse to breathe. Panic spread across Rike's face, her hand pressed to her chest, her lips pressed tightly together as bubbles drifted erratically from her nose and up toward the surface. Aveline prepared to jump out, to push Rike back toward the waiting passage, until -

"You have to let it happen," Morgana said, bracing her hand on Rike's shoulder. Her voice echoed through the water, warbly and deep. "You'll suffocate yourself before the water even has a chance."

Rike gasped, but no strangled cry came after. The water drifted down her throat as easily as air would have, and every muscle in Rike's body relaxed as she sagged against Morgana. "Oh, thank the gods."

"Thank your ancestors," Morgana grumbled, making sure Rike was steady before backing away. "There aren't many cases of sea folk and the people of the land having children together, definitely no others since I've been alive. Even I couldn't be sure what would happen to you in here, especially since your sea blood is as diluted as the heirs."

"I'd be furious if you'd said that five minutes ago," Rike panted. "But right now I'm so relieved, I don't even care."

The portal had deposited them into a field about a mile outside of Thalassa, and they trudged forward in silence. Aveline waited several minutes, until she could barely make out their shapes illuminated by the glowing algae, before following on featherlight feet. They climbed the hills of the sea floor in near darkness, bouncing from rock to rock and using the buoyancy of the sea to their advantage. The familiar sensation of the water around her tugged at Aveline's heartstring, regardless of how unfamiliar it was on her new skin. She may not have been in a sea person's body anymore, but she'd always have a sea person's soul.

They crested the hill, and Aveline stumbled to a stop, realizing that Rike and Morgana had frozen ahead of her. She threw herself to the ground, forgetting she was no longer on land, and ended up drifting down to the seabed at an agonizing pace. It took far longer than Aveline would have liked for the dancing seaweed to swallow her whole, but Morgana was too enthralled by the view to notice anything.

Thalassa was not asleep. It wasn't quieting down in the late hours of evening as they'd hoped it would be. It was bustling with people, lights flashing around the palace as the sea folk danced in the street. Shouts and laughter drifted up the hill, music filtering through the water, and it was clear that nobody in the kingdom would be retiring for a good, long while.

Aveline ran the dates over in her brain, but she couldn't figure out for the life of her what holiday it might be. What could they possibly be celebrating? There were many holidays celebrated in Nysus, independent of the land, such as the winter solstice, the darkest day in Calypdon when Nysus felt as far from the land as could be. Or Haloea, a festival in honor of the god of the sea. But the solstice had passed two weeks ago, and Haloea wasn't until the summer.

"What in the world?" Morgana muttered under her breath, shifting to look at Rike. "The place wasn't even this chaotic during my welcoming ball."

Rike ran her fingers through her hair, using her other hand to grip her knife. "I don't know, I don't know any of their holidays."

Morgana pressed her lips together, inhaling deeply, before bracing her hands on her hips. "This is fine. This is good, actually. If there's a celebration, it might be easier for us to gain access to the palace."

Rike motioned to herself wildly. "In case you hadn't noticed, we're dressed as guards. I don't think guards would be showing up halfway through what seems to be a really important celebration."

Morgana straightened. "Then we won't go as guards. We go as guests."

"Wearing *what*?"

Morgana turned to Rike, just enough so that Aveline could see the grin on Morgana's face, perhaps the first one Aveline had seen since they were both young. "I hope you have money on you. Allow me to bring you on a tour of what would have been your city if your king wasn't such a murderous madman."

Chapter Eighteen

They spent the next few minutes trying to alter their appearances as much as they could, given the circumstances. They shrugged off their jackets, leaving them in black undershirts, boots, and deep navy pants. After so long crouched in the seaweed, Aveline's back was starting to lock up, but she wasn't willing to shift even an inch for fear of gaining Morgana's razor-sharp attention. She exhaled a sigh of relief when they appeared satisfied with their appearance and headed toward Thalassa.

"It might help to act a little drunk," Morgana murmured to Rike. "If his security is set up the same, there's one line of guards to get past around the perimeter of the city, by the gates, but if we act out of our minds, they'll just think we got lost on our way to the party."

Rike motioned to herself incredulously. "And lost our party clothes in the process?"

Morgana rolled her eyes. "We have to fool them into thinking we went off together. You make the connection, Rike."

Aveline's blood boiled as Rike's cheeks colored.

A small unit of soldiers stood guard at a small perimeter outpost. Getting to her feet, Aveline let Morgana and Rike walk a good distance away before following, trying to project a casual air, while keeping a sharp eye on the pair. Once they came close to the guards, though, Morgana let out a sharp giggle and pretended to stumble. She and Rike fell into each other, Morgana slinging her arm over Rike's shoulders.

Aveline had to look away. Instead, she listened to their bubbly laughter and slurred words.

"No, it's *this* way," Rike said to Morgana. Only Aveline would have been able to recognize the strain.

"No, you have to follow the *sounds*. We're going back to the *party*."

Rike laughed gleefully, but Aveline could hear the sharpness in it. "I think we need to go home and find new dresses, though."

The two of them burst out laughing, and Aveline looked up just in time to see the closest guard shaking his head, leaning over to murmur something to his partner. They didn't say anything as Rike and Morgana passed, stumbling and holding each other up. Aveline wondered if Morgana had ever actually been drunk. If she could even *get* drunk.

Counting to ten, Aveline saw the moment that they both straightened, separating, and Aveline sighed in relief that they'd made it through. But the thought that they would be recognized still haunted her, the memory of Morgana's distinct eyes flashing in the back of her mind.

She told herself to take a steadying breath. None of these guards knew what Morgana looked like, the same with Aveline. So long as Morgana stayed out of sight of the king himself, they would be alright.

They would be alright.

Propelling herself forward with one eye on the pair slowly disappearing into the distance, Aveline shed her cloak and left it stowed under the cover of seaweed. She piled a few rocks on top as well, so the tide wouldn't pull it out of hiding. She stood tall, putting on a blank face, and adjusted her cap. This was an act she knew well.

Wearing the uniform Helah had worn two hundred years ago, she moved forward with her head held high, her legs falling easily into that steady march she'd learned two centuries ago.

She paused at the pair of guards, nodding. She wouldn't speak first. Speaking unnecessarily would give her away.

"And where are you coming from?" a bored-looking guardswoman asked. She sounded almost jealous, as if she wished she had a job that allowed her to wander the city.

Aveline sighed. "Orders were to sweep the outskirts of the city, to send any stragglers back to the party. We don't want anyone going missing tonight, that'd sure put a damper on the festivities."

The other man laughed. "I get it. The king doesn't want the people having fun that doesn't involve him, eh? Tonight's a night to honor him, not to sneak out to do gods know what."

They're honoring the king?

Aveline kept a straight face, letting the corners of her mouth lift. "Indeed. I'm heading back to my post. Shouldn't be long now."

"I don't know about that," the woman sighed, glancing over her shoulder. "He doesn't like it when a party dies down early."

The man chuckled. "Come back and give us an update, will you? I'd like to be in bed by the morning bell."

Aveline cracked a smile, said, "Wouldn't we all," and slid past them.

The streets began to steadily fill with people as Rike and Morgana approached the center of Thalassa and the grounds of the palace. As party goers dressed in elaborate finery started to crowd around them, Aveline pushed closer, only allowing a dozen or so people to separate her from the pair at any given time.

"And where exactly are we going to get fancy clothes in the middle of the night?" Rike called to Morgana over the roar of the crowd, jostling past a man who must have lost his shoes somewhere and sending his drink flying.

"You live in a desolated city," Morgana responded, steering her down another street. "Look around. You'd be surprised how many stores stay open late into the night when there are people who come to them at those hours. It was only once, but I've been." Morgana jerked her chin up. "Here we are."

Aveline recognized where they were immediately, and her heart pounded against her ribs, stuttering in a weird rhythm. How was this place still in business?

They'd arrived at the same dress shop where Aveline had once bought Morgana, the silver dress that had taken Aveline's breath away. Aveline had known the owner of the shop, a woman named Reyna. She wondered who ran it now. Who had taken over when Reyna grew too old to sew the dresses?

Though it wasn't nearly as busy as it probably had been earlier in the day, several customers dallied in the shop, getting their dresses fixed or buying accessories. A woman swam from the shop with one of her friends, so excited she let her feet lift from the ground, buzzing about how much better she felt with her new shoes.

"I could dance the night away now," she said, twirling under her friend's arm. Her dress lifted up in the water, and she giggled, pushing it back down.

"And we will."

They smiled and glided away. Aveline felt a tug in her stomach, the longing to know what this new celebration was. To be a part of what was once her home. Sometimes she wished she could go back to a time when she'd loved this place freely, without the deep-seated fury that haunted her now.

She turned away in time to watch Rike catch the door the woman had left open, and she and Morgana disappeared inside.

Aveline didn't dare follow, instead positioning herself across the street, trying to look official even though there were no other guards in sight. She counted down the seconds and wondered how the hell they would get to the crown without anyone noticing.

When they came back out, Aveline barely recognized either of them. Partly because she'd never once seen Rike in a dress. They'd never had any reason for a celebration, never any reason to dress for anything other than convenience. Rike looked stunning in a deep navy blue. Mostly, though, they were unrecognizable because they both wore masks over the top half of their faces. The shimmering purple gems reflected the surrounding green lights in such a way that any indication of Morgana's odd eyes was hidden. Aveline wouldn't have known the woman dressed in the pale pink gown was actually the witch at all if she didn't recognize the hard set of her mouth, the stiffness in her shoulders. Aveline noticed there wasn't even a hint of green on her outfit at all. Probably for the best.

Morgana looked so unlike herself, her hair hidden by a golden wrap. The veil hid every unique feature, and she hugged her wrap close to her chest, as if she could hide her entire being, too.

Rike caught Aveline's eye, briefly, and Aveline nodded. *I'm with you.*

They set off toward the palace.

***

Aveline wondered when King Daegil had stopped vetting guests who came to the palace during celebrations, or perhaps the guards were slacking off so late into the evening, but they made it to the gleaming front gates with no issue at all. Aveline walked along as confidently as possible, nodding to every guard she passed and praying they wouldn't stop her.

Miraculously, they didn't. They barely batted an eye, and she slipped through the doors.

The palace looked exactly the same, but … *more.* Everything had been made bigger and more glamorous, the entrance hall towering above her with golden accents. Guests spilled out of the ballroom onto the staircase above, far more disorganized than any celebration in Aveline's time. The balls used to be formal and contained, with a small dance floor that most didn't utilize, instead choosing to spend the night trying to talk themselves up the ladder. Toward the king and nobility.

Morgana and Rike exchanged a glance.

"I don't know where the throne room is," Morgana murmured as they maneuvered through the crowd, Aveline squeezing by and following them. "That seems like the most likely place to find the crown."

"Or the ballroom," Rike said.

Morgana sighed. "I know where that is."

They started up the spiral staircase, and dread curdled in Aveline's gut. The sense of foreboding built with every step she took up the steel staircase, every nerve in her body vibrating.

Because if the sea king wasn't in the entrance hall greeting his guests, there was only one other place he would be on a night like this.

Morgana kept a firm grip on Rike's arm, guiding her to ensure they weren't separated. They weaved through halls crowded with people dancing and shouting; the guests screamed toward the ceiling, and for the first time, Aveline's ears registered their words.

"Down with Calypdon," they cried, raising their glasses, stabbing toward the kingdom above. "*Victory to Nysus*!"

A rock sank into Aveline's stomach, because she suddenly knew exactly what they were celebrating.

The anniversary of a two-hundred-year-old battle.

Aveline watched in horror as Morgana stalked into the ballroom, head held high in her disguise, before promptly freezing. Aveline followed, peering through the open double doors, and let her eyes slip closed.

The crown was, indeed, displayed where everyone could see it, but not in a case, or even at the top of a statue.

Instead, it sat on the King's head, sturdy and straight, as if it had always been his.

***

Morgana turned on her heel as soon as she saw the crown, exiting the throne room quickly as Rike scrambled after her. Aveline ducked behind a tapestry, pressing herself to the wall as she listened.

"Well," Morgana breathed. "That certainly complicates things, doesn't it?"

Rike's chest rose and fell more rapidly by the second, whipping her head back and forth. Aveline wanted to curse her, to tell her not to look so damned guilty. The girl wasn't used to this. To real missions, to real stakes. She'd spent her entire life waiting, not acting.

"A drink, ma'am?"

Morgana jumped, turning to see a servant carrying a tray of flutes, covered to separate the alcohol from the sea water. The servant smiled pleasantly. "Yes," Morgana breathed out. "Thank you."

She took the drink and downed it in one go.

Rike stared at her, but Morgana only wiped her mouth. "I discovered this stuff about sixty years ago. I missed out on quite a bit during my years in hiding."

"I imagine you did," Rike said quietly, still panicking.

"I don't think I've ever seen you before," a man said to Morgana, taking one of the other drinks from the servant. The music quieted enough out in the hall that conversation was possible, but he still had to shout in order to be heard. "I think I would have remembered someone so beautiful."

Aveline thought that was a pretty lame line, since most of Morgana's face was hidden beneath the mask.

Morgana gave the man a glowing smile, though her jaw tightened. "That's very kind of you, but I'm sure the mask is misleading."

"Indeed, it is," the man smiled. He wore a formal coat, black as night, trimmed with a vibrant blue. His bow tie sat perfectly straight around his neck. "I'd love to see you without it."

Morgana winked, the gesture barely visible through the gems of the mask. "You and everyone else."

And then she turned, grabbed Rike firmly by the forearm, and began to push through the crowd once again.

Aveline raced after them, trying not to look like she was running. If people saw a guard running after guests, other guards would start running, and people would start getting captured, and they'd never make it out of there.

The crowd didn't thin out when they spilled out onto the palace grounds, and Morgana whipped her head around before deciding to veer right, creeping around the side of the palace and into the shadows. Sharp breaths escaped from Aveline's throat as she tracked them down a path shared only with a few scattered pairs that had escaped from the revelry. Aveline spotted a gate, and when Rike glanced over her shoulder, Aveline pointed.

"This way," Rike said, directing Morgana to the exit. Guards waited there, but they'd gotten past them multiple times now, they just had to -

"Excuse me, miss."

Morgana nearly ran into the guard that seemed to materialize onto the path out of the shadows, and the guards positioned at the gate moved to join him.

Clearing her throat, Morgana wrapped her arms around Rike. "Apologies. My friend here was feeling sick, and we didn't want to disrupt the party. We thought it best to leave through the back."

On cue, Rike swayed, twining her arms around her stomach and gagging.

The man didn't so much as spare a glance in Rike's direction. "We received word of a woman refusing to take off a mask who ran from the ballroom. Would that happen to be you?"

Morgana barely moved a muscle. "It couldn't have been. A lady never runs, as I'm sure you know."

His eyes narrowed. "I'm afraid I'll have to ask you to take off your mask—"

"I'd rather not," Morgana said curtly. "It's part of my outfit, you see. You wouldn't ask me to take off my dress, would you?"

The man exchanged a glance with the other two guards, and Aveline didn't like the look on any of their faces at all. The corner of his lip lifted, and it reminded Aveline eerily of Joao. "Maybe, maybe not. Let's go somewhere more private, shall we? Maybe you'll be more willing to reveal yourself there."

"That's rather unlikely," Morgana said coolly, but before she could say anything else, the man had grabbed her roughly by the back of her dress and shoved her toward the gate, leaving Rike behind.

Rike kept up her act, keeling over and dry heaving into a bush until they disappeared into the darkness. Aveline darted out, helping Rike up from her knees.

"What do we do?" Rike breathed, eyes wild.

Aveline looked over her shoulder; she could still hear the sounds of the three guard's footsteps, dragging Morgana behind them. Aveline jerked her head toward the gate, and they crept after Morgana. Barely lifting her feet, Aveline glided over the seaweed, swimming up a few feet to squint through the murky water. Four vague outlines gathered several feet away. Aveline couldn't hear anything, could barely see their movements as the main guard put his hands on his hips, clearly telling Morgana to do something.

"Aveline..." Rike trailed off. "What if they try to -"

"We wait," Aveline cut her off. "And hope Morgana knocks them out with her powers."

"And if she doesn't?" Rike asked nervously. Because even though Morgana was a witch and a monster, she was still a woman. A woman like them. Rike knew as well as Aveline what it was like to be approached by unsavory men in the run-down parts of Briarwood. They knew what it was to be backed into a corner.

Aveline set her mouth into a thin line. "Then we knock them out ourselves."

They watched the guards taunt Morgana, surrounding her on all sides, but Morgana didn't shrink down. She squared her shoulders, folding her arms across her chest. As Aveline's eyes adjusted to the darkness, the predatory look on the guards' faces became clearer, and Aveline gripped her sword. Rike reached through a slit she'd cut in her dress to bring her blade out as well.

The moment one of the guards touched her, Aveline wanted to pounce, her blessed magic rearing up in the face of battle, but she gave Morgana a chance. Gave her a chance to defend herself, to bring them down with the magic she held back. But she made no move to do so. The guard pulled her roughly against him, and she snarled, shoving him, but all of the guards remained standing. They remained alive.

Only when his hand crept lower, snaking down toward her hip, did Morgana strike, using the way she cowered to reach beneath her dress, bringing her sword out and arcing it through the water. But the blade moved slower in the water than through air, and the man had time to jump back before it sliced his neck. The blade cut across his stomach instead, through his uniform. Blood billowed through the water between them, and the two other guards were on her before she could swing again.

"Why the hell won't she just use her powers?" Aveline hissed to no one in particular before jumping into the fray.

Pulling her sword out, Aveline slid over the seaweed, catching what could have been a fatal blow to Morgana's back with a parry. The witch was distracted as she fought off one of the other guards. Rike wrenched the third guard off balance to fight several feet away.

Morgana stared wild-eyed at Aveline, even as her sword kept jabbing and parrying. "Ailani?"

Aveline didn't look at Morgana again, focusing on her opponent, the guard that had touched Morgana. Her vision had gone white with an unexplainable fury. She stared at the man with a snarl, but the guard didn't back down. He fought her with one hand and held his guts in with the other.

She would tear the rest of him apart herself.

"What are *you* doing here," Morgana gasped, barely managing to defend herself in her surprise. "*How* -"

"Not the time," Aveline said through gritted teeth.

Aveline hadn't fought in earnest for several lifetimes. She'd had to settle for training with the other soldiers or running through drills on her own. Fighting against real swords, against real enemies, was quite different, and she felt like a young guard again, protecting a witch she barely knew with her life.

And yet, the sensation of fighting in this body, *really* fighting, was entirely new. Despite how much she practiced, she hadn't faced a true opponent since she'd been blessed. The moves and maneuvers flowed out of her without thought, acting on pure instinct and faster than she ever could have before. The magic coursed through her veins, propelling her forward. She sliced through the water and marveled at the way the world faded around her, leaving only her, the goddess, and the battle.

The only thing slowing her down was the distraction of the two women fighting to her right. "If you felt like using your powers for good for once," Aveline grunted, breathless as her arm began to ache, "now would be the time."

Morgana sliced at one of the remaining men, tearing open his sleeve. "I might just let them take you, as punishment for lying."

"*Morgana*," Rike barked, sinking her knife into her own opponent's chest. His body floated up, blood clouding around his torso, and Rike didn't linger over him, moving on to help Morgana.

"I can't," Morgana snapped breathlessly. "Not while I'm fighting this way."

Growing impatient, Aveline pulled a knife from her waist and twirled through the water toward Morgana's opponent, narrowly missing the witch as she lodged the blade in his neck. She barely even looked at the final guard before dodging his swing, rolling, and feeling her blade sink into his back.

Morgana stood still, sword extended as she watched the guard try to fight with the knife in his neck before shuddering to a stop. "I - "

"There's your limitation for you," Aveline said, tossing her head back and squeezing her eyes shut, trying to quiet the ringing in her ears. The power ebbed out of her, her skin and muscles slowly calming down as she came back down to the seabed beneath her feet, as she settled back into the mortal world.

"What?" Morgana asked, irritated, waving a cloud of blood away from her eyes as she turned to Aveline.

"You asked for me to let you know if we noticed limitations on your power. The fact that you can't use it when you're distracted is a pretty big one."

"It's not that," Morgana sighed. "It has nothing to do with being distracted, and everything to do with my power getting confused over fighting the body versus fighting the soul."

"You should have gone for their souls to *begin* with," Rike sighed, hands holding the back of her head as she gasped for breath.

"I don't -" Whatever Morgana had been about to say died in her throat, and Aveline glanced back at the witch to see that her mouth had fallen open, eyes wide and the light within them guttering, anguish painting her features.

Confused, Aveline started, "What -?"

Morgana spun on her heel, faster than Aveline had ever seen her move, and lunged. Aveline didn't even have time to think about defending herself before Morgana's elbow flew out, colliding with Aveline's wrist. Pain burst up along her bone, and her fingers fell open, her sword tumbling from her grasp.

Morgana caught it before it hit the ground, as if she had summoned it to her flesh. She spun it around like a fifth limb, sweeping Aveline's legs out from under her, and pressed her knee into Aveline's chest.

Chapter Nineteen

The air flew from Aveline's lungs as she stared up at Morgana's seething face, her skin blotchy with rage. Sputtering, Aveline tried to move, but between Morgana's weight and the weapon threatening to slit her throat, she could only stare up in panic. The goddess vibrated within her, willing her to fight back, but Aveline knew if she tried, Morgana wouldn't hesitate to take hold of her soul.

"Morgana," Rike gasped, and Aveline could barely see her over Morgana's shoulder, reaching for her weapon.

"If your fingers even brush against that knife," Morgana growled without so much as looking up, her eyes still trained on Aveline's, "I'll make sure it's the last thing you ever do. And I'll make your leader watch."

Rike froze.

Aveline's hands tensed helplessly at her side, not daring to fight against the hold Morgana had on her. Any questions lodged in her throat, terrified at the foreign, monstrous look of vehemence behind those mismatched eyes. The yellow one seemed to glow from within, a cat ready to pounce on her prey.

"Who are you," Morgana hissed, baring her teeth in Aveline's face. "Where did you get this?"

Aveline's heart fell into her stomach.

Because when Aveline looked at the sword Morgana held to her throat, straining her eyes to see the hilt, it wasn't the one she thought she had grabbed earlier, in the darkness of her bedroom. Actually, she hadn't thought about it at all, moving by instinct as she rushed from her room and tried not to think of all the ways everything could go wrong. She simply grabbed the sword that she'd found a screwed-up comfort in for two hundred years.

Aveline gazed in horror at the sword Morgana had held to her throat on one other occasion. The same one used to slice open Aveline's stomach.

It wasn't her eye that was glowing, Aveline realized. It was the sword, reunited with its true owner after two hundred years. It illuminated the circle around them, pulsing with power and highlighting Morgana's jawline, reflecting off her mask. The snake on the hilt seemed to dance, taunting her for what might be a fatal mistake.

"I -"

"Do not lie to me," Morgana warned, pressing the blade harder against Aveline's throat, drawing a line of fire along her skin. "I know exactly who was in possession of this sword the last time I saw it."

Aveline knew, too. Helah had said that Morgana had fled during the skirmish, when she and King Daegil had fought over the blade. It made sense that she assumed Helah had failed to keep it out of the sea king's hands. Helah had claimed she never knew quite why she fought so hard, why she had refused to hand the weapon over.

"I think it's because I needed to keep the weapon that killed you," Helah had said once. "At the time, I thought you were actually dead, and I needed … something…"

Aveline hadn't made her explain anymore; she had just enveloped her sister in a hug.

Except now she had no idea how to explain herself. No idea how to talk herself out of this, how to get out from beneath Morgana without that sword killing her a second time.

It didn't matter. Morgana kept talking, unable to stop the deluge of words as her eyes glistened. "I *know* he got it back, more than I've ever been sure of anything. The fact that he had it was the reason for *everything*. He would not have left it behind. It should have been here, with him."

"It was not. But how kind it was for you to bring it back to me."

Morgana sprang off of Aveline, whirling her sword around to fight whatever intruder came next, but she stumbled to a halt. Aveline jumped to her feet but froze just as quickly.

Aveline had been so busy staring at Morgana, trying to come up with something to say, that she hadn't seen Rike slip out of view. Hadn't heard the approach of more soldiers, of the sea king himself.

There must have been thirty soldiers surrounding King Daegil, all armed with longswords. The two men closest to the king held Rike, her arms pinned behind her back. Her eyes were wide, but no sound could make it past the hand clamped over her mouth. Terror dropped into Aveline's stomach at the sight of Rike being held, at the fear in her last remaining relative's eyes.

But Aveline was ashamed to admit that it was nothing compared to the fear she felt knowing that it was King Daegil who had her, his smiling face unchanged in two hundred years. Sleek and evil, and most importantly, weaponless. So confident that he hadn't bothered to arm himself.

Morgana remained rigid, her sword poised. "You will *never* get your hands on me again."

The king ignored her words, clasping his hands in front of him. "I have been waiting for you."

"I'm sure you have been," Morgana snarled.

The sea king grinned, feral and animal-like. "Part of me thought you'd return." His gaze shifted. "You, on the other hand."

The sea king looked right past Morgana, right past Rike, to Aveline. To a woman that he shouldn't have recognized at all.

Aveline couldn't find any words. She was too busy trying to figure out how the king had recognized her. Had her body shifted back to her old one when she came through the portal? No, that couldn't have been it, otherwise

Morgana would have recognized her.

"I don't know why you would be waiting for me," Aveline decided to say. "I'm not nearly as interesting as the witch."

King Daegil folded his arms over his broad chest; muscle corded over his forearms. "Oh, I don't know about that. I got what I wanted out of her."

Morgana bared her teeth, glancing at Rike, most likely contemplating how best to set her free without getting both of them stabbed in the process. Aveline was reminded of another situation, years ago, when Morgana had been forced to contain her powers in order to keep a knife from going through Aveline's throat.

The king tilted his head, his jawline glinting in the glow of the shimmering algae, turning his dark hair blue. "But you? You took her from me in the first place. You made my plans … a lot more complicated."

So, he knew. No amount of denying would change that, and she couldn't take her eyes off Rike, at the weapons threatening her. "You seemed to manage alright regardless."

Morgana's brow furrowed, mouth opening slightly as she tried to follow the conversation, trying to figure out how the sea king could know a woman born in Calypdon twenty-five years ago.

The king's smile turned cloying. "I did."

"How?"

He knew what she was asking, that it had nothing to do with Morgana. "We are the same, you and I," King Daegil drawled, spreading his arms wide. "Made anew from the blessings of the gods. Don't think I can't see past this nice new face of yours."

Morgana whipped her head around, staring at Aveline. Her sword hand began to shake, and she squinted, trying to see past whatever mask the sea king seemed to be referring to.

Aveline pointedly avoided Morgana's gaze. "Magic's a funny thing. Either way, her magic can do more for you than mine ever could."

His eyes flashed. "Don't think I don't know that." He turned slowly to Morgana, who still stared at Aveline with a mixture of confusion, suspicion, and perhaps a little fear. "I'll get her in the end. But you -" He snapped his gaze back to Aveline. "One of my most trusted soldiers, who betrayed me when I needed her most."

"Because you lied to me," Aveline snarled. "I'd say we're even."

King Daegil stared at her steadily. "We'll see."

Aveline tried to move, to lunge forward with her sword and put the skills the goddess of battle had bestowed upon her to a real test, but she found she couldn't. It wasn't that her arms weren't working, she could feel the muscles under her skin flexing and reacting, but every time she tried to move, she found a sort of wall pushing back at her. She whipped her head around, her head and neck the only parts of her body with any freedom of movement at all and realized that the water around her had become completely solid.

King Daegil watched with a dark laugh. "You should have thought better when you decided which god to pray to." He glanced at one of his soldiers. "Chain her."

The soldier dashed over, reaching easily through whatever barricade the king had built around her, enclosing her wrists and ankles with what she would assume were shackles of iron. Aveline remembered the moment Morgana had revealed that iron had no effect on her, but the same wasn't the case for Aveline. She felt the blessing go dormant, sinking down to her feet where it would wait until it was freed. She closed her eyes, heart hammering, because she was trapped. Well and truly trapped.

The king approached Morgana, who shoved the sword closer to him, ensuring that there remained at least a meter of space between them. This only seemed to entertain him. "Are you sure you want to put that blade so close to my hands?"

Aveline furrowed her brow.

"Sure," Morgana said, though her voice trembled. "If you're willing to grab the sharp end of a sword, I won't stop you."

The blue and green lights from the sword reflected onto his face, casting the crooks and crevices into midnight sapphire shadows. He regarded Morgana, the most powerful being in the entire world, as nothing more than a mouse. "You're mine."

"You can't hold me," Morgana bit out, though her hand quaked harder than ever. "You've tried before."

The King's smile didn't fade. "No. But what I *could* do is keep you trapped in this kingdom, forever hunted. You have no ability to open portals anymore; you have no way out." His eyes flashed. "And you know what happened the last time you fell into my hands."

For perhaps the first time, Aveline found nothing but fear written across the witch's face, blatant and true.

"And," the king added as an afterthought, "I have your friends."

"They're not my friends," Morgana said, though it came out as more of a question.

"Maybe not this one," he conceded, running a finger down Rike's cheek as she wrestled against her bonds. Aveline wanted to tear him apart. "But her, on the other hand."

Morgana didn't dare glance back at Aveline. She simply spat, "I barely know her."

A sick glee flared in the King's eyes. "So, you really don't know."

"I've been told I know very little for an immortal being."

Aveline could think, through the mess of fear and anticipation clouding her mind, that Castor would be very happy to know that Morgana had remembered that.

King Daegil let his tongue slide over his teeth, eyes glinting mischievously. He glanced at Aveline. "Why don't you tell her your real identity, hmm? I'd call you by the new name you chose, but I don't know what you told her it was."

Breaths stuttered out of Aveline's chest, and she had no idea what to do. She had no idea what would happen if Morgana found out who she was, the destruction that would follow. If *anything* would follow.

The king grinned. Aveline wished he would stop smiling. "Oh, come on, tell her." He paused wickedly. "Aveline."

Morgana sucked in a breath, and her arm dropped to her side, sword and all. Aveline braced herself for an attack like the one before, but it didn't come.

Because Morgana was shaking her head. "No. If this was Aveline, I'm fairly sure I'd be dead by now."

At least the witch was relatively smart.

The king tutted. "Us sea folk know how to bide our time. Even with our killers."

Anger flared in Morgana's face. "You've got a lot of nerve calling *me*—"

"Oh, I'm sure she'd be biding her time with me as well," the king waved her off. "If she knew. Because if I'm right about this as well, I'd say you haven't told any of them the truth."

Morgana's jaw twitched.

King Daegil let his head fall back, laughing toward the surface of the sea. His chest rumbled with it. "Oh, I'll never stop being entertained with the youth, with the humane. The ways in which guilt can further condemn an already tortured soul."

Mind galloping at high speeds, Aveline tried to catch up. Tried to decipher the anguish on Morgana's face and the cool entertainment on the king's. Tried to figure out how he could ever think of Morgana as humane.

Unless…

Aveline watched in horror as the king drew even closer to Morgana, and the witch stumbled back a step. If he was calling two-hundred-year-old women youthful, how old could he possibly be?

"Guilt is a powerful thing. But I should think you wouldn't be concerned over what your body did. Your power has only ever been concerned with the soul."

Morgana's throat bobbed, and her voice came out ragged. "I am more than my power."

"I see that," the king said, reaching out as if to touch her, but Morgana jumped back. He clicked his tongue. "You will learn one day, I'm sure. Soon enough, you'll be as old as me, and you'll understand." He glanced at Aveline. "Maybe her, too."

Morgana turned slowly to look at Aveline, mouth open and brows creased in the center, her lips attempting to form words, though unable to come up with anything. She looked at Aveline in a new light, seemed to see past the face and body, and read her soul again. The shock on her face told Aveline enough.

Morgana clearly recognized the feel of her soul. Knew it like the back of her hand, now that she reached for it.

Aveline thought she might know Morgana's soul, too. Might understand something after decades in the dark, the puzzle pieces that never quite fit finally clicking into place.

The shock on Morgana's face turned to understanding, and then rage, and for the first time in two hundred years, Aveline knew they were on the same page. Morgana turned back, a newfound fire in her eyes, the king looking far too pleased with himself for his own good.

The man savored tearing apart his enemies. Even more, he reveled in watching them rip each other apart so he didn't have to do it. That's exactly what Morgana and Aveline did. What they continued to do, even though Morgana hadn't even known who she was.

Morgana raised her arm again, and this time, it stayed steady. "You can't hold me, and you won't hold her."

The king lifted his brows, along with a knife that Aveline hadn't noticed. "Can't I?"

He gave the witch one last smile, letting the iron blade dangle between them for only a moment, before turning it on himself and plunging it into his own side.

Chapter Twenty

The scream Morgana let out could have shattered kingdoms.

She fell to her knees, slowly, as though the king had stiffened the water around her. She wrapped her arms around herself as she bowed over. Her mouth stayed open long after she screamed herself hoarse, eyes squeezed shut against the agony as she howled.

Aveline rushed toward her, free from her watery prison, but she only fell forward, forgetting that her legs had been bound as well. Her face collided with the seashell studded walkway, and she craned her neck, shouting for Morgana, but Morgana couldn't hear her over the pain, her arms now wrapped around her head.

The king was on Morgana in mere seconds, shoving her down onto the ground, digging his fingers into her shoulder. She winced with every movement, and it had nothing to do with his harsh touch. Something burned within her.

"Iron might not hurt you the way that it does the Hallowed," the king hissed into her face with a haunting smile, despite the blood draining from his face. "But it hurts me, and your magic is linked to mine. Even now."

Your magic is linked to mine. Aveline still didn't know how he had done it, but there was something about the massacre two hundred years ago that Aveline didn't understand. Something about Morgana's magic, and Morgana's choices.

You know nothing about my choices. That's what Morgana had said to Aveline only days ago. She thought of Morgana's pained face in Wendell's room, of her near-constant blank stare.

Perhaps she had never had a choice at all.

King Daegil spoke through the pain of his self-inflicted wound. "Iron coursing through the blood of a Hallowed causes more pain than a mortal could ever imagine. Being surrounded by iron chains is one thing, but this… The iron isn't just dampening the magic. It's *corrupting* it. Our souls are irrevocably bonded, Morgana, and so is our magic. I imagine you're feeling that corruption in every part of your body and soul. It's probably even worse for you; a witch whose soul relies on her magic. Does it feel like your power is trying to escape through your pores? Like an outside force is squeezing it from your body?"

Morgana's whole face contorted with torment, but she managed to open her eyes, looking around the clearing. "Jokes on you," she croaked out. "You're useless, too."

"For the moment," King Daegil said through ragged breaths. "Not once I take back what's mine. Maybe I'll just kill you this time."

"You don't want this power permanently," Morgana spat.

"No," King Daegil conceded, looking her up and down. "No, but a king must do what he must. And you have long since become a liability."

He moved, reaching for Morgana's sword. With the movement, he shifted enough to free her arm, and she rolled out of his grasp. It was an odd fight, the battle between two injured immortals. Slow and painful. Morgana didn't bother attempting to stand, panting, on her knees. King Daegil winced as he tried to lunge after her, and the soldiers scrambled toward Morgana.

But Aveline saw a familiar glint in Morgana's gaze. A lethal one.

"Maybe you'll take me," Morgana snarled, almost foaming at the mouth with the effort to stay still, to keep from tearing her throat apart again. "But not yet."

With the dregs of her power, she managed to collect through the pain, Morgana sent the soldiers flying back, the only one who remained unaffected being King Daegil, who seethed mere inches from her. All the color drained from the witch's face with the effort, but she gritted her teeth and looked to Rike, who scrambled to stand, her arms free. Aveline moved to rush toward Rike, but Morgana had other plans, whirling her sword around and flinging it through the water, over the king and toward Rike's empty hands.

Aveline had a brief moment of fear, where the sword twisted and sliced the life out of the only family she had left, but Rike was trained well. She ducked down, narrowly avoiding getting her neck slashed open, and curled her fingers around the hilt.

"*Take it*," Morgana shouted as the king whipped his head around with a growl, the words tearing out of her throat, tears drifting from her eyes like rivers, bleeding into the sea. Aveline wasn't sure she'd ever seen Morgana cry before. "If you've ever cared for the safety of your kingdom and your friends, take it and *run!*"

They'd left the portal between kingdoms open. They'd told Morgana it was because they didn't have a way of contacting Aveline on the other side. But Rike knew she'd left it open in case they needed to make a quick escape. A quick escape where Aveline didn't make it.

She'd just never considered that Rike would return with a sword and nothing else, and Aveline's heart pounded at the fear on Rike's face, at the agony on Morgana's. But Aveline could see it now, in both Morgana's eyes and King Daegil's face as he struggled against the witch. Rike wasn't his goal, it wasn't even Morgana. His eyes followed the blade as Rike hugged it close to her chest, swallowing hard.

Morgana kicked the king in the groin when he tried to stand, knocking him over, but he landed a blow on her jaw just as quickly. She coughed, blood drifting, but she didn't take her eyes from Rike. "Take it and go! NOW!"

Rike didn't look to Aveline for confirmation. She must have seen something in Morgana's eyes, in her crumpled form, in the vengeful look on King Daegil's face. Swiftly, she said, "We'll come back," turned on her heel, and took off into the dark, murky water.

King Daegil didn't follow, grimacing with a hand on his wound as he stood and looked around at his fallen soldiers, at Morgana staring at him with more hatred than Aveline had ever seen on her face before.

And Aveline watched, unable to escape her cuffs, as Rike vanished into the darkness, the sword with her, and resigned herself to being sacrificed for the sake of a piece of metal.

***

Only a few seconds after Rike disappeared, the soldiers rose, rubbing their heads before jumping to action. They found King Daegil lying on the ground, pinning Morgana down with his remaining energy, but it didn't matter. Morgana had lost consciousness.

Aveline stared at her, tears mingling with the salt water where she lay in the mud, her chained hands digging into her stomach beneath her. Even in unconsciousness, Morgana's face contorted with pain, twitching as the king shook her.

"Find her!" King Daegil bellowed. He may have had more energy than Morgana because he tried to use his magic, but his face paled with the effort, drained of blood as he stood and ordered his soldiers. "Find the sword and bring it back to me!"

Half the soldiers saluted and disappeared after Rike, but Aveline laughed maniacally. By the time the soldiers tracked Rike to the right portal, she would have already gone through to Calypdon, where they wouldn't be able to follow. Aveline had studied their necks and found no breathing artifacts there.

She wondered why that was, as the other half of the soldiers roughly wrenched Morgana and Aveline up, carting them back toward the palace. She would have thought King Daegil would give artifacts to everyone he could. Perhaps he just remained confident that it would never come to a battle in Briarwood.

Or maybe he'd sent all those soldiers out, to the mystical land springs, and they'd come back empty handed.

The ball was over by the time they got back, though the streets still echoed with cheers and laughter. Aveline swayed at the sound, and it rattled around her skull, sounding otherworldly and *wrong*.

For the first time, they brought Aveline not upstairs, but down. She'd never even seen the dungeons until the moment they unceremoniously threw her into one.

King Daegil had been brought up to his quarters, but one of the soldiers hissed through the bars. "You tell your witch that he'll keep that iron flowing through her veins until the moment she gives up that sword, no matter how many times he has to hurt himself."

***

Morgana didn't wake up for several days.

Aveline sat in the same spot for all that time, her ankles and wrists still bound with iron, her head leaning against the stone wall as she stared at the witch's unconscious form sprawled in the corner of the cell. After a while, she couldn't stand it anymore, crawling forward and rearranging Morgana's limbs, positioning her arm to prop up her head. She shivered in her sleep, pressed against the cold floor. Aveline shed her guard's jacket and lifted the witch into her lap, draping it over her shoulders and torso.

She could do nothing but sit in silence and eat the two tiny meals brought to her daily.

When King Daegil visited them in the dungeons, Morgana was still unconscious.

His footsteps echoed over the stone, reverberating as he approached. Two guards flanked him, and though they hid it well, Aveline could tell they were discretely holding him up. She surveyed his body, searching for the wound, but he'd masked it in layers of finery, somehow standing straight while Morgana remained flat on her back.

Aveline didn't bow, didn't even bother to stand as he knocked against the bars.

"Don't bother," Aveline said flatly. "She's in a pretty deep sleep, and won't rouse for the likes of you."

King Daegil smiled, but it was weak, his face white as a ghost. "I'm not here to speak with her."

"Oh, then you're even more out of luck," Aveline snapped, shifting against the wall. She thought the shape of her spine began to shift, to mold into the edges of the dilapidated stones. "I don't even know anything about that stupid sword."

"I'm sure you don't," he drawled. "I'll bet you're itching for her to wake, if just to get an explanation."

She did her best not to look at Morgana, to keep herself from revealing the truth of his words. "And I'm assuming you won't give me one?"

"Not unless you give me something in return." He leaned against the bars, feigning nonchalance, but there was a slight tremor in his hands. What could possibly be so important about a sword that he would sacrifice his own magic, his own strength, for it?

Although she knew the value of Morgana's power, and perhaps that tradeoff alone made it worth it for him.

Aveline's mouth was rusty from days without talking, but she swallowed and said, "I don't suppose I really have anything you want."

"I suppose not," the king mused. "But I do know that the girl you sent running was your niece."

Every muscle in Aveline's body tightened, and she clenched her fists, the shackles rubbing over her already raw skin. She didn't respond, couldn't, because her throat had completely closed up.

King Daegil's eyes sparkled. "No witty retort where family is concerned?"

Aveline wished she could spit at him, but she didn't have enough saliva in her body to do it, nor could she cross the distance of the cell between them. "You won't lay a *hand* on her, or I will find a way out of these chains, and rip that hand from your body."

"Oh, I'm sure you already wish to do so, after what I did to your witch."

Aveline's heart pounded. "And what did you do to my witch?"

Drumming his fingers along the bars, he said, "I'll let her tell you. She won't stay unconscious forever, and you won't be getting out of this cell any time soon." He lowered his voice, drawing his face down until it was shrouded in shadows and level with hers. "In the time that you have to … think over your options, you can decide what's more important to you. Your niece, or your witch."

He disappeared down the dark hall before Aveline could comprehend the threat.

Steeling herself, trying to shove the pants of her legs beneath the manacle to ease the friction of the iron, Aveline floated across the cool floor, grateful that she didn't have to drag herself as she would in Calypdon. Still, she sagged with exhaustion. Even with nothing to do, she could barely get a wink of sleep without waking with a scream, hurrying over to Morgana to check for signs of life.

Aveline checked now, maneuvering her shackled hands until they pressed against the side of Morgana's neck, and she found a familiar, steady heartbeat thrumming against her fingertips. Aveline sagged down, trying to reconcile the relief seeping through her veins with the hatred she'd spent years building. All she could do was try to put together the puzzle pieces of King Daegil's words, of Morgana's pain, of everything that hadn't added up since Aveline found Morgana pretending to live a life in her little shop.

She'd seen Morgana making connections, too, in those moments before she fell unconscious. Looking at her, really *looking* at her, for the first time in … a long time.

Those days alone in the cell shouldn't have felt so long to her, after two hundred years alone. But without explanation, she felt that if Morgana never woke up, she'd have lost her in an entirely new way.

Aveline shook Morgana's shoulder, but nothing happened. Her lips parted slightly, for a moment at peace, before the pain came back.

It always came back.

Lying down next to Morgana, Aveline curled into her side, letting her cuffed hands fall over Morgana's stomach. Her skin flickered in the light of the bioluminescent algae crawling up the walls of the dungeon, sending the hollows of her cheeks and throat into shadows.

Aveline let her eyes flutter closed, unable to look any longer.

"What didn't you tell me?" she whispered into Morgana's shoulder, her lips brushing against cool skin.

No answer came.

INTERLUDE
Two Hundred Years Prior
Flashes of a Woman Enslaved
Morgana

Chapter Twenty One

That night with Aveline was the closest Morgana had ever come to sleep.

She laid with her eyes closed the whole night, content to listen to Aveline's steady heartbeat beneath her ear, the covers pulled up to their chins, as if a blanket might protect them. She had collapsed into a sort of stupor, a dreamlike state where she thought of everything and nothing all at once.

Only when something stirred within her, hunger, perhaps, did she let her eyes flutter open. Disoriented, she sat up. Aveline snored at her side, cheek pressed into her pillow, so deep in sleep that Morgana knew she wouldn't be up for quite some time.

Delicately, she shoved the covers away, disentangling her legs where they were still intertwined in Aveline's. She smiled as their skin slid against each other, even as her head pounded. Rubbing her eyes, she stumbled off the bed, catching herself on the nightstand

As soon as her feet touched the ground, she knew something was wrong. Her feet turned to ice as the floor hummed beneath her, sending vibrations through her bones, and Morgana listened. She dug her heels into the wood beneath her, and knew who called to her.

Ice settled into her bones, trickling down her spine as she blearily looked around. Why did her head hurt, and why was the light so damn bright? She stumbled forward, yanking on pants and a shirt, blindly following the call. Her magic responded, as if it recognized itself in the summons.

Morgana looked back at Aveline as she reached the door, and thought about waking her for only a moment before she remembered the plan. Wendell didn't want her to go with them, didn't want to risk a distraction. And as she slid her boots on, securing them as fast as possible, she knew he was right. She could feel him, his presence, far closer than he would feel a kingdom away. He was near.

But this didn't make sense. They were supposed to know when Nysus invaded. How could the sea bring soldiers into Calypdon unnoticed?

Unless he didn't bring soldiers.

With a silent promise to come back, to always come back, Morgana left Aveline, still asleep, and sprinted down the hall. The silent palace still slumbered around her, and she found that she didn't need to think at all about where she was going. Her magic seemed to know, the tie between her own soul and Daegil's pulling taunt, leading her steps through hall after hall, in a pattern she eventually recognized. She'd only been there a few times, when she was looking for Wendell, even though she never found him there. She had never heard of him holding any kind of audience in the palace.

Wendell wasn't waiting in his throne room this time either. Morgana almost felt relieved. But then movement flashed in the corner and two figures emerged from the shadows. Morgana sucked in a sharp breath.

Joao stood in the back of the throne room, holding an unconscious Helah to his chest, his arm wrapped around her neck. He smiled wickedly at Morgana, and tightened his hold, flashing his sword.

Only when Morgana saw the weapon did she realize what she'd forgotten. What, in her panic, she hadn't even taken the time to look for.

Lifting her gaze, Morgana found King Daegil sitting on Wendell's throne, with Morgana's sword hanging loosely from his hand, as if it had belonged to him all his life.

***

Morgana's mother had passed the Serpent Sword down long before she had passed down the powers themselves. Always fascinated by the bone color of the weapon, Morgana had constantly stolen it, slashing at the trees in the woods and learning the different moves she had seen her mother practice.

Finally, when Morgana came of age, just as her mother's sickness had settled in, her mother sat her down outside, drawing the sword from its scabbard.

Morgana hadn't snatched it up. As she had gotten older, she had started asking her mother to borrow it, noticing that it made her nervous when it wasn't near her hand. "It really is a beautiful sword," Morgana had said after a few moments of silence, her fingers itching for it.

"It is," her mother agreed, gazing down at the weapon. There was no love or awe in her gaze, but rather a harsh resignation. "It's thousands of years old. It dates back to the beginning of our line, the beginning of our powers."

Morgana' eyes widened, shocked. "I don't believe you. It looks as good as new."

"That's for two reasons," her mother had said. "The first is because it's rarely been used. I myself have never used it beyond practice. The second is the magic that was forged into it upon its creation."

Morgana jerked back, suddenly not as inclined to touch the weapon.

Her mother had sighed. "I'm going to tell you a story. A story that my mother told me, and her mother told her, all the way back to the beginning. When our powers came to us, they were too much for an ordinary human to handle. Because that's what our ancestor once was, right? Everyone with magic was once as ordinary as anyone else."

Morgana had felt a pang of longing, then, for a life that could have been if it weren't for someone else's choices. Someone else's fate.

Her mother nodded in understanding. "But when the curse set in, it ate at the body. A curse is different from a blessing, the weight of it can tear a person apart. And had it torn her apart, it would have released a catastrophe beyond our wildest nightmares upon the kingdom. Remember, there was just one kingdom, back then. And so, the bestower of the curse, the god of death, built in a failsafe. He sent down a sword, etched with one of his sacred animals."

"A serpent," Morgana whispered, gazing at one of the snakes. At its glinting red eye and gaping mouth, in such fine detail that she had always had a hard time believing it was man made. That made sense now; it wasn't.

"Half of the magic remained in our ancestor's veins," her mother had continued. "We hold as much of the soul as we can handle without burning up from the inside out." Then she lifted the sword. "The rest of the magic, and the rest of each soul, lies here. This sword keeps us alive, but it also holds the power to destroy us. It can extract the power from our bodies, and transfer it to the new bearer of the sword."

Morgana had snapped her head up, mouth falling open. "*What?*"

Her mother had ducked her head solemnly. "A precaution at the time, but what could now be a dangerous vulnerability. If someone were to get their hands on this sword and strike me down with it, my power would be siphoned from me and into them. The same will soon be true for you."

"I don't understand. Why?"

Morgana's mother had run a reverent hand down the blade. "If we were to die, every other soul in the kingdoms would die with us. Since we are the bridge bringing down the gods' powers, giving energy to their souls, they can only live if we live. It is why my own soul could not fade until I bore an heir." She had stroked Morgana's cheek, then and it had felt like an apology. "But no one is meant to live forever. Even the other Hallowed can be killed, and when they are, they are returned to the earth like everyone else."

"But we can't be killed. Not like that."

"No." Morgana's mother hefted the weapon. "Only with this. And this power we have? It has to go somewhere."

"So that's why you're so protective of the sword," Morgana said. "Because it is the only thing that can kill you."

Her mother had hesitated. "In part. I have no desire to pass this curse to another; it is ours to bear. But it would be over quickly, and you would be free. There are times, though I'm ashamed to admit it, that I've considered doing just that. So you could have a chance at a life."

Morgana's throat had tightened, and though she wished for that life, she knew she would never give this one up. Not if it meant she doomed another.

Morgana's mother gripped her hand. "But, listen to me. To be killed by this sword would be horrendous. But to be wounded by this sword … that is another matter entirely. Someone stabbing you in the stomach, with any sword, would not kill you. Just as the wound is temporary, so would be the consequences. You would not lose your powers to the person who attacked you, not permanently."

Dread had curdled in Morgana's stomach, knowing deep in her gut that whatever her mother was about to say would be so much worse than dying.

Morgana's mother licked her lips. "That wound would open something up between you and your attacker. That connection that already exists between your souls would be heightened, leaving an opening that would grant them temporary control of your power. Of *you*. You will have the ability to control others, though we try to never use our magic in such a way. And when someone can control you, they control that magic within us, too."

Morgana had felt so heavy then, heavier than she'd ever felt in her life as the realities of her fate had begun to set in. The danger that came with it, and the true reason they stayed in the shadows. "Then why don't we destroy it?"

"It can't be done," she had sighed. "This sword channels the souls of the living in the same way we do. Take the sword away, and the rest will go with it."

Morgana had run her hand along the blade, the bonelike hilt, and had thought she could feel a slight thrum of power from within it that she had never noticed before. "I will protect it," Morgana had said firmly, knowing what this conversation was. The beginning of a goodbye. "I'll never let it out of my sight."

"No one is meant to have as much power as we do. There must be a method to take it away," her mother had said, affectionately tucking a strand of hair behind Morgana's ear. "Consider this a good thing. Protect the sword and yourself at all costs, and never forget your vulnerability. Moreover, never let someone else know it, and never let them abuse it."

***

Those words echoed in Morgana's mind as she stared in horror at the earthen dais, at the man staring down at her. He looked unnatural on Wendell's throne, dressed in his blue finery, the silver threads gleaming in the sunlight. He didn't belong here.

"Did you know that there is a portal between the land and the sea, directly linking the throne rooms of the two palaces?" the king asked nonchalantly, reclining back on the throne.

"That doesn't seem right." Morgana forced herself to stare up at King Daegil, even as her eyes burned with the sight. She longed to rush to Helah, to make sure she was alright.

"Perhaps," King Daegil waved her concern away. "But it was an arrangement made years ago. By a very old land king, and an even older sea king." His eyes flashed. "We folk of the sea play the long game. Especially me."

Morgana wanted to rub her eyes, to massage some sense into her head, but she settled for blinking, trying to catch up. Trying to think of a plan, but her mind dragged.

"Still feeling a bit under the weather, are you?" the king asked mildly, catching Morgana's wince.

Morgana narrowed her eyes, heart pounding, stuttering in her chest as she tried to decide which horror to look at. Deciding she couldn't stand to see her sword in his hand, she looked to Helah, still slumped in Joao's arms. She'd scanned Helah for injuries, for blood, but found nothing.

"Ah," the king said. "She'll be like that for a while, I'm afraid. A similar state as her sister, actually. It was all the same poison."

At those words Morgana's heart froze, and she turned slowly back to the king, breath catching in her throat. "Poison?"

"Not lethal, of course," he assured her, with no kindness. "They'd be no use to me dead. Then you couldn't save them."

"I can save them?" she asked before she could stop herself, her voice hoarse as if it'd been rubbed raw with sandpaper.

He flipped the sword in his hand. "Of course. If all goes well, I won't even need to use this."

There it was.

"How did you know?" Morgana whispered. How could he possibly know that he could control her powers with the Serpent Sword? She was the only person alive who knew the weapon's secrets.

"It was only a theory," the king said airily, spinning the sword around as if he'd been practicing with it for decades. "A myth that your lifeline was tied to an object, a weapon that might kill you. Technically never confirmed, but your desperation to retrieve it in your escape was enough to ensure there was some truth to the stories."

"No," Morgana said, shaking her head in desperation. "No, that's not enough. *No* one knew that besides my line. Who told you?"

"That sword extends far beyond you and your mother," the sea king said with a slippery grin. "I've lived longer than you most ancient ancestors, and I'll long outlive you."

Morgana's heart stopped as she understood.

"Who blessed you?" she asked flatly. The only way to gain immortality was to be blessed by a god or goddess. And it explained the age behind those eyes, the eldritch aura that had made her skin crawl from the moment she first felt his soul.

He stood, spreading his arms. "I'm the king of the sea. There's really only one answer."

The god of the sea, then. Morgana's head swam.

"I concealed the portal here," the king said, motioning to two innocuous pillars situated against the right wall. "Generations ago, after Nysus was created in the Rift, with a Calypdon king suffering from advanced senility. He died only days later, and never had the chance to tell his advisors of the new portal. I knew there would come a time when I could put it to good use, and it came the moment you strode into my kingdom."

She tried to think of a plan. Where was Wendell? Surely, they had poisoned him as well. Perhaps they'd dosed the entire palace, and that was why the place was so quiet?

As if he could read her thoughts, the king sat forward, tilting his head as if he was watching a vaguely entertaining game. "Our dear Aveline won't wake for quite some time," he drawled. "Probably for far longer than Helah here. I gave her a much more powerful dose with her dinner. It had to be done, for it to linger on her lips and pass to you."

Morgana felt sick. She'd taken to eating in her room, staying away from the mess hall to avoid the strange looks from the guards. "Everyone?" she asked hoarsely.

"Everyone who ate in the great hall. Which, inconveniently, was everyone but you. The isolation of your line has been a thorn in my side for centuries now, but I managed to find a way around it.."

"Aveline -"

He cut her off smoothly. "She knew the risks. It was a sacrifice she had to make."

A dense metal ball dropped into the pit of Morgana's stomach, and her legs wobbled with the weight of it. "She knew the risks?"

His mouth opened, slack for a moment, and then his head fell back as he laughed freely. It was a horrible sound. "Oh, you poor, young being. Immortal as you are, you have so much to learn. Aveline is, and will always remain, a child of the sea. For all of her days, she will answer only to me."

Morgana's stomach roiled, retracing every detail of her evening with Aveline. "No. No, Aveline is *nothing* like you."

"Perhaps not," King Daegil admitted. "But I think she realized that *you* are quite a bit like me. It didn't take long for her to eventually decide you were worse."

"But I'm *not*," Morgana ground out, voice wavering. "I'm not the monster that you are, and Aveline said -"

King Daegil's eyes widened with glee. "She said you weren't a monster? That, alone, should tell you everything you need to know." He sat forward, elbows on his knees. "We *are* monsters; both of us. It is irrevocable. Perhaps you could tamp it down; suppress it and act like one of the humans you can control. But it has always been there, and it will always *be* there. Aveline knows that, and so do you."

No.

Morgana screamed, the wretched sound tearing from her throat and her heart and all the tiny chinks in her armor that she'd somehow let Aveline carve open. Lifting her hands, she tore at her head as she roared loud enough to bring the ceiling down. She gathered every ounce of magic, pushed through the lingering poison and blazed with all the power she'd been cursed with. Maybe it'd all be worth it, if she could do this. The curse, her life, her love, everything she'd lost … it would all be worth it if she could just kill him. If she could stop this.

Hollering toward the sky, toward the sea, she sent her magic cascading toward him, letting it sink into flesh and bone, to find the life inside him. That pain came back, the same agony that had made her magic whimper the first time she had assessed him, but she gritted her teeth and pushed through it, squeezing her eyes shut. She didn't need to see when she could feel him, and she drove deeper, searching for his soul, for something to take away. She twisted her power, nestling it inside -

Only for it to recoil from him.

Her magic came flying back at her all at once, nearly knocking her off her feet as the air flew from her lungs. She gasped, stars dotting her visions as her magic settled back inside her, cowering, not willing to endure that again.

"Nice try." His voice floated to her from far away, and she blinked the darkness from her eyes to see him still standing, as though she hadn't even touched him. "I see that you've never gone up against a Hallowed. Not surprising, since I'm the only one left."

She swayed where she stood, trying to decipher what had happened.

"You can reach me," he said, the smile growing somehow bigger. He kept stomping her down, and she kept being surprised when it happened. "I was once human, as all your little subjects are. My life force is tied to yours, yes, but it's also tied to his."

Realization dawned on her. The moment he'd been made a Hallowed, been granted immortality, he was not only of this world. He had become linked to another, one she could not reach, one she had no control over.

She could not defeat a god.

The Serpent Witch channeled life into humanity. That had always been the curse, that she gave life to those who needed it to survive. The humans that she cared for, that she gave life to, had such a profound connection with her that she could bend their souls to her will. They were all within reach. Perhaps Daegil had no humanity left.

She couldn't stop him, then. Strength sapped out of her, and she crumbled to the floor, horror and sorrow and an avalanche of other emotions driving her down, grinding her down as her knees collided with wood. Her eyes burned, sending rivers cascading down her cheek, blurring her vision.

She could see well enough as he smiled though, relishing the moment, basking in her agony. He took the steps of the dais slowly, pausing at each one, a predator stalking his prey. "You were never going to win. Once Aveline had taken you to bed, getting the sword was … perhaps too easy. I thought you'd be more of a challenge."

He hopped down onto the floor, a resounding *boom* echoing around the chamber. Morgana gazed up at him, unable to move as he drew closer, power radiating off him. Just as she had noticed it in the sword as soon as her mother had told her of its power, she found herself shocked that she hadn't realized how deep the darkness within the sea king went. Her shoulders shook with suppressed sobs, and she thought of Aveline passed out in her room, enduring the repercussions of her betrayal.

Daegil stopped a few feet away, wiping the gleaming blade of her sword on his shirt. "I understand your sorrow at the truth, and I'd be even more understanding of your anger."

Morgana didn't have the awareness to be angry. She couldn't feel anything.

"But you need not be angry with me. I've only wanted what's best for my people."

Morgana remained silent.

"Will you serve me willingly?" he asked, louder, and Morgana recoiled from the words. "Now that you know the woman you've fallen in love with was serving me all along?"

Morgana was dead inside, wounded beyond repair, but she summoned enough strength to croak, "Never." She would never serve him, never bow to him. She may have been on her knees, but she wouldn't lower her head.

The king didn't look surprised, but he still snarled as he crouched in front of her, close enough that their noses brushed. His breath smelled of brine, the saltiness threatening to suffocate her. She suffocated under all of this, steadily drowning in the knowledge of what must come next.

She couldn't fight. She couldn't even try. The poison remained in her system, making her sluggish, but that wasn't all. She had no weapons and her magic was useless against him.

Morgana was useless against him. Even if everything else in their plan had gone right, they still would have lost.

The thought was almost enough to make her give up entirely, to collapse and close her eyes, as if she could stop what was coming. But she stayed on her knees, kept her eyes trained forward, and wondered what would happen to Helah after this. Had she been working for the king, too? Probably not, she thought, given that Daegil had decided to use her as leverage to keep Morgana from killing Joao.

She hoped Helah would survive.

King Daegil stared right through her into whatever soul a witch could possess. "There's something you should have thought about before ever stepping foot in my kingdom." His voice was almost a whisper.

Morgana didn't ask him to elaborate. She knew he would.

His crown blazed red in the rising sun peeking in through the windows, as if it had been dipped in blood.

"Serpents drown in the water," he hissed, and plunged the blade into her stomach.

Chapter Twenty Two

The first thing Morgana noticed was that her mind still belonged to her.

She wished it didn't. She always thought she would fade into nothingness, that she would be taken over entirely and be none the wiser.

But when the pain exploded in her gut, when that weakness paralyzed her muscles, she found that she could see just fine. The king still stood in front of her, and he was still smiling, and her sword was still embedded in her flesh.

"No," was the last thing she said with any free will at all. She remained silent after that. Everything was silence.

***

Every time she blinked, she was somewhere else. Not physically, but her mind chased each soul he forced her to destroy. King Daegil stayed at her side through the torture, flicking his wrists to direct her, her own personal puppeteer. If she could have, she would have told him that he didn't have to use his arms. There was no use pointing or directing her. He just had to rear up the magic like a tidal wave, and it would strike down each soul in its path. All he had to do was think about something, and Morgana would do it.

And she did. She killed for him. She tore apart an entire kingdom for him.

He wasted no time in having her cut down the army, reaching out to every soul who lived in the palace. The souls evaporated from her hold, one by one, but she couldn't feel it as she once had. They belonged to the sea king now.

Morgana killed thousands from her knees, head bowed as she tried and tried to stop it, tried to rein her power back in, but it wasn't hers anymore. Her blood flowed onto the throne room floor, spattering her knees and hands when she keeled forward.

The king caught her roughly by the collar of her shirt, wrenching her up. Agony tore through her stomach. She stumbled to her feet, wondering why he didn't just make her stand with her powers. Perhaps he liked to feel the physical control that he had over her, to feel the blood in her pulse that now belonged to him.

"Good little witch," he murmured in her ear as she swayed against him, his smooth jaw jutting into her cheek. Repulsed, she tried to move away, but she couldn't. Tried to scream at him but couldn't speak. Tried to stop the carnage, but she *couldn't*. She couldn't stop any of it.

The sword remained in her stomach, the hilt pressed against the raw, throbbing skin at the edge of the wound. He kept his hands wrapped around the hilt, twitching and tearing a maze of slashes through her. Morgana howled.

He let her.

Did he have to leave it in her body? Did he have to keep hurting her to keep the power? Morgana didn't know all the secrets of this sword. It'd never been used like this before.

Apparently, it didn't have to stay in the wound, because the king twisted the blade one last time before pulling it out.

Slowly.

Morgana gritted her teeth as her treasured sword grated against her spine, cutting along bone and through muscle. She refused to scream for him again, refused to cry. But then she remembered the control he had over her and realized she didn't have a choice in her feelings at all. Not anymore.

***

She felt through it all, the agony pulling at what was left of her heart, what was left of her soul. Would her soul disappear, if the king kept on like this? If he kept killing through her, using her body as the weapon she always feared it would become?

Morgana caught sight of Helah again, where Joao had dropped her. She laid still, whatever drug he had given her clearly still coursing through her veins, but Joao wasn't concerned with her anymore. He fell to his knees before his king, bowing as low as he could go without pressing his forehead to the ground.

"My king," he murmured to the ground, his voice low and gravelly. "My king, you did it."

King Daegil smiled, and in Morgana's delusion, the red of his lips looked bloody.

"I did."

With a snap of his fingers, he made Morgana snap Joao's neck.

***

A sharp *"No!"* sounded an eternity later as someone rushed into the throne room, throwing open the doors.

"Ah," King Daegil drawled, but Morgana couldn't see who had spoken. She still faced the throne, and she couldn't turn of her own accord. She couldn't move at all, not unless he told her to. Despair cracked through her bones, dripping into her veins, and she wanted to break the palace in half. To break the kingdoms in half to make it stop. With a lazy smile, King Daegil said, "Right on time."

"What is this?" Wendell's voice floated through the fog clinging to the corners of her mind. "Morgana?"

Morgana's heart was cleaved. What would he think? Surely that she had betrayed him, had betrayed them all. She was suddenly grateful she couldn't see his face, how the reality of the situation would slowly dawn on him.

Or, rather, what would he believe to be the reality.

Perhaps no one would ever know the truth. Perhaps Daegil would find a way to keep her as a slave forever, with her mouth sealed and her magic his.

King Daegil would surely do everything he could to frame Morgana as a willing participant, because he would always be inclined to cruelty over mercy. Without a word, without a verbal order, Morgana felt her legs move beneath her, standing and turning. Every step was agony, as her torn skin shifted with each movement.

Wendell wore his night clothes, a sword at the ready. He didn't bother trying to hide the shock on his face, the despair. "What is this?" he asked again, not knowing that Morgana couldn't explain.

But then something bubbled up in her throat, and though she tried to clamp down on it, biting her tongue so hard she thought she might bite right through it, it came bursting out anyway. "This was always the inevitability," Morgana found herself saying, and when it came out, it sounded cruel. Cruel and sharp as King Daegil's voice always had. In her mind, she could hear his voice beneath hers, as if their two voices were merging. Maybe, in the end, they would become one person. "You were foolish to trust me."

Wendell's face crumpled. Daegil's words, coming through Morgana's lips, crushed any hope he might have had. He tightened his grip on his sword. "I suppose I was."

It made it so much worse that he truly *had* trusted her. As if he had never expected this.

Wendell moved forward first, and though Morgana thought King Daegil would make her attack, she stayed still.

"Stand down," King Daegil said for nothing but show, and Morgana's hand dropped limp to her side. "As much as you'd like to kill him, this one is mine."

Bastard! Morgana tried to bellow, and she could feel it in her throat. Her mouth was set into a hard, determined line, and it would not open. *You lying, disgusting bastard, you—*

It was useless. Perhaps King Daegil could hear her thoughts, but he gave no indication of it as he swaggered toward Wendell, brandishing the Serpent Sword still slick with her blood. Wendell wouldn't know it was hers, of course. He would believe it was just another victim's. Helah in the corner, perhaps, or Joao. It would never occur to him to see a monster as a victim. In his head, he'd already made that mistake once.

Morgana found herself following King Daegil's advance as he stalked toward Wendell. It was as if she was in a trance. Morgana noticed that though King Daegil was the one armed, Wendell leveled his sword at her.

King Daegal lunged, drawing Wendell's attention at last. The duel was quick, Wendell's weapon clattering across the throne room, where it would remain for several years, untouched, along with the rest of the palace. Wendell didn't back down, though, swinging his fist at King Daegil's jaw.

He only got one good hit in. King Daegil lashed his arm out, catching Wendell's wrist and wrenching his arm up. Bones snapped, splitting through the skin of Wendell's forearm. He moaned, dropping to his knees. Blood trickled down his arm, and Morgana's arms longed to reach out, to comfort him as he had once comforted her.

"Look in her eyes," King Daegil growled, shoving Morgana forward and wrenching Wendell's chin up. "Look at what being kind wrought on your kingdom."

Wendell spat at the sea king's feet. "My kindness is not responsible for her actions."

Yes, that's right, Morgana sobbed in her mind. *Your kindness gave me something to fight for. Thank you for that.*

And then Wendell turned, spitting at Morgana's feet as well. "You may cause the downfall of our world, but you will surely go with it."

I'm sorry, Morgana tried to say. No words came, and she was left to stare at the look of hatred on Wendell's face as the sea king plunged her blade into his sternum. The regret and loathing that he would never be able to take back.

Still, she recited her sorrow like a mantra in her head, until his eyes glossed over, as his blood spread beneath her feet.

I'm sorry I'm sorry I'm sorry I'm sorry.

He died believing her his enemy. But he would never be hers.

***

"She really did leave for you, you know."

Daegil whispered in Morgana's ear as he shoved her down the hallway. Morgana couldn't respond. Her voice had been stolen, and she couldn't even open her mouth. The king kept her face completely impassive, staring straight ahead as their footsteps echoed along the hallway. He didn't bother trying to hide the sounds; there was no one left to hear.

She walked like a puppet strung up on taut strings. Inside her mind she screamed against every movement. The halls of the palace were silent, the people either dead or poisoned.

She couldn't feel Aveline's soul, no matter how hard she strained. She couldn't feel any souls at all, as if the bridges linking her to the mortals had been destroyed. The cacophony of lives had been a constant presence. To have that ripped away was almost more painful than the wound in her gut. The silence was unbearable. She hadn't realized before how loud living was, how the souls rattled within her bones.

"Back when you escaped from my kingdom, that wasn't an act," the king went on, swinging the sword at his side. Morgana could only hear the blade slicing through the air, unable to make herself turn to see it. "She truly helped you escape, truly wanted to help you." He scoffed, and the sound skittered down her spine. "It didn't take her long to see things for how they were, for you to remind her of the monster within you."

I'm not afraid of you. I'm not afraid of you. I'm not afraid of you.

Lies, lies, lies.

"She came crawling back to me weeks ago," he hissed to her, his voice filling the emptiness around them despite his hushed tone of voice. "She said she would do anything to see you defeated."

What had she done? When had Aveline changed her mind?

The king seemed to hear her. "She heard what you did to her people when you came to take her sister. Their bodies were scattered across the ocean floor. She saw what you were capable of, then."

I didn't kill any of them, she wanted to say. *I swear, I didn't kill any of them.*

Perhaps Aveline thought she had. Perhaps Aveline hadn't believed her claims that her hands were clean of blood.

They weren't anymore. She'd never be able to scrub it all off, even if none of her victims had bled even a drop.

***

Aveline was where Morgana had left her, lying in the bed Morgana had promised to come back to.

She remained sprawled out over the sheets, the blanket tugged up to her chin, the smallest of smiles gracing her lips. Her hair fanned out across the pillow, muscles completely relaxed, entirely ignorant of the slaughter sweeping throughout the kingdom.

Not ignorant, Morgana reminded herself as the king made her walk into the room, prodding her with the sword. He didn't need to, he could make her do whatever he wanted, but Morgana thought he enjoyed driving the blade into Morgana's skin, the pain it caused her. It sunk briefly into her skin, but King Daegil sent her shooting forward, blood dripping down her back.

And Aveline knew.

She knew, she knew, she knew -

She did this to you, she did this to you she did this to you -

The king rounded the room, the sword slack at his side as he admired Aveline's figure. Aveline's breath was steady and calm despite the poison. Had the poison begun to set in last night? Had Aveline been hallucinating when she came to Morgana's room? Or had it all been a calculated seduction?

Morgana didn't know which was worse. It hadn't *felt* fake when Aveline kissed her. How could it not have been real? She couldn't think about it, though, because King Daegil tightened his hold on her thoughts, and tore them away from any doubts.

King Daegil placed the tip of sword on Aveline's shoulder, drawing it down her body into it rested in the divot of her hips. Morgana waited, waited for the moment the king would plunge that blade down, but it didn't come. The point of the blade floated back up, hovering over her face, dragging over her neck and cheek. In the end, he just stepped back with a click of his tongue.

What do you want with her? Morgana wanted to scream, but her lips remained sealed. King Daegil clearly didn't want to hear from her right now and kept her silent. *If she's on your side, what more could you want from her?*

As though he heard her thoughts - perhaps he did, they *were* connected, after all - King Daegil settled into a chair by Morgana's bed. The same chair Aveline had spent so long in, waiting for Morgana to wake up. He placed the sword across his lap. "She came back to me, yes, but I can't have my soldiers doubting me. I can't have them bringing precious weapons to my enemies."

That's me. That's all I am. A weapon, something to be used, and nothing more.

Morgana wished she would lose consciousness, wished he would take her entirely so she didn't have to bear the pain anymore, wished that he would just kill her already.

He won't. If he kills you, he becomes everything that you are. You're a weapon, and no one wants to be a weapon. No one wants to be used. There's a reason he only wants these powers temporarily.

"Rebels must be punished," he said, bracing his hand against his folded leg. "Allowing defiance without retribution causes the ruination of kingdoms."

Ruin the kingdom, ruin me, ruin the whole damn world. Just leave her alone.

She couldn't control the instinct to protect Aveline. It came before she could stop it, before she could remember that Aveline no longer thought Morgana was worth protecting.

Faster than she could follow, the king lifted the sword and threw it. Morgana didn't know why she bothered trying to flinch, but she wrestled against the bonds, needing to run from the weapon barreling at her. She had no choice but to watch as it came.

But it didn't hit her. It struck true, though, lodging in the wooden floorboards, between her feet. The vibrations reverberated through her bones, through the soles of her feet, but she couldn't look down at the waiting weapon. The king wanted her looking at him.

He bared his teeth. "Take. It."

Morgana took it without thought, and for the first time, the hilt was cold and unfamiliar in her grasp.

Because right now, it has a different master. It doesn't belong to you.

The king sat back, anticipating the show, and he didn't bother saying his next orders. When he looked at Aveline, Morgana knew what he wanted.

Kill her, his voice echoed in her mind, unwelcome but loud and dominating all the same. *Kill her and let the both of us be rid of her.*

***

Something splintered in the back of Morgana's mind.

She thought she had blacked out for a moment, her ears rushing, because when she turned to Aveline after what felt like an eternity, the woman's eyes had fluttered open, and she was sitting up.

"Gods, I have the headache of a lifetime," she said, rubbing her eyes as she leaned forward against her knees. Her eyes must have been bleary, filled with sleep, and she rubbed at them, blinking it away.

Morgana's hand didn't shake as she lifted the sword. How could it? The king was as steady as ever, and she had become the king. The king had become her.

Aveline looked up again, freezing when her half smiling expression fell on Morgana. Confusion sparked in her eyes, a moment of hesitation. Her brows furrowed, her mouth contorted with confusion and fear. But then Aveline sensed the other presence. She flicked her eyes to the corner to find King Daegil watching with his arms folded over his chest, an impious smile gracing his features.

She turned back to Morgana, and Morgana wondered what her face looked like, if it gave anything away, or if the king had so much control that even her gaze had hardened into something cold and distant. Aveline searched her face for something, any sign of explanation.

"No," she breathed out at last, inching back in the bed, kicking the covers off. She wore only a thin, simple nightgown that she'd thrown on at the end of last night, and it lifted up her thighs as she moved. "*No*."

Yes, Morgana thought. *He betrayed you.*

You shouldn't have betrayed me.

Morgana took a step forward. Then another.

Aveline looked wildly between King Daegil and Morgana, but the king showed no indication of interfering. She took another step.

"Morgana," she said frantically, scrambling from the bed, falling to the opposite side so it separated them. Morgana adjusted her path, rounding the bed. "Morgana, what is this?"

She did this to you, the smallest of voices said in the back of Morgana's mind. *She gave you to him. She's responsible.*

But the voice was very small, and the rest of her was focusing on the night before, the weeks before. She kept close to her heart that vision of a woman who had talked with her, laughed with her, fought with her. A woman who not twelve hours ago had insisted she wasn't scared of her. That she wasn't a monster.

Perhaps, even if it wasn't the truth, she was still grateful to have heard it.

"Morgana," Aveline gasped again, eyes wide, and her heels hit a wall. Morgana didn't stop walking until she was close enough to press the blade to the center of Aveline's chest. Aveline's gaze flickered down to the blood painting Morgana's torso, and something guttered in her dark eyes. "What did you do?"

Morgana wished she could cry. A deep anguish welled up in her, and her eyes burned with tears trying to break free, but the barrier between her soul and her body remained. She struggled against the cage of her being, but she couldn't escape.

Aveline didn't run. She couldn't, not with Morgana boxing her in against the wall, King Daegil lingering behind them. Aveline simply stared down that sword, as Morgana lifted it until it was wedged beneath the seashell embedded in her skin.

She's no woman of the sea, the king said in her mind. *Make it so.*

Aveline gagged at the pressure on her throat, hands flying up as if to push the sword away, but where on the blade could she grab without slicing her hand open? Morgana tried to speak, but the king wouldn't let her, pushing the sword in further until it broke skin.

Morgana's soul vibrated, screaming in protest, but her body remained perfectly calm. She saw it in the stillness of her hand, the steadiness of her strike, when it came.

Her body belonged to the sea king, but her heart was still hers, and it jumped and resisted with everything it had.

It wasn't enough.

She didn't feel Aveline's soul leave her body. The lack of magic was like a missing limb, a sense turned off, and Morgana felt empty without it. She, alone, was no longer enough, and hadn't been since her mother died. Even knowing she wouldn't find anything, Morgana felt desperately around for Aveline's soul. It had been such a beautiful thing, the first time Morgana had reached out to touch it when they were alone in her cabin.

But she couldn't find it and instead had to feel Aveline's life fade with her hands, as the warm blood of what had once been her only friend washed over her skin.

***

A scream shattered the silence of the room, but Morgana barely heard it. She couldn't take her eyes off the blood painted over her fingers, painted over her soul. It would tarnish her forever, sink into her flesh and bones, and remain there until the end of time.

Daegil made her turn too soon, before Morgana was ready to stop gazing at Aveline's lifeless face. He redirected the sword now dripping with Morgana's, Wendell's, and Aveline's blood toward the woman crying in the doorway.

Helah swayed on her feet, the poison still coursing through her system, but she was alert enough to stand up straight, to know what she saw was real. Her hands clawed at her face as if she might strip the sight of her sister crumpled dead on the floor away from her memory.

It's not real, Morgana cried. *It's not, it's not, not in the way you believe it is*.

The sorrow melted into pure fire as Helah lifted her gaze to Morgana. Morgana would wonder for the rest of her days what the woman found there.

Weaponless, Helah lunged.

Morgana made no move against Helah, allowing the attack to come, but King Daegil didn't make her move, either. Perhaps he thought Morgana would have some instinct of self-preservation, that Morgana would easily dispatch an unarmed opponent and the whole ordeal would be done with, but that didn't happen. No, Helah fought with practiced precision, her punches swift but hard, especially when the king didn't make Morgana fight back.

His order for action came late, and by the time Morgana moved to defend herself, Helah had already kicked Morgana's sword hand, loosening her fingers and letting the blade fall. Helah grabbed it with barely a pause in her attack, lunging for Morgana's neck, but Morgana was moving now, rolling and dodging out of the way of the weapon. She jumped over the bed, sprinting across the room, but Helah ran hot on her heels, slashing wildly through the air. She was screaming something, but Morgana couldn't make out the words

Morgana's foot tangled with something on the floor, slowing her down, and she caught herself against the wall. Bile rose in her throat when she looked down and caught sight of what she'd tripped over, Aveline's shoulder twisted at a horrible angle from the impact of Morgana's foot. The distraction was more than enough to give Helah an opening, and she finally made contact. The blade dragged across Morgana's forearm. A single, deep cut, more than enough to draw blood.

Morgana's innards churned within her, getting tugged every which way. Her very soul was being pulled in two directions. She slapped her hand over this new wound, trying to stem the flow coming up between her fingers, before she froze. Black spots popped up over her vision, but she could still see well enough to notice King Daegil suck in a breath from across the room.

He hadn't ordered that action.

Whatever Helah had done, breaking her skin with that same sword was enough to break whatever bind the king had on her.

She didn't have the time to marvel at it. Helah reared back, ready to make the killing blow. But that would mean that Helah would be the one to inherit her powers. Not in a million years would Morgana allow that to happen.

Not to Helah, who was so kind, and who didn't deserve any more suffering.

Morgana leaned back against the wall, kicking both of her legs up and shoving with all her might into Helah's stomach. Helah flew across the room, landing in the corner opposite King Daegil.

The sea king clenched his fists and stood, storming toward Helah and the Serpent Sword.

Morgana held the wound in her stomach, her body swaying now that King Daegil's will wasn't holding her up. Helah scrambled to her feet, stepping forward to meet the king's assault. Helah stood in the center of the room, with a monster on either side, but didn't so much as blink. Her sister lay dead at her back, and that was enough to keep her standing.

Helah didn't release the sword as she whipped her head back and forth, clearly not knowing whether to point it at the witch or the king. In the end, she jabbed it toward King Daegil and hissed, "*Leave now*."

The king eyed the sword, glittering in the sunlight streaming in from above, his fingers twitching as if he wanted to lunge for it. But Helah's arm was steady, and she was a member of the king's guard, trained by the best. He didn't move toward her.

"That's enough, anyway," King Daegil said wickedly, staring down the length of the sword into Helah's eyes. He flicked his gaze to Morgana. "I already got what I wanted from you, and you will never come back from this."

Morgana didn't know whether he spoke of the kingdom or her. Either way, she believed he might be right.

Morgana backed away, stumbling into the wall, the sound sending Helah twirling back to her. Helah brandished the weapon to fend off an attack, but Morgana just kept retreating as Helah looked between her and her dead sister.

"I'm sorry," was all Morgana croaked out as Helah lifted the sword higher, anguish and fury lining her features.

King Daegil seized his opening. He struck out with his elbow, sending Helah flying toward the wall, the sword clattering from her grip. Morgana watched in horror as the king moved across the room, fingers brushing along the hilt, and the sight was all Morgana needed to see, to know how this fight would end.

She ran, and now that Daegil had the sword, he didn't bother pursuing her. The palace halls were silent, filled with dead bodies she refused to look at. She raced through a destroyed kingdom, doing her best to hide the trail of blood she left behind her. A breath of sea mist drifted past her as she went, a phantom laugh on the breeze, and she just kept going, trying to ignore the salty tang relentlessly surrounding her.

She ran until trees rose up around her and swallowed her whole. She blended into the shadows of the forest, tucked herself beneath the boughs, and didn't resurface for two hundred years.

PART THREE
Two Hundred Years Later
Aveline

Chapter Twenty Three

Aveline had stayed awake as long as she could, but eventually exhaustion clung so heavily to her limbs that she couldn't stay awake a moment longer. She'd collapsed into sleep with Morgana still in her lap, both of them huddled in the corner of King Daegil's dungeon. Morgana had haunted her dreams, an image of a woman unconscious, a woman possessed. In the dream, Morgana radiated a dark emerald light as she brought the sword up to Aveline's chest, tears glimmering in her eyes as she mourned.

It's not what you think. It's never what you think. Green hair and a yellow eye remained transfixed in the back of her mind even as Aveline opened her eyes, the pain of lying on stone seeping back into her limbs.

At first, when she looked around, she found only darkness. She sighed into the emptiness at the thought of another day sitting alone, running over the details of a mystery she would never be able to solve. Not on her own, at least.

But then the light adjusted, filtering from the algae embedded in the cracks of the stone walls, and a soft face came into view as Morgana leaned over her from where she was crouched at her side. Aveline nearly broke out into a sob, reining in a waterfall of emotions she couldn't explain as Morgana's yellow eye caught the purple glow, her green hair fanning out in the water.

"Morning," Morgana said with a guarded expression, that empty stare of recent days a fading memory. Morgana didn't smile, but she didn't glare, either, and she raked her gaze over Aveline, probably taking in how horrible she looked. "Are you okay?"

"Really?" she huffed, her voice a mere croak as she pulled herself up. Her throat cried out in protest. "You've been unconscious for who knows how long, and you ask if *I'm* okay?"

Morgana cleared her throat, the water thick around them. "It seemed like the right thing to say. How long *have* I been out?"

Aveline shrugged, turning her body away from the guards as if she could pretend the only eyes on her, were Morgana's. "Your guess is as good as mine, but I think it's somewhere around five days." She had counted meals at the beginning, determining the longest stretch of time without one as night, but she had begun losing track rather quickly.

Morgana blinked, shifting to sit back against the stone wall, and she winced, hands flying to her chest. Aveline surged forward by instinct, but Morgana raised her hand, shaking her head. "I'm fine. I … I'm fine." She shifted again, her body jerking as she tried to keep the pain at bay. "I'm glad my body kept me under for the worst of it."

Aveline didn't know what to say. She didn't know anything, anymore.

Morgana seemed to toy with what she wanted to say next before plunging forward when Aveline couldn't. "I've been told we know each other. But I'm having a hard time believing that you're … her."

Aveline ducked her head, at a loss for words even after spending two hundred years imagining what she would say if she ever had the chance to speak to Morgana again. She'd never heard Morgana sound so timid, but it might just be the disorientation still plaguing her.

Stomach churning, Aveline waited, not knowing exactly what she was waiting for. They should be screaming at each other, tearing each other apart for what the witch had done to her, but something held Aveline back. Held them both back.

This woman murdered you, Aveline reminded herself. Even so, the familiar fire that she'd spent two hundred years tending, feeding, didn't rear up as she had thought it would. Instead, it was replaced with a trickle of doubt.

Did she? Did she murder you?

Sorting through the events of that day, Aveline remembered the blank look on Morgana's face. The way Morgana gazed at her as if she was *nothing*. Morgana had looked her in the eye the whole time as the witch had cut her open. For years, Aveline had believed that disdain on Morgana's face had been directed at her.

But the blank stare behind Morgana's eyes had haunted Aveline for two hundred years. The unexplainable bleakness, the jerkiness of each of her movements.

"Tell me," Morgana said, voice harsh again, though the hesitation remained. "What did my dress look like for the one ball we attended together?"

Aveline was surprised by the absurdity of the question, but the image of the gown flashed into the forefront of her mind, even after all this time. "It was silver and covered in embroidered flowers." Aveline swallowed roughly. Morgana had looked beautiful that night, more a sorceress than a witch. More a goddess than a human. "It was as if you'd managed to bring a shooting star from the land, down into the sea."

Morgana's breathing sped up, but she nodded curtly. "Okay. Where did you find me for the first time, and what did I make you do to gain my trust?"

Warily, Aveline asked, "Is this a test?"

"Yes."

"I found you in a cottage in the Abandoned Forest," Aveline said, because for some reason, she found Morgana's suspicion reassuring. "Where you'd been living for years, first with your mother, and then alone."

Morgana's throat bobbed, but she pressed on. "Answer the second bit."

"You made me hold your pet snake," Aveline went on, remembering the cool scales slithering over her skin. "As an act of good faith."

Morgana's mouth opened and closed, momentarily distracted from whatever pain still haunted her.

If this was a test, Aveline could do her one better. "I went back, you know."

This startled Morgana enough into snapping her mouth closed. "What?"

"To your cottage." After the goddess had transformed Aveline into one of the Hallowed, she'd journeyed out to the part of the Abandoned Forest that remained untouched by the tide. She'd walked slowly, adjusting to her new legs and the new shadows cast by the wall of water when the sun tried to shine through it. It had taken her weeks to complete the journey, sluggish in her new body.

She had found Morgana's cabin after several more days of wandering. It sat right at the edge of the invading water, but otherwise remained untouched. The leaves had fallen as cold weather moved in, summer disappearing with any lingering traces of their old reality. Tall grasses and ferns hid the rickety door entirely. Aveline had imagined this had once been a cozy home, but time had worn it down. It seemed to whisper through the silent woods, telling her to turn around, that she didn't belong here. No one belonged there anymore.

The Abandoned Forest had become entirely abandoned the day Morgana left, and Aveline had known in her bones that she was the only person for miles.

"I waited there for … two weeks, I think, but it was all sort of a blur. I thought you might have gone back, too, but you never returned."

Morgana was staring at her wildly now, eyes wide. "I did. I did go back. But when I got there, Coby wasn't there…" Morgana swallowed roughly. "I thought maybe I'd killed him, too."

Aveline's heart hammered in her chest. "You didn't kill him. I just found him first."

Something cracked behind Morgana's eyes. "You did?"

The snake had been curled up on Morgana's pillow, hissing when Aveline finally got up the nerve to cut down the nettles blocking the entrance. But this time, she had found no fear inside her when she looked at Coby's tiny eyes, only a muted sorrow. She wouldn't waste any of her hatred on animals. "He never left, I don't think, but he recognized me. I brought him with me back to Briarwood, because I couldn't bear for him to be left alone." She blinked. "Like I'd been left alone."

Morgana covered her face with her hands.

"He died six years later," Aveline said. She'd been hoping, back then, that he would last a few more years, but he must have been old already when she scooped him up and took him home. "But that trust test you forced on me when we first met paid off. I was never afraid of him after that."

Morgana looked up, eyes shining. A million emotions washed over her face, mouth opening and closing like she couldn't catch her breath. Her fingers flexed, reaching forward and then back, but never quite making it all the way to Aveline. "You're in this cell with me," Morgana finally said breathlessly.

Aveline nodded slowly, growing more confused by the moment, but there must have been a reason Morgana had been so willing to come out of hiding. She needed to hear this. *Really* hear it. "Trust me, I'm aware."

"I don't entirely believe that you're Aveline."

"And I don't totally believe that you won't try to kill me again," Aveline shot back, but Morgana just stared at her intently, still holding her stomach as if she could push down the pain, as if she could hold herself together. Aveline let her hand flutter up to her neck, brushing over the shell. "Fine. You want to know the real reason we didn't just attach this thing to Rike and be done with it?"

"Because you didn't want to risk her…"

"Because it wouldn't have worked even if we tried," Aveline corrected her. "This is *my* shell, my artifact. Once it's been bonded to a soul, it can't be bonded to another. I was worried that my new body would make things complicated, but…" She shrugged. "As they always say, 'It's what's on the inside that counts.'"

Morgana stared at the shell, at the soft fingers holding it, swallowing roughly. "So you … you've been in Calypdon this whole time..."

Aveline furrowed her brow, her hand falling to her side. "Where else would I have been? I escaped Nysus just as surely as you did."

Morgana looked away, eyes shining in the candlelight. The fire turned her yellow eye orange. "Daegil told me that you went back to him," she whispered, as if she couldn't quite believe it herself. "I thought he only made me kill you to hurt me."

Horrified, Aveline sat up straighter. The chains on her ankles clattered as she tried to move, reminding her just how trapped they were. "No. *No*. Once I left Nysus with you, I never served him again."

"I see that now," Morgana said, also looking at the chains.

But Aveline wasn't done, the words bubbling out of her. "I would *never* have served him after all that, I -" She cut herself off, raising her gaze to meet Morgana's shattered eyes. "What do you mean, he *made you*?"

You know nothing of my choices. That was what Morgana had said.

Morgana tucked her chin into her chest, tugging her knees up to her stomach. She'd never looked so small, the iron still coursing through her soul deepening the shadows under her eyes, the slump of her shoulders. "You have no idea what really happened that day, do you?"

Apparently not.

"I need you to tell me everything," Aveline whispered.

Morgana sucked on her front tooth. She glanced at the guards who still flanked their cells, and she motioned for Aveline to come closer, lowering her voice to almost nothing. "You should know, actually. I imagine you are immune to my … lethal powers in the same way he was."

Aveline jerked back, tilting her head. "You're unable to kill the Hallowed?"

Morgana nodded slowly. "My powers can't hurt them. If I could have, it never would have happened. He would have been dead before he could do what he did."

Aveline wanted to scream, "*What did he do?*", but her jaw had locked up.

Morgana went on before Aveline could even wrench open her mouth. "But that's not the point. I couldn't kill him and he had me backed into a corner." She swallowed, closing her eyes. "That night, where you and I…" she trailed off, biting her lip so hard she broke the skin, blood blooming through the water. "He stole the sword, took it from my room. I thought you had been sent to … distract me."

Aveline remembered the thoughts that had gone through her brain in the moments after she woke and found Morgana standing over her, a strange weakness in her body, thinking Morgana had done that to her. Wondering what Morgana had done the previous night while Aveline happily slept.

"Funny enough," Aveline said blankly, "I sort of thought the same thing." Morgana closed her eyes miserably, and Aveline felt sick. "But … what about the sword? Why is it so valuable that you risked your one chance at escape to go back for it?"

Morgana looked to the ceiling, pressing her lips together. "For the record, I wanted to get Rike to safety as well." She squeezed her eyes closed, as if she couldn't bear to look at Aveline anymore. "The powers of my kind … are too much for a human body to handle. Because, yes…" She opened her eyes to look at Aveline. "Before my mother died, and her magic passed to me, I was purely human. We all were at one point."

Aveline had gone through that sort of transformation, her entire body igniting in pain as the weight of magic and immortality settled onto her shoulders. Morgana must have gone through something similar, alone in her cabin after the loss of her mother.

Morgana saw the understanding in Aveline's eyes. "But because of that humanity, the power had to be linked to a sacred object. Something to keep us grounded, to *keep* me from becoming the monster the world believes me to be. Without it, I would be torn apart by the magnitude of the power in my veins."

Aveline's heart wrenched, and she suddenly remembered every moment that Morgana had panicked over the whereabouts of the Serpent Sword, how she had nearly gotten herself killed for it when they had first escaped Thalassa. How many details of the story had she pushed away in order to believe the one the sea king had painted for her?

"What can it do?" Aveline asked shakily.

Morgana ran a trembling hand through her hair, and Aveline wondered how much what King Daegil had done was hurting her. How much was she holding back? How deep was this hold that Daegil had on Morgana? Their souls had tangled from what had happened two hundred years ago, and the iron was coursing across that bridge, corrupting Morgana's soul.

"What can it do?" Aveline asked again.

Morgana stared at Aveline, biting the inside of her cheek as she hesitated.

"You can't use your power to test me this time," Aveline spoke into the silence. "You're just going to have to trust me."

She knew it was a tall order. She was having a hard time trusting Morgana, too. Her instincts to strike for the kill kept threatening to take over. But wars were often caused because people refused to listen to each other. They'd lived long enough to avoid that mistake.

Seemingly thinking the same thing, Morgana exhaled. "Killing me doesn't get rid of this power. If that were the case, killing me would kill everyone, because the existence of someone like me is what keeps life tethered to this world."

That's a lot of pressure, Aveline realized. She could see it in Morgana's face, how the years had worn on her.

"That sword holds half of my life, just as it holds half of every life in both kingdoms. It's almost impossible to kill me, but technically, someone could do it. They would have to use that sword. After all, after thousands of years, my mother finally left this world. She became mortal when I was born, and in cases like that, where it happens naturally, the power is transferred to the heir." She motioned flatly to herself, as if to say she had received the worst gift from her mother possible. "But if one of us is murdered, instead of the power fading with me, it gets transferred to my killer."

Aveline's skull rattled with this new information. "But … the sea king didn't kill you."

"No," Morgana said bitterly. "No, but it turns out that wounding me pretty badly does the trick. At least temporarily. It's as if he turned me into a puppet, and…" She trailed off.

The blood that had been on her shirt, collecting only around Morgana's stomach and nowhere else. Horror and disgust had churned through Aveline's veins at the sight, and she'd racked her brain as she tried to decide who the blood could belong to. Wendell? Helah? One of any number of innocent guards? She'd spent her last breathing moments sending a prayer up for that poor soul, the only person other than her that Morgana had killed with her hands instead of her magic.

But the blood had been *hers*, pouring from Morgana's own skin. The proof of King Daegil's attack.

The king took over her body. The realization clanged through Aveline's bones. He took over her body, and all the magic that came with it.

The rage that had been on Morgana's face that day flashed behind Aveline's eyes, but what she realized now was that the rage wasn't directed at her. It was for the king who had watched with a wicked grin from the corner of the room, the one who'd apparently taken … everything from her.

Aveline knew she should question it, that she shouldn't believe the woman who she'd spent so long thinking murdered her. That she shouldn't take her word for it just because so much seemed to back up her story.

But for the first time since everything fell apart, the world made sense again. Everything that she'd spent two hundred years agonizing over … It made sense.

"And I'm sorry that you got stuck here, too," Morgana murmured, bunching the hem of her shirt in tight fingers, "but I'd rather spend the rest of my long life getting tortured here than let him use my body to … to…" She couldn't finish, shaking her head. "I won't let it happen again."

And there it was. Morgana's body was tainted with iron through her unholy bond with Daegil, her magic dampened to nothing, but her words were strong.

Because they were true.

The space between them seemed to lessen and grow at the same time, and Aveline's fingers itched once again to reach out, as they had two centuries ago. Apparently, even a new body wasn't enough to erase all that she'd felt in the past. But she didn't reach out, unable to pass through the barrier that still remained between them, that wall of secrets and pain.

She simply spoke, because that was all she could do to offer comfort. "You didn't let it happen the first time," Aveline said, more fiercely than she intended. "He … he…"

Aveline felt sick for Morgana, for the stab wound to her stomach and the control that had been mercilessly stolen from her.

But Morgana shook her head. "He used my many mistakes against me," she whispered. "I never should have come out of hiding."

Perhaps she shouldn't have, Aveline thought once again, but for entirely different reasons. Not only because of the thousands of lives lost, but because of the piece of herself *Morgana* had lost. Aveline rubbed her eyes, trying to ease the nausea of the situation. "That would be my mistake, actually."

Morgana laughed hollowly but didn't deny it. "You came for me, but I went. I swore I never would, that I'd stay in my little hole forever and learn to live a half-life. But I'd seen my mother go out and help when she was needed, risking herself in the process. I wanted to help, too, even though I saw who she was before, and who she was after the world knew her, and they weren't the same person."

"But you still came," Aveline whispered. "You still came with me."

"Young and naive, I guess," Morgana murmured, but Aveline needed more than that. Needed to know why. Morgana seemed to sense this and sighed. "My mother told me that I would know when someone was worth it, when it would be the right decision to go … I felt your soul that day, reached out to feel what you wanted from me, and all I found was a woman who wanted to help a kingdom that wasn't her own, who was selfless and needed my help."

Aveline's throat bobbed. Ah, how the mighty had fallen.

"But I felt you, not the king. It didn't even occur to me that you could serve someone so wicked when you were so … *something else*." She swallowed and averted her eyes. "I don't think I'd even be able to count the mistakes that led us here."

Silence fell between them, and they both leaned away from each other. Morgana tipped her chin up, gazing at the ceiling as if she could see all the way outside, out of the sea and into the waiting stars above their home. Perhaps she sent up a prayer, and Aveline wanted to know what Morgana would wish for after all these years. Who she prayed to.

"Why didn't you tell me this earlier?" Aveline said brokenly. She wished she could feel souls, too, if just so they could be even, but she didn't need it. She could see the devastation written all over Morgana's face now that the numbness had fallen away.

"Because I did kill them," Morgana whispered, crumpling into herself.

"No. You *didn't* kill them," Aveline said, to herself as much as Morgana. In the moments passing between them, she rewrote their history in her mind, beneath her skin.

She didn't, she didn't, she didn't.

Morgana inhaled a sharp breath, as if she was having trouble breathing. She curled her hand toward her chest, pressing down. "It may not have been my mind, or my soul, but it was my magic. It was my decisions that led to every soul lost that day. And I carry it with me." A breath stuttered out of her chest, letting her cloud of hair float in front of her face as she gathered herself. "Besides, I didn't trust you before I knew who you were. Hell, before today, I might not have trusted you no matter who you were."

Aveline held her breath. "And now?"

Morgana looked up between billowing strands of hair. "Don't keep secretly plotting to kill me, and we'll see."

Chapter Twenty Four

Morgana wolfed down her first meal in days as soon as the guards dropped it off. Not that the plate had held much. The plate's meager contents barely provided enough sustenance to keep their strength up, but Aveline supposed that was probably the point.

"Is the food helping?" Aveline asked. They'd separated further, leaning against opposite walls. "Helping the pain, I mean."

Morgana wrapped her arms around her stomach. "It's helping the weakness. But the pain, it's like … a deep vibration just beneath the surface of my skin … *everywhere*." She spoke through clenched teeth, gripping the plate so hard Aveline feared the plate of driftwood would snap.

"You're doing a good job of hiding it," Aveline said, looking Morgana up and down. "You look almost normal." She paused. "You don't have to, you know. Hide your pain."

Waving her off, Morgana said, "Honestly, this is definitely troubling, but it's nothing compared to…" she trailed off, ghosts of agony flashing across her face.

Aveline folded her legs beneath her. "Still, just because you've grown accustomed to being alone doesn't mean you have to be that way for the rest of your days."

"There are not many immortal beings in this world," Morgana murmured. Aveline wanted to point out that she was immortal now, too, but she didn't know where they stood yet. Whether they would make it out of here at all, let alone live to see a thousand years. "And even fewer people who will listen to a strange woman running a reptile shop."

The corner of Aveline's mouth lifted. "Yeah, I actually wanted to ask about that."

"The shop?"

"More specifically the name."

Heat rose in Morgana's cheeks, and she ducked her head. "Right. I painted it in a moment of emotion."

"Good emotions?" Aveline asked delicately. "It was a good name."

Still avoiding her eye, Morgana said, "I was very confused, for a very long time. Part of me didn't believe what King Daegil had said about you, but I couldn't help feeling so … *betrayed* -"

"Tell me about it," Aveline said flatly. "You *killed* me."

Morgana ran her hands through her hair, sending the strands billowing through the water. "And if the king had been telling the truth, and you really had betrayed me, you might as well have killed me. I thought you'd given him the opportunity to do so. And…" Morgana trailed off. "And yet, you were dead, and I was alive. I suppose I wasn't ready to dismiss that the time you'd spent with me had meant *nothing*." Her throat bobbed, and she finally looked up to meet Aveline's eyes. A silent question.

"It wasn't nothing," Aveline whispered. She didn't know what it was now, if it ever could be something again, but she could at least admit that much. "I felt betrayed, too, for that very reason."

Morgana managed a laugh. "I'll bet you did."

Melancholy filled the space between them once more. Would it ever go away, or were they doomed to an eternal tragedy by the manipulation of one man? Aveline had a hard time speaking with Morgana now that they knew each other once more after spending centuries as strangers.

"Tell me more about it," Aveline blurted out before she could stop herself. At Morgana's questioning look, she added, "The day it all ... happened."

Morgana hesitated, that darkness falling back over her, but Aveline just slid her plate, with the pathetic remnants of her own meal, toward Morgana. An offering. She sighed, accepting the morsels. "He stabbed me in the stomach."

Aveline took a sharp breath, but she'd suspected that. Had seen the blood, although at the time she'd thought it came from some other victim. Wendell, perhaps. She'd never let herself think too hard about it.

Morgana scoffed. "I think he could have taken control by stabbing me in the leg, foot, whatever. I've thought about it a lot, and I'm pretty sure any wound would have done the trick. Maybe it wouldn't have lasted as long, but I don't think that's what it was about." Morgana stared at the food in her hands, her appetite faded completely. "I think he wanted to cause me as much pain as possible."

Aveline imagined Morgana run through by the sword she held so dear and shivered.

Morgana tapped her own forehead and chest. "But to kill me, it'd have to be a strike to the head or the heart." She did a double take, eyes widening. "I probably shouldn't even be telling you that. You know too much already."

"I was never the one who tried to kill you," Aveline pointed out.

Morgana conceded. "Fair, although you *were* planning on killing me after all this, weren't you." It wasn't a question, and Aveline's silence told Morgana enough. She didn't seem surprised. "I can't say I blame you."

"I won't now, though," Aveline scrambled to say. "In case you were wondering."

Morgana gave her a wan smile. "I wasn't. Mostly because I'd still deserve it, even if you did." Before Aveline could respond, Morgana returned to the earlier topic with a rough exhalation. "Anyway, it was … the worst pain imaginable. Not just because of the sword, but because I could feel him … sucking my magic away from me. As if he was squeezing it out of me with his bare hands, and I was starting to wither away. Ever since my mother died, my magic is what has kept me alive. I'm tethered to it in the same way everyone else is."

What a life to live, a life that didn't even belong to her; to be connected to thousands of souls at once.

Morgana sucked on her bottom lip, biting down with the effort to keep some sort of control over herself, to keep her emotions at bay. Aveline became suddenly sure that Morgana had a lot of practice with that. Aveline did, too.

"And I remember it," Morgana finally whispered, eyes glazing over. "I remember … *all* of it."

Aveline covered her mouth with her hand, leaning forward in horror. "You -"

Morgana nodded. "Every death, every soul … you."

Aveline didn't know how to respond to that. Perhaps magic really could destroy more than it could heal. It had torn Morgana apart.

"My turn for a question," Morgana said roughly. "Why didn't *you* tell *me* who you really were?"

"Because I thought you'd kill me again," Aveline said honestly, adjusting her legs into a more comfortable position. It was getting more and more difficult as the chains seemed to gain weight.

Morgana nodded bitterly. "Good answer."

"And do you believe me? That I am who I say I am?" Aveline asked.

"Do you believe that the king was controlling me that day?" Morgana shot back.

"Yes," Aveline said without thinking. She didn't know what that meant, but she found it to be true.

Morgana sat back. "I think I do. Now that I'm looking for it, there are shades of Aveline … in every part of you."

"There should be," Aveline said. "I still have the same soul."

Morgana shook her head. "But you look different, you sound different. You even *talk* different."

"So do you," Aveline whispered. "Compared to when I first met you. I think it's the whole immortality thing. People can change a lot in two hundred years."

"I'm trying," Morgana said brokenly. "But you could be faking this whole thing, somehow, and I'd have been fooled by you *twice*."

"You're more suspicious than you used to be."

Morgana looked at her incredulously, and the darkness came back. Aveline saw what the world saw again, a witch shrouded by the night and cloaked in the souls of thousands. "Wouldn't you be?"

Aveline just stared, and if she hadn't believed Morgana before, she believed her now. Morgana's fingers curled into the fabric of her shirt, digging into the skin of her stomach, as if she could still feel the lingering presence of a phantom wound, an imprint of what she had lost. If Aveline lifted her shirt, would she find a scar there, like the ones that marked her own body?

The thought made an idea rise in the back of Aveline's mind, and she jerked up. "Wait. Show me, and I'll show you."

Morgana's brows rose. "Show you what?"

Morgana healed like a normal human being; she'd said so herself. Her body would always be human.

"Here." Aveline slid toward Morgana, who watched her warily. Aveline pointed to her face, to the scar lining her cheek. "Do you remember giving me this?"

"I mostly remember the killing blow, but you … fought. I must have sliced you several times before…" She didn't need to finish. They both knew what happened.

No matter. Morgana had left her with more than one scar. With some effort due to the chains on her wrists, Aveline unceremoniously pulled her shirt over her head, letting the fabric gather at her wrists above the iron. Morgana sputtered, but Aveline just shifted into the candlelight, baring the skin. Adjusting her undergarment, Aveline lowered the cloth enough to reveal the ugly, bulging scar just over her heart, and Morgana sucked in a breath. "This is where you did it. You must remember this, because you …I mean, the king took his time lining it up, so it would go right through my heart."

Morgana stared at it. The wound's width matched the blade of her sword. "I remember," she finally whispered.

Aveline pulled her undergarment back up, going to put her shirt back on but getting tangled in it. With the fabric still blocking her sight, she felt gentle hands guide the shirt over her with ease, fingers brushing against Aveline's cheek as Morgana directed her head into the hole.

Morgana's fingers lingered, grazing over the scar on her face. "I don't remember giving this to you. There was so much blood…"

"Don't," Aveline stopped her, taking her hand and lowering it. "It's okay."

"I'm still sorry."

"You can't be sorry for something you didn't do. Not really." She nodded to Morgana, who sat back slowly. "But you should have one, too. This is where you prove it to me."

Not understanding, Morgana asked, "Prove…"

"Prove to me that the king stabbed you. I believe you about the power of the sword, the fact that you sacrificed both of us for that blade says enough. But let me see that he did what you say he did."

Understanding, Morgana grabbed the hem of her shirt, rolling it up to her chest, exposing her curved stomach. And there, just above her navel, Aveline found a raised, angry scar. But Aveline clapped her hand over her mouth, words caught in her throat, because it was more than just a simple stab wound.

The king had torn her apart. Aveline's eyes raked over each mark the blade had left upon the skin, the path the king had carved into Morgana when he twisted the sword within her. Morgana didn't look at it, instead choosing to gaze toward the ceiling.

"It's bad," Morgana breathed. "I know."

Aveline's fingers twitched, willing herself to reach out as Morgana had, but she couldn't bring herself to do it, couldn't even move as she looked at the turmoil Morgana carried on her body. "He did this to you?" She expected her voice to come out wavering, but instead it rang out sharp as stone as ice settled within her.

Morgana rushed to lower her shirt, and Aveline blinked, drifting back into reality and looking at Morgana's face instead. "While he was … whatever you'd call what he did to me, I couldn't really feel it. Well, I *could*, but it was like he'd immersed me in someone else's pain. Each of my senses was distracted by what the souls around me were going though. The agony they felt." She looked up through her lashes. "Maybe I was feeling yours."

Aveline licked her lips, searching for a reply as images of the horrific scars lingered behind her eyes. That was enough for her. "I believe you."

"I thought you believed me before."

"Yeah, well, I really believe you now."

Morgana swallowed. "I believe you, too."

The malaise within her still remained, waiting for the king to return, but when she looked back at Morgana, it eased. "You said it was your decisions that led to the horror of that day. That you'd always carry it with you."

Morgana looked down.

Aveline leaned toward her, and though they still didn't touch, Morgana leaned back. "It was my decision as much as yours. So, I'll carry it with me, too."

***

Aveline had been lying awake for hours, so she was spared the panic of waking to Morgana's screams of agony. Aveline scrambled up, slipping over her cuffs as they scraped across the floor, rolling over to see Morgana thrashing on the floor, pulling at her skin, sobs racking her body.

"What's happening?" Aveline said urgently, reaching out to try and hold Morgana down, to keep her still. Morgana stared up at Aveline, deep-seated panic and pain in her eyes. "Morgana, what is it?"

Morgana couldn't answer, senseless cries coming out instead of words every time she opened her mouth. Aveline had no idea what to do, scared to put too much weight on Morgana for fear of the iron chains on Aveline's wrists doing *more* damage.

Iron.

"Morgana," Aveline said, turning back to her and gripping her wrist. Morgana jerked back so aggressively, she feared her arm might wrench out of its socket. "Is it the iron? You've done this before; you've conquered this pain.

You can do it again."

Writhing on the floor, Morgana struggled for breath, her hands folded over her heart as if she could make it beat normally again. Gasping, she tried to lift herself, squeezing her eyes shut, but fell back to the floor.

"Just stay still," Aveline pleaded, slipping her hands up from Morgana's wrists to her shoulders, pressing her into the floor as delicately as possible. "Stay down and try to breathe."

Morgana's arm flailed out, digging her fingers into Aveline's thigh. Only then did Morgana start to calm down, locking up her muscles and taking a shuddering breath. Aveline clamped her hands over Morgana's and held her there.

Only when Morgana's eyes finally opened again did she try to sit up again, this time succeeding with Aveline's help. "He must have done it again," Morgana gritted out, scooting back and collapsing against the wall, using it to prop herself up. "Stabbed … the iron …"

Of course. King Daegil surely loomed somewhere above, with a knife once again lodged in his side and grim satisfaction on his face.

King Daegil had stabbed himself again, and the iron corrupting Morgana's magic was back with a vengeance.

"So, he's weak, too," Aveline finally said. "Well, we have that going for us."

Morgana gasped in pain. With a sarcastic grimace, she muttered, "Yay."

"Does it hurt like it did when he took your power? As if he's extracting the magic?"

Morgana shook her head, gnawing on her lip and screwing her eyes shut. "No, the power is still mine, but it's as if it can't decide who it should belong to, so it's gone … dormant. But it's fighting to stay with me. It's as if … my veins are on fire."

Aveline shuddered. She didn't want to know the agony of iron coursing through her system.

"My weakness will always be the people I influence," Morgana breathed, gasping between every word with the effort. "Maybe they control me a little bit, too."

"That's not true," Aveline started, but Morgana shook her head.

"I suppose it's a fair trade off," Morgana whispered. "Because so many see me as all-powerful, as this … other worldly witch who holds their lives in her hands. But they hold mine, too. Of course," she huffed out, "I always knew that would become a less helpful weakness for the world to exploit when I stopped caring about my life altogether."

Aveline inhaled. "That won't happen."

Morgana stared into the corner of the cell, her body quaking. "It happened long ago."

Before Aveline could answer, before she could explain away the grief pulling in her chest, the door to the dungeon clattered open. Footsteps approached from down the hall. The guards straightened, saluting.

King Daegil didn't bother to hide the fact that his soldiers were supporting him this time. He floated between them freely, and he smiled all the while. "Painful, isn't it?" he asked by way of greeting. "The sacrifices we make for power can be immense."

Morgana tried to growl, but it came out as more of a gurgle.

The sea king motioned to himself with some difficulty. "I agree, but I imagine the iron hurts you that much more, drinking all that power you have inside. More power than I have, I hate to admit."

"Did I mishear you, or did you just admit I'm stronger than you?" Morgana snarled.

"Stronger, perhaps," King Daegil said with a glint in his eye. "But clearly vulnerable, too. They come hand in hand, as I have no doubt you've realized."

Morgana swallowed, chest heaving, and didn't say anything.

Aveline moved from where she sat beside Morgana with some difficulty, shifting so she could look the king in the eye. "Did you come just to mock us? To show us what we already knew - that you're *insane*?"

King Daegil pressed his thin lips together. "Mortals think of the Hallowed as insane because they don't understand us. You simply haven't lived long enough. Not yet." He nodded his head to Morgana in the corner, squirming as she tried to push away the pain coursing through her soul. "I believe *she's* well on her way. Her sanity began to slip the moment I wrenched her magic from her. "

"Do not claim to know *anything* about who I am because of what you did to me," Morgana snarled.

Silence stretched. Anxiety bubbled in Aveline's chest, and she looked at Morgana as she felt the king's gaze turn on her. As she realized he was focused not on Morgana, but her.

Aveline knew why. After all, he'd already taken care of Morgana.

King Daegil jerked his chin to the guards. "Take her. We have business to attend to."

"No," Morgana moaned, trying to move, but she fell to her side as soon as she left the wall, curling in on herself. "*No*, don't - don't take her -"

But the cell door had already swung open, a pair of guards surging in to wrench Aveline off the ground, her chains shifting around her as she tried to fight. The skin around her wrists and ankles flared in agony as they scraped against the cuffs, digging into the torn flesh beneath. She thrashed around, looking over her shoulder to try to find Morgana, but the guards barely even blinked, pulling her from the cell.

The door clattered shut behind them, and one of the guards slammed her into the bars. Morgana was splayed out on her stomach, coughing as she inched her way across the stone floor. She screwed her eyes shut as she frantically shook her head, but her body wouldn't move faster. Aveline choked on a sob at the sight of Morgana trying to reach her with everything she had, the floor scraping her knees and forearms.

Aveline collapsed into her guards as her knees gave out. "Morgana," she tried to say, resigned, the words wrenching out like broken glass, too sharp and yet too quiet. "Morgana, stop."

Morgana opened her eyes, looking up just in time to see King Daegil secure the lock with a click. He could have taken Aveline away while Morgana had been unconscious, but Aveline knew why he waited. He wanted Morgana to watch, to make sure she knew that, once again, she would be trapped and alone.

Morgana's arms shook as she tried to lift herself, but the corruption of the iron in her soul pulled her down. How long would this bout of pain last? The first had been … days long.

King Daegil grinned down at her. "Apologies that I had to do this to you again, but I couldn't risk that you were feigning your weakness. I had to be sure you wouldn't escape. I'm sure you understand."

Morgana coughed again, trying to swim her way toward Aveline when crawling proved futile. "I wouldn't. I've never held anyone captive."

Not for the first time, Aveline wanted to know how long he'd cursed the two kingdoms with his existence.

The king's eyes darkened. "You will."

Morgana let out a strangled cry full of anguish and fury. She pulled herself up by the bars of the cell, reaching through her nearest gap. Her arm spasmed as she lashed out at the king, but it was a weak attack, and all she managed to do was knock the crown to the floor.

King Daegil just laughed as the land crown clattered against stone. One of his guards scooped it up and placed it delicately back on the king's head. Only then did King Daegil sneer down at Morgana, "How does it feel to become less than human?"

With a snap of his fingers, the guards wrenched Aveline down the hall, her heels dragging as she tried in vain to fight them. They tugged her away, and the last thing she saw before they rounded the corner was Morgana giving up, collapsing into a pile in the middle of the empty cell.

A witch, now only a mortal woman.

Chapter Twenty Five

"Is it the same as when you left?" King Daegil asked as they walked. Or, rather, as they were both dragged. "Or does it seem different because you look through different eyes?"

Aveline screwed her mouth shut to keep from answering, her eyes burning holes in the back of his neck as they moved. She'd given up on trying to walk with the chains weighing her down, letting the guards carry her full weight, if just to cause them all the trouble she could. Flashes of Morgana collapsed in the cell haunted her, and she sagged further, her heart weighing her down.

The king looked over his shoulder. "You don't feel like a talk? But I hear you and Morgana have been so chatty recently."

Aveline yelped when one of the guards kicked her hard in the leg, a silent command. Nostrils flaring, she pulled a few quick words from her throat. "We had a lot to catch up on."

"I'd imagine," King Daegil rumbled. "So many lies, so many secrets, so many betrayals to unravel over the past two hundred years."

"There was a lot to sort out," Aveline mused, after a sharp jab to her stomach this time. "Turns out we never lied to each other after all."

"*You* did, from what I gathered," he responded. "I can't say I blame you. I, too, pretended to be someone entirely new when the gods transformed me."

Now that she wasn't so focused on Morgana, Aveline found she couldn't take her eyes off his head, off the crown situated on his dark mess of hair. Golden and embedded with forest green stonest, it glittered in the light of the algae lining the stone hallway. The earth tones stood out so starkly against the colors of the sea, the blue bioluminescence tinting everything around them. The land crown didn't fit here in this kingdom, and the water around it agreed, swirling as though repelled.

The king noticed her stare, lifting his hand to brush along the gilded relic. "Oh, this? It's rather nice, don't you think?"

"It is," Aveline growled, remembering how it had looked on Wendell, how he had constantly messed with it because he hadn't quite grown accustomed to its weight. "It would be nicer on someone worthy."

"You have no standing to judge my worth," the sea king said.

"Fine," Aveline snapped. "It would look more fitting on its rightful owner."

The sea king cocked his head, musing, "Ah, yes, the missing heir. From a line that faded into obscurity two hundred years ago."

"And they'll stay a mystery," Aveline growled. "Anything to keep them away from you, to keep you from finishing what you started."

"Oh, child," he said with a light laugh, pausing in the entrance hall. The guards carrying Aveline jerked to a stop with him, and his own guards positioned him so he could face her fully, mere inches separating them. "You still have the patience of a mortal. Heir or not, that barrier will fall someday."

Aveline wondered if he kept track of the wall's movement, if he had people reporting any changes back to him.

He leaned down with a sneer. "This heir has continued to be a thorn in my side even after I won against their ancestors. I promise you, they will be mine. Once I find them, they won't live another day."

"*Someone* will die when we find them, surely," Aveline said. "Fate will decide who."

His face twisted wickedly with something as close to glee as a man like him could get. "You know nothing of fate. This story was written ages ago."

"The gods don't write stories," Aveline spat. "They send down a blessing and let the Hallowed decide what happens for them."

He shook his head, and Aveline delighted when he twitched in pain. "I suppose that's why the Lord of the Sea sent me. I've spent years gathering what we're owed."

"You gained humanity," Aveline said incredulously. The Ancient Rift had been brutal, the defining moment where one kingdom had been torn asunder. Half of humanity had been plunged into a drowned realm of eternal darkness, and they were all weaker for it. "You gained a kingdom. The god of the sea only fought for fairness in those days. He only wanted what the land had."

King Daegil came closer, their arms brushing. Aveline bristled, as if his touch was poisonous. "You know, I was born in Calypdon, before Nysus even existed."

Aveline's breath stuttered. "You were alive during the Ancient Rift?" *How old was this man*?

The sea king grimaced at the memory. "I was born on the shore, in a little village called Thalassa. It doesn't exist anymore, of course. Wiped off the map not long before the Rift."

"Thalassa?"

King Daegil ducked his head with a chuckle. "Yes, perhaps naming our capital city after my place of birth was a tad self-absorbed. But I suppose I wanted to bring every part of myself into the sea. No part of me could belong to Calypdon anymore. It never really had."

"Why are you telling me this? I already know how much you hate the land."

"I was born in the days when the god of the sea began to rage against the lands. Storms and giant tidal waves ate at the shore. On the day my village fell into the ocean, I had been sent out of the village. We traded with a nearby town, and my parents always sent me on the ten mile trek. But a storm hit, and I watched from the peak of a hill as the sea swallowed everything, and everyone, I despised.

"He spared me," King Daegil hissed, baring his teeth. "He let me live that day, and then he chose me to rule his kingdom. The gods send down blessings to finish their work, as the goddess of battle did for you." He spread his arms briefly before letting them fall back to his sides, water rushing around his limbs. "And I have struggled for every hour of every day to fulfill what he asked of me. To give the sea *everything* it is meant for."

"He didn't let you live," Aveline snapped. "*So many* villages were destroyed in the days of the Rift. You were just lucky your parents sent you away to do the grunt work." She took a chance with a step forward, and to her surprise, her guards moved with her until she could stand on her toes and snarl into his face. "Many people get less than they deserve. Sometimes, they don't even get that."

King Daegil only lifted his chin, reaching out to grab her. "I'll see you in just a few days," he said in a low voice, digging his fingers into her shoulder. "When I can pull the life out of you without distraction."

The guards wrenched the two apart as she protested, eyes wide. But with a harsh blow to her head, the image of a king forged at the beginning of time swirled up and away into nothing. The world around her faded away.

***

Aveline woke to a song.

Sliding her eyes open, she tried to roll over only to find she wasn't lying down at all. Her body had been awkwardly propped against a wall, shoulders digging into rough marble. The stone pressed cool against her bare skin. She peered down at herself.

She sat in a pile of chains. In addition to the one that already bound her limbs, new ones had been added to hold her body to the corner of an empty chamber, the iron hooked to the wall. The king hadn't returned her to the dungeon, though. He hadn't brought her back to Morgana. They'd placed her in a much larger room, with barren white walls streaked with murky green, empty except for her and her chains.

Furrowing her brows, she strained her ears, itching to hear whatever melody drifted beneath the crack in the door. Perhaps the king was throwing another party, although she couldn't imagine how he could host anything in his current state, weak and depleted as he was from the iron. She couldn't think too hard about that, because the music grew louder, weaving through one ear, around her skull, and back out into the waiting water again just for new melodies to replace the old.

Straining against her chains, she tried to move toward the sound, her body steadily accruing scrapes and slashes as she thrashed about. Desperation filled her as the music grew louder. A young woman's voice and a gentle violin grew more distinct, soothing her soul while somehow awakening a fire within it. It burned through her stomach, her chest, her veins, and suddenly she struggled to draw breath, as if her ears were the only parts of her still working.

The door creaked, and everything stopped. The music, the wild desperation, the fire. Aveline collapsed back against the wall, gasping desperately. The cold pressed reality back into her as the door swung open, slowly carving through the water.

Morgana stood in the doorway, darkness swallowing the hall behind her, and the music began again.

"Morgana," Aveline gasped, the word barely out of her mouth before she lunged forward, pulling against the chains attached to the wall, but the marble wouldn't give. The chains dug into her skin, shocking her as she fought forward. "*Morgana*, how did you—"

Morgana didn't move, simply standing still as the music flowed around her, steadily taking over Aveline's senses. Her hair cascaded over her shoulders, so unlike the matted mess Aveline had seen in the cell only … was it minutes ago? Hours? Days?

Aveline dragged her eyes further down, noting the different clothes Morgana wore, a simple blue dress flowing around her legs in ripples, swaying in a current Aveline couldn't feel.

The burning returned, welling within her as the singing grew louder, and Morgana took a single step forward.

"Morgana!" Aveline shouted, surprised to hear it come out as more of an anguished shriek than anything. The chains tore at her as she struggled. "*Morgana*!" Her voice faded as reality sunk in. She couldn't say anything other than her name. Suddenly, it was the only word she knew.

Morgana took another step and came into the light.

It wasn't Morgana at all. Except it was; she looked the same. She looked soft and lovely as she smiled, as if Aveline sat in a bed of flowers instead of a bed of chains. Morgana's skin was the same, her soft lips, her sharp nose, the curves of her body; it was all there.

But Aveline never looked at any of those features first. She'd never noticed until this moment as she scrutinized Morgana's face, the calm planes of it, more at peace than Aveline had ever seen. Not until she looked to her eyes and found them both yellow.

Aveline reared back, pulling her chains close to her chest, a shield to protect her from whatever had stalked into the room.

"You're not … you're not—"

The tears came in full force, as if they'd never gone away. Had she been crying before? Her face felt raw when she brushed her arms against it.

Morgana reached her, kneeling down and stretching out her hand. Her fingertips brushed over the shell at Aveline's throat, fingernails stretching over the edges. "Shh," she soothed, and the voice was Morgana's, too. "Shh, it's okay." Morgana's nails dug further beneath the shell, as if she was trying to pry the artifact from Aveline's skin.

"*No,*" Aveline sobbed. "No, you're not -"

Morgana blinked, and only when Aveline managed to wipe her blurry eyes did she look up again, finding that Morgana's green eye had returned. "I'm not what?"

Aveline dug her fingers into her chest, as if she could scratch right down to her ribs, to her heart underneath, and bring this constant aching to an end. But she didn't look away from Morgana's eyes. Didn't dare blink, for fear the green eye would disappear.

Only when her own eyes were burning did she finally allow herself to blink, and when she opened them again, Morgana remained.

A strangled sob escaped Aveline, and she fell forward as much as she could in the chains, reaching for Morgana.

Morgana didn't reach back.

"Aveline," Morgana said softly. "You always knew it would end this way."

The music grew louder and louder, screaming in Aveline's ears, but Morgana's whispered words were somehow louder. Still, Aveline could only hear the ringing in her ears.

"W-what? I don't -"

Morgana stood again, smoothing her dress from the rippling currents. "You do. You know."

Aveline swallowed, the shaking returning as she looked left and right, searching for an escape, an explanation. The words came from Morgana's mouth in icy waves. Though Morgana had spent the past weeks with Aveline aloof, and perhaps a little distant, she had never been malicious. The voice sounded wrong, as if it belonged to someone else. "Morgana -" she started, as if saying her name again would help, as if she could snap the woman back into the Morgana she knew.

Morgana didn't look at her, raising her eyes to the blank ceiling. "You will die in that corner there, Aveline, and no one will come to save you."

The music confused her, making the words shatter against Aveline's skull, grinding into her ear drums. Her vision began to blacken at the edges, the world fleeing from her. "Haven't you come to save me?"

Morgana smiled slowly, head still tilted back. "And haven't you realized that though I'm the one with the powers, *you're* always the one saving *me*?"

"I've never minded saving you," Aveline whispered, but the music drowned it out. Aveline thought, for a moment, that she'd had this conversation before. That this all seemed eerily familiar.

Morgana lowered her gaze again, and Aveline flinched at what she found there. The yellow eyes were back, but this time Aveline saw that they were unlike Morgana's yellow eye. These glowed from within, eyes you'd fear to see alone in the dark when you ran from real monsters.

And Morgana wasn't a monster.

She knew that for sure now. She would never doubt it again.

"Get out!" Aveline screamed then as the music cut off, the smile on the monster's face spreading ear to ear, disturbingly wide. The creature was reveling in Aveline's pain. Morgana left, then, backing from the room with featherlight steps, the door swinging shut behind her on a phantom current. "LEAVE ME ALONE!"

The words tore from Aveline's throat into the empty room as she collapsed, pulling at the roots of her hair, and as the music stopped, she realized her throat was raw from screaming. She'd yelled those words before. Over and over, every time this Morgana paid her a visit.

Sirens.

Humans may have conquered the sea a millennia ago, but those creatures still lingered. They haunted the depths, drowning out the noise of the waves, and maintained the mysteries of the deep.

She had just enough sense to realize what the creature was for what must have been the sixth time, to move to plug her ears before the music started once more, and she forgot all over again.

***

She eventually remembered exactly what was happening to her each time. In the spaces of time between when the siren sang to her, the silence filled her and all that could occupy it were memories. The siren had come in the shape of Morgana countless times by now, but each time she came back into the room, her song made Aveline forget.

Sea creatures like the siren were rare in Thalassa, most of them exiled to the dark corners of Nysus after the Rift. They dwelled in the uppermost parts of the sea kingdom, in hollowed out caves on the underbelly of Calypdon. Though she'd seen a siren on two other occasions, she'd never heard them sing before.

It was not always beautiful, as the stories said. In times when Aveline was fully lost in the siren's song, she heard a light voice singing a language she couldn't understand, a gentle chorus of strings fiddling along. But each mirage cracked from time to time, and the screeching of the siren's real voice pierced her down to the bone. It was a horrible, high-pitched cry, and it made Aveline's body tremble, her teeth chattering with the volume and rhythm. Blood clouded around Aveline's head, and she reached up to her ears, running the pad of her thumb over the crust of blood coating the side of her face and the inside of her ear. Her ears bled from the siren's constant song, and Aveline pulled her fingers away, staring at the dark red and brown lingering there, a sign of the damage being done.

How much time has passed? Days, weeks, months? Was the real Morgana dead?

No, Aveline reminded herself. She couldn't be, because she couldn't die unless the sea king took her powers on himself, which Morgana insisted he had no desire to do. The thought wasn't as comforting as she thought it would be. Perhaps the fact that Aveline would eventually die was the only thing helping her to survive. Eventually, this torture would kill her and her suffering would come to an end.

She imagined Morgana, still in that cell, perhaps worse off than before. Were they feeding her? A lack of food wouldn't kill her, but it'd certainly be painful, especially with the iron weakening her system. An artful form of torture in its own right.

The door began to open, and Aveline braced herself, cowering against the back wall as she waited for her mind to once again succumb to the siren, to fall into the sweet lull of song. But instead of music, she heard footsteps, and she remained exhausted but alert as the sea king stepped in.

Her question of how much time had passed was immediately answered as she observed him, standing tall, with no need of assistance. The answer drifted through her foggy mind: *too much.*

She watched without movement as he came in, dressed in a clean, trimmed blue shirt and black pants. The vision of a strong, comfortable king. He stood on his own this time, using his staff to hold himself up.

He stopped in the center of the room to take her in: she knew she must look horrible. And he smiled. He smiled far too often for her liking, for the amount of pain he caused.

Aveline's voice was jagged, dragging along the sandpaper of her tongue and throat. "You're a wonderful host, you know. Just lovely accommodations you have."

He looked around. "I think it's a rather hospitable room." He turned his eyes back to her and sneered. "I hear you've had some … company. We like to keep our guests entertained."

Visions flashed in her mind, and it occurred in the back of her torture-addled skull that this might not be real at all, that it could just be another means to tear her mind apart.

She paused. This was the longest stretch of time between the siren's visits in gods knew how long. She actually had time to think about the situation she'd landed in. *Was this how Morgana felt when he stabbed her, when he took her mind as his own?*

Aveline swallowed with some difficulty, her throat swollen. "You're a cruel, conniving bastard, and I will *end you* or die trying."

He laughed. "You might not die trying. I might just keep you here forever. It'll probably feel like you're dying."

It already does.

"Where is Morgana?" Aveline asked, heart wrenching at the feel of the name on her lips. She'd said it so many times since they'd returned to Nysus, screamed it and cried for her help, cried for someone to help *her*. "Is she safe?"

The king huffed, folding both his hands on the top of his staff. "There is nowhere in any part of the two kingdoms where you two are safe. She is simply enduring another … experiment."

"But why isn't she *here*?" Aveline asked again, ashamed at how broken she sounded.

"Partly because if you could look over and see her, the siren's illusions wouldn't be very effective, would they?"

Aveline's stomach flipped. "Is she in another room, then? Is that where the siren goes when she's not in here?"

He waved her off, irritated by her questions. "Oh, the siren never goes far, never leaves for long. Your sense of time is simply not what it used to be, I imagine."

Aveline rattled her chains against the floor, and a heavy sound echoed around the chamber. "*Where is she?*" she snarled.

"Where we left her," the king said easily. "Screaming in the corner of her cell. Crying out for you, of course." He moved casually across the cell to lean against the wall beside Aveline, folding his arms over his broad chest. "You see, I've spent two centuries carefully calculating how I would break both of you. You are two very different people, you know, with very different weaknesses. Other than the weakness you have for each other, that is."

He didn't need to tell her about the weakness Morgana inspired in her. She had spent two hundred years cursing herself for it.

He went on, drumming his fingers along the muscle of his forearm. "You've felt your own body get torn to shred by the gods, so physical torture holds no horror for you. But that bodily pain is exactly what Morgana is enduring, and I don't give a damn if I have to hurt myself in the process." He bared his teeth. "Like I said, I learned how to play the long game."

"And you don't think the siren's song would hurt Morgana," Aveline said blankly. She couldn't imagine how someone might resist falling apart in this room. She felt herself on the edge of a precipice, dangling between the sea and the land, between the king in the tallest tower and Morgana in the dungeons.

"Oh, I think it could," the king said with a dark chuckle. "It just wouldn't be nearly as effective and I'm not entirely sure she would succumb to the siren's songs as you do."

Aveline glanced at the iron chains, her magic simmering deep with her, down where she couldn't reach. Would she be so susceptible to the siren's power, if it weren't for the cuffs suppressing her powers? "Because of her magic?"

He clicked his tongue, the pride in his tone sickening. "Because I've already torn apart her mind in every way I could. I've delved into every nook and cranny, and I know that short of getting my hands on that sword again, she'll never let me back in."

Aveline let her eyes flutter closed, overcome with fatigue, before they flew open again in a panic. She needn't have worried, though. The king hadn't moved, and she shouldn't have been surprised. He'd just explained how physical torture would do nothing to her, that she'd endured much worse than anything he could carve into her.

He was right.

"And why don't you just kill me?" Aveline finally asked, head rolling back against the wall, her neck too tired to support it. "I'm no help to you."

The king held up a finger. "Ah, but you are. Need I remind you that your niece escaped with something I want dearly?"

"In case you haven't noticed, you're holding me prisoner here. I don't know where she went."

"She ran back to the run-down remnants of your palace," King Daegil scoffed, his fists clenching. "It's not an issue of finding her, it's an issue of getting her."

Something clicked in Aveline's mind. "I noticed that, actually; the shell artifacts missing from all your little guards' throats. The blessed rocks aren't feeling too generous, I gather?"

The king growled and reared out with his staff, the contact sending her chains into her gut. Aveline keeled over, trying to clutch her stomach, but the iron was in the way. The king dropped to a squat, gripping Aveline by the chin and wrenching her up.

He held on tight, not letting Aveline move at all. "The lands have never answered to me, and I wish to change that."

"The lands answer to the good and just," she spat with an almost hysterical laugh. "You'll never change that. The blessed rocks that hold the shells are blessed by the Lady of the Lands, the same goddess you're challenging, linked to the same lands that you tried to destroy. We'll find a way to bar you from Calypdon permanently."

"Perhaps," the king said, pushing her away. Her head knocked against the wall. Skin split open, and more blood darkened the water in front of her eyes. "But you are a woman of the land and sea, made from both worlds. Your soul was born in the sea, but your body was forged on land. Perhaps we could make the gods hear you." He ran a finger over the shell at Aveline's throat. "Perhaps they'll recognize that they blessed you once and provide you with more."

"I think the gods are done listening," Aveline said. She leaned forward with everything she had left, the chains rattling around her. "But *you* listen: *Never*. I will *never* search for you again, and you can't force me to, no matter how long you hold me, no matter what you do."

His eyes glinted. "I think you'll find that's not a challenge you wish to set me." He stood. "I'll come back in a few days, I imagine. We'll see how you're faring then."

He left, and the siren came back. She kept coming, and coming, and coming. Different every time, but somehow the same in that she kept breaking her heart.

***

Days or weeks or months later, after an uncountable number of visits from the siren, they came together. The king and Morgana, with the latter held to the King's chest, a hand clamped over her throat. Aveline didn't scream, didn't cry out for her, just sat and stared blankly at the scene playing out before her. Perhaps she'd lost the ability to comprehend, to be surprised by horror.

Because Morgana bled out in the King's arms, hanging limply with red swirling in the current around her, her feet dragging over the pristine white floors.

And yet Aveline still didn't react. "What is this?" is all she asked in a faint whisper.

The king opened his arms, and Morgana's body fell to the floor with a resounding *thud*. Blood washed over Aveline's feet.

"Oh, this isn't her," the king said, and with his words, Morgana dissipated from beneath him in a wave of mist. A mirage. "I just thought you should know what's coming. What your lack of cooperation will bring your witch."

He left, the siren made her entrance, and the cycle started again.

***

The last time Morgana came to her, the music didn't come with her

But she crept in the same way, one foot after another, slow as the snakelike monster this siren was. Aveline wished she'd known how much time had passed, how many weeks she'd been here. She knew at this point they'd long passed the marker of mere days. She wondered if she'd now spent more collective time with this fake Morgana than the one she'd left behind.

"Go away," Aveline croaked out, too exhausted to notice what was off. That it was odd that she could remember this was a siren at all. But perhaps the lack of music caused that discrepancy. Could a siren present herself to humans without singing?

"I can't," Morgana whispered, placing her feet carefully, as if she walked on a tightrope. "I couldn't leave you."

"You will," Aveline said, staring at her. She couldn't see her eyes yet, and she found she didn't want to. Every time she saw those monstrous yellow eyes, she forgot more and more what Morgana's eyes looked like. The precise shade of green that seemed plucked right from the trees of the forest where Aveline once found her, the yellow that could have been bottled from the glow of a sunset. "You always do."

She could see movement behind those eyes, but at this distance, she couldn't make out the color yet the siren sped up, reaching Aveline, her chin resting on Aveline's shoulder.

The siren whispered in her ear. "Okay. The easy part was getting in, the hard part will be getting out. I need to hear that you're with me."

"I'm not with you," Aveline murmured blankly. She couldn't reach beyond the surface of her own soul, let alone find Morgana's. "You'll go soon, and then you'll come back. Coming back means nothing if you leave every time."

She could feel Morgana swallowing, her chin moving over Aveline's skin as a strangled sound escaped Morgana's throat. "That wasn't me, that was the siren. Do you remember the siren? You should, memories come back when they leave, right?"

"*You're* the siren," Aveline said, as if she recited a script written by the sea king. "You're the siren, but you're also Morgana, and you'll go. You'll go and hide like you must, but you'll go all the same."

"*No*," Morgana hissed, still not pulling away from Aveline's ear. "No, I did, but not now. The king put thoughts in your head before, don't let him do it again."

It wasn't him, it was you. It was your voice telling me you'd leave, it was your mouth saying you hate me, that you wished you'd never come out of hiding. It was you*!*

"You're not who you say you are*!*" Aveline finally cried, and the burning sensation behind her eyes came back with a vengeance as she clenched them shut. She didn't want to see the siren's eyes.

Morgana's fingers trailed hesitantly up Aveline's arm before wrapping around her bicep, squeezing in a way that might have been reassuring under other circumstances, but now just acted as another restraint on her. "No, no, if anyone in this room isn't who they say they are, it's you. Which one of us took on a new body and pretended to be someone else for several centuries?"

The vague attempt at a joke soared in one bloody ear and out the other. "I don't know what you really look like. There's only been speculation on the sirens' true appearances, but no one can ever be sure that a siren is in their true form. I think seeing you as a monster would be less painful, somehow."

"What did he do to you?" Morgana muttered, holding herself very still. "What can I do, what can I - ?"

"You can go," Aveline said brokenly. "You can go and bring the music with you when you come back. At least then I can think it's really her, even for a moment."

"We don't have much time," Morgana said, panic edging her voice as she looked over her shoulder toward the door. That was unfamiliar. sirens had the patience of immortals. The siren never panicked. "If I tell you something only the two of us would know, would that convince you?"

"It won't help," Aveline said dully. "You're in my head, remember? You know everything I know."

"But I don't," Morgana cried as quietly as she could, looking once again over her shoulder. Aveline still could barely see her, though, and settled for staring ahead, at the blank wall in front of her and the door that Morgana had closed behind her when she came in.

That was odd as well. The siren always left the door ajar. Aveline imagined King Daegil had to empty out an entire wing of the palace to keep anyone else from succumbing to the siren.

Instead of the door, or the wall, or the cell itself, she pictured Morgana there. The real one, with her real eyes and her real smile and her real words. If Aveline squinted hard enough, if she let her tears blot out her vision, she could almost see her. Could almost feel her.

And it hurt.

"Go," Aveline whispered again. Her hand lifted aimlessly to her ear. "I miss the music."

Morgana wrenched back then, and Aveline could suddenly see her. And she realized she'd somehow retrained herself, focusing on Morgana's left cheekbone first, then her hairline, then her lips. It took several seconds for Aveline to finally drag her vision to Morgana's eyes, prepared to wince -

And found solid green and a soft yellow staring back.

"I may not care about my life," Morgana whispered at the awestruck look on Aveline's face. Somehow Morgana wrenched the chains from the wall, the stone cracking, and Aveline didn't have the wherewithal to wonder what magic Morgana had drawn on to do it. "But I care about yours."

And as Aveline had once carried Morgana out of the sea kingdom, Morgana wrapped Aveline in her arms and brought her home.

Chapter Twenty Six

Only when they'd made it through the portal did Morgana's legs buckle beneath her, sending the two women sprawling into the snow. Winter had still had its clutches on Calypdon when they had left, but the air had since grown warmer. Still, it was well past nightfall when they stumbled into the forest, and the evening chill pierced Aveline's sopping wet skin, goosebumps tingling all over, and she clung tighter to Morgana beside her.

Raising her hand to her throat, she brushed her fingers over the shell there. She remembered vaguely that the siren had tried to remove it at some point, but it was lodged into her skin in a new way this time; forged by a different type of magic, a rougher kind. The shell obeyed her touch, and they watched as the water in the river swirled and churned. Pebbles rained down into the chasm as it shifted, waves folding over each other as the water worked to bend back into itself. It wove back together, the fresh water of the river blotting out the salty smell of the ocean, leaving only a scar of sea foam in its wake.

"That was too easy," Aveline gasped, pressing her hand into her chest as she rolled off of Morgana, laying on her back and facing the stars. In the moments of sleep the siren had allowed her, she'd dreamt of them, of seeing the clear night sky again. She drank it in, counting the sparkling dots above.

Morgana scrambled up, chest heaving, and her words came out as wheezes. She leaned over Aveline, hands roaming over her face, wiping the blood from her ears. "Are … you … what … happened?"

Aveline just shook her head, eyes wide, because she still couldn't believe that this Morgana was real. She realized in the back of her mind that manacles still encircled her wrists and ankles, but she wouldn't have been able to move even without them, so she didn't particularly care. "Tell me why that was so easy. Was it a deal with the king?"

Morgana groaned with disbelief. "*No*, it was *easy* because every guard in the kingdom was *unconscious*."

Aveline swallowed, trying to remember the quiet journey through the shadows of the palace. Aveline had barely been conscious for most of it, too frightened to worry too much about where they were going. They had moved too fast, the surroundings blurring around her, and she couldn't process it. Vague flashes of slumped figures came back, but she'd thought at the time that her mind had been playing cruel tricks on her. "And how could you do that?" Aveline asked in an accusatorial voice, but she didn't try to move away, to widen the space between them anymore. "And why didn't you *kill them all*?"

Morgana dug her fingers into Aveline's arm, using her grip to steady herself. "I couldn't. Besides, you're still treating me as though I'm a stranger. Would the Morgana you know have killed every person in that palace, especially since it wasn't necessary?"

"The Morgana I know technically killed me."

"Let's not worry about the technicalities for a moment. I've never willfully killed anyone."

Aveline swallowed, and the shuddering that had overtaken her since they came through the passage diminished. "Then tell me how you could put them to sleep at all."

Morgana ran fingers over her torso; in the same place the king had stabbed himself. "The effect of the iron through my bond with Daegil has lessened, but it's still … *there*. I could access just enough of my power to put them in a temporary sleep. They're probably already awake by now."

"How did you get access to your powers at *all*?"

"I remembered what the king had said when he came to get you," Morgana breathed, still assessing Aveline for any signs of serious injury. "He thought I might fake the pain, to fool him into believing each dose of iron would weaken me for longer than it actually did." She shook her head, peering down at Aveline as if she couldn't quite believe her eyes. "The sea king is an inherently selfish man, and he couldn't have liked the pain his plan caused him. He went too long without lacing himself with iron. The effects began to wear off after about six days, and on the seventh I could feel hints of my power again. So, I'd pretend to be powerless for eight days each time it happened. When I pretended for those additional two days, he was eager to believe it, because he didn't want to put himself through any more pain than necessary."

Aveline blinked, catching the phrase "*each time it happened.*" "How long were we down there?"

"I lost track," Morgana sighed, before hesitantly adding, "but I'd say about two months."

Aveline lurched up then, nearly knocking her skull against Morgana's. Morgana reared back, hands raised in innocence as Aveline stared, wide eyed. "Two…"

Morgana nodded, throat bobbing. "I take it you weren't conscious for most of it?"

Aveline shook her head. "You … you…" She clamped down on her lip to stop it from trembling.

Morgana reached out, but her hands stalled somewhere between them, looking down at Aveline's frail form. "It wasn't me. Whoever it was you saw, it wasn't me."

"It was you," Aveline whispered, the torrent of emotions she had suppressed during her time with the siren tumbling out in full force. Exhaustion dragged her down. "It was … so close to being you."

Morgana stared warily. "And do you believe I'm really me now?"

Fear crept back into Aveline's veins, weighing her down more than the chains ever could. "I'm still deciding."

The truth was, every time the siren had come in taking Morgana's form, she'd prayed that that time would be different. She'd prayed that Morgana would come to save her, come to take her away from the torture and tell her that everything the siren had said was a lie. But each time it hadn't been her, and eventually Aveline had stopped hoping.

Two months.

"Listen," Morgana said breathlessly. "Look where we are. Look around, we're not in the sea anymore. If I was a siren, I'd never have made it through that portal, and if I did, I'd be shriveled up by now. You were born in the sea, you *know* that's true."

It was. Sea creatures had no way to survive on land; they'd suffocate, skin drying up in the air.

Aveline's breathing steadied. Her vision cleared.

Aveline raised her hands, her chains clanking. "Tell me what the hell happened, all of it, while you take these off."

Morgana flicked out a dagger with a long, thin blade that she must have stolen from an unconscious guard. Though Aveline longed to be free of the iron, she knew why Morgana had waited until they'd made it to safety to try to get these off. It would be slow going. Morgana probably didn't have much experience picking locks.

She began at the cuffs around her ankles, delicately holding Aveline's legs in her lap as she stuck the sharp point of the blade into the keyhole. "I heard the siren," Morgana finally said. "Those things are ... loud, but I knew what they were. I could feel it on days when the iron started to fade. Remember, I'm linked to *all* creatures, not just humans."

The unspoken words drifted between them. I'm linked to the monsters, too. *Another reason people believe me to be one of them.*

Aveline sat perfectly still, not just because of the dagger millimeters from her skin, but because she thought if she moved, she'd break the mirage, and Morgana's eyes would change back to that sickly yellow.

The sound of the dagger grinding against the lock irritated Aveline's already ruined ears, but Morgana leaned close enough that she could make out the words. "Once I got the timing right, I could do something with my magic each time I reached that eighth day. One of the times, I tracked the siren. I couldn't track you; the iron chains blocked me, but the siren was loud and boisterous, and the king never moved you. I did that twice, tracking her, to make sure they weren't moving you every week."

The chains around her ankles cracked open, flaked with dried blood, and they collapsed into the dirt. Morgana wasted no time, moving up Aveline's body toward her hands. Aveline shoved her wrists out silently. "I didn't knock the guards out immediately. First, I used them to get me out; I made one of them unlock the door. Once the cell was open, I didn't waste any time. I put a blanket of magic around the palace, knowing it wouldn't do *anything* to the king besides tell me where he was, and came to you."

"And you pretended to be the siren," Aveline finished for her. "In case you timed it poorly, and the king came to visit me at the same time."

Morgana bowed her head, unable to look Aveline in the eye, instead choosing to scrutinize her work. "I came to you, and I took a chance that it was me you were seeing all that time."

"Why?" Aveline said weakly, her throat threatening to close up. "Why did you think it might have been you?"

Morgana finally forced the lock to give way, and Aveline felt the chains on her wrists fall away, cool air biting into the ruined skin. "Because I would have seen you."

Aveline's heart skipped a beat, and though her wrists burned from the icy air hitting the wounds, she reached out and took Morgana's face in her hands. Morgana stared at her, dropping the dagger between them, where it landed in the mud with a squelch. "Would you have seen me?" Aveline asked, indicating her new body. "Or would you have seen … *me?*"

Morgana knew what she was asking and raised her hand to press Aveline's hand into her cheek. Her fingertips were cold to the touch. "I would have seen your soul, because that's all that matters to me. Your soul is the same in any body."

"Have you felt it?" Aveline asked, unable to look away from Morgana's eyes. Her real eyes. They drew her in, the soft green and buttery yellow. "Reached out with your magic to test that it's me?"

"Yes," Morgana admitted softly, but Aveline wasn't offended. She was glad for it, for one secret to be blown open completely, one wall to be knocked down. "But not because I didn't already believe you."

"Why then?" Every word took effort, her throat was completely raw.

"Because I wanted to feel you again," Morgana said, as if she was ashamed of it. Aveline held Morgana tighter, her cheeks blushing beneath the fingertips. "Not just to make sure you were the same, but to make sure I was the same, too. I reached out to you, and I felt young again."

Aveline held her breath, eyes burning. Exhaustion threatened to overtake her, emotional and physical, but she needed to hear this. Needed to keep her hands on Morgana even as her arms quaked with the effort, to make sure she didn't disappear. "And are you?"

Morgana nodded, her lips parting, her breath startlingly hot in the cool of the night. "In the ways that count."

Aveline didn't know what she'd have done, then, if her mind hadn't gotten in the way. If the chaos of the past two months hadn't caught up with her all at once, a sudden memory bursting to the forefront of her mind.

They'd gone to Nysus for a reason

"The crown," Aveline rasped suddenly, lightning striking through her. "The *heir*, we have no idea who -"

"I know," Morgana said quietly, hand dropping to her side. "I know who it is."

Aveline tried to lurch to her feet, but her legs betrayed her, and she began to crash back into the dirt at the shock of the statement. Morgana rose up to catch her by the waist, and Aveline's legs trembled beneath her as she attempted to stay upright, unsure whether they could take her weight. Aveline twisted around to face her, her head spinning from moving too fast. "You *what?*"

Morgana had the good sense to look guilty. "Sorry. I probably should have led with that."

"Probably," Aveline agreed, although her heart wasn't really in it. Instead, it jumped all over the place, confused by the torrent of emotions that had been pummeling her throughout the night. She pulled up short. "Wait, you *know* who the heir is?"

Morgana held her hands up and palms out. "My power is strong, and my bond with Wendell was strong, too. I just needed to touch the crown, that was all it took."

"You … *when did you get your hands on it?*"

"It was brief," Morgana said, running a hand through her hair. "When he took you and I knocked the crown off his head." Keeping Aveline steady with one hand wrapped around her hips, she shook out the other arm's sleeve. It fell to her elbow, revealing slashes all along her forearms. "One of the guards took a knife to me, so I didn't try that again, but it was enough. I could feel her through the kingdoms."

Aveline swallowed, swaying even as Morgana held on tight. "Her?"

***

They stayed silent as Morgana led the way, racing through the night back toward the palace as fast as Aveline could handle. She wanted to ask if Morgana was okay, if agony still coursed through her, but the ability to speak and move at the same time evaded her. A thousand thoughts fought for space in Aveline's mind, where was Rike? How was the rest of her team? How was she possibly going to explain everything that had happened?

But she couldn't deal with that right now. The heir was the priority.

Aveline only paused once, at the entrance that the guards had thrown open for her, shooting her worried glances but not daring to say a word. She turned at the top of the steps and gazed out at the wall of water. It had made too much progress in the few months she had been gone. She imagined that Morgana's tiny shop would be underwater any day now. "It's speeding up," she said. "It shouldn't have made that kind of progress in two months."

Morgana gazed over her shoulder at the towering sea threatening to overtake them. "The heir grows closer to death every day, as we all do, and she doesn't have a child," she said, the wave reflected in her eyes. "As she ages, the barrier weakens. Magic knows. I'd say we have one year at most before it begins to flood the outskirts of Briarwood."

Aveline turned away. "All the more reason to hurry up."

Aveline took the lead now, knowing her way to this room better than Morgana, having walked the route more times than she could count. "You're sure?" Aveline murmured, slowing down slightly, as if she could push back the inevitable.

"My powers don't lie." Morgana glanced at her. "I doubted that for many years, but it turns out they've been right all along."

Right about the sea king. Right about Wendell. Right about Aveline.

"Okay, then," Aveline said, pausing at the door and taking a breath. She looked to Morgana. "I believe you."

Morgana smiled, and it was genuine.

The door swung open moments after the knock, the woman inside summoned by the pounding knuckles that rapped harsher than usual. She'd clearly been sleeping, wearing soft night clothes, her braided hair all a mess from her pillow.

Rubbing her eyes and not bothering to look at exactly who disturbed her, Verona groaned impatiently, "This better be important."

Chapter Twenty Seven

Any other words Verona might have wanted to say died in her throat as she realized who it was that stood in her doorway, covered in dried blood and seawater, skin filthy with mud

"Aveline?" she asked weakly, any hint of sarcasm and sleepy irritation gone.

Aveline managed a smile. "Hey, Verona. Long time."

Verona surged forward, and a surprised, if slightly pained, laugh shot from Aveline's mouth when Verona flung her arms around her neck. Morgana reached out, steadying Aveline as the two women rocked back and forth, Verona's tough facade a memory. Suddenly, she was just a girl in Aveline's arms, clearly tired of fighting and even more tired of losing.

Verona wrenched back, squinting incredulously into Aveline's face. "Where have you *been*, we've been worried *sick* ever since Rike got back -"

"Rike," Aveline interrupted harshly, all thoughts of the heir - of *Verona* - momentarily evaporating. "She got back okay?"

Verona blinked. "You didn't go see her first?"

Aveline's throat bobbed, longing to run toward her niece, to find her and see with her own eyes that she was okay, but then she remembered what she saw, the progress of the invading sea. There was no time to waste.

"Morgana," Aveline murmured. "Can you get Rike and the rest of my crew for me?"

Morgana folded her arms. "Sure, just tell me where to find them."

Verona's eyes grew impossibly wide. "You'll send her *alone*?"

Aveline dragged a hand down her face, unable to keep up with all the new information from the past two months herself, and unsure of how she expected Verona to do so. "I'm going to tell you a lot of things right now, and you're just going to have to believe me."

***

Verona burst out laughing.

After sending Verona's four roommates to spend the night in Aveline's room, Verona had listened patiently as Aveline told the whole story from her spot on the floor, unable to stand any longer. She cleaned her ears in a full-length mirror with a wet cloth, sighing as she removed layers of dried blood from the insides and the side of her face.

Only at the end of the tale had Verona dropped down to sit against the opposite wall. Aveline didn't blame her for keeping her space, she knew she probably smelled horrendous.

Now, Verona shook her head frantically, standing and stalking back and forth in front of her. "No. *No way*. I don't know what she got from that crown, but it's wrong."

"Her powers aren't wrong," Aveline said softly.

"Then she's lying," Verona said, flinging her arms in the air. "That possibility must have crossed your mind, she's a *witch*."

Aveline sighed, looking toward the ceiling. It hadn't occurred to her how difficult it would be to convince Verona. "Did you not hear my entire story? She doesn't lie, either."

Verona scoffed. "You're the one always going on about stories, and that's all that is. Another story."

"Verona -"

"*No,*" she shouted, hands on her hips, probably wondering if Aveline needed to visit an apothecary. She looked over her shoulder at the closed door, worried about her neighbors, and dropped her voice to a hiss. "You disappeared for *two* months, come back trusting the witch, and you expect me to go along with whatever she says?"

"Not whatever she says," Aveline said, cheeks heating. "Just … this particular fact, yes."

Verona placed a hand on either side of Aveline's face, as if she could squeeze the logic out. "Did they put a spell on you?"

"No. Well, technically yes, but not about *that*."

"*What*?"

"Well, the siren -"

Harsh, hurried footsteps echoed down the hall, and someone skidded to a halt at the end of it. Aveline turned to see Rike only a few feet away, tears already flowing freely down her face. Micah and Castor waited behind her, but Aveline only had one focus.

"Rike," Aveline sobbed, and they met each other halfway, arms wrapping around each other as they cried into each other's shoulders. The adrenaline sapped out of Aveline's muscles, and she squeezed her niece tight, fingers digging into her back. "You're … you're okay. Thank the gods, you're okay."

Aveline echoed the words as Castor and Micah slipped closer, the first grinning ear to ear and the latter looking like he might cry from relief. Morgana lingered further away, hugging herself, but smiled sadly at the scene. At a scene of people loving and being loved in return.

Aveline pulled back, cupped her niece's face in her hands, and kissed her forehead.

"I've been so worried," Rike said, wiping her eyes. She paused. "You look terrible."

Aveline pushed her feebly away with a snort, turning to beam at Micah and Castor. "You kept things running okay without me?" she asked Micah.

"It's been a wreck," he said easily.

Morgana clapped her hands together once before fully joining the group, folding her arms. "Good, that was a nice reunion," she said pointedly to Rike. "Now, where's my sword?"

Rike glared at her, not letting go of Aveline's hand. "Oh, the sword that you sacrificed everything for? That one?"

"Yes," Morgana said, voice flat. Half of the life had been sapped out of her, once again in the presence of people who hated her. Perhaps she couldn't control it. Maybe her feelings were manipulated by the sour ones of those around her. "That one."

Aveline wiped her eyes even as they widened. "Oh, yeah, you'll probably want to give that back."

Incredulous, Rike's lips thinned out. "I don't think that's a good idea."

Aveline lifted a finger, but Morgana beat her to it. "I think you'll find it would be an even worse idea to try to keep it from me."

Rike looked around the room, spreading her arms. "Don't you think we have the right to have a little insurance here? I say we keep it until it's absolutely necessary, so you don't turn on us."

"And I'm telling you to give it to her," Aveline pleaded, harsher than she intended.

Rike spun to Aveline with a question in her eye, but then she scoffed, jutting her chin toward Castor. "Go get the sword, will you? You know where it is."

Castor leaned back against the wall and shoved his hands into his pockets. "No, you should have just grabbed it when the witch told you to. Get it yourself."

Rike scowled. "I didn't know if Aveline would want me to give it back."

Aveline ignored both of them, motioning back down the hall. "Morgana, go ahead."

Rike's eyes widened. "She's *not* gaining access to my rooms -"

"She saved your life," Aveline said, voice level. "She'll go wherever she pleases."

Rike's eyes darkened, and Morgana looked back and forth between Aveline and her crew, noting the irritation on Verona's face. She shook her head and stalked away. "Good luck convincing them."

Folding his arms across his chest, Micah said, "Convincing us of what?"

Aveline told the whole story of her time in Nysus again, and Verona rolled her eyes at all the right parts. Morgana came back about halfway through the tale, clinging to her sword like an old friend. She lowered herself to the floor with her chin in her hands and, to her credit, kept her face completely straight.

"You told them about the sword?" Morgana asked when Aveline finished, although she needn't have bothered. Each person in the room now looked at the sword as they usually looked at Morgana: like it might lash out and behead them at any moment.

"No way that thing has that much power," Castor said, shaking his head as he knelt down to get a better look.

Morgana shifted, moving the sword to her other side and blocking it from his view. Castor just moved with it, with the intent of getting a good look. Morgana said, "Many would probably say the same about me."

"So … you're saying you didn't kill Aveline?" Rike asked weakly, eyes rapidly moving from Morgana to the sword and back again.

"I mean, how technical do you want me to -"

"No," Aveline interrupted with a glare at Morgana that had no real anger behind it. "She didn't."

They fell quiet then, looking back and forth between Morgana and Aveline. Aveline swayed under their gazes, but she thought she'd gathered herself relatively well, all things considered. At least she'd stopped flinching when she looked at Morgana. That would have made convincing them much more complicated.

"Okay," Micah said when the rest of the crew looked to him, and Aveline tried not to be offended. After all, he'd been leading them for two months now. "Okay."

"Okay?" Aveline asked warily.

"Okay," he repeated, glancing at Morgana. "She's not evil."

"What?" Morgana asked, shocked. It didn't help her case.

Castor shrugged, although he looked the most hesitant of them all. "If Aveline says you're not evil, then odds are, you're not."

Morgana leaned back, and her muscles relaxed. "Wow. You lot were much easier to convince than she was."

"Exactly," Micah said, although Aveline didn't miss how he refused to look Morgana in the eye. "If you convinced her, you've convinced us."

Aveline smiled, hearts swollen at the amount of confidence they had in her, the team she'd cultivated for half a decade. She'd given them a home, and they'd made this place a home for her in return.

"I still don't believe you about the heir thing," Verona said.

Micah spun toward Aveline, mouth opening in a wide O. She hadn't gotten to that part in the story yet. "You found him?" he asked, hoarse.

Morgana answered instead. "Her, actually." She nodded to Verona, who was fuming on her sheets.

Castor's jaw unhinged, and he jabbed Verona. "How is it that you do *nothing*, and you're the one who ends up with a crown?"

"Just because you don't value my ability to keep the people in check," Verona said icily, "doesn't mean I'm any less worthy."

"I'm just saying -"

"*Verona*?" Micah cut them off in shock. "You're sure of this?"

"I'm not entirely sure why you're asking her instead of me," Morgana said, balancing her sword on her knees, although she kept a tight grip on the hilt. Aveline didn't think she'd ever let go of it again. "But to answer your question, yes. It's her."

"But -"

"If you trust me that I didn't kill Aveline," Morgana said over him, "trust me when I say this. When I touched that crown, it was like a spark that came back from the past, burning into my soul. I was overwhelmed by the familiarity of it. Not just because of Wendell, but because of the time I spent here with all of you. They felt the same, like … two generations had suddenly been linked."

Verona swallowed. "I can't be queen," she muttered. "I'm not made for it."

"From what I've gathered," Morgana said, "none of you were made for the life you got, and yet you crawled your way here. To the first clue you've had in two hundred years."

Quiet settled around them once more, before Verona finally cleared her throat and said, "Let's move to the council room, shall we?"

***

The guards and soldiers greeted Aveline as they walked through the corridors, the younger children running up to her in concern, asking if she was okay. She waved them off with a smile, telling them she was better than ever. Verona snarled each time and said she disagreed.

The hour was early, and the tower was bathed in a soft morning light. They fell into their usual circle, Morgana striding over to the fireplace and settling down to build a fire. Aveline smiled at her back, at Morgana once again acting at home here. Only once Morgana fell into her seat did Verona speak.

"So, you found the hei- me. What does that mean for us?"

"It means we have the means to make a real kingdom again," Aveline said, eager at the prospect. "Before, even if we'd beaten the sea king, the two territories would have been in complete disarray, more wars would have broken out to claim land. It would have been ugly."

"Especially our people," Micah said. "They're bitter, and they're rougher after the life they've had. We've only been able to bring so many people into Briarwood, we got lucky that Aveline found us when we did."

"This place needs a ruler," Rike agreed. "And it needs a good one."

"Having a drop of royal blood doesn't make me a queen," Verona snapped, flinging her hands in the air. "Couldn't we just put someone else on the throne? As long as I'm alive, and I know that I need to have children to pass on the bloodline, then the magic still works, right?"

"Right," Morgana conceded. "But it's much weaker. It's a magic that is inherently linked to royal power, and without you swearing that oath, it *will* die eventually. You can see it now, with that damn wall getting closer every day. Once you're reunited with the crown, the power will be strengthened."

"Unfortunately for us," Castor said dryly, "you failed to retrieve the crown."

"Oh, yes," Morgana said sarcastically. "Next time we'll just *not* get held and tortured for two months. Good plan."

"It *is* a good plan -"

"And," Aveline added hesitantly, speaking over them and leaning back into the cushions of her chair, "the king wants you just as much as we do."

"He doesn't want *me*, he wants me *dead* -" The words died in Verona's throat, and realization dawned over her features. "You mean to use me as bait."

Aveline shifted uncomfortably. "Well, if you want to be blunt about it."

Rike was already shaking her head. "No. *Hell* no. That is *way* too risky."

"I agree," Micah said roughly. "Two of our people just escaped from King Daegil's clutches, and you want to throw another one of us in?"

"No," Aveline said, leaning forward and entwining her fingers together. "No one is going into the sea king's domain, not until he's dead. But that means that in order to kill him, we have to bring him here." She glanced toward Morgana, who's eyes glinted with repressed mirth as they both remembered what Aveline had once said.

I invited you on a mission to unseat a corrupt king. I'm still game if you are.

Morgana nodded now, as if to say, *Yeah. I'm game.*

"And there's only two people he would come for," Morgana said to Verona. "You, and me. So, we'll give him both."

Verona turned to glare at Morgana. "You'd do that? Use yourself as bait?"

Morgana gave her a patient, placating look. "I'm fairly sure that's what I did when Aveline and I got captured. But yes. I'd do nearly anything to see that man fall."

"Short of what?"

Morgana stared right back. "We'll see."

That should have scared Aveline, should have made her wonder what Morgana would do, if they'd reach a fate similar to last time. But she wasn't, because she knew what Morgana's limits were. She'd known it then, and she knew it now.

Verona bit her lip, turning away from Morgana to look at Aveline, who simply nodded. She tipped her head back toward the ceiling. "Gods help me."

"They won't," Morgana said.

"But we will," Aveline added, glancing at her crew. "We won't let you get hurt."

Verona looked between Morgana and Aveline, observing their half dead state. "Forgive me if I'm not filled with confidence."

"Come on," Castor said, kicking her. "Your superiority complex will love wearing a crown."

"You're not allowed to attack my person anymore," Verona said, and a hint of a smirk graced her lips. "I'm your queen."

A slow grin spread over Aveline's face. "You are?"

Verona rolled her eyes. "Yeah. Tell me what the damn plan is, but anyone who tries to call me 'Your Majesty' gets castrated."

Chapter Twenty Eight

Aveline didn't hesitate. She'd been planning and scheming for decades, contemplating exactly what would draw the sea king out and where he would go.

And what would kill him.

That last piece had eluded her through all these years. But as she looked at Morgana, something the sea king had said clicked into place.

They didn't leave the council room for many hours, not until the sun passed its peak and Castor snoozed against Verona's shoulder. Verona was the only one still fueled with adrenaline, more alert than Aveline had ever seen her. Something suspiciously like purpose lurked behind her eyes. Something they'd all been sorely lacking for years.

They all stumbled off to their own rooms. Aveline slowed as she got up, watching as Verona held Morgana back, the two of them whispering by the fireplace. Aveline lingered by the doorway, trying to hear what they were saying, but Micah sat up again, reaching out to her as Rike and Castor slid by.

He gripped her hand in his, squeezing tightly. "I'm so glad you're back," he said softly as his eyelids drooped, surprising Aveline. "You were gone, and I just … I hope you know how much we missed you. How important you are to this kingdom."

Aveline's eyes burned. She'd be lying if she claimed to not feel like a bit of an outcast with her group sometimes, an outcast from a different time. She encircled his hand with both of hers. "I missed you, too. Although it helped to know I left the crew in capable hands."

He swallowed, squeezed her hand once more before collapsing into his pillow.

Morgana appeared at her shoulder as Verona slipped past them, not bothering to tell either of them goodnight. Or rather, good midday. Aveline watched her go before spinning to face Morgana. "What did she say to you?" she asked, although it came out more like an accusation than she'd intended.

"She was threatening me," Morgana said simply, but she looked completely at peace, maybe even a little amused.

Aveline jerked back, searching for Verona, but she'd disappeared around the corner. Morgana's fingers wrapped around Aveline's wrist, pulling her back. "Not in a bad way," she assured her.

"There's a *good* way to be threatened?"

Morgana shrugged, starting down the hall and taking Aveline with her. "She's very protective of you. They all are."

Aveline's cheeks warmed. "We've become very close."

"You're like their mother and sister all at once. A mother when they remember how old you are, and a sister when they need someone." Aveline stuttered for several moments, and Morgana laughed. "It's nice, what you have with them. That you found a way to build relationships with others despite your … new situation."

Aveline felt stronger than she had since emerging from the portal, but her legs were still shaking beneath her. Her time with the siren felt like ages ago, but the lingering effects weighed her body down. "The relationships I have with the people in my crew were built on trust. It helped that I didn't feel the need to keep my magic a secret." She glanced at Morgana. "We're similar, you and I, but…"

"Not similar enough," Morgana breathed.

"Will you return, then?" Aveline asked, holding her breath as their footsteps echoed in the wide hallways, covering up the way her heart jumped into her throat. "To hiding?"

"I don't see how I have a choice. The desire for power produces conflict, and the easiest way to gain power is through me." Her shoulder brushed against Aveline. "I cannot put the kingdoms at risk for my own benefit. I've done it once before, and…"

Aveline's breath stuttered. "What about for *my* benefit?"

Morgana looked pained, but she jerked up as they reached her familiar door. They stalled together, and Morgana gazed at the door like an old foe. Aveline stood behind her, heart beating. It felt like a crossroads, and Aveline wondered what Morgana would say. Would they go their separate ways or continue down this … convoluted path they'd managed to salvage.

"I don't want to go back in there," Morgana finally said, taking a step back, closer to Aveline.

This wasn't what Aveline expected. This hadn't been one of the many possibilities running through her head. She furrowed her brows. "What?"

Morgana swallowed, and Aveline realized what this meant. For Morgana to show even a sliver of weakness. Morgana looked over her shoulder, her face ashen. "That room…" she trailed off. "It holds many good memories, but all I can seem to see are the bad ones."

Oh.

Running her fingers through her hair, Morgana shifted her weight, not quite looking Aveline in the eye. "Can I … I…" She swallowed the rest of the words down, but Aveline knew the question.

A question that was also an answer. At least for Aveline.

"Okay," Aveline whispered. "Come with me."

Morgana followed Aveline to her rooms, far from the ones she'd occupied two hundred years ago. They wove through the quiet halls, silent as the rest of the occupants gathered in the mess hall for lunch, the women's hands and shoulders and elbows brushing.

Aveline pushed open the door, allowing Morgana to enter before following. She walked around the small room, lighting candles and lanterns to shed light into the dark, empty space. But she pulled up short at a mirror and stared at herself in horror.

She was suddenly amazed that they'd allowed her to sit through such a long conversation in this state. There was blood … *everywhere*. It matted her hair, darkening the strands even more and weighing it down with thick clumps. Red smeared over her forehead and cheeks, down her neck with dried pools gathered in the hollows of her collarbone. Wherever blood hadn't reached, dirt covered her instead. She found cuts she hadn't even realized she had, up her arms and across her neck and chest, some fresh and others crusted into scabs. The skin around her wrists rubbed raw, and she gagged at the sight.

The king had said Aveline's torture was internal, in her mind. But seeing herself now, no one would ever guess that.

Morgana came up behind her, observing her own reflection. She didn't look quite as bad as Aveline, but her eyes still sparked in alarm at the sight. She lifted her hands, brushing the haunted shadows beneath her eyes.

"Come on," she finally said, her hand a soothing presence against Aveline's back. "You need a bath."

"I need sleep," Aveline said, a dizziness coming over her as the past months crashed back into her, and she stumbled back.

Morgana caught her, capturing Aveline in her arms and bearing the weight. "You do. But you'll thank me later once you scrub off what looks like your body's entire supply of blood."

Aveline reached out, catching Morgana's arms and squeezing tight. "But you -"

"I'm fine," Morgana said softly, steadying her arm around Aveline to steer them toward the washroom. "Dirt is dirt. You'll feel better when the blood is gone."

Aveline's shoulders slumped as she gave in to Morgana's touch, allowing her to walk them across the room. Her vision blurred, black stars bursting forth behind her eyes, but she pushed them away, praying a hot bath would expel some of this heaviness.

She had thought the siren would haunt her more, but that wasn't what stuck with her, not when the real Morgana had her arms around her. It was the feeling of being confined, of not being able to move freely, of having no escape.

But as Morgana lowered Aveline's frail body into the large porcelain basin, she felt none of that fear. She didn't feel trapped, even by the weakness in her body or the smallness of the room.

She felt safe.

She tried to pull her shirt off, but her arms wouldn't lift above her shoulders, her fingers trembling as she tried. Morgana gave her a questioning look, reaching out, and Aveline nodded tiredly, muttering, "Nothing you haven't seen before."

Morgana laughed quietly. "It is, actually. New body, remember?" Bashfulness rose within Aveline, but Morgana soothed her with a brush of her fingers, pulling off the blood-stained shirt and tossing it across the room. It landed with a crunchy *thud*, and Aveline made a mental note to burn it all later.

"Stop worrying." Morgana's words brought her back, and Aveline searched that gaze with her hooded eyes, trying to find clarity in this confounding woman. "I'll take my time relearning your body another time."

Aveline didn't have the energy to smile back at that, but she was sure she'd relive those words a million times over tomorrow.

Slowly, Morgana peeled the clothes from Aveline's body, having to take the dagger to cut off the pants, leaving them in a crumpled heap in the corner. Aveline held no fear of the dagger held close to her skin. She felt no fear when the rest of the clothes were stripped away, and Morgana guided Aveline into the already full wash basin.

She sighed into the surrounding warmth, falling deeper into the basin as steam curled around her skin. Her eyes began to flutter closed, but she forced them open as Morgana worked around her, pouring soap into the rising water. Her hair hung around her, and Aveline didn't care about the mud or the scrapes on her cheek. She just kept staring until Morgana's eyes flickered to hers.

"Why didn't you want to stay in your old rooms?" Aveline asked, gazing up at her through her lashes.

Morgana paused at the sink but then continued wiping her hands with a towel. "I can only see it as it once was. All I could see was you…" She trailed off, ducking her head.

The images came flooding back, like she'd watched it play out from above instead of being a part of it. Of Morgana's sword running Aveline through; of Aveline bleeding out on that floor. "Ah. You mean when -"

Morgana winced, turning back to Aveline and leaning against the wash basin, folding her arms. "I wasn't surprised when you had me stay there, but it was very difficult to find peace in that room," she whispered. "Especially when I believed you were dead. In the night I'd stare for hours at the spot where I'd dropped your body, until my vision grew bleary and I couldn't see anymore."

Aveline blinked, the words were enough to turn the water cold. "I forgot it all happened in there." She shook her head, sinking further into the tub until the water covered her shoulders. Morgana came over and shut off the tap, perching herself on the edge. The silence in the room without the running water was deafening. "It's amazing what a person can focus on after … tragedy."

Morgana nodded, and when Aveline made no move to wash herself, reached for a bar of soap. "I focused on you."

Aveline's breath hitched in her throat. She couldn't tell if it was from her words or the contact she made with her neck, scrubbing away flakes of red. The water turned a murky burgundy, and Morgana turned the faucet back on and unplugged the drain. "I'm sorry," she murmured, craning her neck for Morgana to reach, and the soap lathered over her skin, Morgana's fingers holding her steady. "For putting you in there."

"Don't be," Morgana said, sniffling. "I'm sure at the time you would have been glad to know it was torturing me."

Aveline laughed weakly and tried not to moan in relief when Morgana started on her hair, combing away the knots and washing away any evidence of what had happened in Thalassa.

Morgana's fingers tightened ever so slightly on the strands as she said, "You were the one who kept me alert at night. Thousands of souls I took, and yet if I could dream, you're the one I would have dreamt of."

The words shattered something in Aveline's chest, and she lifted a shaking hand, wrapping freshly clean fingers around Morgana's wrist, calming her. Morgana turned her face away, trying to hide her tears. If Aveline had had the strength to reach up and wipe them away, she would have. "I *did* dream of you."

Morgana swallowed down a strangled cry and went back to washing Aveline's hair.

"I wish you'd stayed," Aveline whispered through her constricted throat, biting down on a wobbling lip. "That you'd explained -"

Morgana's fingers combed through now untangled strands, and she started on the next section. "I would have, if I'd known you would be there for me to explain it to."

"You could have explained it to Helah," she croaked out. The water in the basin had turned a much deeper red, and Aveline marveled at how much blood must have been in her hair. "She would have listened -"

"Even if that were true," Morgana said delicately, "it was no longer a world worth saving." A tear slid down Aveline's cheek, and Morgana took care to wipe it away. "And I believed I'd done enough damage."

Aveline's throat bobbed, and she sat back, allowing Morgana to finish her work, scrubbing away the blood until the water finally ran clear, and Aveline could touch her arms without finding a layer of grime.

Morgana lifted Aveline's hand out of the water, delicately touching the tortured skin where the cuffs had been. Aveline hissed in pain but didn't try to pull away.

Exhaling roughly, Morgana rested the hand in her lap, padding it dry with a towel. "Those chains really did a number on you."

"I think the whole ordeal did a number on me."

Morgana looked up, the concern that she'd been holding back settling onto her face. "Are you okay?" she asked brokenly. "The siren -"

"The siren could have done much worse if I'd thought you were dead," Aveline said softly. "But I knew you were alive, and I knew everything she said was a lie."

Morgana bit the inside of her cheek, battling within herself until she finally decided to ask, "What did she say?"

As Morgana reached for a roll of bandages she must have found in the cupboard earlier, Aveline said, "The stories about sirens aren't true, they don't necessarily show your deepest desire. They just pull from your thoughts, and whatever it is they find in most abundance is what they portray. This can often be a person's true desires, but more often it's their fears."

Morgana sucked in a breath. "And you saw me..."

"*No*," Aveline scrambled to say, finding the energy to sit up in the bath and fall forward against her knees. "*No*, not like that. I meant what I said that night. I've never been afraid of you."

"You were, when you met me."

"It didn't last long," Aveline said, voice shaking. She remembered that initial meeting well. She'd been on the edge of hyperventilating through the entirety of their first conversation, Morgana's eyes and hair a constant reminder that she spoke to something *other*. It had only been when Morgana delicately lifted Coby up and handed him to her that Aveline had calmed, recalibrating her brain to remind herself that monsters didn't love their pets. "It wasn't you trying to hurt me that I saw, it was you..." She swallowed, looking away as her entire body heated in embarrassment. "It was you leaving, telling me that we..."

Morgana took Aveline's other hand and started wrapping it. "That we were nothing?"

Aveline's hand twitched, and she curled her fingers around Morgana's, making her pause in tending to the wound. Aveline searched for the right words. "She was very convincing."

Morgana paused to give Aveline an incredulous look and squeezed her fingers back. "I believed you'd betrayed me. The sea king said you were responsible for him gaining access to me, and I fed that resentment for two hundred years. Yet all it took was for a strange woman to come and say your name, and I damned both of the kingdoms to find out what had happened to you." She turned, and brushed Aveline's wet hair from her eyes. "I've done it twice now, and I'd do it a third time. I'd do it every day for the rest of my very long life."

Aveline's tears mingled with the bathwater clinging to her eyelashes. "For so long, I thought... I thought..."

"I know," Morgana said, softness and vulnerability overtaking her expression in a way Aveline didn't often see. "I never would have hurt you." She shifted her hold on Aveline's forearm, tightening her grip. "And I didn't mean it. When I said I shouldn't have come out of hiding that first time. Clearly, I didn't, because I went and did it a second time. Even if it destroyed the whole world, even if it took me with it, I'd do it all over again to find you."

A mixture of sorrow, relief, and an odd sort of happiness that Aveline hadn't felt for just about two hundred years flowed through her veins, and she leaned further forward, pressing her forehead to Morgana's arm, the only part of her body she could reach. It was the only thing she could think of, when she couldn't move further and the words wouldn't come.

"You will, though," Aveline finally whispered when Morgana threaded her fingers into her hair. She didn't have to say the word *leave* aloud. They both knew what she meant. "Eventually. You have to."

She felt a stutter in Morgana's chest, and her arms wrapped around Aveline's bare shoulder. She didn't hug her, didn't hold her. She did it just for the sake of touching her, of being close, and Aveline sank into it. "Yes," she whispered. "I do not have a choice. Or, perhaps I do, but I've made too many wrong choices. Neither I nor the kingdoms can afford more."

Aveline nodded absentmindedly. It had been the answer she had expected, and yet she still somehow felt like her chest had been cleaved in two. It somehow hurt more than her ringing ears, more than her torn wrists. "I know."

"You don't sound angry," Morgana observed, even as her eyes closed in pain at the thought. At the truth in Aveline's statement.

"I'm not," Aveline said honestly. "I can't be. I spent so long being angry at you for thinking you did a horrible thing. I can't be angry at you for performing a selfless one."

"Let me be entirely clear." She pulled back, then, and Aveline would have collapsed into the side of the tub had Morgana not caught her face in her hands. Her hands were warm against Aveline's cheek, somehow warmer than the still steaming water, and she sighed into the touch. She could easily fall asleep like this, with Morgana as close as she could ever hope her to be. "I will hide from the world, but I will not hide from you."

Aveline's slack face crumpled. "You're saying so many wonderful things, and it's not fair."

Morgana smiled. "Why? Because I'm supposed to be a monster?"

"No, you were never a monster, the world wouldn't be right if you were," Aveline said, and her words began to slur with exhaustion. How much had she slept when she'd been subjected to the torments of the siren? She must have only caught minutes at a time, falling asleep whenever the siren gave her a moment alone. "No, it's not fair because my mind isn't coming up with the right things to say in response."

Morgana's thumb brushed over Aveline's cheek, but then she stood, pulling Aveline with her and wrapping a large towel around her shoulders. "You'll get your chance, I'm sure. You've always done more talking than me."

Aveline tugged the soft towel tighter, leaning into Morgana as they navigated out of the bathroom. "Wait, but don't you need to -"

Morgana lowered Aveline to the bed, and she collapsed down into the sheets. "I can manage to wash myself." She fiddled with the sheets, until she managed to pull the duvet over Aveline's body, pulling the wet towel free.

Aveline smiled. "Just another way you're stronger than me, I suppose."

Morgana bent over her; arm braced against the side of the bed. "Don't ever fool yourself into thinking I'm stronger than anyone. Power does not equal strength." She pressed a featherlight kiss to Aveline's cheek, so close to the corner of her mouth that Aveline let out a strangled sigh. "Goodnight."

"Good evening," Aveline replied, her voice almost nothing, and the last thing she saw before sleep overtook her was the sun dipping beneath the crest of the towering, frozen wall of water outside her window.

***

By the time Aveline woke, total darkness had fallen outside, and she was grateful. She didn't think daylight would help her pounding headache. Only a single candle at Aveline's bedside illuminated the room, casting an orange glow in a small circle. The blanket slid from her body, and she started, realizing she'd never got dressed after the bath. Her cheeks heated, and she rolled over in the bed, hurrying to pull on a shirt and pants from a drawer within arm's reach. Only when she'd managed to dress herself did she straighten and look around, kicking the covers fully toward the end of the bed.

Morgana was nowhere to be found.

Panic seized her, and she jumped from the bed, pausing only momentarily to appreciate the strength that had returned to her limbs as she whipped her head around, searching the dark corners of the room. The cool floor bit into her bare feet, and she started toward the closed door of the bathroom just as it opened, a square of light cascading over the floor and illuminating Morgana standing there.

"What?" she asked, alarmed, looking around the room for some kind of threat. She was wearing simple clothes, but she still held the sword at her side. "What is it? Who -"

"Nothing," Aveline sighed, rubbing a hand down her face. "I - you scared me when you weren't here."

Morgana looked over her shoulder. "I was taking a bath of my own." Her hair indeed hung sopping against her shoulders, dripping onto the floor. Aveline wondered how long she'd sat alone in the bath, letting the water slowly erode the dirt and grime away until nothing else remained. "I didn't think you'd appreciate me watching you sleep."

Aveline fell back onto her bed. "You've done it before. Twice, actually."

Morgana snorted, but she didn't move, her bare feet shifting on the cool floor. "I didn't watch you then, either. Sleep is … unfairly vulnerable for humans."

Aveline smiled wanly. "Too bad I'm not human."

"From what I hear, being human is overrated."

Aveline shifted, leaving the spot beside her open as an invitation, and Morgana took it, flinging her hair from her shoulder and getting it out of the way. Droplets went flying, sparkling in the candlelight and wetting the collar of Morgana's shirt.

The room was quiet and calm, dark where they sat just outside of the circle of candlelight. "You're feeling better, then?"

Aveline nodded. "Is it late?"

"You slept for a day and a half. Morning should be approaching soon."

Resisting the urge to groan, Aveline rubbed her hand down her face. Morgana reached out and pulled it away. "More scheming can wait until tomorrow."

"I know," Morgana murmured, bringing both of their hands down. "I suppose it's become a life of one scheme after another."

Aveline squeezed her hand tighter. "Is this a scheme?"

Morgana's eyes flashed in the candlelight. Green and yellow, somehow soft in their fiery glory. "No." She didn't say anything more, because she didn't have to. Her words from hours before came back and lingered between them. "A break from the schemes can be just as necessary."

Aveline smiled, heart thundering in her chest. Though these past two hundred years were too long to wait, these past two minutes had been much more painful. Her soul wrenched toward Morgana like someone had buried a magnet into each of their chests. She lifted her hand, the one Morgana wasn't holding, and pressed her palm into the other woman's cheek. She wiped away the lingering water dripping from her hairline, thankful to have something to banish other than tears.

"Not a scheme," Morgana murmured again. "But if you don't kiss me, I might just have to figure something out."

Letting out an excruciating sigh that sounded more like a whimper than anything else, Aveline drew her in, and two hundred years folded together, and again, they were one.

"Where are all the nice things you promised me?" Morgana whispered into her lips, soft with a hint of teeth.

A laugh rumbled out of Aveline's chest, and she felt the sound vibrate from her own body to Morgana's. "It's not my fault I keep getting distracted. It's yours."

Laughing, a soft and true sound that came from the deepest parts of her soul, Morgana pulled her back in, and they were done talking. They spent what was left of the night re-exploring each other, Morgana relearning the things about Aveline's body that had changed, the soul that had stayed the same. They took their time in a way they never had before.

Morgana kissed her, and she felt human again.

PART FOUR
Now

Chapter Twenty Nine

Morgana took to joining Verona in her room for lunch on the days when neither of them felt like dealing with the chaos of the dining hall and Aveline was too busy to take a break. Things moved so quickly after that first night back, Morgana barely had the chance to take a breath.

But Verona had pulled her aside after that first meeting in the council room where they'd tried to convince the irreverent girl to be queen. While Aveline wasn't watching, caught up in a conversation with Micah, Verona had kept Morgana by the fireplace, even as Morgana had wished for a long bath and an even longer lie down.

Still, Verona's hold on her elbow had been insistent and warm, her soul soft and open, and Morgana had trusted her instincts.

Verona hadn't spoken for several long moments as the rest of the crew cleaned up the space, considering Morgana with her sharp, dark eyes, hands on her hips. The silence stretched, and Morgana had lifted her brows in confusion.

Verona's lips had begun to curve into a smile, and she bent at the waist, holding her hand to her chest.

Baffled, Morgana had reached out as though to pull her back up, starting to ask, "What are you—"

Verona had simply shaken her head, looking up at Morgana through her eyelashes. "You were right."

"Yes," Morgana had agreed. "I believe that was what this meeting was about."

She shook her head again. "No." She'd paused, exhaling. "I won't bow to monsters."

Morgana's lips had parted as the meaning behind the words set in, and without thinking, she'd bowed back, bending her knees until their eyes were level. "Neither will I."

Verona glanced at Aveline, who still leaned against the doorframe, before turning back to Morgana. "I suppose it would be futile to ask you not to hurt her again?"

Morgana wished it wasn't useless, wished that she wouldn't have to be harsh in the end. "I don't think I could do anything as bad as killing her again," Morgana said, evading the question.

Verona laughed. "You could say that again." Sobering, she continued, "I understand what you think you have to do. And even if you must do it … make sure she knows, this time."

Morgana had nodded, Verona's gaze so sharp that she didn't dare say anything more.

"Or I won't hesitate to banish you," Verona had added in an attempt to lighten the mood. She had patted Morgana on the shoulder before joining Aveline, leaving Morgana by the fireplace, thinking how ironic it was that the witch would soon have to banish herself.

Now, all talk of serious topics had been banished instead as Morgana and Verona sat at the small table in the corner of her bedroom, cutting into the chicken Verona had snuck from the kitchen. "I have a headache *all the time* now," Verona said around a mouthful of food, rubbing at her temples. "If you even *mention* the festival, I'll see to it that you're never welcome near me again."

Morgana pushed food around her plate. "You could do it, too. I'm surprised you haven't kicked someone out already, just for fun."

"It's crossed my mind," she sighed, dropping her fork with a clatter. "Every time Aveline comes up with some other thing that could go wrong, I think, '*You know what, I see why Morgana killed her*.'"

Morgana threw her hands in the air. "You're not allowed to make those kinds of jokes."

"Sure I can. I'm queen."

"Not yet, technically," Morgana said. "That's what the festival is for: to crown you." Morgana paused. "Well, the second festival. Not the first."

Verona pointed her knife at Morgana, warning. "What did I say?"

Morgana lifted her hands in surrender. "Although, I still think it's silly to call it a coronation when we don't have a crown."

"And whose fault is that?" Verona asked innocently. She shook her head. "Besides, we'll get the crown before it comes to the actual..." She motioned to her head with a grimace. She'd asked on more than one occasion if she'd have to wear it at all times and kept asking hoping she would eventually hear a 'no'.

"We will," Morgana agreed. And they would. Hopefully. "And, let me be clear, it was *not* my fault that we didn't get the crown. You can take that up with Aveline."

"Didn't you get captured because you attacked her?"

"She deserved it at the time," Morgana waved her off. "We would have gotten captured anyway."

She looked up at Verona, expecting her to fight back, but instead she just stared out the window to the streets below. They were empty now, but soon they would fill. Soon, these ramshackle ruins would become a city again.

"Do you think the people will be angry?" Verona asked a moment later. "It won't be much of a festival if they're throwing tomatoes at the crown."

"It's getting harder and harder for me to not talk of the festival when you keep bringing it up."

"I'm allowed to bring it up. And if I do, you're allowed to respond."

Morgana sighed, sitting back. "The festival doesn't need to be fun. In fact, you'll be able to tell them after the fact that *no one* had fun."

"You know better than anyone that perception is everything."

Morgana snorted bitterly. "Indeed. But what we've also learned is that people don't stay angry."

"Aveline stayed angry for two hundred years."

"Aveline had a personal stake in the matter. But what I meant is that people don't stay angry if a proper explanation is given. Which you will give at the *real* festival you'll hold after the dust settles."

A festival that Morgana would probably not attend. She tried not to dwell on that.

The door creaked open, and Morgana stiffened, but relaxed when Verona didn't seem alarmed. Castor peeked his head in before the rest of his body followed, throwing himself onto Verona's bed.

"I have not slept in seventy hours."

"I haven't slept in two hundred and twenty something years, but who's counting?"

He jerked up, noticing Morgana for the first time and scrambled off the bed, leaning cautiously against the wall. Morgana sighed, turning away. She was fairly sure Castor and Micah were still afraid of her, although they didn't seem to hate her as they once had.

Rike was the only one who still kept her distance. She would leave the room whenever Morgana entered, avoiding her eye whenever Morgana tried to bridge that gap, to make some sort of peace. Not only did the fear remain in Rike, but the loathing, too.

"I've explained it so many times," Aveline had despaired one night, not long after the women had returned from Nysus. "She just won't listen; she doesn't believe me."

Morgana clicked her tongue. "Which means she doesn't believe me."

"She's started avoiding me, too," Aveline had whispered, hugging herself. "We used to have at least one meal together every day. Dinner, usually, in an attempt at some sort of normal family life, but…" She had trailed off, shaking her head.

"I'm sorry," Morgana had murmured, heart aching. Perhaps what had happened was too much to make right on all accounts.

Castor was still eyeing Morgana warily, but at least it wasn't with hatred. Just a watchful curiosity. Verona scoffed, throwing a piece of chicken at Castor. He did an exceedingly poor job of dodging it. "Stop it."

Castor's wary eyes didn't put Morgana off, though; didn't anger her in the way they would have during her first stay at the palace. She remembered how much it had made her ache, to know that she would never be trusted. To know that she had the power to ascertain the intentions of others, but she couldn't give them that comfort in return.

Stealing a piece of celery from Verona's plate, Castor took a few tentative bites. He was easily the most timid of Aveline's crew, better suited to working in the background and planning. All things considered, Morgana was fairly impressed that he looked her in the eye at all. "I believe your story, you know," he finally said.

Morgana chewed on her lip, considering him. "Are you just saying that because you think I'll kill you if I think otherwise?"

Verona threw her hands in the air. "Not helping!"

"No," Castor said, and Morgana sensed the honesty. "I actually do believe you. I don't think you consciously hurt all those people during the war. But that doesn't mean you won't now."

Morgana folded her arms. "And why would I?"

He stood again, the celery still in hand. "I don't know. I suppose that's the problem. No one knows how a witch's mind works but you. Come on, we're gathering in the tower."

With a soft goodbye tap on Verona's shoulder, he sped from the room.

***

Aveline stayed through lunch in the tower, mostly to fixate on the many ways everything could go wrong. She thought of Morgana, of her confidence during the day. But she would grow silent in the night. Anytime Aveline brought up crowning Verona for real, testing the waters of building a true life, Morgana's expression would shutter, and she would change the subject. No matter what they did, this war would follow them, and Aveline didn't know what was worse: prolonging this fight or finally reaching the end of a conflict that had tied the two women together for two hundred years.

Morgana had come back to Briarwood to finish what she had started. She had always planned to do what needed to be done and then go back to the quiet life the Serpent Witch was meant to live. Once Aveline remembered that any semblance of an appetite always abandoned her.

A knock sounded on the door, and Aveline jerked up from where she'd been mulling over her notes. Rike stuck her head in, looking around the room before deeming it safe to enter.

Aveline snapped her journal closed and stood. "We missed you this morning."

"I overslept," Rike said softly.

"For the third day in a row."

Rike pressed her lips together, looking away. "I've been busy."

Aveline took a step forward, hugging the book to her chest. Rike had been keeping to herself since Aveline and Morgana returned from Nysus, never quite looking anyone in the eye. "Okay. Why don't you tell me why you've actually been avoiding me like death?"

Rike blinked, chewing on the side of her cheeks before she said, "That's what she is, isn't she? Death?"

Pulling up short, Aveline gave her a questioning look. "No. No, the god of death holds that title. She believes he is the one who cursed her."

Rike scoffed. "Cursed?"

"You think the power she possesses is a *blessing*?" Aveline asked incredulously. "No, she has the burden of maintaining *life*. Nothing more, nothing less."

"Having control over life sounds a lot like death to me," Rike said, a muscle in her jaw twitching wildly. "She will always be a threat."

"And so will I," Aveline said patiently. She couldn't get angry, not really. She understood any frustration that her crew might be having right now. After all, she'd been unknowingly feeding them vile, and horribly wrong, information about Morgana for years. "The blessing of battle courses through me, I could kill any one of you at any given moment without a second thought. The only difference is that I would use my hands, and you'd see it coming."

Rike shook her head. "I don't understand your willingness to just … accept what she said. She left you for *dead* for the sake of a *sword.*"

"First of all," Aveline said, holding up a finger as she reminded herself that, despite their age difference, Rike was just as protective of Aveline as Aveline was of her. Spending most of their recent lives having only each other made it something of an inevitability. "I was already in chains. There was nothing she could have done for me. I couldn't fight out of that without my magic."

"You might have," Rike said harshly, eyes flooding. "You were a good fighter, even before the blessing."

Aveline took another tentative step forward, almost within reach. "I was. But I've been relying on magic for two hundred years. There was no way I could have fought off fifteen guards while my hands were shackled. Morgana knew that, and so do you. And even if I *had* stood a chance at holding them off, Morgana also knows that I wouldn't have wanted it any other way. I wanted her safe, and I wanted you safe. And keeping her safe meant protecting the sword."

Rike's lip wobbled.

Taking the final step forward, Aveline took Rike by the shoulders, her skin familiar beneath her fingertips. "If the king took control of her again, many more people would be dead. Not only that, but all my leverage would have been gone. The king couldn't kill me because I knew where you were. She did what she had to do."

"You're making excuses for her -" Rike's voice broke.

Aveline pulled her niece into her arms, squeezing tight, and Rike hugged back with a vengeance, fingers digging into her back. Aveline tried to soothe her, brushing down her hair, but Rike trembled too hard to feel it.

"You stayed there instead of coming with me," she sobbed. "You could have come with me. You could have tried."

No. She couldn't have. She couldn't have even tried.

Instead, Aveline murmured back, "I'm sorry. It was the best way to keep you safe. I'd do anything to keep you safe."

They stayed like that for a long while, making up for the missed moments and the time lost over the last two months. Rike eventually pulled away, shaking her limbs out and sniffling. Aveline squeezed her hand before finally letting go, ruining the day that would someday come where Aveline would lose another family, another loved one.

"We're okay, right?" Aveline asked. "I only ever -"

"I know. Me too." Rike wiped her eyes, straightening. "I should go."

"No, you should stay. We're gathering in the tower after lunch, you should -"

But Rike was already heading toward the hall, hugging her jacket close. She paused in the doorway, looking over her shoulder. "You know I'd do anything to keep you safe, too, right?" Her voice was harder than before. Determined.

Aveline nodded with a sad smile. "I know."

As soon as the words came out, Micah slid past Rike into the room, beginning to greet them before noting Rike's red-rimmed eyes and lowering his hands. "Am I interrupting something?"

Aveline opened her mouth, but Rike shook her head. "No, nothing. I'll see you all later."

She disappeared down the hall.

Micah turned to Aveline with a raised eyebrow. "What was that about?"

Aveline stared at the empty doorway, her heart aching. "We haven't had much time to talk about everything that happened, how long we were apart. We've never been apart that long."

Micah clicked his tongue, shaking his head. "I don't understand why people get mad in situations like that. She should have just said she misses you."

"I think she's afraid of losing me again."

Micah huffed. "Considering how you look at our dear witch, I wouldn't be surprised if we *all* lose you."

"Don't call her that," Aveline snapped, if just to avoid the other topic. Still, she hated when they called Morgana that, even though she felt like a hypocrite, having spent years calling her every foul name she could come up with.

Micah raised his hands. "And what do you suppose we call her? She's not human."

"I suggest her name, although if you want to get on her good side, she might be flattered by *sorceress*." Aveline's gaze caught on something in his fist, a rolled-up piece of parchment. "What do you have there?"

"Updated map of the streets," he said, waving it in front of her face with a grin, and it immediately made her feel better. "Freshly delivered from Verona's scouts. There's been a few collapses in the past months or so, and construction on the western edge of the city is still ongoing."

Sniffing, Aveline nodded and pushed Rike from her mind. She jerked her head, and Micah followed her over to the counter.

***

"We need to make a new plan."

Morgana's voice was urgent as she found Aveline pouring over a long scroll in the council room, pointing something out to Micah. Castor was already there, folded into his usual chair with a journal, listening to whatever Aveline had been saying. They jerked up at her entrance, and Morgana's breath flew from her chest at the smile Aveline gave her; it was bold and unrestrained. She'd received many of those in the past few days, but knew she'd never get enough.

The smile slid from her face as she processed Morgana's words, lifting her pen and pointing at her in accusation. "Is the one we have now not good enough?"

"No, not about that," Morgana said in exasperation. She glanced at Micah as Verona came in, too, perching on the couch to watch the show. "It's about him. We have a problem."

Micah sputtered, nearly falling over in the process of trying to back away from her, and Aveline reached out to steady him. Morgana tipped her head up toward the ceiling with a groan of frustration.

"Oh, good job," Aveline said to Micah with a smirk before returning her attention to Morgana. "Do go on."

Realizing how that probably sounded to Micah, Morgana scrambled to say, "Not a personal problem or anything." She jabbed a thumb over her shoulder. "It involves him, too."

Caster didn't move. Perhaps he'd been expecting this.

Aveline hopped up to sit on the table, the heels of her boots kicking at the leg beneath her as she lifted her eyebrows. "Okay, what's the problem?"

Morgana leaned against the table, spreading her fingers out over the smooth surface as she looked back and forth between Castor and Micah. She'd heard from Aveline how each of them had come to the palace. According to her, they hadn't been particularly trusting of Aveline in the beginning, either.

"What did you do?" Morgana had asked a few nights ago, after Micah had once again declined her offer to join them in Verona's room for lunch. "To win them over?"

"First of all, they're slightly different situations, so take what I say with a grain of salt -"

"What do you mean?" Morgana had asked with a grin. "A mysterious witch who destroyed their kingdom versus the almost normal woman blessed with the power to *protect* their kingdom?"

Aveline rolled her eyes. "It's even more different than that. They knew me first as a regular, mortal woman, remember? By the time I told them I was

Hallowed, we were already something close to friends. They knew me, and they understood why I had kept it a secret for so long. You need them to know you, too. You've convinced them *what* you are, not *who* you are."

"Okay," Morgana had said. "Is there advice hidden somewhere in there?"

Aveline shrugged. "I let them fight me."

Morgana's eyes had widened. "What?"

"Yeah, we'd been training with wooden swords up until that point, their fighting techniques were sloppy and untrained at best."

"Castor doesn't fight," Morgana had pointed out.

Aveline had snorted. "He tried for a while. So stubborn." She'd paused, chewing on her lip. "Anyway, I gave them a real sword and fought back with only my fake one. I think there was something about me putting my life in their hands that made them think … trust runs both ways."

Morgana had sat up on her elbows. "And they both won?"

"No, of course not," Aveline had laughed. "I'm blessed by the goddess of battle, Morgana, they didn't have a prayer. But that wasn't the point. The point was that I trusted them, and I was willing to put my life in their hands."

"But you didn't," Morgana had pointed out. "They never could have beaten you."

"Yeah," Aveline said with a conspiratorial smile. "But they didn't know that at the time."

Morgana shook the memories away and forced herself back into the present, to Aveline's question.

"The problem," Morgana said loudly, "is that I've upset how you all work as a team."

"Morgana," Aveline began to protest, but Morgana simply held up her hand.

"Don't tell me I'm wrong, because I'm not," Morgana said sadly, looking at the two men in the room. "I was … quite literally created to be alone, and I can't say I blame you both for treating me that way. But in the time I spent here before the truth came out, when it was all five of you against me, it became clear that you all trust each other like family. That family you've made is devolving because half of you trust me, and half of you don't."

None of them mentioned that Rike was nowhere to be found; that she wasn't even included in those numbers. They all exchanged glances. Aveline looked like she wanted to pull her hair out.

Morgana rested her hand on the sheath at her waist and squeezed the hilt; her sword hadn't left her side since she retrieved it from Rike. The metal cooled her fingertips, the sensation soothing despite the deadliness of the weapon. "You don't trust me," she went on, "and that's a problem."

Micah eyed her sword warily and didn't say anything. Castor just looked intrigued.

"In my defense," Micah said after a pointed glance at Aveline, "we've heard far more bad things about you than good. And you're quite literally always armed, even without your sword."

Morgana shrugged. "Fair enough. But so are you." She jerked her chin toward his sleeve, where she knew a knife waited. He stiffened and shifted his arm behind his back.

"You want us to trust you," Castor said, swinging his legs down from where they'd been hanging over the arm of the chair, and standing. "Is that what this is?"

Morgana pressed her lips together. "Sort of."

Yes, she wanted them to trust her. But mostly, she wanted them to stop fearing her, to stop looking at her like the monster she'd spent the last several months trying to prove she wasn't. She knew she was struggling against a storm wind, battling against the earliest impression she had given them, colored by the hollowness she had displayed when she had first arrived. But she would keep fighting.

When she first arrived at the palace, she hadn't given a damn what any of them thought. In retrospect, it was startlingly different from how she acted during the first war. This time, she'd moved through those weeks as if in a daze, waiting for this strange woman to tell her what exactly had become of Aveline. Waiting for an excuse to go back into hiding.

Now, she had begun to look for an excuse to stay. And she found that to be, perhaps, a great deal more worrying.

She couldn't dwell on that. She could never stay if Micah's muscles kept tensing whenever she walked into the room; if Castor avoided her eyes but kept studying her behind her back, trying to pick her apart like a mystery to be solved. She supposed she had it coming. Maybe people thought she was a monster because she'd given them no reason to think otherwise. She'd spent so long running, so long hiding. So long feeling guilty.

She looked at them, swallowing down the panic. But even as she broke out into a sweat, she pulled the sword from its sheath.

Castor's eyes widened, looking at it as if it might jump out of her hands and cut him open all on its own.

Morgana gave him a flat stare. "I can control *you*. Not the sword."

Aveline fixed her with a glare. "You're *horrible* at this."

Morgana pushed herself off the table and turned to Castor first. "Bear with me. My experience with human relationships is … limited. Limited to exactly one person over the course of my very long lifetime."

She glanced over her shoulder in time to see Aveline's eyes soften.

Castor looked ready to sprint away, eyes focusing on the point of Morgana's sword. "Is threatening me with a weapon supposed to make me trust you?"

Rolling her eyes, Morgana said, "We might have bigger problems if you think that someone casually holding a weapon in your immediate vicinity is a threat."

"Castor could look at a tiny knife sitting precariously on a table and think his life was in danger," Verona said from the couch, the first time she had spoken since coming in. "Don't take it personally."

Morgana braced herself as the room fell silent. Aveline moved forward, mouth opening in a concerned question, but Morgana didn't let her speak.

If she couldn't trust them, they would never trust her.

Steeling herself, her blood running cold with anticipation, every single hair standing on end, Morgana flipped the sword in her hand until she offered it, hilt-first, to Castor. "Take it."

Castor stared at the weapon with wide eyes, his fingers flexing at his side. "I don't understand -"

"Take it, and I'll explain," Morgana gritted out. "Before I change my mind."

Tentatively, as if the sword was now the monster instead of her, Castor wrapped delicate, uncalloused fingers around the hilt, clutching the snake coiled around the grip with both hands. Morgana pressed her lips together, and as her stomach plummeted, forced herself to step out of arm's reach of the blade. She felt the separation in her gut, the way her power stretched thin at someone else possessing the weapon. But she kept her feet planted on the ground.

Morgana swallowed, her tongue dry as sand. "Right now, you have all the power over me that I usually have over you. You could strike me dead with that sword, or take my power as your own, and I could do nothing to stop you."

Castor shared an incredulous look with Micah, hands trembling around the hilt. Micah came around the table for a closer look at the sword, reaching out to run his fingers along the shining metal. He looked up at Morgana in shock. "You're serious?"

"About it killing me? Didn't you listen to our story at all -?"

"No," Micah cut her off. "About letting us hold on to this."

Morgana straightened. The sword flickered in the light, taunting her, as Castor turned it toward himself to get a better look. "Give it back to me tomorrow," she said, spinning on her heel and heading toward the door before she could lose her nerve. "If you haven't killed me by then, I'll assume we're on the same page."

Chapter Thirty

Aveline found Morgana panicking in the hall several turns away from the council room. She had slid down the wall, trying to catch her breath with a hand to her throat. The lantern blazing on the wall above her illuminated the area with a soft glow, and her free hand skittered along the wall as if she might grasp hold of that light.

Racing toward her, Aveline skidded to a stop a few feet away from where Morgana sat huddled, her breathing loud and unsteady. Aveline raised her hand warily, murmuring, "Morgana…"

Morgana whipped her head up, eyes wild. She gasped and swallowed down her surprise. She must not have heard Aveline's approach over her panic. "I'm sorry," she managed to breathe out. "I just need … a minute."

Aveline dropped into a crouch, whispering, "It's okay, you're okay. I promise they won't hurt you."

She huffed. "Stupid idea, right?"

Aveline remembered, then, the advice she had given Morgana the other night. This must be Morgana's version of … putting her life in their hands.

Recognizing the understanding on Aveline's face, Morgana exhaled slowly, breathing in and out of her nose. "It was the only way. It was the only way to get them to trust me."

"Are you absolutely sure about that?"

Morgana shrugged. "No. But it was the only thing I could think of and being cooped up in this palace with the majority of its occupants hating me, I'm running out of patience. And sanity."

Sitting down, Aveline scooted until she leaned against the wall at Morgana's side, pressing their shoulders together. Morgana reached up, placing a shaking hand on Aveline's thigh, and Aveline covered it with her own. "You are … insane. Just in case no one has told you that."

Morgana let out a half-hysterical laugh. "I'm fairly sure you've probably thought the same on more than one occasion." She rolled her head to the side, until their noses were millimeters apart. "But probably with less affection."

"Who says there's affection involved now?"

Morgana let her eyes flutter closed, and Aveline relished that Morgana had calmed down enough in her presence to do that; that she could let her guard down without her sword at her side. Without thinking, Aveline leaned forward and pressed a kiss to the corner of her mouth, and Morgana's eyes flew open again in surprise.

"What?" Aveline asked.

Morgana smiled. "Nothing."

Aveline turned away, leaning her head back against the wall. "Are you worried about them giving it back?"

"No." Morgana paused. "Well, I mean, of *course*, but that's just instinct. I feel that sword as if it's another person, like it has its own soul. It's … uncomfortable … having it in someone else's hands."

"Then go take it back," Aveline said, creasing her eyebrows. "You've made your point."

Morgana shook her head. "No. They have to be the ones to give it back, otherwise, it would have been for nothing."

Aveline considered her next words carefully, thinking of all the interactions Morgana had had with her crew before they were taken by the sea king. They'd consisted mostly of either glares or intrigue from her team's side. For Morgana's part, she'd been entirely indifferent. "Can I ask…"

"You always can," Morgana said without thinking. "Secrets have caused more harm than the sea king himself."

"It didn't help that most of the secrets stemmed *from* the sea king," Aveline pointed out, before clearing her throat. "I just … why do you care?"

Morgana jerked up from where she rested against the wall, turning to face Aveline completely. "About what? About the war?"

Aveline huffed. "No, I know why you care about *that*. But why do you care about Micah and Castor trusting you?"

Morgana furrowed her brows. "I thought that would have been obvious."

Shrugging helplessly, Aveline asked, "Spell it out for me."

Morgana drummed her fingers along her ankle, and Aveline reached out to stop the fidgeting. Morgana caught her hands, entwining their fingers together. "I said it just now: my presence has disrupted the way you all work as a team. But not only that, it's disrupted your friendships."

Aveline began to protest, to insist that wasn't true, to make sure Morgana didn't assume responsibility for another thing that wasn't her fault. But then she remembered Rike, her avoidance of not just Morgana but Aveline herself, and swallowed the words.

"I'm like an obstacle between you and them that they don't know how to pass. It's not as if I can just leave, not now. I had to change myself from a blockade into a bridge. I don't want the guilt of breaking something else on my conscience."

Aveline felt a burning behind her eyes, a feeling of impending loss overwhelming her. "Because I'll need them when you're gone?" she forced out.

Morgana smiled sadly. "You need them whether I'm here or not."

***

Aveline returned to the meeting while Morgana went back to the room they shared. Morgana dragged her fingers along the wooden walls as she went. She admired the design of the boards, detailed engravings of trees and plants and flowers, rivers and mountains. A map of nature beneath her hands, spread out over the entire palace.

The place was beautiful, even as dilapidated as it had become over the passing of two centuries. Morgana remembered the grand palace she had seen during her first visit, the air of grandeur and nobility, lords and ladies dotting the halls as they dealt with policy and drama. The ghost of that impression still remained, an echo of a vibrant moment in time far removed from the lives within these walls now. It reverberated through Morgana's bones, a conviction that something more awaited this palace.

Something better. A kingdom built upon happiness, and people who lived in the sunshine instead of the shadows.

Morgana gazed out at the wavering wall of water towering over them from the bedroom window. It cast more shadows on their kingdom than the trees ever could. In that moment, she swore she would never pass through another portal into Nysus again. She'd die before she let them take her. She would find a way.

She stared at the wall of cerulean blue, trying to see past it toward a waiting horizon, until she heard a knock on the door. Morgana started. How long had she been caught up in her thoughts? Surely, the war council couldn't have come to an end already. Aveline's crew could talk themself hoarse. Stalking to the door, she wrenched it open before remembering that she was unarmed.

Coming face to face with her sword, Morgana jumped back, hands flying up before she recognized the three faces behind it.

"You scared me," Morgana exclaimed, heart pounding in her chest.

Verona smiled and pushed into the room, leaving Castor and Micah to stand in the doorway, the latter holding the Serpent Sword. "That was the idea, I think. A taste of your own medicine."

Morgana didn't know what to make of the casual air the three of them now radiated. She didn't know if she should be nervous or relieved. Micah held the sword loosely, as if he'd already grown comfortable with it. As if he wasn't afraid of it. And because her brain was tripping over itself at being with all of Aveline's friends for the first time *without* Aveline, she stammered, "I don't take medicine, I can't get sick."

Verona burst out laughing and flung herself into a chair. "Yeah, we know, you're super special, and you're full of life instead of death."

"Oh, sure," Morgana said, watching as Verona sprawled out in the chair, picking up the book Morgana had left on the nearby table. "Make yourself comfortable. This isn't even my room, you know."

"I'm the queen," Verona said as she flipped through the pages. "It's my job now to put my feet up." She held up the book. "This is a good one."

Micah cleared his throat, and Morgana spun back to see him and Castor still standing in the doorway. She had forgotten they were there, and her focus snapped back to her sword.

"Sorry," Morgana said, stepping away to let them in. "It's just that I'm already friends with her."

Verona perked up. "Oh, are we friends?"

"Tentatively," Morgana said without taking her eyes off the men. She did her best to keep her attention on the men instead of the sword, but her eyes kept flickering down without her permission. "What can I do for you?"

She thought about asking if they'd come to kill her, but she held back. Just in case the answer was yes.

Micah and Castor exchanged a glance, and with a slight nod from Castor, Micah flipped the sword around in the same way Morgana had, earlier. It flashed for a moment, and she had a sudden vision of the blade slicing through her neck, her magic bleeding away along with her life. She tried not to flinch.

But he caught the blade with a steady, gloved hand, and presented it to her, hilt-first. Morgana didn't grab it, though. She kept her fists clenched at her side as she held Micah's gaze.

He licked his lips, searching her eyes, and seemed content with what he found there. "We don't need twenty-four hours."

Morgana still didn't move. "What's the verdict, then?"

"I tried to think of every way this might have been a trap," Castor said honestly, folding his arms across his chest. "Instead of talking about the festival, we discussed you instead. For two hours, while Aveline watched and didn't say a thing."

Morgana lifted her brows. "And why's that?"

"Because she didn't want to sway our opinion," Verona said, staring at the ceiling as if she was bored again. "Something about not wanting to seem like she was making excuses for you."

"So, what? You couldn't think of any ways I might be trapping you?" Morgana asked Castor.

He shrugged. "Sure, I could. We thought of dozens, half of them involving the sea king."

Morgana's heart pounded in her chest, the sword still a wall between them, the sharp blade separating them in more ways than one. She tried to read their eyes, too, as they had read hers, but she didn't have enough experience with people. She longed to reach out with her powers, but she held back, thinking that if they ever found out, they might change their minds and turn the sword around again. "At least I'm joining a clever team, whether they trust me or not."

Micah smiled. It was hesitant, and not far from a grimace, but it was there. "We trust you."

Morgana blinked. "Why?" She directed this question at Castor, because he was the thinker, the planner. He wouldn't have been easily convinced.

"Every possibility that this was a trap involved at least one of two things." Castor held up a finger. "One, Aveline's death."

Morgana cringed, and she saw on Micah's face that it was the right response.

He lifted his other finger. "And two, you turning yourself over to the sea king. And if there's one thing I've believed this whole time, it's that you'll do anything to keep you and this thing," he jerked his head toward the sword, "out of his control."

"But you still gave it to us," Micah finished for him. "Monsters don't take risks like that."

"Probably because monsters aren't stupid," Verona put it.

Morgana made a mental note to tell Verona that their trial friendship was on suspension. But she didn't take her eyes off the two men. Delicately, she reached out and accepted her sword.

Micah tucked his hands into the pockets of his jacket, and Morgana slipped the sword into its sheath. She'd never taken it off.

Castor's eyes snagged on it. "You're still wearing the sheath?"

Morgana looked down at herself, balanced once more with the additional weight on her left side. "I am."

"It's heavy, isn't it?" he asked incredulously. "Were you planning on sleeping with it?"

"I don't sleep," Morgana said. At the same time both Micah and Verona said, "She doesn't sleep."

"We've covered this," Micah said as he held up his hand before Castor could object. "*Filled with life and the energy of others*, and all that."

"Glad to see you're catching on," Morgana grinned.

Castor considered Morgana, and after a moment of concentration, he let out a huff of a laugh. "You knew we'd give it back today."

Morgana shrugged. "Call it an educated hunch. Most people wouldn't hold something so valuable to its owner for longer than necessary. And I didn't think *you'd* want to sleep with it in *your* room."

"So, it *was* a trick!" Castor exclaimed.

"No," Verona groaned, standing and popping her back. "She would have let you keep it for the full day if you'd tried. She just sensed your disgusting human decency."

Castor shrugged, but he smiled, too. "Just checking."

Morgana waved him off. "I know, witches and their trickery." She glanced at Verona. "Be careful though, I've completely won over your partner. I might ruin your chances of being king."

Castor sputtered, and the blush on his cheeks confirmed her suspicions. "I have no intention of being king," he said, too loudly. Verona cackled with glee.

"Ha! And I have no intention of *making* you king! You'll be prince-consort or nothing."

Another knock sounded on the door, and they all turned to see Aveline standing in the empty doorway with her hands on her hips, looking both irritated and fond at the same time.

"This is nice and all, but are you done here? We're behind schedule, and we move tomorrow."

Verona saluted, standing as the mood in the room sobered at the reminder of what waited for them when the sun next rose. "I'll obey for now, but only because I'll be in charge soon."

"Oh, you're going to be insufferable," Castor groaned as the two of them followed Aveline from the room. Morgana made to go after them, but a soft touch on her elbow held her back.

Morgana's hand went to her sword, but not for defense. "Do you want it back?" Morgana asked Micah. "I meant what I said, about letting you keep it—"

Micah shook his head and backed a step away. "No, no, it's not that."

Straightening, Morgana narrowed her eyes. "Then…"

Still, he glanced at the sword. "I need to know that you care about Aveline more than that sword."

The weapon suddenly felt heavier at her side. Morgana licked her lips as she tried to hide her surprise at the question. "What?"

Micah folded his arms, and none of his nervousness from before remained. "You saved the sword instead of her. Back in Nysus."

Morgana's stomach lurched as she realized what he must be talking about, what saving the Serpent Sword back in Thalassa must have looked like to Rike, and she lifted her chin. "I saved the sword when it was the only thing that could be saved."

"Okay," Micah said calmly. "But what would you have done had she not been in chains?"

Considering him, Morgana thought of Aveline in her chains, of the raw skin at the wrists that had only recently begun to heel. Of the haggard look in her eyes as she'd collapsed after their escape. Flashes of Aveline dead in her arms appeared before her eyes.

And then Morgana thought of her own sword lodged in her stomach, the lurching sensation of her deep-seated magic being wrenched from her very bones, killing thousands as she screamed silently, locked in her own mind. She thought of the crushing grief that had plagued her for decades after, that still followed her in the deep hours of the night.

She raised her eyes back to Micah. "You do realize you're essentially asking whether I would save her or myself. And in the worst-case scenario;

her, or the rest of Calypdon."

He swallowed. "I do."

"Good," Morgana said with a nod of approval, and she started for the door. "The answer is her."

***

Aveline waited for Morgana in the hallway, watching with raised eyebrows as Micah passed her and hurried after Castor and Verona. Morgana let him go, waving goodbye with a small smile.

Glancing between Morgana and Micah's disappearing form, Aveline pressed her lips together nervously. For all Morgana's talk about building bridges, Micah had run out pretty fast. "What was that about?"

Morgana's smile and slight roll of her eyes immediately put her at ease. "That was the second of your crew to threaten me," she said, bracing her hand on her hip and leaning against the wall. "Should I be concerned?"

Aveline grabbed her by the arm and tugged Morgana with her. "Only if you don't do what I say."

Morgana jogged after her with a laugh, and Aveline marveled at the normalcy of it. If she didn't think too hard, she could convince herself she was dragging her normal partner to a normal meeting on a normal day in a normal kingdom.

Except she wasn't normal. Neither of them were. They would live and die as one kind and yet worlds apart.

Aveline slowed to a walk, dragging a hand through her hair as she examined Morgana's profile, her cheek dimpling in a slight smile, as if she was waking up from a pleasant dream. She didn't see the siren when she looked at Morgana; she could barely remember the creature. All she saw was a woman who wanted to be happy and yet would never allow herself to be.

I may not care about my life, she'd said when she took Aveline from the siren. *But I care about yours.*

The words still made the breath snag in Aveline's throat, and Morgana looked at her, sensing the change in emotions.

"What is it?" she asked as they walked.

Aveline huffed and looked away. "It's creepy, how you do that."

"Do what?"

"Read me."

"It's not anything to do with my powers, if that's what you're worried about—" Morgana started.

"I wasn't," Aveline said, and she stepped in front of Morgana, effectively cutting off her path. Morgana stumbled into her arms with a surprised yelp, but Aveline just tightened her grip on her waist.

Morgana's pupils widened as she cocked her head, clutching at Aveline's arms.

"Stop defending your magic to me," Aveline said softly. Their faces were so close she barely needed to voice the words. "It's not something you need to apologize for."

Morgana's cheeks reddened, and she averted her gaze. "I just meant that I won't use it on you without you knowing. In any way."

Aveline cupped Morgana's cheek, gently lifting her gaze once more. "I wouldn't particularly care if you did. Your power isn't violent, Morgana, it's not inherently destructive. If you were to reach out to my emotions to make sure I was okay? I wouldn't fault you for that."

Morgana swallowed hard, her throat bobbing. "You told me once that you weren't scared of me."

"I meant it," Aveline whispered. "I meant it then, and I mean it now. You don't need to put that sword in my hand to get me to trust you."

"Even after I killed you?" Morgana joked weakly, but tears gathered in her eyes. Aveline didn't mind it as she watched a slow tear fall, grateful to see Morgana feel openly after spending so long walking through a tranced life.

"You'd saved me before, and you've saved me since."

Morgana squeezed her eyes shut, shoulders trembling.

Aveline leaned forward, and Morgana's forehead fell against hers, as if her neck had simply given up. "Your powers are more than the damage they've done."

"I know," Morgana breathed out. "I know that, now."

They stood there for several long moments, breathing in each other's breaths, listening to the other's heartbeats. She wondered if Morgana listened to Aveline's soul instead of her pulse, now that she had permission. If it soothed her in the same way.

When Aveline drew back, she asked, "So if you didn't use your magic, you just knew, then? That I was panicking about tomorrow?"

Morgana reached out and brushed her thumb over the planes of Aveline's face. "I've made it my mission, these past few weeks, to relearn and love this new face of yours like I did the old one. I've done a decent job of it."

Aveline smiled, her heart soaring. The meeting would wait. Tomorrow would come no matter what time they arrived.

They entered the tower room twenty minutes later, to a mix of exasperation and smirks, the latter courtesy of Verona. The women stopped as the crew stared at them, dropping each other's hand.

Breaking the silence, Castor asked, "What, no excuses? We've been *waiting*."

Morgana looked at Aveline. "Is there any way to make them scared of me again?"

The meeting went on with more laughs and smiles than they'd had in weeks, a small distraction from what would come when Verona got on that balcony and put herself on display for both kingdoms to see.

***

"I need to ask you something."

The palace had an impressive library. During one of the many nights Morgana had no one but herself for company, she had wandered in search of … anything, stumbling upon the array of books. It was sequestered in the uppermost corner of the palace, sealed off for many decades. Morgana practically had to break down the door and was probably the first to peruse the bookshelves since Wendell's reign. Dust covered the leather, the titles mostly from her time, which made it all the more enjoyable. In the evening when the rest of the palace slept, she would remain awake and read for hours, just to keep her mind busy. Usually, the time passed uninterrupted. Aveline was an extremely heavy sleeper, but tonight after only an hour, Aveline sat up with tousled hair and whispered her name, startling Morgana from her perch.

Morgana closed her book, unfolding her legs from where they'd been curled in an oversized chair. "Aren't you going to ask if I'm awake?"

"Funny," Aveline said, scooting up under the covers to make room for Morgana. She settled at the foot of the bed, crossing her legs beneath her.

"Can't sleep?" Morgana asked. "Are you nervous about tomorrow?"

Aveline shook her head, even as she said, "Of course I am. But that's not what I have to ask you."

Morgana shifted, pulling the blankets from beneath her and draping them over her legs. Now that she had permission, she reached out toward Aveline'e soul and felt her nerves trailing over her spine. Even so, Morgana's muscles relaxed at the caress of Aveline's life force; her own soul breathed easier. Souls ebbed and flowed all around her, but she felt Aveline's more than all the others, a crystal-clear note drowning out all the other noise.

Morgana homed in on Aveline's soul, and the woman's sorrow reached out. Morgana wished she could take it all away, replace it with something better.

Aveline looked down, entwining her fingers together in her lap, her knuckles paling. "Did you mean what you said?" she finally asked.

Morgana's mouth opened, then closed again. "I've said a lot of things, and meant most of them," she said. "I suppose it depends on when I said it." She wondered how many half-truths she'd told in her time at the palace before the real truth came out. She'd been so absorbed in her guilt that she couldn't bear to say that she hadn't done what they all thought she'd done. Not when she technically had.

Aveline fiddled with the hem of her blanket. The silhouettes of her hands danced along the wall, the lamp hanging in the corner casting an orange glow across her skin. The moment darkness fell each night, Morgana lit up the room. She needed to be able to see Aveline in the bed and her sword at her side.

"Aveline," Morgana prompted, pushing forward. "What did I say?"

"About not caring about your life," Aveline blurted out, her eyes fluttering closed as if the words caused her physical pain. Perhaps they did. "You … when we were in Nysus…"

Morgana sat back, mouth clamping closed as she remembered her frantic words, when she had feared Aveline wouldn't go with her. She'd tried to hide the panic, then, to stay calm for Aveline's sake. She would have said anything to get Aveline to go with her.

And yet...

"Did you mean it?" Aveline asked, voice cracking.

Morgana looked down and knew that she couldn't lie. She'd lived alone for centuries, wallowing in the guilt of what she'd done, the loneliness of a woman who would live forever and feel each soul around her fade away. She knew, from the moment the curse had settled into her bones, that it was not her life that mattered. That she only lived for the benefit of others.

"For a time, yes," Morgana whispered.

Aveline choked on a soft sob, and the sound was enough to make Morgana look back up and move closer, regretting the words as soon as they came out. Aveline shook her head, back and forth faster than Morgana could follow.

Morgana tried to explain shakily, fingers trembling at her side. Her entire being felt as if it would never settle, that she was doomed to a life on the edge until the world finally decided it didn't need her anymore. "Some consider me greater than any other human, but in actuality, I'm less than all of them. You included. I'm alive for a purpose, and it's a good purpose. To give life, to keep the world living and breathing. And for a long time, I believed that I was meant for nothing more. That I *couldn't* be anything more."

Aveline blinked rapidly. "Morgana -"

Morgana lifted a hand. "Let me finish. I thought that, and so I shut myself away. I did what I was meant to. I breathed for myself so that I could breathe for them, and that was enough." She gazed at Aveline, at the soft orange light reflected in her glossy eyes. She felt Aveline's soul, and she was the same as the woman she had known two hundred years ago. "But I'm a part of this world, too. I'm human, too."

A trembling smile spread over Aveline's face. "Was convincing Castor and Micah of your humanity that much of a life changing experience?"

"Yes," Morgana murmured honestly. "I've never had more than one person care about me at any given time." Her mother, then Aveline briefly, before the world had exploded at her own fingertips.

Aveline exhaled. "You deserve a life. You should not be punished for the actions of an ancestor born millennia ago."

Morgana shifted and gently laid down beside Aveline, pulling the other woman down with her. They sank into the pillows, heads curved toward each other and strands of hair winding together. "I can't keep seeing it as a punishment, as a prison," Morgana whispered. "Without me, you wouldn't be alive, and that alone makes it impossible to see my magic as inherently bad. It is not a curse, Aveline. It just is."

"I know," Aveline murmured back, reaching out to hook her index finger with Morgana's. "But how do you plan to live with it?"

"I don't know. Not yet. But I plan to live with it, not just endure it. I will find a way."

Aveline's eyes had begun to droop, exhaustion coming back for her after the adrenaline sapped away, and she curled closer against Morgana's body. "Make sure your way gives me a life to live, too."

Chapter Thirty One

Trumpets blared throughout Briarwood, shaking the trees as the streets hummed with anticipation. People peered from behind tattered curtains and looked to the palace. News that a person of royal blood had come forward after all this time spread like wildfire and was more than enough to bring the people out of their hovels. They came in great droves, their clothes worn and threadbare, stitched and restitched countless times.

Aveline watched from the balcony, staying in the shadows so people wouldn't mistake her for the waiting queen. People paraded down the streets, calling and shouting toward the palace with words Aveline couldn't decipher. They were too far away, and Aveline wasn't ready to hear them.

Micah came up to stand by her shoulder, peering down at the people below. "There's even less than I thought there would be," he said weakly. "There's never been an occasion to gather all these people that fled to Briarwood in my lifetime."

"Each generation is smaller than the last," Aveline murmured. "And I can't say I blame people for not wanting to have children in a kingdom that gets smaller by the day."

Micah's jaw hardened, glancing up at the roiling wall of water he had lived under all his life. "We'll change that today. That shadow will be gone by tomorrow."

Aveline wished she was as confident. She wished she could reach out and find Morgana with her fingers, but she hadn't seen the woman since daybreak, when Aveline had slipped from the room with a wink and a small salute. "It will," she finally said, more for Micah's benefit than her own.

"Do you think you will, when the wall falls?" Micah asked.

"Will what?"

He hesitated. "Have children."

Aveline bit her lip before shaking her head. "No, I wouldn't. But not for any of the reasons you might think." She swallowed before knocking her shoulder into his. "You should, though. Once this is all over and done with. You should get away from the planning and the worrying and just … live a normal, human life."

Micah's eyes softened. "You should too, you know."

Aveline smiled bitterly, remembering Morgana's words and all the questions they'd left unanswered. "I'm not human, remember?"

He reached out, squeezing her arm, as if he had forgotten that she was anything more than what she appeared to be. She was grateful for it. "I've come to believe that *human* is an entirely relative term."

She thought of Morgana and muttered, "I might just agree with you."

***

Morgana crept through the halls of the palace and felt eyes on her. She knew that she was probably imagining it, that she was simply waiting for the inevitability of the king, but she couldn't help but look over her shoulder the moment she bid goodbye to Castor and Verona. A few guards accompanied them, but their role for the day would keep them far from the palace.

After that, she had been alone, and the hairs at the back of her neck stood on end as she stopped at the various rooms Aveline had laid out for her, picking up what she needed as she chewed on some crackers. Her stomach wouldn't tolerate more.

She paused only once, at a window on the ground floor, and she gazed at the balcony above, where Aveline waited. But when she couldn't make her out, couldn't see past the pillars lining the veranda, Morgana instead watched as the people came. They craned their necks up at the newly repaired, freshly painted balcony, trying to get a glimpse of their new queen.

Morgana knew that, in the long run, she would have no place here. The generations of Serpent Witches that had come before her had always declined a seat at the palace. That was indicative enough of the choice she should make. But still, the floors had become comfortable beneath her feet once more. Aveline's bedroom had become her own.

She would play the part that her kingdom required of her today, and she would decide the rest after.

Swallowing, she looked away from the people and the mass of waves towering over them, and headed toward the stairs. The halls were emptier than normal, the guards sent out to monitor the festivities. In actuality, they'd just needed the soldiers out of the way, out of potential danger. In general, the fewer people who knew of a deception, the less likely it was that it might go wrong.

Still, even as she crept through silent hall after silent hall, her nerves wouldn't calm down, her skin turning cold and clammy as she tapped the familiar sword at her side, peering around every corner before actually moving on. She climbed the floors, fingers trailing over the railings as she reached her destination, rounding a corner when -

Morgana staggered back as she almost ran into a tall figure. She tore her sword out of the sheath, her heart pounding.

"Whoa," Rike said, holding her hands up in innocence. "It's just me."

"Rike," Morgana gasped, pressing her hand to her chest in relief as she lowered her sword. "Gods, don't sneak up on a woman when she's acting as bait."

Rike lowered her hands to adjust a scarf she had wrapped around her neck to ward off the morning chill. "If you're acting as bait, shouldn't you be ready for an attack?"

Morgana shook her head. "Not yet. He's not here yet."

Rike pressed her lips together, glancing over her shoulder in the direction she'd come. Probably from the balcony, where Aveline waited for Morgana's update. "You can definitely tell?"

Morgana settled back on her heels, her pulse calming. Rike may not like her, but that was just another thing she'd deal with after. Another bridge left to mend. "I may not be able to kill him, but our souls are still bound together. My impression of him is faint, but I can feel him even now."

"What's he feeling, then?" Rike asked.

Morgana let her eyes close and reached out, extending her powers through the space separating their two kingdoms to find him, brushing over his life force. Her eyes flew open at the single touch. "He's angry. And … ready. He knows we found the heir." She paused. "Earlier than I thought. Perhaps our connection flows in both directions."

"And you really believe he will come?" Rike said, skepticism written all over her face. "He must know it's a trap."

Morgana folded her arms, thinking that if Rike had been more tolerable of her presence, she'd have been there for the many arguments they'd already had about this. "I'm sure he does, but he also believes he's more powerful than any of us. He believes this connection he has with me neutralizes even me as his opponent. He won't consider any trap of mine to be a threat."

Rike's face twisted. "Okay, then." She studied Morgana, who shifted uncomfortably. "If this gets her killed, I'll never forgive you."

And though Morgana had a hard time believing Rike would ever forgive her for anything, Morgana just said, "I know."

Pressing her lips together, Rike drew herself up and said, "Good luck. Don't get killed. She'd never forgive you for that, either."

That startled a smile out of Morgana, and she nodded in return. "You too."

They passed by each other and headed in opposite directions.

***

Aveline felt fingers wrap around her elbow, and she was pulled silently away, off of the balcony. She stumbled over a pile of tools and leftover paint as she was dragged into the waiting hallway, leaving Micah leaning against the railing, gazing at what was left of the populace. He didn't notice them leaving as Morgana swung Aveline around, bringing them both into the shadows.

Giggling, Aveline swatted her away. She hadn't panicked at being grabbed, recognizing Morgana's familiar hands immediately, falling into the touch. "You do realize that if Micah had seen that, he might have tried to kill you before he realized you weren't a threat."

"Then it's a good thing Micah knows I wanted a moment alone with you," Morgana said. "We're on the same wavelength now, me and him."

Aveline snorted. "I'll bet." She exhaled, gazing over Morgana's head at the arched window propped open, the wind ruffling Morgana's hair. If she ignored the sounds coming from below, the world was almost peaceful. She could waste away years standing still like this, never moving but not actually stuck. "You have something for me?"

Morgana gave it to her, and she looked lighter as if she got rid of the weight. Aveline admired the sword Morgana now held compared to the one she'd been given, the precise detail work, silently admiring Castor's craftsmanship.

"Rike sends you her well wishes," Morgana murmured against Aveline's shoulder, wrenching her gaze back up. "I think she's more nervous than the both of us combined."

Huffing, Aveline trailed the pads of her fingers over the exposed skin of Morgana's wrist. "That's not surprising."

"She thinks I'll kill you again."

Aveline pulled back, narrowing her eyes. "She doesn't, not really. She'll be easier to get on your side when this is all over."

"Says who?" Morgana grunted. "She has your blood in her, and you took two hundred years to convince."

"You didn't spend two hundred years *actually* -"

Morgana laughed, reaching up to place a delicate thumb over Aveline's lips, pulling at the soft skin there. Aveline swallowed her words, her heart doing somersaults.

Aveline snagged at Morgana's wrist. "You can't distract me right now. I'm already nervous enough as things are."

"I wasn't distracting you; I was shutting you up." Morgana exhaled, sucking on a tooth. She looked like she wanted to tell Aveline to stop panicking, that everything would be fine, but Morgana had promised to never lie again.

So instead of reassuring her in return, Aveline squeezed Morgana's wrist tighter. "This time, we both survive."

Morgana's eyes softened, and she stretched onto her toes, pressing a soft kiss to Aveline's mouth. Aveline drank it in. Morgana's lips were chapped and yet somehow still soft, her breath fanning out along Aveline's cheek. It all made sense in that moment, how Morgana had the power to give life, and Aveline took all she could fit within her.

"If the people see you, they'll never believe our charade."

Aveline and Morgana didn't jump apart at the sound of Micah's voice. Their lips separated, but they stayed close, clinging to each other while they could. Aveline glared pointedly at Micah. "That's why we came in here where we would be alone."

Micah rolled his eyes. "I was getting antsy out there, the crowd is getting restless. We need to act."

Aveline glanced at Morgana, catching her eye and deciding to focus on the yellow one, the eye that, despite its otherworldly color, held just as much humanity as the green one. Morgana nodded back, and they stepped away from each other, the spring air flowing into the space between them. It acted as surely as a wall as the barrier that separated the two kingdoms.

Swallowing hard, Aveline turned her gaze to Micah. He stared at her like the world was about to end. She made to take a step toward him, to thank him for everything, but he'd already extended his hand. "Ready, my queen?"

Aveline watched as Morgana took the offered hand with a sour look, allowing herself to be pulled toward the balcony. Micah pressed his lips together and bowed his head to Aveline. "Go," he said. "I'll see you when we crown the real queen."

The air between them grew colder by the second, and Aveline turned away, unable to watch them walk away.

"Good luck," Aveline whispered as they moved toward the light.

"I have both the luck and misfortune of thousands," Morgana called back, flashing her one last smile, the only thing that could keep Aveline's nerves at bay. "We can only hope the scales tip in our favor today."

Chapter Thirty Two

The sunshine hit Morgana as she and Micah came out, climbing to the low platform they'd built to make sure the people in the streets could see her clearly. She stepped over an overflowing basket of supplies, leftover from repairing the balcony. An assortment of spikes, mallets and scrapwood had been thrown haphazardly into the corner, tangled with a long coil of rope. She eyed the crowd below warily, sound drifting up to them, her skin crawling at the sheer number of people waiting below. Waiting for her.

"I didn't think they'd be so … welcoming," Morgana said. "It's been so many years. I wouldn't blame them if they were angry."

"They are," Micah said softly. "But after all this time with nothing, they're glad for anything, even an inkling of hope."

Morgana chewed on her lip, squinting at him through the sun. "Is that why you came so easily, when Aveline offered you shelter?"

Micah's breath caught in his chest, but he didn't shift his gaze from the horizon. "She found me when I was barely eighteen, living off whatever I could

find. My father was sick, our home less than a mile from the water. Our days were numbered in more ways than one."

He looked warily up at the looming water. The sun was cresting high in the sky, peeking above the waves. "But I was handy with a weapon. I'd been hunting for years, since my mother died, and Aveline found me one day in the woods, snapping my arrows in half because I couldn't find a single sign of game." He shifted. "She said she'd been watching me, that she'd never seen better form from someone without training. She said she could offer me a place to stay, a job, somewhere that could become home until we could all find a better one."

"And you went," Morgana said softly.

Micah shook his head. "Not at first. I told her to get lost, that I'd never abandon my father. But I made the mistake of mentioning this crazy woman to him, and he wouldn't let it go. He said he'd heard about her; a woman descended from a soldier who had survived from the war, trying to make an army."

Morgana let out a puff of air, imagining Aveline trekking across the remaining villages, pretending to be an ordinary woman, searching through the poor and the sick and the wounded for anyone who could help. Who might still have enough hope in them to put up a fight. She figured Aveline must have come through her village half a dozen times, and neither of them had ever known the other was there.

"I thought it was ridiculous. I was prepared to live my life in the small hut we shared with another family and drown with my village when the time came." Micah sighed at the painful memory. "But the wall had pushed into our village, taken over half of it, and that time grew closer and closer every day. I didn't even think my father would live to see it happen." He took a moment, steadying his breath. "I swore when he got sick that I would be with him when he went, but he wouldn't have it. He kept telling me, '*You have to go. Find a way to fix this world.*'" Swallowing, he closed his eyes against the sun. "And so I went, and I found Aveline. Three days later, Verona reported that my hut had been swallowed. The water took my father with it."

Tears pooled in Morgana's eyes. She imagined Micah much younger, barely a man, leaving everything he knew for the chance at something better. "I'm sorry," Morgana croaked out. "The death of a loved one is the true curse of being human."

Morgana had stayed human long enough to know that, at least.

"Indeed," Micah whispered. "Mine is a common story. There are almost no happy ones left in this kingdom. I intend to see the day where we can bring happy stories back."

Morgana's ears homed in on the sounds of the crowd again. Shouts of excitement and anticipation mingled with cries of fear and sorrow. Morgana thought of the families ripped apart, of the lives ruined. Generations living in poverty, wracked with starvation. Decades of living on top of each other, with nothing more than desperate love and half shredded hope to live on.

"Stop," Micah said under his breath.

Morgana jerked up. "What?"

"Aveline's right. You can't blame yourself for our hardships any more than she can."

Morgana lifted her brows. "How could *Aveline* blame herself?" She'd been unconscious from the poison for most of the nightmare, and dead for the rest of it.

He gave her a sad look. "People find a way. Guilt and regret can spin the most convincing illusions." He rocked back and forth on the balls of his feet. "I know them well. Perhaps not as intimately as you, but…" He trailed off, choosing his words carefully. "He took something from you, that day. He took your control. He took your peace of mind. Don't let him keep it for a second longer."

Morgana's throat bobbed as the words sunk in.

"Well," Micah backtracked. "Actually, use that anger today. But tomorrow…" He smiled. "Anger and guilt and regret will only be obstacles for the new lives waiting for us."

Morgana squinted at him. "You're awfully wise for a young human."

He smiled. "I know too many immortal beings for my own good."

Morgana patted his hand. "I'm sorry about your father, and how hard you've all had to fight for the lives you deserve. You shouldn't have had to."

"For many years now, I've been preparing to fight." He looked at her more closely, observing the embroidered cape sitting on her shoulders. "You would be an excellent ruler, actually."

Letting out a startled laugh, Morgana shook her head. "The people need to relate to their ruler, to feel that their queen is one of them." She motioned to herself, blinking her mismatched eyes. "I would scare them."

"I'm fairly sure Verona will have her own reign of terror."

Morgana gazed out at the trees beginning to sprout with green after the long winter. "We immortals are not meant to rule over humans. We've seen that well enough."

"We have," Micah sighed, and extended his arm once more. "Nevertheless … ready to become queen?"

"Ready to be attacked in front of hundreds of people," Morgana answered, and he led her up on the dais.

***

Aveline listened from a floor below as Micah declared Morgana as queen. She closed her eyes and leaned against the palace wall outside of the throne room, momentarily unable to move at the thought of how vulnerable he and Morgana both were, dangling themselves out on that balcony for everyone to see. The roar of the crowd ebbed and flowed, cheers crawling through the hall of the palace as they welcomed Morgana.

But confirming the existence of the Serpent Witch was enough to stun the crowd into silence.

"I thought I was doing the right thing," Morgana was saying to the people below her on the balcony. Aveline craned her neck toward the nearest window, trying to hear better. "I've spent centuries in hiding, believing it was where I belonged. That I could do more harm out of the shadows than help. A part of me feared this kingdom to be too far gone. That it was no longer able to be saved."

Shouts of anger followed then the first signs of unrest, but they quickly quieted when Morgana raised her voice once more.

"I knew that I possessed some royal blood, dating back to some of my earliest ancestors, but I had no idea the power that that blood could possess. This wall of water that's been haunting us…" Aveline imagined Morgana closing her eyes, tilting her head toward the sun. "It grew so close because I waited for so long. And for that, I'm sorry. I won't let it hurt you anymore."

Morgana played guilty almost too well.

"After consulting with your general here -" she must have looked to Micah then, "- we know that we can restore this kingdom to what it once was. With my blood back on the throne, that water will finally recede. The blessing once gifted to us by the Lady of the Lands will protect us again, and all of Calypdon will be ours again."

Aveline didn't stick around to hear the rest. She couldn't. Instead, she turned away from the open window and headed inside the throne room, shutting herself inside. She cradled the weapon to her chest, and prayed King Daegil came for *her* instead of the queen announcing herself to the kingdom outside.

***

"I want to hear you," Morgana said, her voice scratchy but booming over the crowd. She gripped Micah's hand to keep herself steady, so hard her fingernails probably drew blood, but Aveline's second-in-command stood strong and stoic at her side, only moving to nod along with her words. "What you have to say, what we all wish for in the years ahead. I will hear your questions and concerns, your pleas, and I will do everything I can. And in more than just Briarwood. Once that water is gone, we'll have a real chance to rebuild the entire kingdom."

This was lasting longer than she'd planned, sweat dripping down her back despite the early spring chill. She scanned the crowd, searching for any familiar face, but couldn't find even Verona or Castor, let alone King Daegil. She reached out to the bond they shared, but he was still too far away, a mere fragment of a soul.

She glanced at Micah. He could only give her an urgent look that was wildly unhelpful. She cleared her throat. Maybe King Daegil didn't want this final confrontation to be in front of the people of Calypdon. After all, he wanted to rule them. He couldn't show them who he truly was.

Maybe, maybe, maybe.

Okay. Backup plan.

She spread her arms and smiled as dazzlingly as she could. "Please, enjoy the festivities, and as you go about your day at the palace, come see me in my throne room. I will hear every petition. Calypdon is a kingdom for us all, and I will rule it as such."

On trembling legs, she stepped down, not paying attention to the mixture of cheers and disdain. She couldn't pay any mind to their responses at the moment.

"He's not here?" Micah asked as soon as they'd turned away, walking through the double doors and slamming them shut.

Morgana shook her head, anxiety crawling up her throat. "No, he … Is it possible he's not coming?"

Micah shrugged helplessly. "I suppose, but I doubt it. It's well known he has ways of getting information from Calypdon. He knew when you and Aveline returned to Nysus. He must know."

"If he knows, then he will come," Morgana said, setting her jaw. "He wants the heir. He wants me. Finding out they're the same person? He won't be able to pass that up. A crowded, chaotic festival before the crowning is his best chance. I don't believe for a *second* that he -"

She felt it, then, a tug from the depths of her soul. She stumbled to a stop, gripping Micah's elbow to steady herself as pure wickedness washed over her. She recognized it at once, in the way they all knew the demons inside themselves.

Immediately, she drew back the power she'd been using to track him, gagging at the entangling of their life forces. Her fingers slipped free from Micah and she fell against the wall as King Daegil's soul ebbed away. It left a final imprint, a whisper of a sea breeze.

You may have Aveline's soul, but she still belongs to me.

"Morgana," Micah said, shaking her shoulders. "What is it, is it him?"

"Get to the doors," she croaked, shaking him off. "Don't let any of the civilians into the palace, you hear me?"

"He's not in the crowd?"

The temperature in the room plummeted. "I don't know. I can't -" Her ears rang, her head pounded, and she tried to make sense of where she was over the noise of what was left of the sea king's soul. It seemed to cry out to her, as if she might somehow have the power to save him from himself. "But he's on land. He's close."

She will come back to me.

The words were like ice trailing across her skull, and Morgana froze. "*Aveline*," Morgana breathed. Throwing off the cape, she left her role as queen behind and resumed her role as witch.

***

Once Aveline was sequestered in the throne room, she couldn't hear anything of Morgana's remaining speech or the events that followed. Her heart beat faster because of it.

She'd situated herself in the rafters of the throne room, set in a low crouch with one hand on a wooden beam and the other on the blade. She kept her eyes trained on the two pillars in the corner of the room; the ones Morgana had pointed out as the hidden passage the sea king had once used. They looked innocent enough, identical to the other pillars lining the room, but if she looked close enough, she could make out a faint glow.

They'd considered destroying it, tearing apart the passage so King Daegil would have no way inside the palace, but there were multiple problems with that, least of all that they didn't know if destroying a bridge between two kingdoms was even *possible*.

When Aveline had suggested it, Morgana had been all for it, but Castor had responded with a definitive no.

"We want him to come to us anyway, right?" he'd said. "This is the way to get him here. We know where to wait for him, all we have to do is draw him in."

Aveline had thought at the time that King Daegil was too smart to assume his plan would work twice, but they'd split up anyway.

"You shouldn't send me to the place he's least likely to be," Aveline had argued when Morgana had suggested Aveline be the one to watch the throne room. "I should be with you, we made the mistake of separating last time -"

"We weren't separated because we *agreed* to be separated," Morgana had said flatly. "We were separated because you were quite literally poisoned and unable to come with me. More to the point, if you think it's the place he's least likely to enter, that's your problem. I think it's the second most likely because he's a cocky bastard, and he loves repeating old tricks."

The thought of Morgana getting hurt had been enough to silence Aveline, and before she knew it, they were agreed.

Aveline scowled at the portal, her legs beginning to cramp from staying in one position for so long, but she wouldn't drop her guard. The moment she did, someone would be there to stab her in the back.

And so she waited, glancing back and forth between the pillars and the great double doors of the throne room. She had pulled them shut when she came in but was starting to regret that now. Her ears strained, trying in vain to hear even an inkling of what Morgana was saying, of a fight breaking out, of the announcement coming to an end. But at the opposite end of the palace, she could hear nothing, all sound from the courtyard silenced by the thick walls.

What if he didn't come?

It was possible. They knew they might get stuck playing the long game, forced to keep up this charade until King Daegil finally decided to make his move. Verona had grunted and groaned about it, insisting she would be the one who had to deal with the fallout of confessing that Morgana was not, in fact, the heir, but Morgana had been insistent.

"He doesn't know anything about my family's past. It would appeal to his own ego if he found that I carried the blessings of the land as well as my curse. He'll be much more confident if he thinks he has a single woman to take down, a woman who he's beaten before."

It had been a fair argument.

Aveline shifted; the wooden beam creaked beneath her, worn from two centuries without repairs. *He would come. He had to come.*

As if on cue, the passage began to glow, and Aveline straightened. She felt a mixture of relief and fear trickling down her spine. She clutched her weapon and watched as the passage widened, a crack blooming in the wooden panels of the floor. It creaked and shifted, and Aveline drew her arm back, ready to impale King Daegil as he came through.

A flash of dark hair came into view, and Aveline tightened her grip, sheer hatred flashing through her veins. It had been festering for two hundred years. A loathing that she'd once reserved for Morgana had finally found its true target.

The glow of the sea faded away as someone climbed out, and Aveline barely had time to stop herself from flinging a spare knife she's sheathed at her waist directly at the invader's chest. She gave herself only a moment to let her mind and vision clear, and everything went entirely blank as she observed the person wringing her hair out, looking around nervously and palming a knife strapped to her thigh.

A woman.

Rike came from one kingdom to the other, and as Aveline tried to figure out why, she lost her footing and plummeted to the waiting ground.

Chapter Thirty Three

Morgana tried to run for the throne room, desperate to get to Aveline, but Micah grabbed her hand. He pushed her against the wall, her vision dotting with stars at the impact.

"Are you insane?" she gasped, trying to push Micah off. "We have to -"

But the horror painting Micah's face effectively cut her off as he gazed with wide eyes over her shoulder to the balcony. His mouth opened with a silent cry.

Morgana followed his gaze, her body moving slowly as if in a dream. As if some part of her feared what she would see. Through the window, she gaped, helpless, as the once beautiful day darkened into a nightmare.

The wall of water that had reared over Calypdon for two centuries began to curl in, as if whatever invisible barrier had held it up had finally shattered. The water bent down like a wave breaking against the shore, bathing the city in shadows and ready to swallow Briarwood whole. The towering wave swallowed the sun, covering the sky, and Morgana staggered forward and pushed back onto the balcony, craning her head up as the sea came crashing down toward Briarwood on all sides. The heaving surge of water swirled as the tops of the walls collapsed against each other, thundering in a glittering spray of sea mist. But not a drop fell onto Briarwood.

Instead, what was left of Calypdon was shadowed by a churning, frothing ocean, held back only by a dome of the same force that had held the seas at bay for two hundred years. Murky waves blocked out the light, leaving Briarwood in the dark, shimmering twilight that Morgana remembered from her time in Nysus. The water began to settle into a dim, swirling tomb, surrounding the people of the land on all sides. Even above.

Only when the roaring in her ears died down did she realize that the cheers of the crowd had been replaced with screams.

"What…" Morgana started, pushing the word out through her constricting throat, trying to make sense of the large bubble of air that remained around them. The people in the streets below were overcome with terror, many fleeing back to the dubious safety of their homes while others cowered where they were, paralyzed with fear. Others tried to make their way into the palace, as if the stone walls were any more protection from a tidal wave. They ran into each other in their haste, barreling over one another, trampling fallen bodies. "Micah -"

"Verona," Micah croaked out, hand raised to his mouth as he surveyed the crowd, desperately trying to find the real queen. "*Verona!*"

Realization hit Morgana as she stared at the dome that had moments ago been the tall stretching wall. Something had weakened what was left of the blessing of the heir that had battled the encroaching water for so long. She reached frantically around the crowd, seeking through the souls of the kingdom for the soul of a ruler. The soul of the one meant for this crown, the only soul that kept the waters at bay.

She almost missed it, the soul barely a wisp of its usual intensity, but she nearly sobbed in relief when she tugged on it and felt Verona tug back. The dome above them shook, threatening to collapse.

"She's alive," Morgana said. Barely, but she was alive.

"*Where?*"

Too far. Morgana whipped her head around, squinting into the depths of the forest where she felt Verona, but she was *too damn far*. Too many flights of stairs away, too many turns, too many steps through the palace. Morgana gritted her teeth, whipping her head around as she tried to think of a plan. She had a hard time getting past the frantic thought of, *Get to Verona. Get to the queen.*

Her eyes caught on the pile of supplies they'd used to fix up the balcony, left abandoned in this morning's rush. She lurched toward it and fell to her knees beside the box, sorting through the tools and spare lengths of wood until she freed the coil of rope.

"We have to go," Micah urged her, this time trying to force her from the balcony, pushing her before him, but she wouldn't budge. "*We have to find her.*"

Morgana yanked the rope free and, as quickly as her shaking hands could move, she secured it to the railing. She took a moment to pray to any god or goddess that might be listening that the old architecture would hold. Nudging Micah, she said, "You said you trusted me. Now it's time to put it to the test."

His eyes flicked between hers and the rope, and his jaw twitched as he nodded.

"Good," Morgana said, and without pause, she threw the rope down the side of the palace and rolled over the railing after it.

***

Aveline couldn't get up at first, her body aching as her left leg and shoulder barked with pain. She winced as she rolled over, dislodging her elbow from beneath her and shifting so the hilt of the sword stopped pressing into her gut. Only when she'd managed to sit up did she remember why she'd fallen in the first place.

Her head cleared, and she whipped around as Rike rushed to her, kneeling at her side. "Gods, Aveline, are you okay?" Rike surveyed Aveline's scraped arm.

Aveline's mind did its best to catch up with what was happening, but no matter how many times she ran over the series of events, they didn't make sense. Had she hit her head when she fell from the rafters? Was this another siren? But there Rike stood before her, in Calypdon, drenched from head to foot.

Aveline sputtered, "Where did you get that?"

She was pointing at the shell glittering at the base of Rike's throat, because it didn't make sense. The blessed land springs had stopped responding decades ago.

But Rike didn't seem fazed, glancing up nervously at the doors, still shut tight, closing them off from the silent hallways and whatever waited outside. "I have your blood in my veins. The land springs recognized me as someone touched by the gods, or they at least saw a piece of you, and they answered."

Aveline gaped, horrified. "But how -"

"We need to go," Rike interrupted, pulling Aveline to her feet. "You need to come with me."

Aveline scrambled to her feet, and Rike rose with her. Aveline's heart pounded in her throat as she glanced at the portal, the cerulean beams of Nysus still dancing within its depths. Aveline ran toward it, bracing her hand against the shell on her own throat to seal it shut. The glow lasted only a moment but lingered as an imprint in her mind's eye. She stared at the healed crevice in the wooden floors, trying to decipher Rike's words. She turned back, confused. "*Go?* But he could come any second -"

"He won't," Rike said quickly, stalking toward Aveline. "He doesn't care about you; it's not you he wants."

"Yes, but -" The words died in her throat as the realization set in. Her legs nearly gave out beneath her as the implications of Rike's words registered. "How does he know I'm the one waiting here?"

And then her eyes fell once again to the shell embedded in Rike's throat, a near twin to her own, and the pieces clicked into place.

Before she could voice any of the questions clouding her mind, Rike's face became masked by shadows. In fact, the entire room fell into darkness, the once-bright windows muted, as if day had suddenly become night.

Aveline hurried to the closest window, pulling herself onto the high sill and gazing up at the sky. It looked as if night had set it, something completely blotting out the sun despite the fact it was midday. And then the sky began to move. It rippled with dim sea green light, waves bearing down on them and threatening to swallow what was left of their tiny kingdom.

Aveline stepped off the windowsill, and she turned slowly to gape at Rike. The girl was just as mesmerized by the dome of water encompassing the city, her eyes wide with wonder.

But she wasn't surprised. Not remotely surprised.

Aveline's eyes widened with growing horror, and she lifted her hands to pull at her hair. "What did you do?" Aveline whispered.

***

Morgana slid to the end of the rope, not caring as it tore at her palms, burning them raw. She dangled more than her own height off the flagstones. Holding the rope tighter, she swung herself back and forth, further and further until she could kick against the wall. She propelled herself forward through the open air, swinging over the crowd. When she was as far as the rope would take her, she let go. Flailing, she braced for the impact.

She slammed into the back of a man, sending them both rolling over the cobblestone, her knees and elbows tearing as she tried to slow their momentum. They stopped at the edge of an emptying street, sliding onto the grass. Morgana let her head fall back into the dirt in exhaustion.

The man shoved her roughly off, furious as he stood. "How dare you—" His mouth snapped closed when he saw Morgana's face, his eyes widening as she stood, pressing a hand against a particularly nasty cut on her arm. "*Hey*, aren't you -"

"No," Morgana said, and pushed him back into the agitated crowd.

Morgana looked over her shoulder, anxiously searching the churning dome of water that hid the sky. She began to turn toward the forest, toward Verona, but Micah's shouted, "Watch out," stopped her. He joined her only moments after, landing easily in a crouch at her side. He stood with a wince and immediately pushed Morgana forward, a silent gesture. *I'm following you.*

"Graceful," Morgana commented as she took off down the streets, dodging around people running in every direction, Micah close behind.

***

"He got to Verona," Rike whispered, grabbing Aveline and pulling her back toward the pillars. "He'll be coming back to take the palace soon enough, once he gets the witch. We have to go *now*."

Aveline dug her heels into the ground beneath her, refusing to move as tears welled in her eyes. "What do you mean, he got to Verona?" The words came out as a mere croak, her voice cracking on her friend's name. She didn't dare take her eyes off Rike to look back at the dome of water, but the memory flashed in front of her eyes, and she knew what it meant. There was only one thing that could have made the wall of water surge in so fast.

She can't be dead, Aveline tried to tell herself, even though it didn't help. *If she were dead, we'd all have drowned by now.*

Rike exhaled, as if she had the right to be impatient, her fingers clenching and unclenching at her side. "She's injured, to draw Morgana in—"

"How did he get to her so fast?" But then the second part of Rike's statement registered. Aveline knew immediately that Morgana would be racing across Briarwood as they spoke, to whatever trap King Daegil had set, waiting with Verona as bait. Aveline swayed on her feet, her reality tilting beneath her, because this was *backwards*.

She'd been prepared to fight the enemy. She was ready to confront the man who had haunted her for centuries.

She wasn't supposed to be standing across from the only family she had left.

Aveline tried to swallow the words, not wanting to hear the answer, but they came out anyway. "And why do you know what King Daegil is doing?"

"Aveline, we don't have time for this -"

She knew. She knew the answer. She'd known since she watched Rike pull herself from the portal. And yet she still couldn't believe it. She couldn't believe that the woman she'd practically raised, the girl she loved with everything she had, had done … what?

"What did you do?" Aveline asked again, her voice deathly quiet. "*What did you do?*"

Rike stared at her, lip wobbling as she braced her hands on her hips, eyes closing. "You were gone for *two months,* Aveline. *Two months*, and we knew *nothing* of what had become of you, we thought you were *dead*."

Aveline stayed perfectly still. "What does that have to do with you turning traitor for the sea king?"

There it was. The bitter truth. She knew it was the truth because Rike hadn't flinched, hadn't moved a muscle. Instead, Rike's eyes were filling with tears, and she burst out, "Do you realize what it was like here while you were gone?"

In only a moment, Rike had transformed into a stranger. Aveline didn't recognize the girl's voice. Everything about this was wrong, like the siren's wretched illusions all over again.

Aveline flinched, scrutinizing Rike from head to foot, but found nothing. Her eyes, her complexion, the little details down to the way her nostrils flared as she cried. Besides, a siren couldn't survive in Calypdon. This was the Rike she knew.

She wished it were a monster.

Rike took a rattling breath. "*I* escaped, and *you* were stuck there, getting tortured or starved to death, or who knew what. He could do whatever he wanted to you."

"But we escaped," Aveline rasped, realizing she was barely breathing, that her lungs had stopped working properly. "We got out -"

"And why do you think that was?" Rike snapped, tears flowing freely now. She took another step towards her, but Aveline just backed further toward the wall. Aveline was two hundred years older than the other woman, but she'd never felt so small. "Do you really think the sea king would have accidentally allowed Morgana to escape after all he'd done to get her?"

Aveline shook her head, as if she could ward off the words. "Why let us go at all, then?" she asked desperately. "You're right. He never would have let her go."

"I said accidentally. But he needed the heir. He needed the heir even more than the witch, and definitely more than you. So, when I came to him, he listened."

"*You* went to *him*?" Aveline shouted incredulously. "You… you -"

"I came to look for you. When everything dissolved into chaos, I did what Morgana told me to do. I went back to Briarwood and gave the sword to the others. I obviously didn't know what that sword could do at the time. And then I went back to Nysus to break you out. But King Daegil was waiting for me."

Aveline shook her head. Back and forth, too fast, as if she could shake the image in front of her away. "But you didn't need a shell for that. I left the portal open specifically for this reason; in case I was captured."

Rike lifted a hand, gently brushing her knuckles over the shell at her throat. "No, he took me there later. The blessed land springs wouldn't gift any of the sea soldiers' passage into Calypdon, but…" She nodded resolutely. "I'm different. We're different."

"No, we're not," Aveline screamed, the words tearing at her throat.

"I knew the Lady of the Land had stopped giving her blessing, but you and I both know blood is everything to the gods." Rike flung her arms out wide. "Look around, Verona's blessing should be proof enough of that."

"But why?" Aveline asked brokenly. "You still didn't need a shell for that; the portal was still open -"

"I needed it for after. So I could get back to him after you and Morgana escaped."

This was worse than the siren. This was worse than Morgana killing her. Aveline thought of all the gatherings Rike had missed, her strange absences. Was she in Nysus during the times she should have been with their friends? "Rike, please, I don't understand. Please tell me I'm misunderstanding."

Rike swallowed. "We made a deal."

"The Hallowed don't make deals, especially not Hallowed like him."

"But he needed someone you trusted," Rike said. "He *needed* me. I couldn't give him the sword; I'd already passed it on to Micah before I knew what it meant. But I would give him your plans, I would give him the witch, and in return, *you* would be safe. You get a home in Thalassa, we both do, and he leaves us alone. That was it, that was the deal."

Her words cleaved Aveline's heart in half.

Stomach roiling, Aveline fell back against the wall. "You … you gave up our friends … You doomed everyone in Calypdon … to keep *me* safe?"

"He never would have let you go," Rike whispered, the despair evident on her face. Aveline couldn't look at her. "You would have lived out the rest of your immortal life as a prisoner; he would have tortured you until you were beyond saving. Was I supposed to just allow that to happen?"

"*Yes*!" Aveline exclaimed, throwing her hands in the air. "*Yes*. I would have stayed there for eternity if it meant the people I cared about were safe."

"It was never you he wanted," Rike pleaded. "You didn't deserve it; it would have been for *nothing*!"

"It *would* have been for something," Aveline insisted sharply. "It would have been for … everything." Everything she'd built here. All the things she had, and all the things she still wanted.

Rike reached out. "I just need you to come with me, we'll be safe in Nysus, we *belong* there—"

"We were safe *here*."

"Not for long. If that wave comes down, it won't matter that we can breathe the water. We'll be crushed. Just … come with me."

Aveline's jaw twitched, a great void opening within her that she would never be able to fill. "I won't. I'll never go back there. And right now, you're the last person I would go *anywhere* with. I know what it feels like to be betrayed."

Rike looked at her desperately. "I didn't betray *you*," she pleaded. "I betrayed *her*."

They both knew she wasn't talking about Verona.

But she'd betrayed them all, and Aveline whispered, "To betray her is to betray me. We're one and the same."

Rike flicked her eyes to the steadily darkening window, to the dome pressing closer as Verona's soul flickered. It was as if the water pulsed with Verona's heartbeats.

Aveline had to get to her. Had to get to both of them, had to get to everyone she had left. She started forward, but Rike was there to stop her.

"We need to move," Rike gasped, grabbing at Aveline's wrist, but she slipped out of her grasp.

"Did you not hear me?" Aveline shouted. "We protect our own. I won't leave the people I care about behind."

"*You're* the person I care about!" Rike's entire body shook now, her hands reaching up to rub at her raw eyes. "That's what I was *doing*."

Aveline remembered Morgana's words, then, her reasoning for staying in hiding for so long. How Morgana thought of herself less than the mortals around her, and that it was her job to protect that magic that gave life to them. They rang true, and she understood Morgana in that moment more than she ever had. She grabbed Rike roughly by her shoulder, pushing her away. "It is never our job to put one soul above all others."

"Right," Rike scoffed. "As if you haven't put your trust in the witch over the safety of everyone you say you care about."

Fury rattled Aveline's bones, sinking deep into her core. Before she knew it, her hand had whipped out, cracking across Rike's face. Rike stumbled back, shocked, as Aveline hissed, "Know this. If Verona dies, it won't have been the sea king who killed her. It will have been you."

Rike had been prepared to kill thousands, just as the sea king had. As the sea king had already forced Morgana to do.

Unable to look at Rike any longer, Aveline moved to rush past her, needing to find the others, to put a stop to whatever was happening, but Rike caught at her arm. "You have to come with me," she cried. "You *have* to, otherwise this will have all been for nothing!"

Aveline's mouth twisted, her stomach roiling, because it would have been for nothing anyway. She spit out, "You'd have to drag my corpse." She yanked her arm back, and Rike's fingers, the once comforting touch of family, fell away like nothing. "If you see the sea king before I do, tell him I'm coming for his head."

She turned away, hands trembling at her side at the thought of leaving Rike behind. Her blood reached out, the shared blood that allowed Rike to do all this in the first place, but no response came. Would Rike go back to Thalassa? Would she follow Aveline and make this all worse? She hesitated as she approached the door as another question occurred to her.

After everything, would Rike really let her leave without a fight? Because Rike truly did love her. All through the girl's childhood, before Aveline had brought in the others, they'd only had each other.

But Aveline didn't have her now. This was a stranger.

Before she could come to any conclusions, Aveline felt Rike's movement behind her, the attack of a trained warrior. Aveline whirled around in time to see Rike pull her knife back and hurtle it through the air.

Aveline dodged, acting on pure instinct, power thrumming through her. The magic of a goddess reared up, possessing her like a puppet designed to wreak havoc. Jumping to the side, she pulled the sword free from her belt and sent it slashing through the air.

The knife embedded itself in the wooden paneling of the wall, but the sword found its intended target.

Blood splattered over Aveline, the sword clattering against the floor after having passed across Rike's neck. She remained standing for a moment as Aveline stared, wide eyed. Rike's hands clawed up to her throat, a bone chilling gurgle escaping her lips, and she collapsed.

Aveline's head snapped around to stare behind her. She gasped at what she found there, sobs wracking her body. The knife was stuck low in the wall, and Aveline blinked away the tears as she saw where the weapon would have struck her had she not moved out of the way.

Her leg. Rike had been aiming for her leg.

Aveline scrambled toward the dying girl, sliding over the blood to where Rike gasped and writhed, her hands trying to stop the blood spurting from above the shell, to no avail.

"Rike," Aveline gasped, crouching and trying to staunch the flow of blood, applying pressure even though she knew it would not save the girl. "Rike..."

Rike choked, her hand moving beneath Aveline's, and Aveline loosened her grip. Rike's fingers spasmed, until her fingers curled around Aveline. She didn't squeeze, didn't have the energy, but Aveline could tell she wanted to.

"No," Aveline said, and squeezed hard enough for both of them. "No, no, I'm sorry, I thought -"

Rike coughed, and Aveline thought she was trying to shake her head. Her eyebrows creased with pain and concentration, her lips moving as if she was trying to speak. Aveline tried to read the unspoken words in Rike's eyes, but she was no Morgana. She couldn't feel Rike's intentions, couldn't feel her lingering soul. Instead, all she could do was watch as whatever message Rike had wanted to tell her flowed out of her, unspoken.

Aveline closed her eyes and tipped her head back to scream at the dark rafters overhead. She lowered her body, resting her forehead against Rike's chest as if she could somehow find a heartbeat. She cried and gripped Rike's limp, bloody hand, and silently told whatever part of Rike might linger that she loved her. Despite it all, she loved her.

Betrayal was not enough to entirely destroy love and loyalty. This was a lesson Aveline had learned twice now.

She rose quickly. Rike was dead, but she would still try to save the people her niece had betrayed. Aveline blinked away the tears, gazing out the window.

"*Forgive me, Helah.*" She whispered her sister's name into the waves, willing the prayer to escape the wall of water closing in on them and reach wherever Helah might wait. "*Forgive me, Rike.*"

Forgive me, and I will try to forgive you.

Aveline stumbled to her feet, slipping in the puddle of blood spreading from the body as she backed away. She had just enough presence of mind to recover her sword, wiping as much blood away as she could.

Trying to wipe the blood and tears from her eyes, she turned from the room.

Aveline may not have been able to feel Morgana as Morgana could feel her, but as she watched that wall of water tremble and pulse, she knew where Morgana would be.

She took one last, long look at Rike's blood-soaked body lying on the floor of the throne room; so similar to how she'd found Wendell all those years ago. But after an agonizing moment, she forced herself to shove the sword back into her sheath and flee the throne room, heading for the streets.

Chapter Thirty Four

Twigs and branches and thorns tore at Morgana's face as she raced deep into the woods, lifting her arms to shield her bleeding cheeks. Lanterns illuminated the people rushing over the winding paths. Whispered prayers surrounded her, drifting toward the sky, and she wondered if the gods could hear them through the dome of water threatening the lands. Wondered if they even bothered listening anymore.

Micah kept close to her heels, periodically calling to ask if they were nearing Verona. Morgana's lungs burned so hard that she wouldn't have been able to give him an answer even if she had one. She didn't dare waste concentration on looking further than the few feet before her as she weaved through the crowd, jumping over roots and rocks. She could only follow the tug to Verona wherever it led her.

"Don't fade," she murmured to herself through gritted teeth. "Just hang on and let me find you."

In response, the dome above rippled, dropping closer to the city.

The crowd thinned as the people around her slammed the doors to their shacks and cottages. At last, they ran through barren streets, and Morgana grappled desperately with how King Daegil had lured Verona so far away. Until a long smear of blood drew her eyes, and she nearly tumbled over herself. Morgana threw her arm out to stop Micah, and he coughed as her elbow dug into his stomach.

"He dragged her," Micah croaked beside her, spotting the deep red staining the dirt as well. "The bastard dragged her."

"She's close," she told him. "Which means he is, too."

All the color drained from Micah's face. "He."

"The sea king -"

"No," Micah said, whipping his head around to search the forest, eyeing the single smear of blood. "Castor. Where's Castor, where's -"

Morgana held up her hand, mind running as she remembered that Castor had been with Verona. Before she could allow herself to panic, she reached out and found his soul thrumming at full force, not faint as Verona's was. "He's fine, he's alive."

"For now. We have to -"

"King Daegil is alone," Morgana cut him off. She went over to the blood, keeping her footsteps light, and the feel of Verona's soul overwhelmed her senses. The blood definitely belonged to her. "Remember what the king said? The blessed springs aren't offering artifacts anymore; he couldn't bring his soldiers here." Though her heart pounded in her chest, she could feel

Micah's hammering at near impossible speed. He needed to calm down before they could do anything. "This is her, but I don't sense him anywhere around here. I'll bet he only took Verona. Castor's probably either running for help right now, or he's unconscious. And unconscious means safe."

"What if -"

Morgana tried to imagine where Castor might have ended up, how he and Verona could have gotten separated. It didn't help her nerves. She tried to sound soothing, but knew the words came out sharp when she said, "One thing at a time. Castor's true role was finished before today's sun even rose. Are you with me?"

He stared at her with desperation, looked at the blood again, and set his jaw. "Where is she?"

Jerking her head toward the cluster of trees to the right of the path, they moved into the grove, the forest denser than it had been closer to the palace. Between the churning water above and the canopy of thick leaves stretched overhead, it was nearly impossible to see. When Micah clung to her hand to avoid being separated, she squeezed in response. She drew her sword as the trees opened up again, and a bit more light filtered onto the grass of the clearing.

Micah drew a harsh breath, and Morgana broke into a sprint, the tug between her and Verona almost unbearably thin.

The future Queen of Calypdon lay perfectly still on a bed of frost-burned wildflowers, her limbs sprawled around her and her chest only making brief, shallow movements. Morgana tossed her sword aside and fell at Verona's side, trying to find the wound beneath her torn, blood-stained clothes. Morgana's knees turned a sticky red as her hands roamed over Verona's torso, searching through the darkness until her fingers slipped against a knife puncture on the right side of her chest. Not directly above her heart, but close. So close.

Verona groaned when Morgana put too much pressure on the wound, her face twisting as Morgana assessed the damage. The earth seemed to shake with Verona's movement, as if the land could feel its queen's agony. The water rippled above, heaving in time with Verona's labored breaths.

The world was painted red, but the water would soon wash it away.

"Micah," she hissed without taking her eyes off Verona. "Micah, we have to get her out of here -"

He didn't answer. Instead, she heard a loud crunch and a shout of pain. She turned around to see Micah crumple to the ground, a long gash along his forehead. King Daegil sneered above him, his shell studded staff dripping with Micah's blood.

***

Aveline forced her mind to think only of her surviving friends as she raced through the streets, dodging remnants of the crowd while tracking Rike's blood behind her. They shouted in fear at the sight of her, disgusted when she had to push through the knots of people with blood-drenched hands, but she couldn't think about them. She couldn't think about Rike, or what she'd done, or what Aveline had done to her in return. She couldn't think about Helah. Aveline used to pray her sister was watching over her, that there was a place souls went after even Morgana couldn't reach them. But now she prayed that they faded into nothingness, so that her younger sister wouldn't have had to witness what Aveline had done.

Aveline would think and cry and mourn about all that later. Now, she searched and searched, hurtling through the streets of Briarwood and climbing trees to look for them, but the darkness made it nearly impossible. She stole a lantern from a nearby door and carried on deeper into the woods. Morgana would likely be by the nearest portal, the one they had used when they had rescued Helah and the others from Nysus so many lifetimes ago.

She had to be there. Gazing up at the roiling dome, she gripped the sword at her side and didn't dare think of what would happen if Morgana wasn't at the portal. What would happen if she didn't find them in time.

***

Morgana rose slowly to her feet, fingers dripping with Verona's blood, and turned away from the panting woman, keeping her own body between the sea king and the queen of the lands. She did not shake. She met his piercing gaze. She looked right at him, refusing to be afraid for another moment.

He seized your power, he stole your peace of mind. Take it all back...

She would. He would see.

Her eyes fell, then, to the sword he held. The sword she had dropped to help Verona. She stiffened at the familiar sight.

"Foolish girl," King Daegil laughed wickedly, and the minimal light filtering through the waves above danced over his skin. His body seemed to ripple with it, bathed in cerulean blue; in the color of the veins branching across his pale skin. "You've always shown such concern for these humans. They don't deserve it."

"Who am I to decide what the humans deserve?" Morgana asked, taking a step away from Verona, wanting to put as much distance between the sea king and the queen of the land as possible. Verona wouldn't survive another wound. She might not survive at all.

As if on cue, the water rumbled above them, sinking closer. She tried to calculate how long they had, how long it would take for the barrier to reach the ground and crush them all, but it was futile. They had only as long as Verona managed to keep breathing.

"So noble," the king jibed. "I've always said; your humanity will be your downfall."

"As it should be," Morgana responded. "Humans are not meant to live forever, and neither am I. When this world ends, I will go with it."

He shook his head incredulously, casting a disgusted look down at Micah laying by his feet. He hadn't moved since the staff had sent him tumbling to the ground. She reached out, feeling his life force respond to hers. She carefully hid her relief.

"Have you ever spoken with the gods?" King Daegil asked suddenly.

"No," Morgana said flatly. "I'm not blessed by them as you are. They don't care about me."

"Indeed they don't," he spat. "Perhaps they would if you had the courage of a true Hallowed, if you saw this world for what it was: small, insignificant, merely a steppingstone to something greater."

Morgana gaped at him as she realized what he said. "You wish to become a god?"

He spread his arms. "Soon, I *will* be. There will be nothing but myself and those who worship me as they would the one who blessed me. This new kingdom will belong to me and me alone. We'll have to worry about balance no longer."

"There will be no one left to treat you as a god," Morgana said plainly. "You will die as all men do, as I will, too. You are no more than I. Nothing but a cursed witch."

He scoffed, taunting her as he swung the sword back and forth at his side, slicing through the air as he would soon slice her. "You're a disgrace to the Hallowed. You've sunken down to the level of these humans."

Morgana shook her head. "The difference between you and me is that I never thought to rise above them."

His eyes flashed. "Our differences go far beyond just that, *witch*. Twice now you have forgotten yourself." He brandished the sword before her as she took a step forward, closing the distance. "Again, you have tossed aside your most prized possession as if it was nothing."

Perhaps he was trying to understand her. Perhaps he couldn't comprehend that Morgana might still consider herself human when she so clearly wasn't. Had he ever been a normal man, one who didn't dream of power and glory, or had he spent his youth praying for immortality, for a long life he would live alone?

Yes, perhaps it would happen one day. The loss of a Hallowed's humanity was an inevitability. Perhaps the monster that slumbered within her would awaken as it had in him. But she would keep it at bay for a good, long while.

Morgana folded her arms in front of her. He wanted her to raise her hands, to surrender, to show some sort of fear at seeing that sword in his hands again, but she stayed perfectly still, perfectly calm. The darkness of the dome swallowed the details of the snake hilt, but she knew it was there. She tracked the sea king's movement as he turned the sword this way and that, letting the sea green light of the waves catch on the silver of the blade.

King Daegil's lip curled as he followed Morgana's gaze, and he leaned back against a nearby tree, holding the weapon in both hands like a treasure. "It is a beautiful thing, isn't it?" he said, running his fingers over the blade. It sliced the pad of his thumb open, and he didn't so much as flinch. "Forged by the god of death himself, I believe?"

Morgana's stomach turned over. Just seeing the familiar shape in his hands made her feel two hundred years younger, two hundred years more naive, but she pushed it away. She couldn't afford to feel small anymore.

"That's what I was told," Morgana said eventually, when it became apparent, he was waiting for an answer. "Made of the bones and souls of the dead to hold the lives of the living."

He hummed, lifting his eyes back to her. "The power is wasted on you. I hope you know that."

"I do," Morgana said, taking one last step. She was unarmed, and they were a mere arm span away from each other. She could wait no longer. "A power like mine is meant to be wasted."

He reached out, tapping the sword against her temple. "Maybe I will take your powers for myself after all."

"I'm shocked you haven't already," Morgana said honestly. She cocked her head. "It must have killed you, knowing I was out there all those years."

His mouth twisted. "Enough chatter." He glanced beyond her. "Our dear heir won't last much longer, and it would be best if we were through the portal before the sky comes down." The smile he gave her then would haunt her for the rest of her life, for as long or as short as that might be.

Morgana took that chance to look around. She caught sight of movement in the trees, the gentle rustling of leaves above her, and she knew it wasn't the wind. The air around them was perfectly still.

She flicked her eyes back to King Daegil. "How did you know she was the heir?" she asked after a moment. He remained still; the weapon held loosely at his side. She was running out of time waiting for help.

King Daegil's face sparked with glee. "Your dear Aveline -"

Morgana shook her head with a huff. "Just stop -".

"- that niece of hers was quite pliable."

Morgana just shook her head at his attempt to manipulate her once more. She was done waiting. With a glance up at the trees, she knew that his time was up, too.

"My humanity may be the death of me," Morgana hissed in his face. "But your bravado will be the death of you."

His eyes narrowed, and at her words, he wasted no more time.

She expected it when it came, the cool sword piercing her heart, but she couldn't help the gasp that flew from her lips. Pain burst inside her chest, spreading through her torso as the blade ground against her ribs. She swayed, only held upright by the pressure of the sword.

"I don't care about you," he snarled in her face. "But your powers are mine now."

Morgana waited several moments to respond as the life sapped out of her, as her heart fluttered like a panicked bird, and then stuttered to a halt. She felt her pulse slow to nothing, but it didn't matter.

Morgana smiled, blood on her teeth. "Wrong sword."

Aveline dropped from a high tree above them, landing easily behind King Daegil with the power of the goddess of war flaring behind her eyes. Morgana had just enough time to be surprised at her bloody appearance, but King Daegil didn't get a chance to turn. Aveline swung the weapon through the air with a strength powered by two hundred years of anger and grief. The blade slashed across the back of his neck, severing his skull from his spine.

He bellowed, his legs crumpling beneath him as blood spurted from his neck, soaking Aveline's feet. Morgana stumbled back when the King's grip slipped from the sword still embedded in her chest, and she slid to the ground as her mind grew fuzzy.

Aveline hurried over to her, holding the actual Serpent Sword so tightly her knuckles had turned stark white. Her eyes were red-rimmed, and Morgana could barely make out the sorrow and desperation beneath the blood spattering her face, but tears had worn away the gore covering her cheeks. Aveline tried to shove Morgana's sword into her hands, but Morgana shook her head as agony spread through her like fire. She didn't care about the damned sword.

"Aveline," she gasped out. The decoy sword had missed her lungs, and she was glad for that. She didn't particularly care to find out how odd living would be without breathing. Her hand flailed out, and she found Aveline's.

"Did it work?" Aveline asked, wiping the blood away from the sword. She hiccupped through her words. "Please - please tell me it worked."

"If it hadn't, I'd be dead," Morgana said through clenched teeth, and she didn't know what made it harder to breathe: the wound or seeing Aveline living and breathing. "Take it out, and if I don't die, we'll be sure."

Panicked, Aveline sobbed, "Are you sure -"

"Please," Morgana rasped out. "I only want to focus on the fact that you're here, and not the fact that a sword is impaled through my heart."

Aveline didn't hesitate a moment longer, pulling the sword Castor had forged from Morgana's flesh. Morgana felt it as it slid through her, dragging over bone and slicing through muscle. Stars dotted her vision, the agony threatening to send her spiraling into darkness, but she focused on Castor's handiwork as the hilt drew away from her. It was completely identical to the blade she had carried all her life. Morgana couldn't find a single detail out of place, except that this sword didn't have the power to kill her.

Morgana sighed when at last the blade slipped free, clamping her arms over her chest as if she could undo the damage to her punctured heart. Aveline tossed the sword aside and leaned over Morgana, cupping her face in her hands. "This was a stupid plan," she cried. Morgana figured she must have noticed the stillness of her throat, the lack of a pulse there. Would it ever come back? She supposed it didn't matter. She could clearly live without it. Except for the tortuous fire branching out from the wound, it was as if she wasn't stabbed at all.

Morgana raised her shaking hands, cupped Aveline's bloody fingers with hers. They were slick and warm, but she held on anyway. "You can't call a plan stupid when it worked."

Aveline's face crumpled further, and she leaned forward to press her forehead to Morgana's, and Morgana clung to her with everything she had.

"Okay," Aveline said eventually, pulling back and wiping away the blood she'd smeared onto Morgana's face. "Okay, can you stand?"

"Miraculously," Morgana muttered, and looked past Aveline's shoulder to where King Daegil waited. Still alive, still breathing, but unable to move, his spine torn open as it was. He stared at her with wide eyes as Aveline helped Morgana to her feet. Her agony was like nothing she'd ever experienced, and she knew the wound would take weeks to heal. But she trusted it would. In this moment, two hundred years in the making, she would grit her teeth and bear it.

She wouldn't lose consciousness as she had the first time she'd been stabbed. She would see this with her own eyes, and she would do it with her own hands.

Aveline stayed close, propping Morgana up until she could stand without support, and even then, staying close enough to touch. With a disgusted glance at the sea king, she held the sword out to Morgana, chest heaving and tears still pouring down her face. "Take it. Finish him."

Morgana hesitated, taking in Aveline's bloody torso and the fire in her shining eyes. Whatever had happened with Rike had incited a brand-new rage in Aveline that Morgana hadn't thought possible. Morgana stepped away from the blade. "I think you might need this more than me."

Aveline took a shuddering breath, body trembling. "I'll get revenge in watching his pain," she whispered. "You need to take yours."

"Aveline -"

All at once, Aveline's face crumpled, more tears spilling down her blood-streaked face. "I don't think I can. I already took a life today, I can't -"

Morgana understood, then. She saw the transformation behind Aveline's eyes; a hollowness that Morgana knew all too well.

Morgana could see that for the first time, Aveline felt like a monster. As if a piece of her humanity had been torn away.

Morgana steeled herself. Killing this man wouldn't make Morgana feel like a monster, not when he'd tried to take everything from her. Not when he *had* taken everything, even if only temporarily.

"Okay," Morgana said quietly, and took the sword. "Get Verona. Help her."

As if reminded, Aveline choked on a breath and scrambled toward the fallen queen. Morgana watched her go before turning back to the man lying amidst the blood and dead leaves.

Several yards away from Micah's still form, the king gasped on the ground, trying to move his limbs in vain. He had watched as Aveline rushed to Verona, assessing the damage and applying pressure to the wound, before returning his attention to Morgana.

"You were right," Morgana said as she stood before him, her sword cradled comfortably against her chest. King Daegil craned his neck up to see her, unable to move anything below the horrific wound. "We differ in many ways. The most important of which being that blessed or not, your body is, and always will be, entirely human."

"No," he snarled. "I'm no human."

"You are," Morgana said, approaching him. "Look at you and look at me. You can die by any sword."

"You can't," he laughed, blood trickling from his lips. Morgana felt better knowing that he could bleed, that he could feel pain. "You've tried before, and you can't kill me."

Morgana stalked forward, twirling her sword around her wrist as he'd done two hundred years ago. "I can. I just can't use my powers.

He tried to laugh again, but it came out as more of a wretched, gurgling sound. "You don't have it in you. The only way you could kill was with me pulling the strings."

Morgana wouldn't give him the satisfaction of explaining how much she loathed him, how much he had hurt her. She wouldn't allow him another moment of life. "You said it yourself. We've been linked together for two hundred years. I won't let you haunt me anymore."

He shook his head. "The gods won't let me die."

She crouched, pushing away the black clouding her vision, threatening to pull her in. Digging her fingernails into her palms, she forced herself back to reality and brought her sword up. "I'm the only goddess that matters right now. I may not be able to take your soul, but I can separate it from your body." She motioned toward herself, to the blood dripping from her wound onto his neck. "I'm the only being who can survive without a heart."

Morgana looked him in the eye. Then, just as he had to her only moments ago, she plunged the blade into his heart.

King Daegil's eyes widened, as if he hadn't expected her to go through with it. As if it had never occurred to him that he might one day truly die. But Morgana felt the moment he took his last breath and watched as the light behind his eyes winked out. The shock and fury of his face smoothed out; without the centuries old soul locked inside, he looked like an ordinary young man.

And in that central part of her magic that held his soul, he faded away at last.

She reached forward and took the crown from where it had fallen beside his head. She didn't say anything as she hooked it around her wrist.

Morgana had just enough time to see the sun filter through the trees above, the wave of water curling into itself and falling away, before the earth tilted beneath her and she collapsed beside the sea king's body.

Chapter Thirty Five

Aveline's consciousness blurred as she took in the four bodies around her, squinting through the returning sunlight to make sure three out of four of them still breathed. Her hands were covered in blood, and she couldn't know what belonged to Rike, what belonged to Morgana, and what belonged to Verona as she stood. She tried to wipe her hands on her pants only to find them drenched in red as well. She stepped away from Verona, taking in the steady rise and fall of her chest that had strengthened slightly after Aveline had wrapped her wound, but the queen wasn't safe yet.

Aveline craned her neck up, watching as the water above them continued to recede, rushing over the dirt and back toward the sea. The land was flooded, the forests drowned and dead, but for the first time in two hundred years, she could see the mountains in the distance, blending into a crystal-clear sky.

Tripping as she backed up, she left Verona and went back to Morgana but knew there was nothing she could do for her. Not really, since the wound would heal whether she wrapped it or not. So even though it went against every instinct, she continued toward Micah, whose face lay in the dirt. The trickle of blood coming from his temple had slowed, a small pool accumulated by his ear, but otherwise he seemed okay. Aveline sighed, realizing it could have been much worse. She was moving to tear yet another strip from her tattered shirt when he moved with a groan.

She dropped to her knees, brushing his hair aside as his eyes fluttered open, blinking into the blinding sun. He lifted a hand to block it, and Aveline smiled. Wiping the blood from his face, she said, "Welcome back. Are you okay?"

He blinked again, bleary and confused. "Did I miss the fight?"

Aveline let out a half-hysterical laugh, leaned over, and crushed him in an embrace.

"Gross," he mumbled into her shoulder, even while hugging her back.

Aveline stiffened, remembering exactly whose blood covered her, and she eased herself away. "Can you stand? We need to get Verona and Morgana back to the palace -"

The trees rustled behind her, and she stood, spinning around before realizing she was unarmed. But when the form flew into the clearing, her eyes closed with a half sob. They were all here. They were all alive.

"Oh my gods," Castor said in horror, his mouth going slack as he took in Aveline's state. Aveline wanted to hug him, too, to ask where the hell he'd been, before she noticed bruises on his neck and his unsteady gaze.

Castor didn't waste any time, looking around with wide eyes and taking in the blood-soaked clearing. They finally settled on Verona, still unconscious across the glade, and he sprinted toward her. Aveline took the moment to crawl across the clearing back to Morgana, who hadn't moved. The only sign that Morgana still lived was the occasional, erratic breath. Aveline pressed her hand to Morgana's neck; there was still no pulse. She squeezed Morgana's hand, and even though nothing happened, Aveline wouldn't allow doubt to set in. She'd watched Morgana get stabbed just for them to gain the element of surprise. She'd been stabbed through the heart and stayed standing. She would survive.

Even so, Aveline used the remainder of her overshirt to carefully wrap Morgana's chest. Her eyes found the crown, and she left it on Morgana's arm for the time being. With Micah and Castor shouldering Verona, Aveline took Morgana in her arms, and they made the slow trek back toward the palace. Though the waters had receded, the people remained huddled in their houses. The crew walked through the silent streets as inconspicuously as possible, sticking to the tree line and shadows.

Only two soldiers stood by the gate when they returned, and Aveline didn't pause for their report. She just nodded, told them to call a healer for Verona, and moved deeper into the palace.

Aveline took Morgana to their room. She began the slow process of doing for Morgana what Morgana had once done for her. Setting the crown gently on the nightstand, she carried Morgana to the bath, lowering her gently in the basin.

She took her time cleaning Morgana, slowly scrubbing the dirt and gore from her skin. The dried blood on her own arms flaked away, until she was clean from the elbows down. But she didn't worry about that. She lifted Morgana instead, wrapping her wounds with bandages leftover from Aveline's own injuries. Dried blood smudged from Aveline's face onto the white cloth, and try as she might to scrub it away, it wouldn't come off.

Only once Morgana was laid out on the bed, dressed and dry, did Aveline walk mechanically toward the mirror, taking in her own worn and bloody appearance. She didn't have the energy to gasp. She just swayed where she stood, swallowing hard.

She looked like a monster, something that had crawled out from the depths of the underworld itself. Every inch of her front was slick with blood, her undershirt soaked through with the stuff. She stared at herself, trying to differentiate which blood was Verona's, which was Rike's, and which was Morgana's. She stared as if there might be a visible difference between blood that came from healing and blood that came from killing.

An image arose, unbidden, in Aveline's mind. She saw Rike writhing on the floor, gasping for breath. She remembered Rike throwing the knife, too, but that image did nothing to soothe her.

She turned away and returned to the bathroom, her feet blindly following the path she had walked a thousand times before. She turned the water back on. The stream was loud and clear, but even a waterfall wouldn't have been able to drown out Aveline's thoughts.

I killed her. I killed her. I killed her.

She took a step into the bath, and the water began to loosen the gore on her foot.

This is all you get, a voice said in her head as the blood washed away. *This is the last part of her you will ever have.*

She got in anyway and waited for the water to rise.

The still water of the bath wasn't enough to wash away the deeper stains in Aveline's soul, but she could scrub away the physical traces. It took her nearly an hour to rid herself of the last traces of physical blood. She refilled the basin over and over until she finally sat in lukewarm, clear water. But the horror lingered, a layer of phantom blood that would never go away.

She got out hours later, drying herself and dressing. She went around the room after, cleaning drops of blood staining the wood, and then went to the hallways to clean their path. Only when every inch had been cleaned did Aveline contemplate returning to the throne room to clean up the worst mess.

But when she took that first step in that direction, her feet froze, and she ended up heading the opposite way.

She returned to her room and took another bath. Only then did she sit by Morgana's unconscious form. She leaned forward and pressed her forehead to Morgana's chest, against the bandages wrapped around the wound. She listened to the silence stemming from Morgana's torn open heart and breathed.

***

Morgana dreamt of the lands soaked with water, of the trees knocked down by floods that rose to the people's necks, threatening to drown everyone left. She dreamt of the sea king, of some far away moment of calm where he sat still and silent, and she wasn't afraid of him. She dreamt of Aveline's face, of her body dropping from the trees at the wrong moment, resulting in getting her skewered, too.

She dreamt of Aveline beside her, of an easy smile and an easier life.

She dreamt of a heart beating inside her chest.

***

Days passed and still Morgana didn't move. Micah and Castor tried to visit several times, bringing food and attempts at reassurance, but Aveline barely noticed. She watched Morgana until her eyes ached, but to no avail. Her love's eyes remained closed, her body still.

After a long fruitless day of watching Morgana's motionless chest, she stumbled from the bed. She saw the crown on the nightstand, glinting in the moonlight filtering in through the window. She picked it up, hesitant to touch it with her unworthy hands. She made her way blindly from the room, ordering a guard to watch over Morgana in her stead. She headed toward Verona's room before she caught herself, remembering the throne room once more. Her stomach flipped as she steeled herself, altering her course toward the site of the betrayal. She battled herself every step of the way -

Only to find the throne room empty and pristine.

The crown nearly fell from her hands as she took in the freshly washed floor, and for an aching moment she thought she'd imagined the entire thing. Had she finally gone crazy? Was immortality beginning to catch up with her?

She wheeled around, ready to run from the room in a panic, before her gaze fell on the wall. The clear mark of a blade sunk into the paneling. The knife itself had been removed, but that notched spot would haunt Aveline for the rest of her life.

She went and stood beside the blemished wood measuring herself up against it. It was level with her kneecap. She turned around to face the wall, craning her neck to see.

Rike had been aiming for the back of Aveline's knee, to slice the ligaments there. Would Rike have destroyed the other knee after Aveline fell, to render her incapable of walking? Would she have dragged Aveline through that portal into Thalassa? Perhaps Rike was convinced Aveline wouldn't fight back, that Aveline wouldn't want to hurt her.

Perhaps, perhaps, perhaps. She would never know.

Gripping the crown tighter, she left the throne room and turned her steps toward the tower.

Who had found Rike's body?

The three remaining members of her crew were exactly where she thought they'd be, spread out around the candlelit tower room. They froze as she walked in, silence falling among them. Verona sat forward with some effort, eyes narrowed and teeth gnawing at her lip but looking otherwise healthy. Neither Micah nor Castor moved as Aveline swayed in the doorway with the crown held against her stomach.

At last, Verona murmured, "She was the one who told him I was the heir, wasn't she?"

At those words, Aveline fell apart. Her friends came around her, her tears answered enough. They stayed like that for a long time.

Aveline eventually gathered herself enough to offer a disjointed explanation of what had happened, pausing more than once as she broke out into ragged sobs.

After, they moved over to the couches, and Aveline collapsed into the cushions, rubbing at her throbbing head. She was beginning to fear the pain would never go away.

"Who…" Aveline's voice came out as a rusty croak. "Who cleaned…" She couldn't finish.

"Castor and me," Micah said softly. "We figured you wouldn't want -" He cut himself off. Maybe none of them would ever be able to speak of this.

Aveline looked away. "And her body?"

"In her room," Castor said. "We didn't want to do anything about the burial without you."

"Now I'm reevaluating whether we should give her a burial at all," Micah said, and Aveline could see in their eyes that they were angry. Furious. But they tried to hide it. For her sake.

Verona settled beside her and took her hand. "You did what you had to do."

Aveline only nodded, turning her attention to Verona's injuries. "You survived, then?"

Verona motioned around them with a small smile, happy for the change of subject. "The lands are ours again."

"I'm sorry I kept sending you all away." She nodded to Verona. "And that I haven't checked on you."

Verona waved her off. "These two have been smothering me enough as it is, it was good to have some space." Her brows crinkled, then. "Though I was worried about you. They said we should leave you alone until Morgana woke up."

"Did she?" Micah put in anxiously. "Wake up, I mean?"

Aveline shook her head. "She was out for two weeks last time, and that wasn't a mortal wound. I think her body has to shut down entirely in order to heal, considering…" She motioned toward her own chest.

Castor winced. "Her heart."

"Yeah," Aveline whispered. She looked around at all of them. "It will probably be quite some time before she wakes up."

"Well, she'd better come around soon," Verona said fiercely. "She's not allowed to play the martyr."

Aveline thought of Morgana actually dying for them, and it hit Aveline all over again. The possibility had been very real, especially with Rike…

Pushing away the fear, Aveline sat forward. "In the meantime, I'd love a distraction." She turned to Verona and held the crown out, nudging her. "Ready for your orders, my queen."

Chapter Thirty Six

A restlessness settled into Morgana's dreams. They turned into something she couldn't follow. They cycled through her mind in a blur, so quickly that a new dream would pass through before she could even finish processing the last one. Some were in vibrant color, others dull and drab. She clung to the core emotions of each, the happiness and sadness and fear, but it all blended together in the end.

Morgana saw flashes of life and death until she couldn't see anything at all.

***

The following weeks passed by at an achingly slow pace for Aveline, but Verona kept her busy and focused, hardly letting her out of sight. Aveline would return to Morgana each night, checking for a heartbeat before curling up at her side, praying she wasn't sleeping beside a dead body.

Because that was a possibility, Aveline realized as Morgana's color began to fade. Without the warmth of blood pumping through her system, wasn't that all Morgana was?

Morgana had insisted she couldn't die unless her own sword did the deed, through her heart or through her head. But the more time that passed, the more Aveline was sure she'd end up mourning the most important person in her life, directly after the funeral of someone else that had meant so much.

Rike's burial had passed without much fanfare. Only Aveline, Micah, Castor, and Verona attended. Aveline had decided not to wait for Morgana; she probably wouldn't have wanted to come, anyway. Even Verona seemed hesitant to attend, massaging her own healing wound all the while.

"You don't have to come," Aveline had told her crew one evening, before they each went to bed. "She almost got you killed."

"She almost got us all killed," Verona had corrected, running her fingers through her hair. "But under different circumstances, at a different point in time, she would have saved my life. I'll honor that."

"We don't honor monsters," Aveline had reminded her.

"I'm convinced monsters don't actually exist," Verona had said, turning away.

At that point, she hadn't been wearing her crown. She only put it on when she finally stood on that balcony and announced the truth to Calypdon at large. The queen laid out what had happened, why they'd lied, and what the future held. Verona did the same thing Morgana had done. She invited them all in to speak with her, and this time they actually made it through the palace doors.

Aveline stayed in her room for that, trying to block out the noise. She curled up on her side of the bed and listened to a kingdom coming back to life while everything within her shriveled up.

A knock sounded on her door long after sunset, and she forced herself up, rubbing at eyes that had glossed over from lack of sleep. She had expected Verona but instead found Castor leaning against the opposite wall.

"Hey," Aveline said. "Did everything go okay?"

He nodded. "It'll be okay."

Aveline nodded back. *It'll be okay.*

Noticing the way her face fell, he stepped forward. "It will be. I have an idea."

Lifting her brows, Aveline's heart skipped a beat as Castor brought the Serpent Sword out from behind his back. Aveline stared at it. She'd left it with Castor to look after but reached for it on instinct.

Castor handed it to her readily. "Can I come in?"

Aveline stepped aside, the blade heavy in her hand. Someone had scrubbed the sea king's blood from it, and she thought once again of his body. Micah and Castor had been the ones to deal with that mess as well, bringing the body to a room in the lower level of the palace. But that wasn't a burial they could have without Morgana. "What happened to you during the fight? You were gone, and we didn't know where you were…"

Castor rubbed his throat. The bruises there had long since faded, but he touched his skin where they'd been. "He found Verona and I together. We never would have separated willingly, but he knocked her out before we even noticed he was on us. I tried to fight him off, but you and I both know I've never been good with weapons. He got me by the throat before I could even draw the knife you forced on me."

Aveline remembered the fight, pressing her own knife into his belt even though he insisted he would never be able to do anything helpful with it.

His hands fell to his side. "I played dead, hoping he would leave, but he didn't until I'd actually passed out. When I woke up, he and Verona were gone" His eyes flicked down, then back to Aveline. "I followed the blood."

Aveline tightened her grip on the sword with a nod. "What's your idea, then?"

He told her, and she stared at him. "It can't possibly be that simple."

He shrugged. "It didn't occur to me until just now, but she's so linked to that thing that it could have been worsening her condition. Just try it."

Aveline shook her head. "It feels like a violation."

Castor gave her a pointed look. "I think she'd be angrier at you if you let her die."

With that, he left, and she was alone again, with nothing but Morgana and the Serpent Sword.

Carefully, Aveline approached the bed, balancing the sword between her hands as she gazed at Morgana's still body. She remembered Morgana's agony over King Daegil taking over her body. She tried to imagine what Morgana's reaction would be, but nothing came, and she pushed her worries aside.

Morgana would want to wake up. Morgana had said as much. She had said that the time when she didn't care about her own life had passed.

And Aveline needed to see her eyes.

Gripping the serpent hilt, Aveline reached out and dragged the sharp tip of the sword across Morgana's arm, from the tip of her shoulder down to her elbow. The skin split, but no blood welled. How could it, when her heart did not beat?

Aveline set the sword down, pressing it to Morgana's skin. She watched Morgana's pained face and decided this would be worth it. It had to be.

The magic came as a small trickle, swelling in Aveline's chest. Whispers of nearby souls clouded Aveline's head; she felt a guard passing in the hall, and a servant cleaning a room a floor above. But the only soul she cared about was Morgana's, and she reached out tentatively along that bridge.

The caress of Morgana's soul was more beautiful than she ever could have imagined. She wondered how Morgana could bear this constant feeling; if the sensation of Aveline's soul might bring Morgana to tears, too.

Steeling herself, Aveline took hold of the small amount of control she'd gleaned by tearing Morgana's skin. She cupped her palms around the trickle of magic and let it accumulate over her fingers.

"*Heal,*" Aveline whispered at last, leaning over Morgana's chest and breathing it over her skin. She sent the word out into the space between them and let it sink into Morgana's soul. The command jerked out of Aveline's core, unnatural and a little bit painful. She thought of King Daegil taking over Morgana's body all those years ago. How could he have endured this on such a large scale? Would this hurt Morgana, too?

The magic twisted around Morgana's heart, and Aveline could feel as muscle tissue knit back together. The body itself listened to the magic, every fiber obeying as Morgana's heart worked to heal.

Aveline waited with bated breath, her fingers squeezed tight, before finally reaching out to feel Morgana's soft neck.

"Morgana," she breathed, and sank to her knees.

The pulse beneath Morgana's skin had thrummed back to life.

***

Morgana woke up slowly at first, but then the heartbeat roaring in her ears was enough to make her jerk up in bed.

She immediately regretted it, a sharp burn spreading out from the deepest parts of her chest. She fell back into her pillows, and when her blurry vision cleared again a figure came into view, and she let out a whimper.

With everything she had, she pulled Aveline's crying form down to her, arms tightening around her back, burying her face into the crook of Aveline's neck. The skin was warm and familiar, while Morgana's entire body trembled with cold. Aveline's heart beat against her own.

Before Morgana could say anything, Aveline wrenched away, and Morgana's arms suddenly held nothing but air, her skin prickling with cold. She shivered under her blankets and regarded Aveline, who stumbled away, falling to the ground

"I'm sorry." Aveline's voice was choked and tight, which did nothing to dampen Morgana's confusion.

"What?" Morgana croaked out, throat like sandpaper as she spoke for the first time in … *how long had it been?*

But she couldn't think about the passage of time with Aveline curled into herself on the floor, burying her face in her hands. "I - I'm sorry," she sobbed, hiccupping through the words. "I'm so sorry. You were dying, and I -" She swallowed her words as her throat closed up.

Morgana still couldn't move without difficulty, her legs frozen, but she shifted as much as she could toward the edge of the bed. Her hip hit something sharp and cool, and she looked down to see her sword. Then Morgana glanced down at her arm; a fresh cut was bleeding onto the blankets.

She suddenly noticed the tug of control burrowing into the surface of her soul. It wasn't as deep as it had been when the sea king had put the blade through her body, but the simple cut was enough to cede a small portion of her power to another's will.

A brief flash of fear flared up within Morgana, a reaction that reached through two hundred years of running from what had happened to her. But the pull within her felt different, softer. She hadn't noticed what Aveline had done before because Aveline wasn't tugging on the power. In fact, she scurried as far away from the magic as possible, as if she could undo the taking of it. But still, their souls were intertwined, and Morgana didn't run from it.

The fear and guilt on Aveline's face told Morgana everything she needed to know.

Without hesitation, Morgana swiped her arm out, sending the sword clattering across the room and away from them. She fell from the bed, her knees striking hard against the floor, and said, "What did you make me do?"

"You were dying," Aveline repeated. "Your body wasn't healing, or if it was, I couldn't see it. Castor said I should -"

Morgana reached out, silencing Aveline's explanations with a soft thumb against her lips. She ran her thumb over the softness there, dragging her finger over her jawline. "You healed me?"

"You healed you," Aveline said, wiping her eyes, looking at Morgana as if she might fade away at any moment. "I just made you do it."

"Then you healed me," Morgana whispered, and it really was that simple. She remembered her dreams, the endless wandering across doomed kingdoms. She would have done anything to be pulled from that nightmare. She never would have thought she'd long for this world that she'd once hated. She said as much to Aveline, moving closer until she cupped Aveline's face in her hands.

Aveline dug her hands into Morgana's thighs, keeping her close as she gathered her breath. "I thought you'd hate me for it."

Morgana wiped away Aveline's tears. "You didn't tell me to kill," Morgana said. She held Aveline tighter, and she thought that perhaps Aveline could be what Morgana treasured most, what she would keep closest. She would forget about her sword, she would forget about the world, if she could just have this.

Aveline choked on a tearful laugh. "You need to raise your expectations, Morgana."

Morgana shook her head. "No, listen to me. You didn't take control for the sake of controlling me, you're *repulsed* by the idea."

Aveline nodded, as if Morgana needed any more confirmation.

"You told me to heal," Morgana whispered. "You didn't make me do anything that I wouldn't have done myself. And you knew that, or you wouldn't have done it." She leaned in to press a kiss to the corner of Aveline's lips. "I don't hate you for it," she murmured against Aveline's mouth. "I love you for it."

Aveline's smile illuminated the room. "I'm not making you say that, am I?"

"I don't think your tiny cut could make me say something I didn't want to say," Morgana said intensely, pulling back to look at Aveline.

Aveline held her tighter and leaned back in, murmuring those words over and over again, in time with Morgana's beating heart.

***

They spent several more days in their room while Morgana gained strength. Aveline held her close for most of it, trying to transfer some of her own warmth to Morgana as her body replenished its blood.

After the initial shock, Morgana started shaking again, trembling so hard that Aveline could barely maintain her grip. Castor came in with the others and piled blankets on top of her, and the two of them snuggled together as Morgana adjusted.

"I'm starting to wish away the part of me that's human," Morgana had said at one point through chattering teeth. "Monsters can't possibly know pain like this; take my heart out and keep it."

Slowly, Morgana began to heal. Verona came knocking at their door as soon as Aveline gave her the okay, with Micah and Castor hot on her heels.

"She lives!" Verona exclaimed, and before Aveline could stop her, catapulted toward Morgana with a hug. Aveline thought Morgana would panic, but to her surprise, she simply hugged Verona back with a quiet intensity.

"I'm glad I can feel your life again," Morgana murmured into her shoulder. "As strong as it ever was."

Verona pulled back. "Oh, that will never stop being creepy. What did it feel like?"

"Unpleasant," Morgana said grimly, and left it at that.

When Aveline brought Morgana outside for the first time, the kingdom looked entirely different than how they'd last seen it. She'd watched the recovery process over the past few weeks through glazed eyes, mind elsewhere. But now that Morgana was up and moving, Aveline watched as the people milled in the streets, basking in the sunlight.

"The sea retreated entirely?" Morgana said in awe.

Castor nodded. "Whatever magic King Daegil used to hold the water up, it died with him. There's a lot to repair, a lot of damage, but…" He trailed off, and his lips tugged up. "It's ours again. It goes on for miles, and from here, you can't see the end. Only the horizon"

Aveline watched as Morgana stared out at the peaceful land, the silence comforting as the setting sun framed her face, igniting her hair. "It will be beautiful again, one day," Morgana said. "I can see it already."

"You'll be there to see it, I'm sure," Verona said. She glanced at Aveline. "Both of you."

"I hope it happens in your lifetime," Morgana told the queen softly. "So, you can see it, too."

Verona gave her a sad smile and reached out to pat her arm. They fell into silence as they gazed down at the people.

"Is there something to eat besides bread?" Morgana asked as she turned away from the streets below, throat tightening. Aveline knew it still hurt for her; for there to be so much that she could never have. The kingdom was healing, but Morgana believed she could never truly be part of it.

Micah raised his brow at Aveline. "You only fed her bread?"

Aveline waved him off. "She kept throwing up."

Verona came up beside Aveline as the men took Morgana inside, and quiet settled between them once more. It was a comfortable quiet, as it often was between them.

"When do you leave?" Aveline asked.

Verona lifted a hand to touch her bare throat, where a piece of willow bark would soon be embedded in the skin. "In a few days. I plan to go directly to Nysus after I visit the willow. They're expecting me?"

"They are." Aveline had forced herself to visit Nysus one last time. The kingdom had devolved into chaos since their king's death, with many elites vying for the now open throne. But Verona vowed to make sure Nysus didn't collapse the way Calypdon had.

"When do *you* leave?" Verona asked softly.

Aveline sucked in a breath and turned to look at her friend. She was giving her that same sad look of understanding that she'd given Morgana, and it made Aveline's heart crack. "The sooner the better, I imagine." She swallowed. "I haven't told anyone yet."

"They know," Verona whispered. "We've … always known."

Aveline looked down, leaning heavily against the railing. "At least I'm leaving the kingdom in good hands," she finally said.

"You are," Verona agreed, giving Aveline a sideways smile. "I wish you weren't leaving at all, though."

"Trust me. You'll have a much easier reign if we stay out of sight."

Verona set her hand over Aveline's. "I can't say I disagree with that."

Aveline turned to gaze at the clear sky. The sun set over the mountains, and the distance called to her.

***

Morgana had gone with Aveline to see Rike's grave only once. They went in the dead of night, with only a torch to light the way.

There was no headstone. They hadn't marked the place where they'd buried her, at the edge of Briarwood. But the heap of disturbed dirt still rose slightly above the ground, the only bare earth in a wide field of grass.

Morgana would be lying if she had said the fury she felt toward Rike had completely faded. As she stared at the grave, she felt a bitter resentment for everything she could have lost had Rike's betrayal borne fruit.

But Aveline knelt by the grave and bowed her head, squeezing her eyes shut.

"I'm sorry it ended the way it did," Morgana finally said, coming up behind her. The orange glow of the torch traced over Aveline's quivering lips.

"She wasn't trying to kill me," Aveline whispered brokenly, and Morgana twitched in surprise. "But I saw the knife, and I just … acted. As if my body moved without my permission. This … power and rage coursed through me. I saw the knife coming, and then her throat was split open."

Morgana crouched down beside her, running her fingers over the rough dirt with one hand and reaching for Aveline's fingers with the other. "She was trying to hurt you. You defended yourself."

"She was trying to save me."

"By hurting you," Morgana said sharply, but then softened the edge from her voice. "I would have done the same thing, if that's a comfort to you."

Aveline lifted her eyes to Morgana's. "It is." She turned away, shaking her head. "Maybe my power is a curse, too."

"All power is," Morgana said, because that's all she could say. In her time, she had only known three people with that kind of power. The two of them had barely survived, and the third had died, a victim of his own power and thirst for more. "But don't think for a second that you didn't do the right thing. Many more people would have died if Rike succeeded in taking you away from this kingdom."

Away from me.

Morgana doubted Aveline believed her yet. But someday, she would. Morgana would spend the rest of her days reassuring Aveline that she was a good person.

They went to him next, making their way to a nearby clearing. A pyre sat in the center, and Morgana clenched her fingers around the torch. The sea king's body lay atop the pyre, wrapped in a cloth of deep black.

"We're nothing like him," Morgana said, both to Aveline and herself. "We'll never be anything like him, no matter the time and no matter the power."

Morgana dropped the torch into the kindling spread around the edge of the pyre. They watched the flames ignite and walked away with the body still burning.

***

They left in the dead of night, when the streets were silent and the palace was asleep.

The new queen watched them go from the highest balcony, flanked by her last two friends. One of the two figures disappearing into the surrounding forest carried a lantern, the light dancing over the cobblestones as they headed toward a new life. The queen sent a prayer up to the stars, hoping not just for a better life for her people, but for a fresh start for the last two Hallowed.

The light of their lantern faded into the distance, and she clasped her companions' hands tighter. The men guided her back inside and let the doors close behind them on the last remnants of an ancient past.

The two Hallowed would watch the world heal and grow from the opposite side of the kingdom. They would fade into obscurity, until no one in either Calypdon or Nysus remembered their faces. The company of each other would be enough until a new threat arose, and the kingdoms would call on them again.

Craig Gallant
Crimson Sand
Crimson Snow

The Dragoon Clan:
Rebirth of Courage
Brandon Rospond

The House on
Dominion Street
And Other Stories

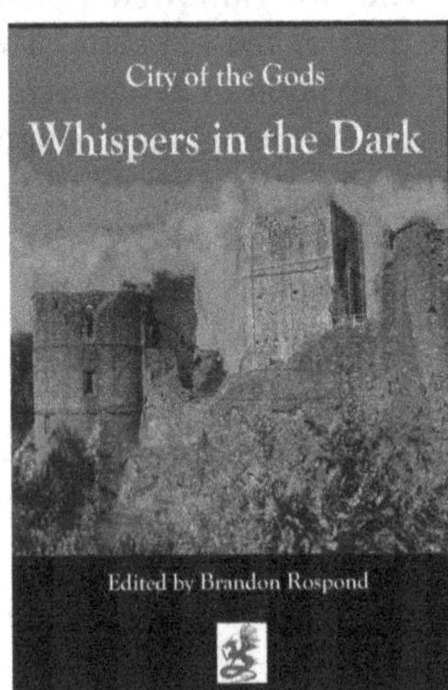
City of the Gods
Whispers in the Dark
Edited by Brandon Rospond